AT THE MERCY OF THE MISTRESS OF THE NEW WORLD . . .

"You're afraid of me," she said abruptly. "You've written that a life of fear isn't worth living. I agree."

He felt the cold steel of a dagger. . . . Despite himself, he shivered. Not from fear of pain and dying; but from not knowing what she would do. Knowing had kept him alive. But now . . . The knife moved down. . . .

Praise for
Legend of the Duelist
by Rutledge Etheridge:

"Action-packed SF adventure . . . There are battle scenes galore, plus some intrigue." —*Kliatt*

Ace Books by Rutledge Etheridge

THE FIRST DUELIST

RUTLEDGE ETHERIDGE

ACE BOOKS, NEW YORK

This book is an Ace original edition,
and has never been previously published.

THE FIRST DUELIST

An Ace Book / published by arrangement with
the author

PRINTING HISTORY
Ace edition / June 1994

ISBN: 0-441-00063-0

ACE®
Ace Books are published by The Berkley Publishing Group,
200 Madison Avenue, New York, NY 10016.
ACE and the "A" design are trademarks
belonging to Charter Communications, Inc.

PRINTED IN THE UNITED STATES OF AMERICA

10 9 8 7 6 5 4 3 2 1

SIMON BARROW

The life of Simon Barrow began to take shape long before the dawn of the human mind.

Billions of miles from the gaseous caldron that would become the Earth, an asteroid plunged full-force into a barren, rocky planet. The stricken world shook, split open down to the core, and wobbled away from its orbit. But the pieces clung together—just barely—bound by a gravity-field that grew continually stronger by dragging passing bits of matter down from the freedom of space and forcing them to become part of the jumble formed by the broken world and the wanderer. Thus was born a new body in the cosmos—running free of ordained orbit and falling, drawn by an irresistible tide, toward the dense center of the Milky Way galaxy.

Eventually, perhaps inevitably, something got in the way. It was a small thing, a tiny comet, which brushed the wanderer-world with just enough force to upset the delicate balance between gravity and centrifugal force.

This time the world flew apart.

Millions of fragments were simultaneously released to shoot through a shattered sky and enter space as a meteor storm. From that one cataclysmic moment—and for billions of years more—the meteor storm raced out toward eternal night; unchanging, unchallenged, flung on its course by unwitnessed violence, destined to rage through emptiness—blindly, forever—on a path that contained nothing.

Until A.D. 2128.

At precisely the wrong moment, a human mind aboard *Utic Shinar* made the decision to bring the vessel back into normal-space.

The ship, therefore, was the intruder.

First to strike was a broad, tumbling hunk of iron and

nickel that rang the outer hull of *Utic Shinar* like a gong. The meteor bulled into the ship's starboard quarter, broke apart as it gored through six layers of plastalum alloy, hurled armies of jagged shrapnel in every direction, and dead-ended in the heart of *Shinar's* Primary Power Junction Box. All ship-wide power systems failed immediately.

That first collision lifted the gargantuan vessel from its course and slammed it hard-over. In machinery areas throughout the ship, soft human bodies were ground to pulp beneath shifting, unyielding metal. Airtight doors banged open and could not reseal as bulkheads compressed, warped, and folded inward. The spine of the vessel snapped; then it too folded. The atmosphere vanished in an instant. Three hundred crew were dead, the rest doomed, before the ship had spent ten seconds in normal-space.

Within those same ten seconds a lifelaunch flew clear of limp hydraulic pinions and was driven to the opposite bulkhead, now thirty feet below. The craft contained a small amount of air, and one sleeping boy.

And then the rest of the meteor storm hit.

Utic Shinar cartwheeled through space as thousands more pieces of the old wandering world ripped through its carcass. Piercing, squealing shrieks of mangled metal tore at the boy in staccato percussion-waves while the lifelaunch that held him tumbled in total darkness, end over end, through the crazily spinning compartment. Finally the craft jolted to a stop, suspended halfway between ship and space, wedged tightly between an airlock's sprung door and its hatchway. In shock and bleeding, terrified, the boy vomited and clamped his hands over his ears, gasping in the last few precious breaths of air inside the life launch.

Dead! he thought. *I'm sixteen, a criminal, and dead!*

The boy groped blindly. Even panic was overwhelmed by the desperate need to breathe. His entire being was focused on one thought: Reach the air controls and set them to Autoflow. Outside this tiny one-thought world within the lifelaunch, oxygen tanks stored beneath the hangar's deck-plates exploded. Flame flashed through the cavernous compartment and died instantly as the unburned gas was sucked into space. The force of the explosion kicked open the airlock door by a few more inches. It was just enough. Boy and lifelaunch were suddenly free, spinning wildly away from *Shinar*.

Disoriented by the sudden loss of all weight, the boy was thrown face-first into the lifelaunch control panel, crushing his jaw. The impact activated the ventilation Auto-flow, and the vessel's distress beacon. The boy drifted freely in the small space, unconscious, globules of his own blood and vomit flying around him in a microcosm of the meteor storm that was passing outside.

The lifelaunch fell away into black, empty space.

Utic Shinar continued its death throes. For a short time, solenoids sparked within servo-control valves in a vain attempt to shut and seal ninety-three twisted airtight doors. Emergency generators whined to life, only to die each time as crushed and shredded cables were unable to transfer current.

For that eternally short time there were men and women aboard *Utic Shinar* who did not know the extent of the damage, and who therefore believed that despite the devastation they could see from their limited vantage points, they and the ship might survive. These were the Ready Crews, who had been standing by in full suits for the shift to normal-space. Now they continued to stand by, helpless, without power for their tools or emergency lights. They spoke to one another through battery-powered communicators intelligibly and calmly for as long as they could. Their deaths were the cruelest, because they would be such a very long time in dying.

The only component aboard *Utic Shinar* that still functioned properly was a self-contained bank of distress beacons. The radio signals would travel for sixteen days before reaching Earth.

When help arrived fifty days later, only the boy was alive. Not one of the 1,180 carefully selected crew and scientists sent out on *Shinar* as "The Pride of ALL Nations" survived. Thus ended the first great expedition under the aegis of UTIC, Universal Terramorphic Industries Corporation. The grand adventure had lasted for exactly nineteen days, forty minutes, and nine seconds.

The death of *Utic Shinar*, and the miraculous survival of young Simon Barrow, would come to be known—for good or bad; opinion would vary—as the single most significant event of the twenty-second century.

2

The eyes of Simon Barrow were bandaged shut against hot lights that seared his face. Gritting his teeth, he answered the questions with a laugh. "Of course I can be silent. But isn't it traditional among the dying, at least to complain a little?"

"You will *not* die!" an old man shouted from the corner of the compartment, clacking an iron-clad heel against the steel deck for emphasis. He said, in a quieter voice, "It hurts, boy. We all know it hurts. Be patient. And don't give her a reason to call me." The door shut quietly behind the old spacer, called Papa by some and Captain by most.

Now Simon was angry. What was wrong with these people? Why didn't they understand that his comment about dying was merely a jest? Why wouldn't they laugh with him, making his humiliation as beneath notice and as contemptible to them as it was to him? Could they really believe that he was afraid of pain?

"Only a minute or two more," the woman said. The sound of her voice was calm, intentionally soothing. It seemed to be her natural tone. Simon Barrow had heard the others, crew serving as guards, walk out shortly after they'd placed the bandage over his eyes and the straps around his body. This was a graduation of sorts; they trusted him now, within limits. When he'd first been brought aboard they'd watched him as if he were some strange animal pinned and wriggling in a net. But he'd seen from the beginning that the gruffness they attempted was awkward for them. Clearly, they had no harmful intentions; all they wanted was his compliance. His course of action, then, was obvious: He would return courtesy for courtesy, and stone-eyed silence for threats. It worked. In less than three days he had established among them how he was to be treated. If only there were more time!

"Moving up the scale a little," the woman said in her musical tone. Nerves and muscles beneath his facial skin were jolted back to life under the probing light. He felt them rising in outrage: a nest of bees kicked open and stirring to frenzy.

"Shall I stop?" the woman asked.

"No!" he gasped back. This one he'd met just before the bandage was placed over his eyes. She was old, eighty or more, and wasn't a doctor—there wasn't one aboard—but an instrument tech with a strong, calm smile and stringy red hair. She was also, he'd heard mentioned, the captain's wife.

"This is all new technology," she said conversationally. "Older than you, but new to me. It's called a gaser. Papa got it in trade just a couple trips ago. Nobody aboard really knows how to use it, but it seems safe enough. And your face doesn't look like raw meat anymore." She coughed and cleared her throat. "What I mean is, you probably don't require the full spectrum to heal. I guess your skin only absorbs what it needs."

"What happens to the rest of the spectrum?" he asked, through clenched teeth.

"Why, I don't know, Simon. The question never occurred to me."

He resented the condescending tone. "It was a joke," he snapped. "Doesn't anyone here have a sense of humor?"

"Yes," she said. Now her tone was agitated. Better, he thought. "Of course we do. But we're all strained just now. The UN Trade Authority forced this contract on Papa. They're not even paying us enough to meet expenses, and because of this trip we're missing out on one of the best deals we ever made. I don't mean to compare your troubles with mine, Simon, but we're set up to carry goods, not strangers. And we're trying to be sympathetic toward you."

"I don't need your sympathy," Simon replied.

The woman's tone softened again. "You're very well-muscled. Decent gravity, that's what does it. And you're tall for your . . . taller than most. You're from Earth?"

"That's right." Tall for his age, she'd meant. He was ten inches over five feet. And his physique *was* good, the result of careful, specialized training—and "decent gravity." His hair was red-brown from his father, who'd also given him deep hazel eyes. From his mother he'd inherited perpetually tan skin and a mouth that was "generous," as she called it— "plain big," as his father described it. His parents had never settled the question of who'd given him his temper, each accusing the other. But both claimed to have bequeathed him the ability to keep it in check.

The woman was chuckling quietly. As he began to speak, his voice cracked. He coughed and made a conscious effort to lower it. "You're laughing at me, aren't you? What's funny about me?" *Damn! What a baby thing to say!*

"Not you, Simon. Me. I asked if you were from Earth. When I was your age, I'd have laughed at anyone asking me where I was from. What planet, I mean. Because it would be so unusual, do you see? I was born on Earth also, but we come from very different worlds. Do you understand that?"

He knew she was talking just to be talking. He didn't mind; his jaw stung like fire and any distraction was welcome. "Where were you when—" His entire body spasmed with the next jolt that went through him. He willed himself not to cry out.

"Almost finished," she said. "Where was I when Lyndon's Locket Rocket went up? That's the one thing no one of my generation will ever forget. I'm easing the intensity." The sting eased to a warm sensation, sore but not sharp. "That was quite a time," she said. "Everyone knew about the attempt, but not many believed that the Rocket would actually travel faster than light. But it did. And I was right there. On F.O.L."

"On what?" He asked to keep her talking, and because she'd had the decency not to call him a "brave little man," as others had. He knew exactly what she was talking about. Every schoolchild knew. And like most people who were not scientists, she had it all wrong. But her voice was soothing and he listened, making polite sounds of interest as she told him what she'd been doing on that day. F.O.L. was Fujiwara Orbiting Laboratory, from which the first hyperspace device had been launched. Aboard the craft, for luck, was a miniature portrait of Project Director Dr. Harry Lyndon's wife, Lydia, encased in a tiny gold heart. Thereafter, the vehicle, which was not a rocket and which did not travel faster than light—it moved through hyperspace—would forever be known as Lyndon's Locket Rocket. That was in 2094, still referred to as the Great Light Year.

Now, only thirty-four years later, commerce was brisk from Earth all the way out to the farthest research station, named after the nearby moon Triton. And the five major settlements between the two were already showing signs of overcrowding. The obvious solution, with the stars newly reachable, was to extend the domain of humankind. And so three years before, in 2125, a hitherto unknown corporation called Universal Terramorphic Industries Corporation was granted an exclusive UN charter to put together an expedition to a promising-looking planet, given the name New Hope, circling Zed Centauri—which was precisely why, nineteen days before his sixteenth birthday, Simon A. Mohamad Barrow had stowed away on *Utic Shinar*. And why, although he was lucky to get them at all, he was enduring these treatments without benefit of anesthetics—which by law were strictly accounted for and definitely not to be wasted on citizens bound for prison.

As suddenly as it had begun, the heat stopped. Simon lay still while the woman folded up the gaser's extension arms. The beehive-itching faded to a mild pins-and-needles sensation in a few seconds. For a moment the woman stepped away, then returned and wiped his face gently with a coarse cloth. He could feel the treated scar tissue balling up and rolling away under the gentle pressure. After several minutes she washed his face with warm water and patted it dry.

"We're finished now," she said, stripping off her plyex gloves with a snapping sound. "You'll stay here until we touch down. I won't see you again."

The transit gravity began to ease off, giving him the sickening sensation of rising, then falling, against the straps. It would help if she'd remove the bandage from his eyes, but he knew better than to ask. Why was the ship slowing its rotation? They were preparing to dock! He coughed and cleared his throat of a foul taste.

"Simon," the woman said hesitantly. "Do you believe in God?"

"This would be a good time to start, wouldn't it?" His mother had been Egyptian, his father Hebrew. Both were atheists, but could never agree on *which* God it was more important not to believe in. "Why do you want to know?" he asked. If she wanted to pray for him, he would accept it as a human kindness and not object, even if it was a futile exercise.

She placed a hand on his upper arm. "I believe it was the will of God that pulled you safely from *Shinar*. I believe there was a reason for that."

"Of course there was," he said bitterly. "So the rest of my life can be wasted in prison."

"Ridiculous. You were saved when everyone else on that ship died. Your life is not to be wasted. Definitely not."

"There's no way out of the Gulag," he said, his voice rising. "They don't even ship the bodies home. What do they do, use them for—" *Stop that! Take control!* He continued in a calm voice, "The only way out for me is if UTIC retracts the lies that are putting me in prison. And you know how likely that is." He forced a lightness into his voice that he certainly didn't feel. "Besides, if there's a God, do you really think he's stronger than UTIC?"

She answered at length, but Simon wasn't listening. He was feeling the full, crushing weight of reality. Ceres, Mercator, and Hermes—the Gulag—circled together in an isolated orbit between the Asteroid Belt and Jupiter. At irregular intervals ships—not like this one, because this was a special charter, carrying only one passenger—docked at the space station called Central to deposit supplies and new inmates. On the three asteroids of the Gulag itself there were no jailers, and no staff. And no programmed release. A prisoner stayed there until he or she was dead. Rarely, an inmate was bought free by a family with great wealth and influence. That meant nothing to Simon Barrow; he had no one.

The woman was speaking as if from a distance. He focused again on her words, searching for a way to suppress, if only for a while, the dread that filled him.

". . . that everything serves a purpose," she was saying. "Everything, and everyone. The challenge is to *find* that purpose, and to serve it willingly. Remember, it was impossible for anyone to survive what happened to *Shinar*. But you did! You—"

"I did *not* sabotage that ship!"

"I know that, Simon," she said, sighing. "None of us believes anymore that you wrecked *Shinar*. But that doesn't free you of all responsibility, does it?"

"What do you mean? I told the truth in court. UTIC lied. About me, and about *Shinar*.

"UTIC had no other explanation to offer."

"What about negligence? Stupidity? Second-rate equipment? Flawed designs? Inferior materials? Inadequate training? Stifling regulations? Political watchdogs in place of necessary crew?" He'd listened, spellbound, to the things they'd said about him. Even more shocking were the "safeguards" and "contingency preparations" that the representatives of UTIC had described to a sympathetic UN Court. Oh yes, they said, *Shinar* was the product of the best minds from every nation of Earth. It was the essence of the great unity bought with the blood of our forebears. A marvel! A bridge to the Universe! "LIARS!" he'd shouted, sealed in a glassite booth. "You didn't build a bridge, you built a political compromise!" He'd pounded on the transparent walls of the cubicle, vainly demanding that they hear him. "Isn't there *one* engineering-literate judge here? Are you *all* so stupid? And the crew you sent out! You called them 'international'? You're right! All they did was argue about political justice on a world they hadn't even seen yet! The only thing that kept them from outright mutiny was that half of them couldn't understand what the other half was saying! Don't any of you understand? Can't you see what UTIC did? *Shinar* was a suicide ship! And you'd better recheck their terraforming procedures, because you can be sure that they're as fraudulent as that ship was!"

But they hadn't heard him. Even with his microphone switched on, they would not have heard him. Only UTIC was heard, along with the bereaved husbands and wives, and the children, of the dead crew. The thousands who'd packed the auditorium for the three-day circus wept and nodded solemnly at every word, and would have killed Simon Barrow right there on the floor of the General Assembly, had not "justice" ruled the proceedings.

Now, wounded and about to enter prison for the rest of his life, Simon Barrow said angrily, "UTIC used me to avoid any blame to itself. And then it convinced the United Nations to subsidize the loss. And triple its investment. The bastards are probably grateful that *Shinar* died."

"Perhaps they are, privately," the woman said. "But remember that you gave them that opportunity. You were there illegally. And you survived."

"Yes," he said. Of course she was right. Blind luck had saved his life, but it was his own actions that had placed him there to begin with. So yes, he was to blame for whatever happened to him. That was easy enough to accept. But it wouldn't end with him. "UTIC and the UN murdered that crew. And the same thing will happen again."

"That's beyond your control, and mine. I said before that life has a special purpose for you. You survived *Shinar*, and you can survive prison. That's what I want you to think about. Now goodbye, Simon. Go where you're led and begin the work you were born to do. I'll remember you."

"Thank you," he said, wishing that her vacuous sermonizing would go on for just a while longer. It was annoying and childish, but it was better than silence. He was close to tears and couldn't understand why. What was prison? Nothing! If he died, he died. Everyone did, sooner or later. "I'd like to know your name."

"It's Alicia. Alicia DurNow."

"Goodbye, Alicia. I'll remember you."

The door shut quietly behind the old woman, and he was alone.

He was sleeping—after a long battle with the fear, which he'd won—when they came for him. The instant the door opened he was awake, although his eyes remained shut beneath the bandage and he kept his breathing carefully slow. There were two of them approaching the bed.

"Gig him, Captain Hartner?" a male voice said.

"Yes." This was a woman, much heavier-sounding than the man. One of her boots clicked against the deck, as she circled the bed to stand opposite the man, on Simon's right side. "Go ahead. Make it hurt."

Simon winced inwardly, wondering where the blow would land. A full minute passed, and nothing happened. Then he heard the man giggling.

"Your heart-rate monitor's going crazy, boy," the captain

said. "Other than that it's a good performance. Now stop the charade and state your number."

"I'm Simon Barrow," he said immediately. "I don't—" The rod came down hard on his left thigh, just inches below his groin.

"She asked your number, garbage," said the man. "And the next word out of your mouth better be 'Captain.' Understand?" To punctuate the command he touched a button on the rod's handle. Simon arched upward in a spasm of agony as the current shot through him.

"Captain!" he said through clenched teeth. "Captain, Captain, Captain! All right?" The charged rod bit into him again.

"Your number!" the man demanded.

"I don't *have* a number! I went straight from the UN to a shuttle and right up to this ship, and all the numbers on this ship are stored in a safe and guarded by wild dogs that yap like you do so I didn't get one, do *you* understand? Captain!" He drew in a deep breath and waited for the jolt. It was far worse than the first two. When it ended he'd bitten his tongue bloody and he was gasping for breath. But not a sound had passed his lips.

"Yes," the captain said mildly. "I understand. You're undesignated, which means that I will send you to whichever unit seems most appropriate. Which would you prefer? Ceres, Hermes? Or—" She paused. "Mercator?"

The man giggled again and moved the rod upward until it pushed into his groin.

Simon squared his jaw firmly and said nothing. The rod jerked to life, going on and on until he lost control and screamed, cursing them both until his breath was gone.

"What was that again, little boy?"

"Captain," he said hoarsely when he could speak. "Kindly go to hell. And take your dog with you." He spit the blood from his mouth in her direction and emptied his mind. With any luck they'd kill him. Now.

"Very well," the captain said. "You've chosen." Her clenched fist drove straight down into his stomach with tremendous force. Then twice more.

Consciousness slipped away as he heard her voice, strangely soft. It sounded almost like compassion. "That's the best you're going to feel for the rest of your life, Simon Barrow. I'm sending you to Mercator."

During seventeen minutes of free fall he bounced from overhead to deck to bulkhead, trussed hand and foot in the pitch darkness of the scouter's cargo hold, trying to prepare for whatever waited within the infamous confines of the asteroid Mercator. He was badly frightened—and grateful to be alone, so that now he was free to let the fear come at him, be explored, and thus be beaten. The fear came in images. The one most persistent—the one routinely depicted in holo epics—was of hands; hundreds of hands. Reaching up from dungeon depths to tear at his unprotected flesh. And faces. Twisted leers and red-run eyes glaring at the youthful newcomer with hunger. And noise. Bars clanging, chains rattling, voices taunting. Noise more soul-jarring than the death of *Shinar*. *That's enough of that. You're thinking like a child! What happens, happens.* The key is to be ready. Take stock of your assets. *Such as?* You're freezing and hungry and you hurt in a dozen places, *But you're alive!* The bandage is off your eyes; if you're ever in light again, you'll be able to see. And no bones are broken. *Yes, that's all true. Any other good news?* No.

The scouter stopped feather-soft and the cargo hold was suddenly and brilliantly lit. He'd have shielded his eyes, if his arms had been free to move.

There came the sounds of a distant door creaking open, and then Simon heard two people entering the airlock from Mercator. The dog-wheels on the craft's inner door spun three full circles and stopped. With arms and legs bound, Simon pushed himself to a position that would put him behind the door when it opened. Then he clamped his boots on both sides of a raised deck-support beam to stabilize himself. But as the door was pushed open, air rushed through it to equalize pressure with the airlock. The unexpected gust—*You should have realized!*—yanked him from the beam and propelled him forward. Suddenly he was flying, with no way to control direction. His head slammed against the dog-wheel in the center of the door.

Laughter from the other side. "Works every time," a man's voice said.

"It's frightful, Gault." The second man's tone said that he didn't approve. Then he added, "But they must learn, truly."

"Come around where we can see you," Gault said.

The second man said, "Hurry! They gas the compartment three minutes after the door's open. Hurry now. Bravo Level is always so cold!"

Carefully, still reeling from the blow to his head, Simon pushed away from the door and toward the center of the hold. He spun slowly and was still moving when a hand clamped the back of his neck and jerked him roughly out through the door. When he was fully inside the airlock, he was released and taken around the chest by large, strong arms. A small man pushed past him. He was quick and wiry and moved with confident control in the micro-gravity. The door was pushed shut, leaving the three in complete darkness as the dog-wheels were secured. A final twist brought a metallic squeak from the wheels and a satisfied grunt from both men. Immediately a hissing sound began from the scouter's hold.

"Damn them!" the small man said. "Less than two minutes and they turned on the hackin' gas!"

"So unfair, Gault," the other man said in a soft voice. "You always do the job so fast." He pulled Simon closer against him as he spoke. As a shield? Simon wondered. The man was large, and fleshy, and smelled like one of the sharp chemical cleaners his father had used in the shop.

"Next time somebody's as slow as this garbage, Clonus, I'll leave 'em inside. I swear I will!"

"That's fair, Gault," Clonus said. "I honestly swear that it truly is. But it would be cruel. And Mr. Tench would be very—"

"*Hack* Tench!" the smaller man said angrily. "And shut

your mouth before you make me sick. Open the hatch and let's get out of here."

From outside the airlock came the sound of the scouter pulling away, metal grating against metal. Then it was gone, and Simon Barrow was carried down into the depths of Mercator.

Tarnon Tench sat heavily, in luxury, on the seat the others jealously referred to as his throne. There was only one other like it. That one was six hundred feet away through solid rock, sitting above the only other gravity generator on Mercator. Like everything else on that side of the world, it belonged to the witch-woman, Talon.

The Duke, as he allowed his confidants to call him, was in a rare good mood. Hartner said the boy was stubborn and smart and would never be bought free. Excellent. For that type there were two alternatives: Train them if they could be made useful, or kill them quickly. Which would it be? He scratched at a rash beneath the hair on his stomach and waited, pleased that the boy was to be his. One thing about Captain Hartner; when she owed a favor, she paid. For the moment Tarnon Tench was content.

He'd just dismissed two women, blessing them silently for the natural gifts of their kind that helped to make his kingdom and his place in it, if not pleasant, at least bearable. The two he'd chosen this time would have the best food today. And they would be allowed to bathe, expecting at any moment to be called again. Would he grant them the privilege? Probably not. In less than two hours they'd exhausted their imaginations and were beginning to repeat themselves. Better to send them to the Core, and use new ones next time. Then why waste food and clean water on them? Good question. He gestured to a personal guard standing a few feet away, then pointed toward the doorway through which the two women had exited. The guard nodded her understanding and followed them through a stone archway. A moment later there was a scream, followed by hysterical pleading.

Turnover, Tench thought, chuckling, as the voices disappeared in the distance. That's what Captain Hartner called it. A fine woman. A fine word. It was a law of life. It was almost his name. Turnover-Tarnon Tench. They die, they're replaced. Always new bodies to train, a few of them good enough to enjoy. A tough system; that's what prisons are about. It's a rare man who knows how to use it.

He scratched leisurely at the itch below his beard. Yes it was tough, he thought. Real hell. You can go from Earth to Triton and you won't find anyone to argue with that. But I rule here, by God. Eighteen years on Merc. I survived. I paid my dues. Now this hell is mine. And that is everything. *Except for Talon. What the hell can I do about Talon?* He inhaled open-mouthed, forgetting himself for an instant. A molar erupted in pain and he went pale.

"Mr. Tench?" a young man sitting at his feet said solicitously.

"Quiet!" he snapped back. "Can't you keep your mouth shut?" Careful, he thought. To be seen as weak is to be dead. He tossed a key to the young man. "Go to the lockers and bring my iodine." He shrugged broadly and smiled. "Tell the guard I'm bleeding again." All but three of his lower front teeth were gone. Those remaining were brown and angled, twisted stumps clinging to his gum line. Above them was a red expanse of scarred pulp.

The young man caught the key and jumped to his feet, careful to stay within the seven-foot dome of gravity. The Duke always kept the terminal at low radius; gravity was a luxury he controlled jealously. "Yes sir, but won't you allow me to call Central? Please forgive me for mentioning it again, but I'm sure the captain would send down something to cure that tooth. Since it's you, I mean."

"Of course she would," Tench said. And then he'd owe her another damned favor. Right now they were even. "But why bother? Who'd cry about a little toothache? You?"

"No, sir!"

"And am I less a man than you?"

"No! No, Mr. Tench, I never meant—"

"Then shut up about it," he said pleasantly. Lately the decay was more painful than it had ever been, driving him to blind madness at times, forcing him to hide his weakness by raging at anyone nearby. Or worse. Only days ago he'd killed beautiful Mary. The sad thing was that just the moment before, he'd decided to give her permanent status near the throne. But he'd had no choice. She'd been there in his private quarters when the pain was too much; she'd seen him cry like a baby, cradled his head against her breasts, and cried with him until the pain went away and he fell asleep. When he woke up she was still there, still holding him, and he remembered. He didn't want to kill her. She'd seen his weakness, so he had to. That was all. He said to the youth, "I told you before. The things we don't control, control us."

"Yes, sir. I'm trying to remember that."

"You're doing fine, Harper. Learn control and patience, and you'll always have what you need." Except brains, he thought. This one's too stupid to live. Doesn't he wonder why I treat him so well? *For Captain Hartner, you fool!* he wanted to shout. I want you healthy, strong, and as virile as your body suggests. Hartner told me that you were a holographer's model before you killed your lover and came here. You'll be my gift to her, as soon as you've been made totally mindless. The drugs are working. Slowly, but they're working. She'll owe me a great deal for you, my young friend. Maybe she'll give me Talon. Yes!

Tench breathed deeply through his nose as the familiar fantasy put a fire in his belly. Yes. Wrapped and delivered to me personally. Dead. None of her so-called Family will know. No one will see us. Yes. And when I'm finished I'll burn her body. After that there'll be no challenge to me. Except Joyner. Never mind him now. I've always won, and I always will. I'm the Duke, by God. This prison is mine.

Simon Barrow arrived in the throne room lashed to an eight-foot section of pipe, pulled by the hair like a trailing carnival balloon behind Gault. The larger man, Clonus, followed and nudged the boy's feet upward when micro-gravity edged them downward. They'd reached this place, Simon memorizing everything, after walking for eight minutes through a sloping tunnel that forked twice and was intersected five times. At each of the intersections were three to five people, mostly men, each armed with a sheathed knife or sword of obviously poor quality. No one spoke to them as they passed, but he saw them all looking at him. Some with amusement, most with dull-eyed apathy, others with blatant hostility. The only ones that angered him were the few who showed pity. He stared back at them all, giving nothing and asking nothing.

The room was an open cavern that appeared to be circular, measuring perhaps sixty feet across, although it was difficult to gauge because of the domed ceiling that arched over to meet the floor with no clean break in color or texture—dark gray, and rough. Two more entrances were visible, separated by roughly 90 degrees of arc. There must be a fourth I can't see from here, he thought. The lighting was surprisingly good. Great chunks of glowstone were inset strategically into ceiling and walls, and into four thick stanchions that quartered the cavern. At each of the entries and at irregular intervals throughout the room were more groups of three to five guards, men and women in about equal numbers. He counted a total of thirty-six. All wore the crude knives and swords he'd seen earlier. Everyone in the room was watching him, except one.

This was a hairy, bearded, and bloated man who sat alone at the center of the cavern in a raggedly upholstered chair. The seat was brown and trimmed in black, mounted on a three-foot pedestal. Obviously it had once been a ship's pilot seat. The man was naked except for a towel draped across his lower belly and lap. His legs, arms, chest, and shoulders were covered with coarse black hair and bore the look of formidable strength degenerated to useless bulk. He was dabbing the end of another towel at his mouth, and it looked as if he was wiping away blood. Then he looked up at Simon, and smiled.

One of the guards approached and motioned for Gault and Clonus to stand aside. He then put Simon's pole-mounted, arrow-straight body on his shoulder and launched him across the room toward the Duke. Clonus sighed and looked away while Gault laughed out loud, contorting his pinched and pockmarked face. He said, "Brisson, you're a hackin' genius."

Simon flew head-first, six feet from the floor and dropping slowly. He struggled to bend away from the imminent impact, but the section of pipe held him rigidly straight. The hairy man was looking to his left and showed no sign of seeing him.

"Move! Move!" Simon shouted, unable to change his trajectory. He was spearing inexorably at the seated man's mid-section.

The Duke looked at him calmly, then raised a hand. "Stop," he said quietly. In that instant Simon entered the gravity dome, and dropped like a stone. He managed to twist his head aside, and came to a stop with his right shoulder crunching against the pedestal of the chair. The cavern filled with laughter.

More than the ache in his shoulder, Simon felt white-hot with anger and humiliation. Two guards dragged him away from the throne. Once free of the gravity dome, they rolled him over so that he was facing up.

One of the female guards sat on his chest—a weight he didn't feel—drew out her knife, and pushed it under Simon's chin. Looking down at him, she showed white, even teeth in a wide smile. "How dare you attack Mr. Tench!" she called out in a loud voice. "Should I cut him, sir?" She pushed the dull blade tight against Simon's throat, obviously enjoying herself.

"Not yet, Corinne," Tench said. This girl was new, another deserter from Talon's side. She'd told the same story all the deserters did. Of cruelties Tench could barely imagine, and of happenings they could not explain. The fact that they preferred—begged—to live under his control was chilling testimony to Talon. This one he kept close to his throne and protected by his order. He planned to have her, very soon. Perhaps after the boy's killing. Or during! He stirred at the thought. "Take off his bonds and stand him up."

Corinne slid the long section of pipe out from beneath Simon's ropes. It took several minutes for the knife to saw through the bindings around his arms. At one point she leaned close to his face and whispered, "You're very handsome. Are you brave?" He ignored the taunt and used the time to center himself, to cool the impulse in his mind and his clenching hands. *I'm being tested,* he thought. *The hairy one is in charge, and he'll decide what happens next. But first he wants to know about me. Very well.* When his arms were free he sat up, careful not to leave the floor. He stretched to restore circulation and finished the movement by snatching the knife from the guard's hand as she bent over his feet. Instantly there was the sound of other weapons being drawn. Simon reacted immediately. "Stand easy," he said in as loud and commanding a voice as he could manage. The guard lunged for her knife. He put his free hand on her chest and easily pushed her away. "Mr. Tench said to release me, not to bore me to death."

"Wait," the Duke said to the guards who were moving in. This was fascinating! The boy was inhumanly quick, and apparently without fear. What would he do next? And would he die with as much courage?

Simon used the point of the knife to unravel the knots in the ropes circling his shins. Within seconds he was free and standing. Turning to face Tench, he tossed the knife underhand toward the guard who'd sat on his chest and taunted him. Startled, she jumped aside and traveled ten feet before reaching the floor again, flushed and staring wide-eyed at the mocking faces that now were laughing at her.

The Duke brought his fist down hard on the chair's arm. He meant to laugh with them. This girl would be great fun! But at that moment his molar erupted again and his face contorted with the agony, despite his will. Panic consumed him as he felt every eye in the room on his face. He acted swiftly to take control of the situation. "You stupid hack!" he bellowed at the guard, diverting attention to her.

It worked. They all misunderstood his expression and looked back at the hapless guard. All, except for Simon. He'd been studying the hairy man's face ever since he'd freed himself. And he knew.

"Get her out of here," Tench said roughly. "Strip her and take her down to the Core. Tell those animals she's a gift from the Duke. And tell them she'd better be dead before I come down there again. Do it!"

The young guard was trembling and white with shock. She turned away from Tench and looked at Simon. Reading her face, he didn't see the expected hatred—what he saw was dismay and astonishment. As if to say, *How could you do this to me? It was just a game!* It jarred him to realize that he'd completely misjudged her actions before. She wasn't malicious. She was playful!

And looking at her closely for the first time, he saw that she was not very much older than he was. A year or two, at most. Her eyes were teared over—soft and brown and looking

at him!—and her body was petite, pitifully small against the
woman and the man who seized her arms and pushed her
ahead of them toward one of the exits. When they reached the
archway the guards stopped and stripped her naked, then held
her immobile while others came to leer and paw at her. The
girl screamed in terror and humiliation, then fainted. The
guards carried out her slumped-over form between them—as
easily as Simon had pushed her away.

Simon turned back to face Tench, ready to shout out what
he'd seen in the man's face. But Tench had already left his
throne and was surrounded by hee-hawing guards as he strode
through the cavern.

"Come with me," Gault said from behind him. Simon
turned to see the wiry man facing him with a knife in his left
hand. Gault took a half-step backward, saying, "You'd better
not try that trick again. I'm dangerous with this knife."

Simon ignored him. He would wait, and see what needed
to be done with Gault. The shorter man released the breath
he'd been holding, grunted in satisfaction, and walked away.
Simon followed. His right shoulder was throbbing where he'd
collided with the chair pedestal. As they walked he realized
that he'd been unconsciously keeping the shoulder immobile.
Moving it slightly brought sharp pain and confirmed his suspicion; it was dislocated. From beyond the exit ahead of them
came the sound of a girl's sobbing, and raucous laughter.
There was no way to know if it was the guard he'd disarmed
or some other inmate of Mercator. It mattered to him; however ignorantly, he'd had a part in that young girl's death.

Simon looked around for Tench, but the hairy one and his
pack of donkeys were gone. *Bastard*, he thought. *Your time is
coming. I know you now.*

4

"Tell me how it is. Truly, now." Clonus's thick fingers released their incredibly strong grip on Simon's right shoulder. Sensation returned slowly to the area. And with it, spreading warmth. "Yes?" Clonus asked.

"Yes," Simon answered. "It's—"

"Good." Without warning Clonus pushed his thumbs below the base of the boy's neck and snapped both of Simon's shoulders back with his fingers. There was a jarring POP! Simon lurched away, and was hauled back and held down by gentle hands. His neck felt like rubber—loose, but strong. And warm. Blissfully warm.

"It's all right, Simon," Clonus said soothingly. "Everything is good now. Honestly. Stand up."

They were seated on a cot, and now Simon stood, slowly, conscious of the sudden stark clarity of the room and everything in it. And the eerie tingling in all of his upper body.

"Well, tell me! How is it?"

Simon straightened and rolled the right shoulder experimentally, then bent his neck, rotating it cautiously. "Good!" he said, amazed. He tested the range of motion. Slowly, then with more confidence. "Very good. Thank you, Mr. Clonus."

"You're welcome, Mr. Barrow."

Gault was seated cross-legged on the stone floor, seven feet from the cot. He coughed and cleared his throat. *"Mister?"* he said, sneering. "I'd bet every hackin' thing I own, no one's ever called either one of your 'Mister' before. Have they?"

Simon ignored him, marveling at the forgotten sensation of blood circulating as it was supposed to—and, for the first time in weeks, feeling no pain. None at all.

"It was a long time ago, Gault," Clonus said. "But yes, they honestly did."

23

"Are you a doctor?" Simon asked.

Again, the rough cough from Gault. "Ha! That's funny. No, boy, he's not a doctor. He's just good with his hands. Other than that he's worthless. Aren't you, Clonus?"

"Yes," the big man answered quietly. To Simon he said, "My mother was a holistic healer. She taught me how to do a lot of things."

Gault snickered, slapping his hands down hard enough to lift him off the floor. He twisted with easy agility and set his feet under him. "She never taught you how to be a man, though, did she? I'll bet she knew all about that, eh, Clonus? And she never taught . . . Ah, hack it. This is too easy. Too easy!" Laughing, he jumped lightly for the overhead trapdoor, caught the edge, and pulled himself feet-first through it and out into the corridor.

"Why do you take that?" Simon asked, after Gault was gone. His question was born in anger, but he was genuinely curious. "Why don't you break him in half?"

Clonus stared at him, wide-eyed. "Oh! I could never . . . no, never!"

"Of course you could. You've certainly got the strength. I'll show you how, if you like."

"Oh, I know how to . . . I understand bones and linkage. My mother . . . but not . . . NO!" He was horrified.

Then I'll do it, Simon thought happily, having made the offer that seemed only fair. During the long walk to this cell that was now home to the three of them, it had become clear that breaking Gault was one of the first things he needed to do.

From the Duke's throne room they'd passed through the same portal the female guard had been carried from. They walked—Simon mimicking their technique of pulling with the front foot and gliding a few inches from the ground, touching down about every three yards—along a gradually curved and downward-sloping tunnel. This one was intersected every seventy yards by narrower passageways set at right angles, only a few of them guarded. Gault stayed ahead of him, never looking back, contemptuously inviting an attack from behind. After eleven minutes they came to an alcove dug into the right side of the tunnel wall, the first of its kind he'd seen. As they drew abreast of it, Gault abruptly turned and jumped into the open space, disappearing from sight.

Simon leaned into the alcove and peered downward to see the wiry man propeling himself rapidly, feet-first, down a thin pole that was centered within a lighted eight-foot-wide well. Were they heading for the Core? He assumed an assignment there was the worst of fates on Mercator. He fought the impulse to run. *There's no place to go.*

As if answering his thought, Gault shouted up to him, "Tench's got more than two thousand people on this side. Think you can hide from all of us? Now stay with me!"

But they weren't going to the Core. After descending a hundred yards—the well went much deeper and ended in a dark circle—Gault pushed away from the pole and again disappeared. Simon entered the well head-down; he wanted to keep Gault's exit point in clear view. He pulled one-handed, keeping his dislocated right shoulder as still as possible, down past level after level, expecting at any moment to be set upon from any of the portals. As he moved lower he noted that the temperature was falling off quickly; by the time he'd passed the fifth level down, with twenty yards to go before he reached the point where Gault had disappeared, it was uncomfortably cold. He shivered when he thought of that young guard, stripped and taken all the way down to the Core.

The lights went out at the same moment a siren's screech attacked his ears. Instantly he was disoriented in the pitch-black well, and fighting an overwhelming urge to vomit. *What? What's happening?* Images from a dying *Shinar* flooded his mind. He clung to the pole with one arm and both legs—*Which way is up?*—suddenly afraid to move and terrified of remaining where he was. The siren wailed up and down its scale, moving from a piercing shriek to pummeling bass. Then the lights flickered, on and off twice in every second, and he saw something dark and big coming down at him—no, *up* at him—fast, filling the well, stopping twice each second in the strobing lights. He crawled backward, up the pole, and when he realized that there was no time to escape, he wrapped his arms around his head and waited to be crushed. Now the lights stayed on.

The siren stopped and left a heavy silence in the air.

"Come back up here!"

The unfamiliar voice came from beneath his feet, a long way away—up. Two yards from his head the dark thing—it was a platform—had slowed and now was inching toward him.

"I told you to stay with me!" a second voice called. This one he recognized. It was Gault.

Simon reversed his position on the pole; then the platform touched his feet and began carrying him smoothly back the way he'd come. Far above him he could see two figures leaning over into the dot of open space at the top of the well. As he got closer he saw that one man's face was grim. The other's was split by a sharp, twisted smile.

The first was a dark and burly guard who pulled the boy out of the vertical tunnel and cuffed him not-very-hard on the left side of his head, warning him never again to wander off on his own. The incident would not be reported to the Duke, this time. Simon remained still and quiet, accepting the blow, surprised that his "punishment" was so light, and over so quickly. Gault put his hand on the guard's shoulder and thanked him with groveling politeness for helping to find the boy.

Simon contained the rage within him, and laughed good-naturedly as the Duke's man shook off Gault's hand, glared at both of them, turned, and left. "Funny," he said in a friendly tone. "I owe you one."

The wiry man spit at his feet. "I'll be waiting." He turned and continued down the tunnel.

Clonus had just come awake from a nap when Simon followed Gault down into the cell. There was a drop of fourteen feet from the ceiling entrance to the center of the floor, with all dimensions of the room identical. Two cots, with a neatly folded blanket on each, lined opposite walls. Simon hoped that a third bed would be arriving soon. At the head of each cot was an eighteen-inch-wide table on which was mounted a small chunk of glowstone. A thin wire connected each light to a drilled hole in the wall next to it. That was for outside control, Simon realized immediately. The amperage required to excite a glowstone was very small; a low-grade battery would power it for decades. Simon assumed that this "lamp" was a luxury item, in the same category as the ancient foot-square holo receiver that was set against a third wall.

Across from that were a toilet and a sink, sharing a common drain. There was nothing else in the cell, which was of the same uniform rough gray and color-flecked rock as every other surface he'd seen on Mercator.

Clonus said, "The shoulder is all right? Truly?"

"Yes. And again, thank you. Will I be staying in here?"

"Griffin said you will, and I'm so glad, Simon. I told him about you and he said it would be all right for you to be here. It will be pleasant to speak with someone besides ..." He glanced upward at the trapdoor. "I don't mean to be harsh, truly, you understand, don't you? Gault is ... he says things the way the others do because he wants to be like them. But he'd never hurt me, you understand. That's why Griffin put us together, because he knew that."

"Who is Griffin?"

"Oh, he's a good man. And *very* smart. You can trust him if you don't make him mad. This—" He hesitated, shivering. "This is a terrible place, Simon. It won't ever be good for me, but some things make it better. Like having you to talk with. Do you understand?"

"Yes. Friends are important." And I'd better find some, he thought. But not Gault. That one was a schemer, a cloying coward with a rat's eyes and a rat's intelligence—he'd "never hurt" Clonus because he knew the big man would crush him like an egg if he ever tried. But there was no guile at all—not even enough for self-protection—in this man. "I'm grateful for your help, Mr. Clonus."

The large man was nearly bald, with wisps of fine blond hair above wide ears. His left eye was blue and the right one very pale, almost white. The skin left uncovered by his clean and pressed uniform jumpsuit was hairless, and his face was unlined. His fleshy, almost infant-smooth appearance was fairly common in people who'd been born and brought up in little or no gravity. Such an environment led to a number of physical problems, including lack of muscle tone, weak circulation, and underdeveloped skeletal systems. And although gravity generators were basically simple devices, they were strictly controlled by franchise licensing regulations, and for that reason were prohibitively expensive for most people. So space-borns were fed massive amounts of bone strengtheners through childhood, and were taught from birth to move in a way that generated continual muscle-opposition. Some, as was apparently the case with Clonus, became exceptionally strong. Simon guessed him to be somewhere near fifty.

"Which of the settlements are you from?" Simon asked.

"New Sarajevo," Clonus said, shrugging. "It's a small place. It's not important."

"I think it is."

"Honestly? Oh, that's wonderful!" The rare—so terribly rare!—chance to talk about his home brought a light to his eyes. "Tell me what you know about it!"

"All right. New Sarajevo is an agricultural colony, begun as an orbital experiment by RyComm Corporation in August of 2069. Originally it was designed to field-test the light-filtering properties of glassite, to demonstrate that selectively bred plant life could grow and reproduce in the part of the spectrum that passed through it. The experiment was enormously successful. In June of 2077 the station was expanded and towed out to where it is now, in orbit between Mars and the Asteroid Belt. Permanent settlers arrived the following month. Soon afterward the settlement became profitable by supplying a number of mining sites in the Beltway with oxygen and food. Quite a few hybrids were developed there." He winced at his clumsiness. The word "hybrid" was used commonly to indicate true space-borns. The epithet was an intentional cruelty, like so many others that grew and spread like infections through human languages.

Clonus showed no reaction to the unintended slight. He said, "You know so much! Then tell me this. Who was the Project Director?"

"Elena-Linda Spinelli," Simon said immediately. "But Dr. Spinelli didn't stay for the orbit-change. She retired from Rycomm two months before, in April of 2077, and control passed to a standing committee of seven. That's still how the colony's governed, even though it moved again. In 2097 the dome's ecosystem began to deteriorate. No one could discover why. All of the people and the movable equipment were re-established on another asteroid, also called New Sarajevo. The new colony is even more successful than the original. It retains the committee of seven, and now has one at-large member who is seated with the Pan-Asteroid delegation to the

United Nations." He stopped, realizing that Clonus wanted something more personal than cold facts; he wanted the *feel* of the two homes he'd known. That was something Simon could not deliver. "But I've never been there," he said. "So I really don't know much about it."

"Oh, but you are so smart! Here's one I'll bet you won't know. Are you ready? What is the name of the first child ever born on New Sarajevo? The original one, I mean!" He laughed like a youngster, clapping his hands. "Do you accept my bet?"

Simon thought for a moment, and realized what the answer had to be. "What is it you'd like to bet?"

"Friend bet!" Clonus said happily. "Just a bet between friends!"

The man's laughter was infectious. "Then yes, I accept!" Simon said, recalling from years before, the game of Doctor Genius he'd played so often with his parents. The enthusiasm was the same. "*Nothing* must remain unknown," Isaac Barrow would intone solemnly to begin the game. When he was four, Simon intuited the rest of the epigram: "But everything else, we *must* know." Neferti Barrow had taken her son in her arms. "Yes. Yes, that is the truth."

Now, remembering his father's solemnity and voice, he closed his eyes and put his fingertips against his temples. "Ah, yes. I see the answer. The first child born on New Sarajevo was a boy. His parents were both scientists who arrived with the first wave of colonists. She was an artist of healing and a sage counselor, and her husband found delight in the secrets of botany, agronomy, engineering, and atmospherics. The child grew to manhood there, and then traveled to the new colony. He bears the family name, which is—" He opened his eyes and said in mock surprise, "Why, it's Clonus! It's you!" He held the amazed expression, waiting for the big man to reason out how he'd answered in such detail. All of it was obvious from what Clonus had told him about his mother, his apparent age, his asking that particular question, and from knowing the history of the two colonies called New Sarajevo; the first settlers had all been scientists, either medical/psychological or agri-engineering.

The big man was looking at Simon in awe. After a long silence he asked, whispering, "Are you a witch?"

"What?"

"A sorcerer," Clonus said, looking away. "One of the witches." When he looked at Simon again, the joy had gone from his eyes.

Simon began to laugh, believing the joke had been turned around at him. But the fear in Clonus's eyes was real.

"If you're a witch," Clonus said, "you wouldn't be allowed to tell me. Is that how it works?"

"I don't know how it works," Simon answered distractedly. He was thinking, hard. *One* of the witches? Do they believe in nonsense like that, here? Is it possible? Why not? Mercator's a world in itself. The people who survive here . . . strong, adaptable. Maybe insane. Some of them, at least. Was that how they were controlled? With superstition? It was important to know; *everything* was important to know. He asked, "Are there witches here?"

"Yes, Simon," Clonus said in a subdued tone. "Will you tell me why you came to Mercator? Did Talon summon you here?"

"Listen to me," he said levelly. "I am not a witch." He explained how he'd answered Clonus's challenge a minute before. Then he added, "I'm a sixteen-year-old boy who reads a lot. That's all. But I'd like to hear about this." *For instance, who was Talon? And what did Clonus mean by "summon"?*

"I understand," Clonus said. "Honestly, you don't have to tell me anything. But I don't think she called you here. You're a man and so . . . I'm afraid, Simon. What are you going to do to me?"

"I'm going to be your friend," he said sincerely, hoping the man could believe that, despite what Clonus now believed him to be. "You have no reason to be afraid of me, Clonus. Or of anyone."

Relief spread across the fleshy face. "Thank you, Simon. I won't become like . . . one of you, I mean, you understand? It's too frightful, the things you have to do, and even the things you have to know. Ghastly! But I can be your friend. There's no harm in that. Is there? Honestly?"

"No, Clonus. And I'm not a sorcerer. Honestly. Tell me about Talon."

"She rules on the other side," Clonus said. "She . . . but

you *chose* to be brought here. Didn't you? So you know about
. . . everything. Don't you?"

Of course, Simon thought. Witches "know" things. But before he could reply, Clonus said, "Oh! You're asking how
much I know, myself."

Simon made no reply. It was useless to deny it again. The
big man would have to see for himself that his new cellmate
was just an ordinary person.

Clonus nodded in understanding and began, wringing his
hands nervously. "I don't meddle in things that are above me,
truly, but I've been here long enough, over five years—did
you know that?—to hear a little. And it isn't bad to tell you
what you already know—who could be angry about that, honestly? And I trust you, Simon. Truly I do." He took a deep
breath. "Talon came here just before I did, when Jacoman
died. That was six years ago . . ." It was a long and rambling
monologue, disjointed and sometimes unintelligible. And
grossly exaggerated, Simon suspected. The key to understanding it was to remember that Clonus was terrified of the people
and the—things—he was describing. Many of the events Clonus related were physically impossible. Others were too ob-
scene, the boy judged, to have happened as he described
them. Even among hardened criminals.

The man was dead. His eyes were glazed over and his last
breath still offended her nostrils, but she held the coat-
wrapped bulk desperately over her. She was dying of the cold
and praying that no one would pull this warm thing away. He
was their leader, the one who'd claimed her when she was
thrown down to them, along with the Duke's whiskey and instructions. Fourteen of the twenty male inmates in the cell had
stood in line waiting their turn, while she shook with cold, her
ankles lashed to opposite sides of the cot, and the leader
stared at her nakedness, getting blind-drunk and eager. But
when he staggered into position, the prisoner who was holding her arms passed out. And as the leader struggled clumsily
to open the front of his reeking overcoat, she'd sat up suddenly and pulled him on top of her. And as the drunken
watchers cheered the thrashing and the screams she gave for
effect, she'd gotten her small hands around his throat. After a
few minutes the onlookers lost patience and wandered away,

looking for more whiskey and a way to stay warm. There were other women in the cell; Tench sent them down almost regularly. These women were as drunk as they were. And they had no one waiting in line.

For Corinne, forever had squeezed into an hour and passed, since Tench and the boy had sent her here. Dozens of times she'd called out, delirious with fear, for her mother. Now she was quiet. Now she was a murderer and she was at the Core of Mercator and her mother wasn't here and it no longer mattered, because now she felt nothing. Except for a floating sensation that was lifting her away from the bone-deep, killing cold. She was near death.

No one in the cell heard the choked screams from above, or heard a giant bolt slide free of the trapdoor fourteen feet over them.

The hatch was lifted and five dark-clad and masked figures slid silently down through the opening. Knives appeared as the figures slowly settled to the floor. Thirty throats were slit and thirty ritual mutilations performed, with no sound from the dying.

The corpse of the cell's former boss was shoved aside and the young woman was cut free of the cot, then taken up gently. She was wrapped in a thick blanket that came down through the trapdoor when one of the figures gestured for it. Fifteen seconds later the six were clear of the cell.

Back inside the main compartment, eighteen of the Duke's guards burst through an entrance that had been bolted shut against them.

"There!" the man who was last through the doorway shouted, pointing. "Get that hatch open. Hurry!"

"Aw, lookut this!" a woman called from the trapdoor entrance to the cell. She was peering down inside. "I'm g'na puke." Then she began slapping frantically at a cloud of red globules drifting down over her. "Mary'n Joseph! There's blood all over the hackin' place!"

The man called back impatiently. "You heard my order. Move!"

"Like hell! They're not gonna cut off my—"

"Sshh! What's that smell? Do you smell something?"

A series of clicks began in that moment, one every two seconds. In panic the eighteen rushed back for the entrance, those arriving first cursing and kicking to get the door open again, screaming for help when they realized that it was now bolted shut from the other side. On the eleventh click that section of the Core erupted into a billowing, gas-fed inferno.

Seventeen hundred feet above, Tarnon Tench felt a mild tremor and opened his eyes. "What was that?"

"I said the boy is causing trouble," Gault repeated. "He needs to be killed, sir." He took a deep breath and asked the all-important question with a casualness he'd rehearsed before coming here. "Do you want me to do it for you?" Then he added, his heart racing, "Duke?"

Tench shut his eyes. "Tell me about it again," he said, and drifted back into sleep.

⇒ 5 ⇐

Maria Regina Hernandez y Estephan was weeping. Her fingertips gently touched the waxen, frozen-closed eyelids of a young girl's angelic face. She whispered, the tone rhythmic and hushed, the words unrecognizable to the few people within hearing. From a small vial she poured drops of a clear liquid into each of the young girl's eyes, allowing her to remove two colored lenses.

Around her the others stood with outward discipline, but all were edgy from waiting, wanting to ask but afraid to speak. They knew that the Family had been violated as never before. They believed that there could be only one response. And they were right.

Throughout the catacombs of Mercator, shrill-pitched pipes sounded three times with enough power to shatter any glass within twenty feet of the speakers. At the same time eighty-one followers of the witch-woman Talon went out in strike-squads of nine, the formations long ago established and the warriors well rehearsed in their roles.

Everyone on the Duke's side who heard the wailing pipes reacted. Nearly all of them believed it was the troop-alarm, too loud and repeated unnecessarily, announcing more trouble from Captain Hartner and her murderous rifle platoons. The Duke's army of guards followed their standard procedure of stowing knives and swords into wall-away lockers, then joined long lines of cleaners, scroungers, and petty thieves, storytellers and artisans, and workers for the farm chambers and sewage centers—common inmates—filing toward the cell-blocks. The guards bolted the others into their cells and returned to the throne room. When Hartner arrived all would be orderly, quiet and passive. Or her platoons would start shooting immediately.

One in fifty, forty-two in all, knew what the signal really was. These forty-two all headed in a common direction away from the cell-blocks. Some were shocked, some were terrified, and more than a few smiled with grim anticipation. Others were jubilant, knowing what was to come. At last. When opportunity arose, they paused just long enough to cut the throats of selected stragglers from Tench's guard force, individuals who'd caused harm to the Family. These were left to die slowly, and alone. Ritual mutilations were not performed; haste was important, and nothing was permitted that might impede the exodus of Talon's fifth-column troops. The spies were going home.

When they reached deserted corridors, they ran with all possible speed to seven prearranged safeholds. There the forty-two met with waiting strike-squads and were rushed through secured tunnels to the cavern that was home to Talon. They entered and found the atmosphere very different from the charged excitement they'd expected. Once warned, they were absolutely silent. Even the oldest among them, a close confidante of Talon, did not dare to disturb the solemn quiet.

At the center of the room a robed woman was kneeling, bent over a wrapped figure whose face was ghost-white. The girl was trying to speak. Her lips were parted in a terrible grimace but she produced no sound. After several minutes the woman straightened, then stood and faced the newcomers.

Her eyes were black, dry now after tears. She spoke in a low voice that was heard throughout the cavern. "This child was at the Core for fifty-one minutes before I knew of it. Tell me why."

"Whaa—!"

Tarnon Tench jerked awake to see three men standing at the foot of his bed. His immediate impulse was to order them killed for breaking into the best of his private fantasies. The dream had happened again! So real, and now gone like smoke. He'd been a young man, strong and healthy, back in the face-plate shop on Luna. Working, sweating, loving the smell of the place, the grind-wheels singing. Business bad, as always. But his own shop. He was happy. Then they came, the same two little bureaucrats, again, with that new hacking Viso-Plast, telling him he needed to invest in all new materials and tools and fittings and designs because the plates he'd been making for eleven years were out of date and unsafe. And they said with those little twisty-mouth we've-got-power-you-don't grins, that they were suspending his license until he made the required changes. His license!

So in the dream he challenged them, just as it had really happened, to put on their new hacking expensive Viso-Plast face-plates and he'd put on one of *his*, and open all the hacking air-seals in the whole hacking shop. And in the dream they laughed, and met his challenge. Just as it had really happened. But *this* was *his* dream! *This* time it was different. The Viso-Plast shattered so beautifully! Like sugar-glaze. The two bureaucrats were dying with their tongues swollen and their faces black, and their eyes . . . *This* time he needed no hatchet; there was no need to rip out air hoses. This time the Peacekeepers couldn't call it murder!

"Duke."

The man who spoke was tall and rigidly straight, with bare arms that were long and hard-muscled. His hair was close-cropped and gray, the same color as his eyes. Griffin Joyner, Tench's Chief of Guards.

"What the hell do you want?"

"To tell you something, obviously," Joyner said. He had no fear of Tench; on three occasions the Duke had ordered his death for precisely that reason. But the former military man had learned of it each time, the Duke's too-friendly manner signaling the plot, and each time Joyner had discovered and personally butchered the designated assassins. He'd never sought revenge; the attempts on his life were trivial and pitifully inept, and therefore as natural to Tench as breathing. To acknowledge them at all was beneath his dignity, and would honor-bind him to kill Tench. Griffin Joyner had decided long ago that when he wanted visibly to hold ultimate power on Mercator, he would visibly take the power. Until that time he'd be content, and amused, to serve as he did.

"Then tell me something!" Tench said, irritated as always by the man's arrogance. If only he weren't so valuable! And deadly. The Duke said more quietly, "What is it, Griffin?"

"Should this be here?" Joyner pointed at Gault, who was sitting on the floor at the bed's baseboard. He'd been writing out an elaborate plan to murder Barrow when the three guards had entered. Now he sat frozen, smiling at a fixed point across the chamber and saying nothing.

Tench sat up and looked. He vaguely remembered the little pest being there, and rambling on about something that was funny and helped him to sleep. He shrugged.

Joyner took Gault by the collar, then heaved him at one of his companions. "Get rid of it. And both of you get out." Gault was hurled through the doorway, followed by the two guards.

"Well?" Tench said. He was sharply uneasy. Being alone with Joyner was always unsettling. Worse, the Chief of Guards seemed to be in good humor.

Joyner spoke in a cadenced, disinterested monotone as he told Tench about the flamed-out section of the Core, the forty-nine dead, all but eighteen mutilated in the usual way and those eighteen burned to skeletons; the six stabbed in the throat and all but one of them dead; the forty-two inmates who were all women, and all—up to now—thought to be deserters from Talon and all of whom were now missing; and about the two fires that had burned out of control until the areas had been evacuated and sealed. And—ah yes—he smiled, showing those maddeningly perfect teeth—all of the Duke's personal medical and food lockers were stripped clean. And lastly, three of the five potable water tanks had something in them that turned the water green and was pre-

sumed to be poisonous. When he'd finished he waited for the
Duke's inevitable curses, threats, and the single question that
defined the man: What does this mean? But instead, he saw
calm acceptance of the situation. And what appeared to be
deep thought. It was enough, almost, to inspire respect.

"I wonder why," Tench said softly. "Why now, I mean."

Joyner has asked himself the same question. He couldn't be
sure, yet. But he thought he knew the answer. It was simple
enough that, given time, even Tench might reason it out. But
that must not happen. If he was right, and if the Duke were
to know the true cause of this war, he'd barricade himself so
tightly they'd have to kill him to get him out—and then he'd
be more useless than ever. Or, Joyner thought, I could tell him
now, and kill him now. No. He's got to be alive for a while
longer. Pity.

Joyner began the story he'd formulated on the walk to the
Duke's chamber. As he spoke he ran the entire lie quickly
through his mind again, and again saw only the one glaring
flaw in it. "It's the boy," he said. "Simon Barrow."

"What did he do that could cause all this?"

Joyner said, with no hint of deception on his face, "In the
past thirty hours the boy's name has been mentioned at least
fifteen times by Talon and her chief advisors. My spies
couldn't get close enough to make sense of what they were
talking about. But it was clear that Talon herself is interested
in him." He lowered his voice and said significantly, "And
listen to this. Talon called Captain Hartner personally three
times in the hour before she started this war." It was a lie
within a lie. Joyner had never been able to place a spy in Talon's camp; insulting and frustrating. It was impossible to
know what Talon was doing. But of course there was a way
to use this. Every situation yielded opportunity, if seen properly. Tench believed, because Joyner had trained him to believe, that there was a well-formed network of spies in place.
And so Joyner was free at all times, as now, to interpret Talon's actions with complete credibility—in whatever way
served him best.

"Talon wants him?"

"Obviously," Joyner said sardonically, pulling Tench in
deeper. "And the reason can only be that Barrow's about to

be paid for. Talon wants possession so she can demand something from Hartner in return."

"But Hartner told me the boy would never be bought free."

Joyner shrugged. "Things change. The question is, why did Hartner tell Talon about Barrow, instead of telling you?"

"But—yes! Why?" The question was enough to trigger the Duke's natural paranoia, and blast away any possibility of logical reasoning. "And why didn't *you* know about it?"

"I'll deal with my own staff in my own way," Joyner said, in a tone that precluded any further questioning by Tench. Then he moved in for the kill. "Let's deal with what we've got. And that is, now we know what Talon's up to."

"Yes," Tench said. "Now we know." Holding back an inmate for barter—threatening to kill him or her, which would destroy the deal for all concerned—was done at times, but it was always risky. Everything depended on the purchase price. Guess too high and demand too much from Hartner, and you threatened her share. Persist, and she'd send in the troops. Felix Jacoman had guessed too high, once too often. But Talon was never wrong. Never. Damn her. If she wanted Barrow enough to start a war, he was worth a fortune. Maybe even release! That was done at times, also. Twice, in the eighteen years Tarnon Tench had been imprisoned on Mercator. And it was about to happen again! He clenched his fists, inhaling sharply and barely aware of the throbbing in his molar. He turned red and wiped spittle from his lips. Talon was trying to steal his freedom!

Joyner noted the reaction and released the breath he'd held. Tench's train of thought had gone exactly where he'd planned for it to go—thundering right past the story's weak point and directly into a mountain of self-pity. The Duke would see another chance at freedom gone, and it would blind him to the obvious: If Talon wanted Barrow, she'd simply take him. Quietly, as she'd stolen others so easily in the past six years. With none of her women ever caught. Not one. Ever. Joyner smiled, thinking of the witch-woman. Now there was someone worthy to follow. Impossible for him, of course. Impossible for *any* "him." He asked himself, Can I beat her if the war goes on after this maggot's dead? But of course Hartner won't let it continue; she'll kill everyone on Mercator to stop it, if she has to. Aside from that, *could* I beat Talon? Very probably. But only "very probably"; the witch-woman was good. But he wondered, not for the first time, *Would* I beat her. Ho, that's another question. Entirely different.

Joyner remembered the day they'd brought her down from Central. Felix Jacoman had just been taken by the rifle platoon—tied and handed over by his own troops, to avoid a slaughter—and all inmates who'd been in his inner circle were ordered to watch what happened next. Joyner was there, so was hatchet-man Tench, and brown-nose Montrose, and brilliant Valdez ... and a woman he'd never seen before. Hartner began the ceremony by crushing Jacoman's fingers in a set of pliers, then his toes. The screams and the begging were sickening; the man had no shame. After that she pushed him into the airlock, spun the dog-wheels tight, and started the timer. He had six minutes to get back inside before the outer door opened to space. No one ever saw Jacoman again. The stranger in the group of witnesses was Talon—called Maria by Captain Hartner. She was the most beautiful woman Joyner had ever seen. He considered himself a sophisticated man, as worldly as his sixty-two years and purposeful bearing conveyed. And there was no lack of women on Mercator. Not then. Nearly half of the inmate population, more than three thousand at the time, were female. But this Maria took his breath away. She was exquisite, so frail-looking he would hold her only gently, afraid of hurting her. Yet full-bodied and soft-shaped, as if taken from his innermost thoughts and sculpted into flesh. Into perfection. Her hair was raven-black, cut short all around and converging in a peak above the bridge of her tiny nose. She was a pixie from the kiddie-holos his nephews and nieces had so loved. The eyes, too, were black. And large. And very easy to get lost in.

There had been no explanation of why she'd been at the execution. He'd watched her and had seen her whispering as they all heard Jacoman sucked into space. A religious rite, he'd thought. If only he'd known, then. If only they'd all known. But they hadn't, and Montrose announced his intention of taking her to his cell immediately, while Valdez claimed the right for himself. The argument ended in a stalemate and a compromise. Tench left to get drunk, shaking from what had happened to Jacoman. Joyner had walked away lost in thought; his most urgent need was to decide whom to back in the coming struggle for power.

Montrose and Valdez both died that night. The rumor was that Tench had killed them—his reputation made it easy to believe—and Joyner advised him to go along with it. He also advised that no action be taken against Maria—to protect the rumor, but mostly because he wanted her. Even though she frightened him; or perhaps *because* she frightened him. Both corpses were missing the left thumb. But stranger than that, they'd been opened at face, neck, and belly, torn as if by the claws of an eagle in frenzy. Or, as Joyner had described it, giving Maria the name she now bore, the talons of a demon.

"Where is Barrow right now?" Tench asked. "She hasn't got him, has she?"

"He's protected," Joyner said. "I've assigned fifty men to stay with him."

"Good. Where?"

"He's safe. The fewer who know where, the better."

Tench reddened. "You won't tell *me*? What is it, Joyner, you're planning to make your own deal with Hartner? I'll—" He stopped, frightened by his impulsive words. To threaten Joyner was to commit suicide.

"You'll what?" Joyner asked mildly. Inside, he was howling with laughter. His contempt for Tench was renewed, and he felt better. "You'll understand why I'm suggesting respectfully that you don't tell anyone where he is? Or was it something else?"

"That was it," Tench said, relieved. If only he had his strength again. He with a hand-axe, Joyner unarmed. But of course he would lose. Stupid, even to think of it.

"Good. Come, I'll show you." Joyner turned to leave.

"I should go with you? Why?"

Because I don't want to knock you senseless and *drag* you! Joyner thought, losing patience. Because I'm not sure yet what has to be done and I won't move openly until I do know. Aloud, he said in a deadpan military tone, "You'll want to inspect the security arrangements. And the men should see you. It will inspire them."

"Yes, I understand." Tench stood and dressed, not understanding at all. If Joyner was planning to use the boy for his own benefit, as he assumed he was, why not stage the mutiny here, now? But that couldn't be it. If it were, Joyner would have told him nothing at all. What was he up to?

Griffin Joyner walked at a steady pace from the chamber and out into the throne room. Twenty guards, all male because all of the women had been immediately suspect and immediately locked up, fell into formation behind him as he crossed to the opposite entrance.

Tench came up quickly from behind. "Wait!"

Joyner stopped, obedient as he always was in public. Tench strode to where Gault stood, fifteen feet from the throne. "What was that idea of yours again?"

"To kill Barrow, sir," Gault said, his sharp eyes brightening. He'd have stopped there, if he'd paid attention to Tench's facial expression. "I've worked out a great plan, sir, I think it will amuse you. I've even written it down. For you." He offered the papers, multicolored bits of scavenged wrapping he'd stolen from Clonus's "box of treasures," along with the pen.

Tench glanced over it. When he'd finished he was smiling. "I like it. Very funny."

"Thank you, sir! I only hope—"

Tench spun away and took the papers to Joyner. "I want this done," he said, loudly enough for everyone to hear. He turned and jabbed a finger at the rapturously staring Gault. "To him!"

The Chief of Guards read the plan and was impressed. There were indications here of clear tactical thinking. Amazing. He looked up from the sheaf of papers and said to Gault, quite sincerely, "You poor bastard. You poor, stupid bastard." Then ordering his men to stay behind, Joyner led Tench to Simon Barrow.

➤ 6 ⬅

A small passenger craft speared down into Earth's atmosphere, like an arrow in search of a bull's-eye. With reckless speed it narrowed its target from Western America to California, to San Francisco Bay, to Four Sisters Island. As it neared the rock once known as Pelican Island, the craft executed a parabolic sweep that carried it directly above the new headquarters building of Universal Terramorphic Industries Corporation. It touched down lightly on the roof landing pad.

The moment it came to a stop a man and a woman emerged from the craft. Both were heavyset, tall, and dressed in classic-styled blue business suits. They were brother and sister, Marcus and Daphne Steadhorne, co-chairs of UTIC. Both were smiling broadly as they were met by a waiting aide and escorted in a private elevator down to the Board Council Room on the fortieth floor.

Six board members stood up from around a lacquered wooden table as the Steadhornes entered the room.

"Be seated," Daphne said, as she and Marcus took their places at the head of the table. Their broad smiles had disappeared.

"Have you heard the news?" Marcus asked everyone at once. He did not wait for a reply. "Very well, we will brief you. Daphne?"

"As you know," Daphne Steadhorne began, "we have all been quite excited about the possibilities in development at Fryeburgh Technologies."

All of the board members nodded, virtually bowing their heads. The expressions among them ranged from worry to hopeful enthusiasm. J. Carter Fryeburgh and his geniuses had constructed a computer model that promised to solve nearly all of the problems still resisting the best efforts of the UTIC scientists assigned to terraformation research. The Fryeburgh model had been produced and then tested on a small scale within a sealed dome on Mars, using only native elements and imported bioforms. It worked. The beginnings of a viable ecosystem had been produced. Fryeburgh had done what UTIC had convinced the United Nations *its* process would do, on any marginally habitable new planet. What Fryeburgh lacked, they all knew, was the political savvy to find and develop the right personal assets within the UN's labyrinth of appropriations committees. That aspect of business necessity was the strength of the Steadhornes. The answer to UTIC's dilemma, then, was to buy out Fryeburgh, or engineer a merger. The alternative was to lose the UN contract, go out of business, and probably go to prison for fraud. It was only luck—the destruction of *Shinar*—that had prevented UTIC's flawed terraforming systems from being tested, and exposed.

"A week ago," Daphne continued, "Marcus and I met with Mr. Fryeburgh. That meeting was not revealed to anyone, including you here, for reasons of security." There was a brief moment before the insult struck the board members. But no one responded. "Mr. Fryeburgh had been extremely reluctant to discuss our offer." She coughed and drank from a steaming cup in front of her. "But a meeting was set."

Relief spread visibly through the room. Daphne held up her hand. "Don't get ahead of me. You don't know—" She was hiding something. Everyone saw that. Whatever it was, it wasn't good.

Marcus put a consoling hand on his sister's shoulder. "Let me," he said gently. To the board he said, "Our top people, including the designers of the *Shinar* project, were included in the meeting. Fryeburgh agreed to bring his seniors, as well. The groups met at Nassau and flew to a private island east of St. Croix. Daphne and I were to join them after two days." He cleared his throat. "My friends, I regret to tell you that the aircraft was lost over the Caribbean. There was an explosion, apparently. Of course there will be an investigation. But I have been informed that no one survived the disaster. Mr. Fryeburgh and his associates, and thirty-two of our dear friends, are dead. I am very sorry." He took a deep breath and let it out slowly. Daphne handed him her cup and he drank from it. "I am very sorry," he repeated. "Now, you all realize what this news could do to our public position on the trading markets. Therefore until I make the official announcement, you will tell no one of this tragedy."

One of the board members said, "There's been nothing on the media, Marcus." The Steadhornes' ability to manipulate or suppress information was well known by UTIC's board members; the Secretary General of the United Nations was a personal friend, and omnipotent ally. "When did this happen?"

Brother and sister looked blankly at him. "It has happened just as he told you," Daphne said, then hid her face in cupped hands. "The board is adjourned," she said, looking up again. There were tears in her eyes. Rising solemnly, the board members stood in silence as the Steadhornes walked from the room.

Ninety minutes later the pair arrived at a hunting preserve they maintained for important guests, on the Upper Peninsula of Michigan. They were singing, very drunk, and deep in the shared ecstasy of a secret.

"Can you find another one?" Simon called over his shoulder.

"Oh, certainly," Clonus said. He felt along the cell wall, testing each sharp pinnacle with sensitive fingers until he found just the right size and texture. When he had defined the borders of the quartzlike stone, he pushed his thumbs beneath its lower edge and grunted. The veins on his neck stood out, pulsing, and his face darkened with the effort. A few seconds brought a clean SNAP! as the shard broke free of the coarser material. Clonus made a game of jumping after it as the powerful push of his thumbs sent the shard flying upward. This time he caught his quarry before it reached the overhead. "Ha!"

When he'd lit on the floor again, he scraped the prize against the wall to file it clean. "Here you are," he said proudly. "Will this do?"

"Yes, it's got a good edge. Thanks." Simon was working on the foot-square holo receiver. He'd broken the case open carefully from the rear and found all the parts there. The circuit boards appeared to be intact, which was critical; there was no way to repair them, here. And the battery, of course, still held power; it was top-grade and only fifteen years old. Caked-on dust was no problem. But several of the lumo-connectors needed to be cut apart to reattach damaged wire-ends. For that, these hard chips were adequate, even though they were impure and wore down quickly. "This is the last connector," he told Clonus. "We'll know in a few minutes." The repair had been made more difficult by frequent outages of the glowstone lamp. Without it, the cell was pitch-dark.

"It will work!" Clonus said excitedly. "Yes, it will! And I know that Mr. Tench will lend us some of his optic tapes. He will! Gault says he has a big receiver, and o-tapes of wild places on Earth. With snow! And whales! And some that were made by Captain Hartner, truly, telling us about the rules here, and some ..." Simon was listening only distantly. He too was excited. But for a very different reason. The last of the lumos was remade, and he carefully replaced the back of the unit. "Finished," he announced, reaching for the power switch. "Ready?"

"But don't you do something first? Say something over it?"

"Clonus," Simon answered in exasperation, "real power doesn't depend on words." Then he thought, *Or does it?* Knowledge is power, and knowledge comes by words. Something to think about. Later. He added, "Incantations are only to impress the gullible."

"Really? I didn't ... Is it all right for me to know that?"

Simon laughed, despite himself. "Don't tell anyone I told you so."

"No, never."

"Good." He snapped the power switch on and was dismayed at the reaction: Nothing. But then he felt the box tingling against his fingers, and remembered that these were ancient sets; they took several seconds to warm up. The vibration increased. It was going to work! He stood away from it and said, laughing with relief, "Do something, Clonus!"

"Me! I can't do anything!"

"We're a team now, aren't we?"

"Why, yes! Yes, Simon, I guess we are! But what can I—"

"Look!" The receiver's screen blinked, then stayed faintly lit. A bar of light formed across the top and began to glow through the colors of its characteristic spectrum—red, violet, blue, green, yellow—one by one. And then a curtain of shimmering white light grew out from the bar and angled down and out from the unit, reaching the floor six inches from the base of the box. "Thank you, Clonus." Simon smiled at the man who was staring gape-jawed at the perfectly functioning set.

"But I didn't . . . how? I didn't!"

"You got the stones," he said. "And I used them. That's what happened, and that's *all* that happened. Don't you understand? The only difference between us is that I've studied these things. But I couldn't have repaired it without your help." There was nothing in the cell that Simon could have used to cut the crystal chips free, and hammering them out would have splintered them to useless grit. He'd never met a man as strong as Clonus.

"But Simon, I used to repair machines all the time, and I even built one of these from a kit. And it worked, honestly! But I couldn't fix this one, and that's because I'm not a sorcerer."

"I know, Clonus. And neither am I, and I know you don't believe me. But you have to believe what I'm about to tell you, my friend, because you just proved it. You're more important than you think you are. You'll cause both of us harm if you ever forget it."

"I won't," Clonus promised solemnly. "Never."

"Good." It was impossible not to see the staggering lack of self-confidence in Clonus. This puzzled Simon, because just the opposite should have been true. Clonus was very much an individual, and remained so, despite the intense pressures a place like this exerted toward sameness. Standing out from the pack in Mercator was a dangerous proposition; it invited attention, and attention was not beneficial here, he had seen. Clonus had a highly developed sense of himself. And he had the rare courage to remain uncompromised in the things that made him unique. But incredibly, he thought of himself as a coward. Then there was his physical strength, which even for a space-born was nothing short of phenomenal. The same fingers that could delicately reseat a dislocated shoulder could just as effectively break rocks apart. Yet courage and strength were qualities he would never attribute to himself. Astounding.

"I think they're opening it again," Clonus said, looking upward. Half an hour before, while they were working on the holo, a guard had stuck his head and shoulders into the cell, looked around for a moment, then pulled away and slammed the hatch. They both heard the bolt slide home. Simon had looked questioningly at Clonus, who had merely shrugged and said that these "lockdowns" happened from time to time.

Now, as the hatch opened, Simon sensed that something unusual was happening. Clonus showed no interest at all. As he'd said before, fixing the holo-receiver was much more exciting than whatever they were doing out there.

"It *really* works?"

Simon nodded, unhappy at deceiving his friend. He wanted to say, *It will, yes, but not as you expect.* Altering the machine from its intended purpose had been child's play. Now he had a blast-weapon that was good for one shot. Maybe more, but certainly one. *In truth, my blaster will make a big hole in one of those scouters, right between the cargo hold and the pilot's compartment. Before they can turn on the gas.* After that? I really don't know. *But you and I won't be here anymore, my friend Clonus.*

As the hatch opened they heard a quick scuffle and a muffled curse. Griffin Joyner poked his head down through the entrance. "Clonus, will you do something for me?"

"Oh, certainly, Griffin. What would it be?"

"Keep this here." He moved from the entrance and pushed down an unconscious Tarnon Tench. "Keep it safe, will you?"

"Of course, Griffin."

"Thank you, Clonus." The hatch slammed shut and was bolted again.

Simon was staring open-mouthed at the hatch. As he watched Clonus carry Tench to a cot and tie him firmly down with long strips that he tore from his blanket, Simon found his voice. "That's Griffin Joyner! Isn't it? General Joyner?"

"Oh, do you know him?" Clonus finished the job and tested all of the knots, pulling them tight until they seemed to disappear.

"Of course I know him!" Every student, every military cadet, anyone who'd studied history or politics ... Didn't *everyone* know Griffin Joyner? Simon recited a student's catechism: "Griffin Joyner was the United Nations Special Deputy who broke the tax revolt on Luna in 2102. He sealed the domes and rounded up all sixty-three conspirators without a single casualty. And in '05 he was the Establishing Governor on Titan; then in '09 he was promoted to Second Command of the UN Peacekeeper Forces. A year later he was appointed First General in the new Exploration Service, but then he published *War with the Mind*, which was—"

"But do you *know* him?" Clonus asked, this time impatient with cold facts.

"No, we've never met. How could we? He went insane in . . . he was *reported* to have gone mad in 2112, the year I was born."

"That is the year he came here," Clonus said. "And . . . can you keep a secret?"

Simon was deeply curious. "If you like," he said casually.

Clonus took him to the far side of the cell, well away from the unconscious Tench, and spoke in hushed tones. "Griffin is the reason *I'm* here. You see, I did a terrible thing. Terrible! Five years ago, or maybe it was six, I rented a ship and came here to ask them if I could visit him. Because he never had visitors, and that's cruel, do you see? Well, as soon as I made radio contact, before I even got to ask, they were shooting at my ship, and one of their guns exploded and two people were injured. Not dead, though! Honestly, they got better. But it was a bad thing, just the same. Do you see?"

"Why did you do something"—he almost said "something so stupid," but caught himself—"like that?" Clonus would never expect to be fired on, simply for approaching Central with a question. Stupid? No; just naive. Incredibly naive.

"I had to, truly and honestly. Griffin is my mother's brother. But he won't let me call him Uncle Griffin, here. Because he doesn't trust anyone, do you see? He says they'd hurt me, because they're all afraid of him."

"You were sentenced to Mercator for *that*? For asking to visit your uncle?"

"Oh no, Simon! It was because those people were hurt."

"But Clonus, you didn't hurt anyone. Those people were injured by their own equipment. And it was probably illegal for them to fire at you at all, since you'd only made radio contact. You shouldn't have been convicted of anything more than trespassing."

"Oh, they never sent me to trial. Captain Hartner reported me dead, and kept me here. She can do that, because she's in charge here, and this is where I committed my crime. Do you see?" His face clouded. "But Simon, it's so cruel, because now my parents think I'm dead and I can't tell them that I'm alive and that Uncle Griffin is not crazy and I still love them and . . ." He turned away.

Simon put his hand on Clonus's shoulder and stood quietly while the big man wept. He understood the man's grief, but there was nothing he could say that would ease it. If his parents were still alive, they'd be as heartbroken as Clonus's parents, and that was intensely painful to think about. He didn't know which was worse: thinking of them in the grave, or thinking of them in torment. Perhaps it was best the way it was.

Isaac and Neferti Barrow had died quietly, knowing it was coming, content to be with him and each other. It was a long, wasting virus, determined to infect only those with a rare genetic irregularity. The disease eventually produced microscopic tumorlike growths in the central nervous system.

Isaac died first. Later the same day, Neferti held Simon's hand as the light in her eyes left him forever. He cried, hugged her a last time, and ran from the room. A week later the small import shop that had been the Barrows' livelihood was seized and sold at government auction, to help pay for research into the disease. With no living relatives, Simon was made a ward of the State. He remained in an institutional home for one day, and escaped.

The virus proved to be fragile and apparently died with its last victim—before any of the rumored curatives were cleared by the dozens of World Health Organization committees responsible for product safety. Research was abandoned when no new cases were reported for a consecutive twelve-month period. The recorded, final death toll was 87,619. But on an Earth of seven billion, it was pointed out in the media, more people than that died every year from bathtub accidents. Yet this "near disaster" served a worthwhile purpose: It underscored the desperate need for more research, more education, and more funding. At that time living alone in Vladivostok, Simon had written a response that was never sent: They should all choke and die.

The only solace was that Isaac and Neferti Barrow would never have to know what became of their only child. But even as he formed the thought he knew it was a lie. They should be alive. *Alive! I loved them and I miss them and they would know I never sabotaged that ship. They'd find a way to buy me out of here. No matter what the cost, somehow, they would find a way.*

Clonus was suddenly quiet, but still with his face turned away.

This man is the nephew of General Griffin Joyner, Simon thought. Maybe that's where he gets the courage to be unique. The difference is that he doesn't understand what he's capable of, while his uncle ... It wasn't the military and administrative brilliance of the man that impressed Simon so much, though that alone would be enough to assure Griffin Joyner a place in history. It was the book he'd written, *War with the Mind*. On the surface it was a scholarly treatise on military tactics, contrasting Imperial China's Sun Tzu of 600 B.C. with the later-born Japanese warrior/genius Miyatomo Musashi, and with the early American guerrilla leader, Francis Marion. Uniting the diverse elements of conflict represented by these three, the book then marched forward through time to the present, demonstrating that in nearly three thousand years nothing truly new had been devised in matters of warfare. And that the same mistakes were repeated, from era to era. The book went on to argue that since this was so, and with the communal "sameness" of knowledge in a transglobal society, future armies would inevitably fight to stalemate—repeating old patterns, wasting lives, and settling nothing—or else destroy the Earth entirely. But the threat of common holocaust or wasteful stalemates would not prevent war; futility had never prevented war. Wars would always be fought, Joyner argued, and therefore they must be won, as quickly and as economically as possible. Barring tactics of total annihilation, the only answer was to shift emphasis back to the individual soldier. Only then would the most vital ingredient of success—unpredictability—once again exist on the field of battle.

Joyner was a classicist, and used the time-honored illustration: "For want of a nail the shoe was lost; for want of a shoe the horse was lost; for want of a horse the rider was lost; for want of a rider the battle was lost; for want of a battle the war was lost . . . and all, for the want of a nail." One soldier, Joyner had insisted—proving it time and again from history—one properly trained and motivated soldier could identify and destroy the enemy's "shoe-nail." It was an old truth, he said, that ought to be understood again as the human species crawled from its cradle and stepped out into the Universe. Humankind must be free, together and as individuals ". . . to *go*, to *reach* for what's out there, and to *do* whatever is necessary to go even further."

But Joyner's next step was into trouble. To achieve what he termed "this lost genius of the singular citizen," he argued that it was necessary first to make war with the mind: to overcome the ingrained conditioning that pressed against the notion of individual initiative; to pass without hesitation beyond learned limits of endurance and achievement; to refute dogmatically the principle that "we" is necessarily wiser than "I"; to reject all modern definitions of what "I" am capable of doing—*if "I" am left alone to do it*. Great nations, he demonstrated, arose and faded into history with the rise and the fall of that one idea. It was time again for the "singular citizen"—who must first wage, and win, a war within the mind. General Griffin Joyner had asked his readers, "Shall this not hold true as ever it has, in the great domain of the Universe itself?" YES! Simon had exulted, putting down the book and pacing his room in excitement. The Great Domain! It would be the Universe itself!

Simon remembered that Joyner, too, had had his day at the General Assembly: Are you, General Joyner, advocating anarchy? No, he'd said, I am not. But isn't the "Mind" you refer to in your title merely a metaphor for our way of life? It is partially that, yes. And, therefore, isn't what you propose a return to lawlessness, a descent to the evils of barbarism, a plunge into total chaos and disorder? No, madam, that is not my intent. With due respect, General Joyner, this Assembly has presented expert testimony to the effect that you are indeed urging a kind of rebellion, a war of discontent, against the established will and mind of society. And that collective mind, General Joyner, is the United Nations itself! Now then! Are you saying that these experts are wrong?

Oh no, madam. In that, the experts are precisely correct.

The judgment was malfeasance against the freely established world order. Not a serious crime, merely foolish. Joyner received one week of counseling and was allowed to retain his rank, for humanitarian and public-relations reasons—but his career was effectively ended. The book was never banned; censorship was unthinkable in a free world. However, because it had been exposed by experts as "Paranoid resentment of order," the book was removed from libraries and bookstores and authorized school-lists, and was never again printed. But banned? Certainly not.

Joyner's signed apology was widely distributed, having been written on the same night he went mad and attempted suicide over the pages of yet another manuscript. Those pages were burned out of respect for the man he had once been. As the media stories said, it was a shared tragedy. For wasn't it society's loss that so valuable a citizen was without a close network of support, there at the end when he was going mad? Oh, citizens, how we need one another!

Simon was twelve when he'd read the book, a birthday gift from his parents. He'd wondered how Isaac and Neferti had been able to afford such a rare, expensive work. He remembered the dealer who'd come to their shop offering his wares. He was a merchant-scholar from the Saharan Republics named Abram Slate, an old and dark man with quick hands and hysterically funny eyebrows. He'd looked for a long time at Simon, then said to Isaac, "Your son carries both life and death in his hands, good man. Life and death by the billionfold."

Isaac had laughed, Simon remembered. Then he'd said, in the spirit of the exchange, "Can you be more specific, O wise one? Is it life or death that our son holds in his hands by the billionfold?" Then he'd exchanged a glance with Simon and Neferti. The old bookseller was putting on a good show. But there was no humor in the bookseller's reply, Simon recalled. He'd replayed the moment a dozen times in his mind. The old man's voice had seemed to roll up from the depths of him, suddenly hollow and weighted with deep fatigue, and cracking like a bone-dry riverbed. He'd locked eyes with Simon and said, "Both. He holds both. I said that, didn't I?" Then he'd broken the strange moment by grinning and chucking the boy under the chin. But Abram Slate had insisted that Simon must read Joyner's book; he refused to sell Isaac and Neferti anything else.

And he'd insisted correctly. The book was dismissed by his parents as far too radical and speculative. And they were bothered by the fact that the author had, in Neferti's words, gone barking mad after writing it. But to twelve-year-old Simon Barrow, the tome was a revelation, a series of detonations in his mind that brought in light and illuminated whole new worlds of thought.

So engrossing was this new knowledge that for months after receiving the book, Simon had nearly abandoned the daily physical routines he'd practiced since the age of one. This became too obvious during a sparring session between father and son. For the first time in years, and to his horror, Isaac Barrow was able to penetrate the guard of his precocious son, and land a blow. That was unacceptable. It was the threats of Isaac and Neferti—Go back to your work, son, or lose the book—that had restored his life to balance.

"Griffin Joyner is here," Simon mused, unaware that he was whispering aloud. "He never went mad. They lied about him, too."

"Oh, yes," Clonus said. "Truly."

7

Before opening his eyes, the Duke had heard a man crying. The thought flashed through his mind that he'd come magically awake at his own funeral. A dark room, a hard coffin, the mourning a terrible thing to hear. But why strapped down? Then he remembered, and his mind cleared in a rage of blood. Joyner! Traitor!

His head throbbed. He felt as if a cubic yard of granite was inside his skull and cracking. He heard one other person in the cell, breathing quietly. "It's dark." He spoke softly, unsure of his ground. "Who's with me in here?"

"No one is," Simon answered.

Clonus lifted his head, coming back slowly, reluctantly, from images of the first New Sarajevo that were more clear than he'd seen in many—so many—years. The playground had been especially vivid: The pipes outside the living-shell, great silver ones and thin, blackened ones that made a "jungle" to be climbed and "fallen" from. The game of tag with its infinite variations, catch the villain, find the hero, hide and seek, escape the monster. There was Joshua with no eyes, and Myrtle who was faster than anyone, and Boma who was trickiest and always the last caught. And the oldest one, who was punished above the others for playing where a single shield failure could mean death, as the grownups said a million times if they said it once. That was Farley Xavier Clonus, the oldest and biggest and strongest child on New Sarajevo. And according to his mother, who ran the school and knew about things, the smartest and the handsomest but also the one most afraid of people, and the one who would never leave here, and who would always be a blessing to his parents. She was wrong about everything.

Clonus blinked his eyes clear and forced his voice to sound as it always did. "Oh, hello, Mr. Tench! How are you feeling?"

"I can't see you. Is it Clonus?"

"Yes, sir.

"And I heard Barrow. Where is Joyner?"

"I don't know, Mr. Tench, truly. He asked me to keep you safe here."

"Yes. And you did what he wanted you to do. But I'm awake now, Clonus. You can untie me."

"I agree," Simon whispered. "Untie him." The sound of Tench's voice made him feel sick. He'd told Clonus about the young woman guard, and Clonus had responded by telling him about other things Tench had done over the years. What Simon wanted to do now could not be honorably done to a man who was strapped down.

Clonus replied, also whispering. "I think that would be a bad idea, Simon. I promised Griffin to keep him safe, remember? Please don't be angry, but I *did* promise. Honestly." It was a tone Simon hadn't heard from him before. The words were mild, but the tone carried the unmistakable message: Don't challenge me on this.

And he was right; Joyner would have a strong reason for wanting Tench hidden away and safe. He said, "All right, Clonus. Do what you think is best."

"Thank you, Simon."

"What are you two talking about?" Tench demanded. "You're a part of Joyner's mutiny, is that it? I'll tell you once: You can save your lives if you let me go *now*. Otherwise I won't stop my men from killing you. They'll find me, and you can depend on that. You can't keep me here."

"You'd rather be at the Core?" Simon asked, speaking low in his throat, taking a step closer to Tench in the darkness. "Just say the word. That's an order I'll gladly obey."

"You young hack! Who do you think you—"

"Please!" Clonus said. "Now just be quiet, truly! There's someone up there."

They all heard the bolt slide back on the hatch. It opened for a moment, admitting a bright stream of light that formed a circle on the floor. Griffin Joyner said, "Close it behind me," and dropped through the lighted column. When he touched down, the cell went dark again. He said, "Your men won't find you, Tench."

"You think they won't?" Tench bellowed. "You're betting your life on that!" There! Now they'd know where he was.

"No, I'm betting yours. And I'd lower my voice if I were you."

"You're not going to kill me!" Tench shouted as before, sure that he'd found the right answer. "I'm the—" His voice was stilled by a hand across his mouth that pressed into his rotting gums and caused his eyes to tear in agony.

"Please, Mr. Tench. Please don't shout. Truly."

"Thank you, Clonus," Joyner said in the darkness. "After I say this, he can scream as much as he wants to. Tench, you have no support. Half of your former guard is dead, and the other half is either hiding from Talon or looking for you. If they find you, they'll kill you. Do you understand that? And understand this. I won't waste myself trying to stop them. It's up to you. Let him go, Clonus."

Tench jerked his head aside as the hand was removed from

his mouth. It felt like a steel clamp opening. He sputtered, "You're lying, Joyner!" He strained against the straps, unable to loosen them even slightly.

"What was that, Tench? I couldn't hear you."

"I—" He hesitated, in turmoil. "Joyner," he said softly. "What's going on? The truth. Please."

"Very well. I owe you nothing, but there are courtesies to be observed. The truth, you mindless animal, is that you started a war with Talon. The truth is that—"

"No! She started it! You saw what she did!"

Joyner let out a long breath and answered with a calm detachment he did not feel. "We're both dead, Tench. It makes no difference to me if you hear what I have to say, and it will make no difference to you. Let him go, Clonus."

"All right, Griffin," The straps came away as Clonus broke them easily.

Tench sat up in the darkness. "Griffin, I'm—" It was difficult to speak this way. "I'm sorry. I want to hear it."

Joyner told him what he'd suspected, and had now confirmed. Tench cursed and then fell into brooding silence.

"Heavens!" Clonus said when his uncle had stopped speaking. "What are you going to do? The killing will never stop!"

"It will," Joyner said. "If necessary, Hartner will come down here and slaughter ninety percent of us to make peace."

Tench coughed and began choking on the blood collecting in his throat. Reflexively, Clonus pushed the Duke's head downward and handed him a towel from beneath the cot.

"But you won't let everyone die!" Clonus said.

"No," Joyner said. "Not everyone." He addressed the choking Tench. "I accept part of the responsibility, because I should have killed you long ago and did not. For that reason I consider both of our lives to be forfeit. And so this is what we're going to do."

Tench's throat cleared and he tried to shut out the cadenced, calm voice of Griffin Joyner. Then he was screaming incoherently. Then he fainted.

Simon spoke for the first time. "General Joyner, I'd like to go with you."

"You're Simon Barrow."

"Yes, sir."

"Clonus told me you're an exceptional lad. But apparently you're an idiot. Didn't you hear what I just said?"

"Yes, sir. I heard you."

"You should take him with you, Griffin," Clonus blurted out. "He's a witch. Not like Talon, but he's a witch. Honestly."

"Oh?"

"No sir, I'm not. I've tried to explain that, but—"

"I understand. Simon, we're not coming back. Tench is going to be killed, and it's nearly certain that I will die, also. Assuming that you're sane, why do you want to go with us?"

"Because I believe I can help." Then he said quickly, "I know you've got something in mind. Or something will happen that you'll turn to advantage. I've read your book. And . . . I know you, sir."

Joyner laughed. It was a low, rumbling sound in the blackness. "You do, eh? And you want to help? All right, Simon Barrow. Cast a spell to keep Tench asleep until we get where we're going. That will be a great help."

"Then I can go?" He was breathless. This was Griffin Joyner, the most original military mind in centuries!

Joyner considered. Clonus had reported to him that the boy was courageous, when they'd talked just after the Duke's asinine "gravity trick"—a joke that had ceased to be funny years ago. And the word had spread about Barrow's reason for being here. The sabotage was a lie, of course, just as his own "madness" had been a lie. The stowing away on *Shinar* was bold enough to inspire admiration—and foolhardy enough to leave a question about the boy's reliability. He said pointedly, "Why ask me? You go where you please, don't you? With or without permission."

"Yes, sir," Simon answered immediately. "And when I'm wrong, I face the consequences."

Joyner was quiet. That was the only good answer. Maybe Clonus was right, almost, about the boy. He was obviously intelligent, not a witch—probably contemptuous of the subject, which was understandable but ignorant, and could be fatal—and he claimed to have read the book. Did he understand it? Joyner had met no one who'd read or heard of it, after his abduction. He asked, "Which is to be preferred, Simon. Long life, or glory?"

"You used that in your seventh chapter, General Joyner. The same question was asked of Alexander the Great. My answer is the same as his." He added to himself, *But only a fool chooses one over the other, if both are possible.*

"Good enough." Joyner's hand found Simon's shoulder. "So long as you understand. Let's go."

8

Twelve died quietly, all but one by their own hands. All forty-two of Talon's newly returned agents had been aware of Corinne's presence on the Duke's side of Mercator. Most had had no direct contact with her. These were harshly disciplined but allowed to live. Twelve, however, had been among Tench's guard force when the monster condemned Talon's daughter to die at the Core. These had failed to alert Talon. Like Tench, their guilt was absolute. For this she could not afford to forgive them—life on Mercator did not allow for failure, or for a lapse in discipline. What had to be done here and now, and in the fight against Tench and his troops, was for the survival of the Family itself. Never again must anyone feel it was safe to attack a person who was—or might be—associated with Talon.

Still, for the sake of those watching, for the espirit de corps they would need in the coming war, Talon wanted the guilty to die with dignity—all but one.

Eleven drank the numbing elixir offered, and after a minute had no physical or emotional sensation as, on command, they watched their own hands plunge long dagger blades into their own hearts. Their need for courage had ended when they drank the potion Talon offered.

The twelfth refused the drink, as Talon had known she would. Older and smaller than the rest, this woman walked beneath the cold, dry stare of Talon, to the shivering girl. A tear fell from her cheek to Corinne's as she bent close and whispered, "Forgive me."

"She will not," Talon snapped bitterly. She too was whispering. Even so, her voice shattered the pall of silence that hung in the chamber. "You, above all the rest. Corinne and I sacrificed everything to protect you. You—" Her voice broke and stopped suddenly, as if a stone had lodged in her throat.

The condemned woman lowered her eyes to Talon's feet. "I know," she said simply. She made no movement as Talon approached her, nor did she flinch as her cousin's hand flashed from beneath her robe. A thin blade drove through her eye and deep into her brain. Consuela Ramona Garcia y Hernandez fell to the stone floor and thrashed involuntarily until she was dead.

Tarnon Tench came awake and screamed. He spasmed, then fell silent as Griffin Joyner's fingers closed viselike around the back of his neck. Joyner half-pushed and half-carried the hirsute man at arm's length ahead of him in the micro-gravity, through the deserted tunnels of Mercator. His other hand rested on the pommel of his sword. He didn't want to kill Tench and thus diminish his value as a gift to Talon. But he knew that a silent, desperate, and passive man could be only one instant away from a shrieking, savage, and inhumanly strong madman. He'd seen it happen often enough. And Tench had made the transition before.

Joyner was oddly pleased that Barrow had come along. The boy's presence did not add to his hopes for personal survival, which were nil, but Barrow was interesting company; he had proved himself to be a radical element in the texture of certainty. Joyner smiled to himself, knowing that if he'd made that observation out loud, Barrow would cite its chapter and page from *War with the Mind*, and then go on to quote the rest of the passage. Maybe that was it, he thought. Simon Barrow understood a dimension of Joyner's being that no one else did. And the boy approved. Ego, he wondered? Of course. And something related, much more difficult to contemplate. Griffin Joyner wanted a friend. But this would not be a long friendship.

Under other circumstances he'd have dismissed the boy's request to accompany him as a foolhardy quest for adventure.

But since Barrow was going to die no matter what happened, it seemed only decent to allow the boy some choice in how that happened.

Simon Barrow trailed four paces behind the two. He was searching his mind for the solution he believed was already at work in General Joyner's actions. There had to be more to it than personal surrender, in exchange for an end to the war. Why would Talon agree, if she already had them in her custody? Of course she would stop the killing at some point, before Captain Hartner arrived to suppress the war with rifles and gas grenades. But by that time, another thousand innocent people—if such could be said for anyone on Mercator—could be dead. Except for Clonus, the noncombatants had been locked in their cells by Tench's men when the alarm first sounded. That was procedure. Later the women guards, all of whom were now suspected to be Talon's agents, were locked away also.

But there was no one to release these people now. Half of the Duke's personal guards were dead and the other half were hiding. Those eighteen hundred or so locked in their cells were defenseless. Talon's forces would simply free those who were her agents, and murder anyone else they found. Joyner was an honorable man and would never allow such a slaughter. Of that, Simon was certain. What was his plan?

Simon had understood, as soon as he'd heard Joyner's assessment of what had begun the war, that he himself would be a priority target for Talon. He had instigated the events that ended with Corinne's death-sentence. Was the girl dead? It was impossible to know, from the flamed-out skeletal remains found in that one cell area. Why was Corinne of special value to Talon? He blamed himself for her fate. Yes, she had come at him with a knife, in a hostile environment. But if he'd looked closer—*When will you learn?*—it would have been plain that she was not a threat; astounding as it was in a place like this, the girl was merely playful. He should have understood. *Would I have found another way to impress that hairy jackass? Was there another way?* He was certain now from what he'd learned that Tench had been planning to kill him that day, for amusement. In a sense Corinne had saved his life. Or more accurately, he told himself coldly, he had sacrificed her life for his.

"Why are we stopping?" Tench asked.

"Quiet," Joyner said. He held himself and Tench immobile.

Simon wondered also, and realized that he'd been much too absorbed in his own thoughts. He hadn't even noted the last turn that had led them to this particular tunnel. *Simpleton!* There was nothing and no one in sight. It was wider here than in the other passageways they'd come through. *Think!* The lighting was no different than anywhere else; glowstones at six-foot intervals. He'd heard nothing, except for the sounds of their own breathing and the drag-step-drag of their feet. Why had Joyner stopped? What was different? Only the air. The air was a bit cooler and fresher. Of course! That was it. Someone had opened a nearby hatchway. Recently.

"Take me to see Talon," Joyner called out. His voice was loud enough to be heard, but carried no sense of alarm. He shoved Tench a few paces forward. The hairy man stumbled and righted himself, looking in both directions and afraid to move. Joyner called out again. "I brought her a gift."

A female voice answered. "You brought her *three* gifts."

"Hello, Elaine," Joyner said, sounding mildly surprised. "So, you were one of Talon's agents? I congratulate you on a fine deception. Now, come out with your people. Don't be frightened."

"Hack you, Griffin!"

"Why, certainly!" Joyner said, chuckling. "But first you must stop hiding. I will do the rest. As ever."

Simon was not at all surprised to see the man smiling. It's not bravado, he thought; Joyner was genuinely enjoying this.

Twenty feet ahead, three women emerged from each side of the jagged tunnel walls. The six were carrying swords, and each had a sheathed dagger. Foolish, Simon thought immediately, if they expected a close-in fight from ambush. Close-in was work for the dagger, not sword. Was Talon sending out untrained troops? Not likely. Perhaps they had something else in mind. And then it was clear; of course they did. They expected Joyner and his party to pass them; then they would stand ready with swords to block a retreat. He tapped Joyner on the shoulder, to warn him that others were just ahead. Before he could speak, Joyner turned and said, "I know. Good observation, Simon." There was something in his eyes when he said that. Was it pride?

Joyner turned to face the closest of the women, now fifteen feet ahead. "If you and your friends attack," he said, gesturing to include the tunnel behind the six, "we'll kill you. Or if you win, Talon will kill you. You would be wiser to obey my order and take me to her." He paused for a second, then shook his head. "Elaine," he said patiently, as if to a child. "Do you need me to explain this again?" Her uncertainty confirmed for Joyner that he'd been correct; Talon wanted him, and Tench and Barrow. Alive.

The woman he'd called Elaine glared at him. "Take off the weapons," she demanded.

"Of course," Joyner said. He unstrapped the belt holding sword and dagger. "But that's stupid."

"Stupid to disarm you?" She laughed. "You're a prisoner, Griffin!"

"Correct." He dropped the belt and stood away from it. "And now if I or my friend here are killed, it cannot be said that we started the trouble, can it? What will Talon do to you if that happens? You *are* in charge here, aren't you? Well?"

"Stop!" Elaine shouted. "No more questions! I know how you twist things, Griffin. Now stop it! Walk toward us. Now!" Joyner smiled pleasantly and held out his empty hands. He stepped toward her, followed by Simon. After two steps she held out a hand to stop him. "Pick up your hacking sword first! Let's go!"

Tench had been standing immobile between the two groups. He was confused, terrified, and enraged. He still didn't understand what Joyner had in mind, but he was certain that his death was a part of the plan. And he was enraged at this mutiny by his Chief of Guards. How dare he betray the Duke? The DUKE! ME! I own this damned prison! Jacoman died, and then it was me. That's the system! Eighteen years! I *paid* my dues! It's mine! He turned and screamed at Joyner, spraying fine droplets of blood from his rotting gums. "Liar! Traitor! Thief!"

Tench squatted and pushed off from the stone floor, launching himself at Griffin Joyner. His hands were outstretched with murderous intent.

Elaine groaned. "No, no." She shouted at her troops, "Stop him! Talon will kill me!"

The troops were too far away to make a difference. Joyner

squared himself to meet the charge, intending to step aside and shove the fool's face into the stone floor as he passed. But Joyner was jerked off balance as Simon caught him by the tunic and threw him roughly back and to the side. As Joyner stepped backward to catch himself, Simon pushed ahead of him and stood directly in the Duke's flight path. Tench flew at him, nearly blind from the blood raging through his brain. Simon bent double at the waist, crumpled himself, and rolled—too slowly, it seemed—onto the floor. He arrived on his back just as Tench's reaching arms passed over him. Using the hard floor as leverage, he punched straight up with both arms. His left fist slammed into Tench's pulpy mouth just as his right buried itself in the man's soft belly. With his inertia and momentum broken, Tench angled upward past Simon. He was caught around an ankle by Joyner, who hauled him down again.

By now Elaine and her troops had reached them. Simon offered no resistance as he was pulled to his feet and held by two of them. The big woman to his right said to him. "Fitting. That was fitting." She squeezed his shoulder with powerful fingers and half-smiled. Her face was wide and attractive, with almond-shaped brown eyes. Central Asia, he thought; probably Mongolian. Simon hadn't seen her before, but apparently she'd heard about his being strapped to a pipe and launched at the gravity dome.

Griffin Joyner stepped close to Simon and stared at him. "Don't do that again, Simon. Do you understand me?" The quiet husk of his voice was chilling.

"Yes sir," Simon answered. "I'm sorry. But—"

"You had a reason for acting. To protect me, and to repay a debt in kind. Whether or not I'll beat you senseless for it remains to be seen." The anger left his voice. Now his tone was that of a teacher. "There is a procedure among warriors in small personal clashes, Simon, which originated with the Samurai. If one wants to take over a particular action, the proper word is *Dozo*—'with your permission.' If it is safe to do so, the other steps aside. You have been told once and will be expected to remember. If we are to work together."

"Yes, sir." Simon weighed the significance of Joyner's words. '. . . warriors . . . we . . . work together . . . we . . .' "Yes, SIR!"

Two of Elaine's troops picked up the unconscious Tench. The four other women formed up around around Joyner and Simon. Ten more emerged from their hiding places and surrounded the group as it reached them. No words passed as they continued through the tunnel toward the dogged-shut hatchway which marked the beginning of Talon's half of Mercator.

"You are a maniac, Marcus. A mad, moronic, murdering maniac. And a mellifluous malefactor, I might add. Were you aware of that, my dear friend?"

"And you're a pretentious bore, Carter," Daphne Steadhorne said, "who doesn't—"

"Who doesn't understand his situation," Marcus finished for her. "We have saved you, Dr. Fryeburgh. No one will ever come after you again."

J. Carter Fryeburgh shook his head. "You saved me, eh? By killing nineteen of my senior people, and thirty-two of your own. Yes," he said sardonically, "of course I see the logic. Right. As I say, you are quite insane." He turned to Daphne. "And since I am apparently addressing two bodies with one mind, please consider yourself identically identified. As it were. Ahem." He faced Marcus again. "My malevolent friend, may I ask from whom you have saved me?"

"From us, of course." Marcus Steadhorne reached under the table set between them and brought up a wide, flat metal box. From it he withdrew a sheaf of papers and offered them to Fryeburgh. "Would you like to examine these?"

"Certainly not. I assume this concerns past investigations?"

"Yes," Daphne said. "Nine years ago you were arrested for killing several people who were linked to your business. We have proof that you were guilty, after all."

Fryeburgh laughed at them both. "As I have said. Past investigations. I was innocent, and was so designated by a court of law. Even if I were guilty, I could not be tried again for the crimes. But of course that is hypothetical. For unlike yourselves, I am not a murderer."

"Yes, you are," Marcus said. "And a liar. Our people have looked into this exhaustively, Carter. There are three killings here you were never charged with. You can be tried for those. We can guarantee your conviction."

"And execution," Daphne added.

For the first time, Fryeburgh was truly alarmed. He had never taken the life of another human being—unless imagining and opining with intimate associates were culpable offenses. But innocence would not protect him from the Steadhornes. The corruption of a court was one of the very few demonstrable successes of UTIC.

Daphne said, "We intended to use the information to force you to provide us with your newest discoveries."

"But we would rather have you as a willing partner," Marcus said. "And—"

"And now we do," Daphne finished. "You can walk out of here, Carter. That's right. You're free to come and go as you like. You can tell the authorities that you had decided against taking that Caribbean vacation, and that you mourn the loss of those who died. You might be under some suspicion because of your past, but there is no evidence of wrongdoing to be discovered in the recent disaster. And so in the end no one will doubt you."

Marcus said, "As our partner your income will increase substantially because we have a very lucrative market for your work. You will be wealthy and content with UTIC, Carter. Until you disappoint us. On that day—"

"You will be arrested for these crimes," Daphne said, pointing at the sheaf of papers. "And you will be sent to prison for the rest of your life. Which will be very unpleasant."

"And very short," Marcus assured him.

"You won't run," Daphne said in response to the change in Fryeburgh's eyes. "We'd find you. We have resources."

Brother and sister exchanged a smile.

"You killed my senior people," Fryeburgh said numbly. His nerve, and his phony accent, had deserted him. "How can I work—"

"Really now, Carter," Daphne said, mocking his affectation. "Do you imagine us fools?"

"I told you, we have resources," Marcus said. "We know that not one of those nineteen seniors was involved in the project that interests us. They were useless."

"And," Daphne added brightly, "all of the people we lost were involved in the details of *Shinar*. You see? We have covered our vulnerabilities."

"And exposed yours," Marcus said. "We own you, Carter. Learn to enjoy it."

J. Carter Fryeburgh was silent for several minutes. Sister and brother watched him complacently, savoring and sharing a complete victory. Then Fryeburgh began to laugh, hesitantly at first, looking from one smiling Steadhorne to the other. He took off his spectacles and mopped his forehead with a sleeve. Then his laugh became spirited. And annoying.

"What—" Marcus began.

Fryeburgh held up a hand. "Oh, give me a moment, won't you?" He took deep breaths, darkening the redness in his face. Finally he said, now fully in command of his nerve and accent, "My dear friends. How wonderfully you have entertained me. And how deeply, how thoroughly, how abominably upon us all, you have shit!" Again he held up a hand for silence. "Yes, yes. I accept your kind offer. We are partners. Done. Sealed. Delivered. And as a token of my good faith, I will reveal to you very sensitive information regarding Fryeburgh Technologies." He laughed again and cleared his throat. "You were quite mistaken to refer to me as a murderer. But, my friends"—he put the spectacles back on and gave them his most dignified smile—"I am assuredly pretentious. And a thoroughgoing fraud, of course."

"It's so unfair," Daphne Steadhorne said, sulking. "We're *all* thieves!"

It was an hour later. All three were drunk. The collective mood alternated between hilarity and depression as they discussed the past, and their new linkage.

J. Carter Fryeburgh had invented, had discovered, nothing. He was a businessman whose success was built around the genius of one nonaccredited lab assistant—who rapidly became a senior scientist—and, as quickly, his wife. One morning he was arrested as a murderer. The media came early, grew thick, and made celebrities of the entire family. Gina Fryeburgh couldn't bear the disgrace. While Carter was in jail awaiting trail she never communicated with him. After the acquittal he returned to their home, and found nothing but silence and a notarized certificate of divorce. Gina had taken their child and gone. The only item on the plus side was that she'd removed her resident relatives, as well. Since that time he'd hired a number of people whose primary function was to interpret Gina's lab notes, a secretive and tedious process. His wife had worked alone, and wrote in a series of codes that she shared with no one. The deciphering process yielded major results, but slowly. It was maddening, how slowly. J. Carter Fryeburgh's "discoveries" kept the business going, but were never really enough. She had never come back, and no agency he'd hired had been able to find her.

"The Martian espheriment was small," Fryeburgh said, carefully setting down a cup of sweet-sour liquor. "Won't work without hyperoxychen ... hyperosha ... canned air. Lots o' hackin' canned air. Usheless on a new planet. Even if you could get us to one, you frauds!" He sighed. "No good without Gina."

"We'll track her," Daphne said for the hundredth time. Again, her mood swung upward.

"If she's alive," Fryeburgh said. Depression set in again.

"We have resources," Daphne said emphatically. She giggled and swallowed more from her cup. She felt better again.

"Name," Marcus said. "Name name again." His pen was poised unsteadily over a sheet of paper covered with wild lines and looping scratches.

"Fryeburgh!" he said defiantly, and sadly, knowing he could never claim her again. "Maria Gina ... REgina ... Maria Regina Hernandez eee Estephanzi ... Eshtephi ... Oh hell, Markey, give me the damned pen. I'll write it down for you."

Hung by his wrists high up on a wall in the Duke's throne room, William Chadwick Gault had never been so frightened in his life. Three feet below him was a thin, sharpened six-foot wooden pole. It was held erect by a loose pile of rocks that hid it completely and formed a wide pyramid down to the floor. Beneath the base of the pyramid, switched off, was the terminal to the Duke's gravity generator. It was set for immediate and maximum power.

This was the fifth and final deathtrap he'd planned for the Duke's amusement. But Barrow, not W.C. Gault, should be dying here.

Tench's guards—*Bastards! I was a friend!*—didn't bother with the first four stages of Barrow's execution. Those steps had a solution. Barrow would figure them out. But this fifth one was a *great* joke. Even Griffin Joyner thought so! Because there was no obvious threat. It was just restraint a few feet above some rocks, no different from other rock piles. It wasn't even uncomfortable, in micro-gravity. It was a brilliant plan! We tell Barrow we'll cut him down later. And then later. And then we say, tomorrow. Maybe. When everyone leaves, Barrow scrapes the rope against the wall. Rope shreds. Wire in rope breaks. Circuit trips. Generator switches on. Rock pile collapses. Barrow slams onto spike like hackin' iron to a hackin' magnet. W.C. Gault becomes important!

His 'friends' had laughed at him. They promised to let him go, it was all a joke, just an initiation. He believed them at first. Why *wouldn't* they want him? He was one of them! Finally, he understood. Bastards. "Tell your lies to Barrow, you hacks!" he'd screamed at them.

Then from every direction had come POP!-POP!-POP!-POP! and the throne room doors clanged shut. The bastards were all running then. And screaming at each other when the gas started hissing out of canisters jetting crazily all through the room. And clawing like animals at the doors. "They're bolted!" he cried out. "It's Talon! You hear me, hacks? You're dead, you hacks!" The smell made him think of a shit-processor. His eyes bulged and teared. Then it was dark, and louder in there than he'd ever heard. He vomited and felt Mercator rolling. Over and over and over.

When he woke up the lights were on again. His first thought was, *They didn't see me!* The gas was gone, but the stink was worse. They were all dead. Brisson was near the Duke's throne, on his back. His throat was gaping open, with a knife still in it. Tench's pet, Harper, was still chained to the throne. He was lying face-down with his arms covering his head. Harper was the only one for whom Gault felt anything but contempt and hatred. Gault had been used by Captain Hartner on his first day in prison. Harper had been promised to her forever. It was better for him to be dead. Most of the other corpses were in a jumbled pile near the door to Tench's quarters. Blood was everywhere. Big and small pools of it, raised in half-bubbles like pimples on the floor.

Unconsciously he flexed his left thumb and felt a little relief. *Still there.* He'd bet anything that all of these dirty hacks were missing theirs. They deserved what they got.

He'd been awake now for a long time. Each and every moment he expected Talon herself to walk through one of the doors and look right up at him. When the shrill pipes began wailing again his heart went off like a rock-shredder and he pissed in his uniform.

The sound of the shrilling pipes caught Clonus dangling in the air, holding onto a ledge, in the act of opening the hatchway at the top of his cell. As the noise began he instinctively slammed the bolt home again and released the ledge, allowing himself to drop slowly to the floor. But by the time his feet touched down, he'd changed his mind. Something fearful was going on up there. He had hoped that Griffin or Simon would come back and tell him what it was. But not even Gault had returned to tell him anything. Gault would lie to him, of course. He would say whatever he thought would terrify Clonus the most. But that was all right. Just seeing *someone* now would be very good. Oh, if the lights would only stay on this time!

He jumped back up to the hatchway and opened the lock again. Very slowly he raised the hatch an inch at a time. *I bet I look like a turtle,* he thought. But this wasn't funny. This was frightful. As the hatch rose he peered in every direction, ready to slam it shut again. There was nothing to see. The corridor was empty in both directions. Not one of the hatches to the other cells was raised. The siren was wailing high and low, hurting his ears and then easing down to almost quiet before starting up again. During one of the quiet cycles he heard the sound of voices. Clonus slammed the hatch, but did not drop to the floor. He was determined to find out what was happening. Not knowing was a very bad feeling.

And then he remembered what Griffin and Simon had talked about. There was a war! Yes, a war! Talon and her witches were killing people. Because Mr. Tench sent a girl down to the Core, and that girl was special to Talon. Griffin and Simon took Mr. Tench and they were going to stop the war. Well, they must have done it. There was no one fighting here, that was plain. He felt better. Opening the hatch again, he climbed out of the cell. It took only a minute to go from one cell to the next, until all eight in the corridor were open. Thirty-six people came out. They all wanted to know what the siren was for this time.

Clonus shouted the same thing to each group. "I think it's telling us that everything is all right now." As he shouted it to the last group he'd freed the wailing stopped, as if to confirm his statement. "Oh, good! That was horrid, wasn't it?" The sudden silence left an odd, empty feeling in his ears that tickled. "Now," he said, "I think we should go unlock everybody's cell." He'd meant for them to go in different directions. But no one else saw it that way.

The inmates followed him from area to area, corridor to corridor. He was glad they did. There were piles of dead guards in many of the passages, and they had all been killed in ghastly ways. They found eighty of the Duke's guards still alive. Most were alone or in small groups—tucked between overhead ventilator ducts, inside closets, and above or beneath or behind anything large enough to hide a person. Some were in cells and had to be reassured before they opened the hatches and came out. A few still refused, and Clonus simply ripped the hatches out entirely. He insisted on releasing the women also; they promised that they weren't Talon's witches, and he believed them. No one challenged him.

Within two hours every cell on the Duke's side of Mercator was opened and all of the wall-away lockers emptied of swords and knives. Storerooms and tool bins were stripped of anything that could be used as a weapon.

Clonus never thought of it in those terms, but he was now the savior and leader of nearly two thousand frightened, angry—and armed—criminals.

The pipes and sirens had wailed again for the same reason as before: to call Talon's people back from the Duke's side of

Mercator. Or more accurately, from what had once been Tench's territory.

Now the hairy man who had once owned a face-plate shop on Luna, who had once been chief hatchetman for Felix Jacoman, who had once sat on a ragged throne and doled out favors and revenge and food and warmth and life and death—now Tarnon Tench owned nothing. Worse, he could not hide from his surroundings within rage and violence. The witch-woman had ordered her troops to pour something down his throat. He choked and spit, but the burning fluid went down. Now he was quiet. He had no desire to scream and curse and fight them. Now he was clear-headed. His thoughts were more lucid than at any time he could recall. And he could re-call everything. But the strange drink did not affect his inner dread. He was terrified. It was a silent, flowing terror pro-duced by every face in his sight. Faces that hated. Teeth and lips that were hungry for his flesh. Eyes that saw his naked soul, saw it writhing like a snake, twisting in fire; blistering and popping open in a thousand places. Eyes that watched ev-ery moment of his life pass before them, hating him for every thought, every need, every desire and decision and impulse that took him from one moment to the next. Eyes that knew he was nothing—NOTHING!—that should ever have lived. Eyes that saw his emptiness, his selfishness, his rage, his loneliness, his hurt—and loved the sight of it—all of him—burning. Slowly, slowly burning. His own eyes were bigger than the world and could see that the watching faces were right about him. He was screaming—not moving a muscle, not making a sound. All the faces were watching. They were all one face. It was small and dark, with eyes that were black. And satisfied.

"How long will he be like that?" Joyner asked. Tench stood alone against a wall. Both arms were stretched in front of him, one slightly higher than the other. His nose was clotted shut from Simon's blow. His mouth was open, breathing in rough gasps, and bleeding. The eyes were red and swollen and wild, twitching like twin cocoons ready to explode in birth.

"Until he is dead," Talon said. She walked behind Joyner, trailing a dark robe. "And then for eternity." She had stepped away from Tench minutes ago, but the wild eyes followed her as she moved.

Joyner was lashed securely to a chair. He could hear Talon behind him, could follow her movements by watching Tench's eyes. Every few seconds he felt her close to him. Twice she had brushed her fingertips against the back of his neck. Once she had brought her face within an inch of his cheek, and then repeated the eerie inspection on the other side. He had expected to feel the hot bite of a blade at his neck at any moment. Now he was sure that when she killed him he would be allowed to see it coming.

"You believe I'm going to kill you?" Talon asked. There was a note of surprise in her voice. She stepped around in front of him. Joyner took in a sharp breath and felt his heart slam hard in his chest. She had removed the robe. "Will I kill you, Griffin?" she asked.

She is so beautiful! Joyner tried to stop, and then ignore, what the sight of her, dressed in a short, clinging tunic, was doing to him. She was as soft and perfect as his dreams had made her. No, he thought. My dreams didn't make her perfect; she made my dreams perfect. He knew he couldn't hide his physical reaction. But that wasn't the battle he needed to fight at this moment. This was the same tunic she'd worn when Jacoman was killed. So. She'd noted his reaction the first time he'd seen her. She's making a mistake, he thought, wearing the same clothing now. It makes her psychological attack much too obvious to be effective. *Good; she's capable of error, after all.* His defense was to prevent her from humiliating him or making him ashamed, and using that to overwhelm his intellect. When she killed him it would be Griffin Joyner who died, not some pitiable creature.

"Will I kill you, Griffin?" she repeated.

"I don't know what you're going to do," he said icily. "You have Tench. There is nothing to be gained from my death, or the boy's. But it's obvious that you enjoy killing."

"Do you believe that?" she asked with no visible sign of anger. "Without verifiable research? Wouldn't *you* call that an irrational assumption?"

He stared at her. All these pointed questions, and especially that last, strange one. Was she baiting him to add to her enjoyment, or was she merely insane?

She smiled down at him. "Use your *mind*, Griffin. You think you're at *war*, don't you?" When she saw his eyes react, she lowered her voice and continued. "Yes, I've read your book. Why didn't you ever understand that? You've had years to reason it out. 'One warrior, unfettered and unpredictable, can destroy the fabric of certainty.' I found your ideas inspirational. I used them. More than that, I mastered them." She laughed softly. "*And* you."

Joyner was astounded that she had read his work. More astonishing was the possible truth of what she'd added. Had she mastered the subject matter? And the teacher? The sudden thought forced him to reconsider everything he believed about Talon—everything they all believed about her—in the now-glaring light of that possibility. Witchcraft. Mysterious mutilations. Eagerness to kill. Even omniscience. Other oddities that seemed beyond rational understanding . . . Real, or calculated effects? It didn't matter, of course. The perception was real. And that was enough to ensure that no one—not himself, the Duke, or even Hartner—had ever attacked her. Until the fool Tench blundered and harmed her daughter. Then Talon moved immediately to send the unmistakable message that this must never happen again. In an unforgiving place such as Mercator, it was exactly the correct action to take. But was it cold logic—or hatred—that had carried her to the right decision?

Another thought came, striking his mind like a physical blow. *She's done nothing on her side of Mercator, that I haven't done on mine. Me, they called a genius. Her, we called a witch.*

Uncharacteristically failing to form an instant assessment, he continued to stare. Logic was weakening, and emotion refused to be stilled. One thing was clear, though. Talon had succeeded in every conflict she had engaged in on Mercator. He'd always known she was formidable—and found that the basis for a deep respect and a strong attraction to her. Now she'd killed at least half of Tench's forces. Mercator was hers. Now Griffin Joyner sat before her, bound and helpless. And, perversely, every part of his being loved her for having the art and the skill to prevail over him. She'd beaten him; he loved her. And it made no difference at all to him that she was only seconds away from taking his life.

"Will I kill you, Griffin?" she asked again. She bent over him and brought her face close to his. "Why can't you think rationally? I find that surprising, and delightful. But do *you* know why?" She kissed the tip of his nose and backed away. "If I wanted your life, would you be alive at this moment?" Her eyes were impossibly deep, like space itself. And she smelled like roses. How was that possible, here? She straightened and brushed his cheek softly with her hand. His heart was racing. "You're trying so hard to feel nothing. But your life *is* what you feel, Griffin. Why do you deny your very being?"

He forced himself to look away from her, up at Tench. *That is what is real. Here, and now.*

"You're afraid of me," she said abruptly. "More than that, you're afraid of yourself." She sighed. "Have I thought too much of you?" Watching him with sadness in her eyes, she walked around behind him again. "You've written that a life of fear isn't worth living. I agree." He felt the cold steel of a dagger pressed flat-side to the back of his neck. Despite himself, he shivered. Not from fear of pain and dying; but from not knowing what she would do. During a long career as a soldier and then a stateman, and as Chief of Guards for Tench, he had always known what his enemy would do. Knowing had kept him alive. But now . . . The knife moved down, giving a hint of razor-sharpness—and was taken away. He felt a tug of the ropes binding his arms, and then his legs. The last rope was around his chest. When it fell away he stood up, momentarily confused, and turned to face his tormentor.

Talon held the knife, handle-first, out to him. "Go ahead," she said. "Do what you believe will end your fear." He snatched it from her hand, furious that she had called him a coward. He knew he wasn't. But she had also treated him like a fool. And she might be right about that.

Five of Talon's troops rushed across the room, swords drawn. Talon held up her hand at them, never taking her eyes from Joyner's. The five stopped.

From twenty feet away, also tied to a chair, Simon had watched the tableau unfolding. He couldn't understand Talon's brazen challenge. Did she believe she could humble General Griffin Joyner? Did she believe she could taunt him into attacking her? Simon knew that if blood were spilled, his would join the flow immediately. He wasn't worried, for the moment; it was a matter of trusting Griffin Joyner. Corinne stood and moved next to his chair. He had the impression that she wanted to speak with him, but was reluctant to be overheard.

Corinne seemed to be fully recovered from her ordeal at the Core. But she was different. Her hair was darker and shorter than it had been. And her eyes were no longer the soft brown he remembered. They were black, like her mother's. She put her left hand on Simon's shoulder. Speaking quietly, she said, "I hope he understands people better than you do."

Joyner took a step back from Talon. He turned to place her on his right side and raised the knife. And saw her eyes go wide. Without a moment's hesitation he snapped his torso to the right, pushed off from the floor, and buried the blade fully into the chest of Tarnon Tench. Joyner's gaze lingered only a moment on the wide and tortured eyes of the Duke. In that moment those eyes ballooned, but did not change in the madness that filled them. His mouth sprayed out a mist of blood.

Tench stiffened until he stood absolutely erect. He whispered, "Yes! Kill it. Please . . . kill it again"—and slumped backward against the stone wall. "Kill it," he pleaded, holding out his hands, staring into emptiness. Then he screamed at the flow of life inside him that would not stop, a grotesque and filthy flow where faces rose up and saw him and drowned and sank again. He ran screaming through a hell where a spinning sky was hurling down torrents of his own ice-clear memory. "KILL IT!"

Joyner struck again. This time the blade entered through Tench's lower jaw and speared cleanly up into his brain. The Duke shook like an unbalanced dynamo tearing itself apart. Then came a high-pitched wail, spraying blood from his mouth and blowing the clots from his nose. He collapsed, and was dead before he settled gently on the floor.

Griffin Joyner turned again to Talon.

There was a knowing look in her eyes. He'd done what she expected him to do. Or had he? There was no question of his killing her; not with Simon tied up and surrounded by drawn swords. Not when the order to stop the general killing could only come from her. Did she expect him to make a noble sacrifice? A demonstration of courage in the face of certain death, and turn the knife on himself? No, he decided. She'd known exactly what he would do. And what about now? Did she expect him meekly to hand over the knife? It was time to learn more about her.

When she held out a hand, he shook his head, turning to walk toward the cluster of guards standing near Simon. "Put the weapon down, Joyner," one of them said. All swords were drawn and pointed at his chest. Three of the guards took a step toward him. The rest formed a protective phalanx around Corinne.

"Who first?" Joyner asked, still walking. He knew he'd made the correct decision. Talon had offered him a death with dignity. This time he was sure he understood her. He stopped and placed the knife on the floor where he could take it up again before any of Talon's forces could reach him. "Corinne," he said. "Please go and stand with your mother." Any threat to her would be suicide—as Tench had proved.

"Yes," Talon said. "Do as he says."

Taking her hand from Simon's shoulder, Corinne stepped away from him and crossed the room. Joyner picked up the knife again when she was clearly out of his reach, then continued walking toward the guards. The women held their position.

"Where do you think he's going?" Talon said to the guards in her low, melodic voice from behind him. "Back to Earth? To Central? Out of this room? Get out of his way."

The guards parted, leaving him a path to Simon. Good, he thought. The boy is entitled to this. He stepped forward, fingers tight and wrist loose on the hand holding the knife at his side. None of the guards moved to interfere. With quick strokes he severed the cords binding Simon. When the boy stood, he offered him the knife. "Can you use this?"

Simon shrugged. "What difference does it make?"

Joyner nodded. "In the end, very little. But there will be a price paid for my life. Your decision is your own, of course."

"That isn't what I mean," Simon told him. He'd been thinking furiously for the past several moments, since watching this man and Talon together. Why wasn't it as obvious to

Joyner as it was to him? But he had seen this type of inexplicable mental lapse before: Isaac and Neferti Barrow had been highly intelligent individuals—but even after eighteen years of marriage they were sometimes as irrational and giddy as children, when they were together.

Talon came to stand near Joyner. "Griffin, your men are waiting for an attack that I will not order. It would be a good idea to let them know."

Understanding flashed in his eyes. "Yes," he said. "It would. Talon, eh, perhaps—"

She took his free hand and held it for a moment. When their eyes met his heart began racing again.

He handed her the knife. Turning to Simon, he said, "Let's go."

"Oh, no," Talon said. "No." She offered the knife hilt-first to Simon. "You will have the chance to defend yourself."

"Mother, I told you, he meant me no harm," Corinne said, crossing the room quickly. "He's a child."

"So are you," Talon said hotly. "That didn't prevent him from jeopardizing your life." She faced Simon again. "Take the knife." She tossed it at him, exactly as he'd thrown Corinne's knife back to her.

Simon caught the weapon by the hilt and turned it to take a fighting grip.

Joyner took a step toward Simon.

"Stop!" Talon said. "I can still order your death, Griffin. And I will."

"I've never abandoned an ally," Joyner said levelly. He stood next to Simon and turned to her, ready. The man and the woman faced one another. Neither would relent, and both knew it.

"Very well," Talon said. She stepped aside, pulling Corinne with her. "Elaine. Ke Shan. Torry. Robin. Kill them both."

"No! It's wrong!" Corinne shouted. Two of the guards took her arms and held her.

Simon looked to Joyner. "If you please, sir. This is mine alone."

"No, Simon. I can't allow it."

Simon smiled at him. "*Dozo*, General. You are expected to remember what it means. If we are to work together." Turning to face Talon, he said, "I'm sorry for what I did to Corinne.

But it was me, not him. General Joyner wasn't present at the time."

"I know that," Talon said. "Tench is dead along with the twelve of my people who were responsible. Your guilt is not absolute, as theirs was. But it must be paid."

"That's right," Simon answered. He turned to Joyner. "By me."

"Simon—"

"With respect, sir, you don't understand the situation. Please let me deal with this. Alone."

"No. I have never—" Something in Simon's expression stopped him. "You are certain?"

"Yes."

Clonus was correct as usual, Joyner thought. This is an exceptional lad. He said to Talon, "I agree to honor his choice. But four of your troops—"

"Three were for you," Talon said. She turned to Simon. "Corinne survived because of her will and her ability. You'll have the same opportunity. The fight will be to the death. If you win, you may leave unharmed." Gesturing toward the four guards, she said, "Choose one."

Simon shook his head. "No one in this room can win against me singly. You choose the life you want thrown away uselessly."

"Insolent braggart!" Talon snapped.

"I've been trained since I could walk, Talon. In ways you haven't seen and won't understand. I'll win."

Talon glared at him for a moment, then turned to her troops. "Ke Shan." She pointed to the biggest among them, the same woman who'd held Simon by the shoulder and told him that his action against Tench had been "fitting."

Instantly the woman stepped away from her companions and toward Simon. Her sword was already trained on his heart. With her left hand she withdrew a dagger from its sheath.

Reluctantly, Joyner stepped away to give them room. Everyone moved aside, giving the combatants a ten-foot free area.

Corinne said urgently, "He's only been here a short while. At least let him fight in gravity."

Talon considered the request and said to Ke Shan, "Do you object?"

"I prefer it," she answered.

The order was given. A guard brought the generator terminal to the free area. "Half standard," Talon said. "Set the radius at ten feet." When it was done, she said, "You have three minutes to adjust."

Simon felt heavy and clumsy at first. He guessed the adjustment would be easier for Ke Shan; unlike Tench, Talon would use the device regularly to keep her troops fit. But his youthful muscles responded quickly as he bent and twisted and stretched. Within the allotted time he was ready. When the moment arrived Talon said: "Commence!"

Ke Shan leaped forward. Her right arm was bent slightly, with the tip of the sword wavering only slightly as she moved, indicating a firm grip and loose wrist. The dagger was clutched blade-down in her left hand and held a few inches out from her breast. Her first pass with the sword was an exploratory move to test him—a spear-thrust aimed at his face. It was a move that Simon was ready for. He avoided the thrust by feinting to his right, stopping short, half-stepping left and planting the foot on that side, then back-spinning to his right. As he came around on Ke Shan's right side, the sword blade passed his neck harmlessly. Still spinning, he changed knife-hands and began uncoiling his right arm. The arm reached full extension as his squared shoulders pushed Ke Shan's sword-arm in toward her body. Simon back-fisted her solidly at the temple, stunning her. As the spin was completed, he brought his left arm around and stabbed downward in a quick, short arc. The knife hilt thumped against her chest. He finished the technique, which had taken slightly more than one second, by dropping his own weapon and wrenching the semiconscious Ke Shan's wrist backward until her knife fell. Simon squared both feet on the floor and shoved the powerful woman away from him. She stumbled to the edge of the gravity dome and then broke free, gliding spastically across the floor until she slammed against the far wall.

Simon Barrow stood straight, and turned to face Talon.

"By all that's holy," Joyner whispered.

• • •

Captain Wanda T. Hartner eased her legs up onto the broad wooden desk that was the centerpiece of the largest office on the space station called Central. With one hand she fiddled with a remote control device set into the arm of her chair. As she twisted the dial to the right, the room's gravity increased gradually. She moved the dial to the fifteenth notch and set the timer for ten minutes. Very quickly, her breathing became labored. The damned thing's broken again, she thought disgustedly. It reads three-quarters, but I know full grav when I feel it. I haven't been out here *that* long.

In fact she had been the commandant of Ceres, Mercator, and Hermes—collectively know as the Gulag—for nearly ten years. It was a dream assignment for a UN Peacekeeper whose primary ambition was not rank but a secure billet that could last until retirement. Only six years remained until Wanda Hartner would begin a life of wealth and total ease. The pension she would receive was insignificant compared to the sums she had put into various Credit Union accounts over the past ten years. The "hazard" pay she received for each trip down to one of the asteroids—to quell a disturbance or, more profitably, to extract a prisoner for release—was good. And the families of those inmates to be released were more than generous, when her Earthside bosses explained to them that Captain Hartner could not guarantee their loved ones' safety due to an already-exhausted budget. Her share was one third.

She twisted another dial in the chair's arm and muted strains of classical music rose to fill the office. Grieg was her favorite composer this month. The soft, pleading wails of Peer Gunt's mother, Ase, always soothed her. On impulse she reached for the monitor panel that formed the left side of her desk. She hit switches one at a time, each activating a hidden microphone on the asteroids. All thirty on Hermes were working. She heard conversation, laughter, anger, copulation, weeping, snoring, cursing, screaming. The usual. Ceres was the same. But the first Mercator switch brought silence. And the second. And the third ... all of them were out. Next she tried the two-way radio links to Tench and Talon. Both out. Another switch ran a diagnostic for the equipment at Central. All perfect. "Damn," she said mildly. How long had the system been off-line? Probably the surface antenna down there.

She'd have to send a repair crew. And a rifle platoon, just in case. There was no hurry. Tomorrow would be time enough.

What Captain Hartner most enjoyed about her assignment was the autonomy. The bureaucrats watched her overtime, supply, transportation, and maintenance budgets carefully, but the job itself was hers. It was her responsibility to warehouse the most dangerous criminals known to humankind. No one entering the Gulag as an inmate was expected to leave again; they all came here with life—or rather, death—sentences. There were new arrivals every month. And because it was prohibitively expensive, and dangerous, to billet Correctional personnel down on the asteroids to coddle murderous criminals, the Gulag's death rate was not a subject of great concern in the upper echelons of her employers.

Her back was beginning to ache. She glanced down at the timer; six minutes to go. The hell with this, she decided. Every week some genius in the medical department issued new guidelines for nul-grav assignments. What did they know? They weren't out here doing a job no one else could handle. She snapped the dial back to the third notch and relaxed as the oppressive weight drained from her back.

The desk's intercom speaker buzzed softly. "Call, Captain." Now what? "Who is it?"

"Home base. It's General Lindemeer."

"Oh? Well, put it through. Then get off the line."

A green light came on at the side of the speaker. "Vance!" Captain Hartner said, stretching comfortably. He was her immediate supervisor. They'd met only once, briefly, but they had a wonderful relationship; they were both getting rich.

"Hello, Wanda. Is this line encrypted?"

"Of course. What have you got?" Her mind adapted automatically to the long delay between transmissions and receptions. There were rumors about a new device that warped space and sent a signal anywhere, with no time lost. She'd believe it when they installed one in her office.

"We have an extraction to perform," the voice came back. "Two, in fact."

Two? This was a first. "How much?" she asked eagerly.

While waiting for an answer, she punched the combination to a top drawer and withdrew a small notebook. She opened it to the last page she'd written on. Lovely numbers, she thought contentedly. And room for more.

General Lindemeer's voice returned. "This is a special one, Wanda. I cannot discuss price this time."

Captain Hartner sat up straight, ignoring the sharp pain in her back. "What the hell does *that* mean?" she demanded. As soon as she'd spoken, she regretted the outburst. Suppose Lindemeer wasn't alone? No, she thought. If someone were with him he'd never use the word "price."

There was a sharp edge to Lindemeer's voice when the interminable wait was over. "Don't argue with me," he warned. "My orders are direct from the Secretary General's office. If *you* want to set a fee on this one, I'll put your call through stat." He didn't break for a reply. "Listen, Wanda. It was made clear to me in the strongest terms that this is important. I pass that admonition on to you. If anything goes wrong, you lose everything. Your commission, your pension, and those special accounts you have. Including the ones you don't think I know about. Further, you can expect to join me and *my* boss for a no-return flight down to the Gulag. Do you copy?" Again he did not break. "We've rerouted a civilian FTL ship from Phobos to Central. It'll be there to pick up the two inmates within twenty-four hours." He gave her the details of the ship and the recognition codes he'd established with the crew. "The inmates' na—" A burst of static interrupted the reception.

"Damn it!" Captain Hartner pounded a meaty fist against the desktop. She glared at the flickering green light. "WHO? WHO?" She had a horrible feeling that these two criminals were on Mercator. And dead. Or would be held by Tench or Talon for a high price. She'd have to send in all five of Central's rifle platoons, to be sure there was no resistance. Not this time.

The voice returned after a second, the reception smooth and loud. ". . . say that again. The inmates' names are Hernandez. Maria Regina Hernandez y Estephan, and her daughter Corinne. Repeat the names back to me, Wanda."

Captain Hartner breathed a deep sigh of relief. Talon. Thank the powers that be, it's Talon and her kid. They'll be alive, all right. And Talon will be grateful to me. In fact, I'll go myself. With the five platoons, of course.

She repeated the names back to Lindemeer. "I'll see to it

personally, Vance. We'll be ready when the flight gets here. Out." She broke the connection and added, "Don't *ever* scare me like that again, you . . ." Then she laughed and stood up to put her uniform on.

In the Duke's private quarters, Clonus and sixty armed inmates crammed the available space and propped Tench's large bed against the entrance. Others waited elsewhere, by twos and fives and tens, in overhead ducts, in lockers, in tool bins and food-storage areas.

The most frightening thing for Clonus was that the lights were out. That was Gault's idea, and Clonus was glad he'd found his friend alive. Gault was positive that Talon was coming back "to kill every hackin' one of us!" So they'd left those poor dead people where they were, divided up all the food and water they could find, and tore the wires out from the lights in the throne room. Now they were waiting. Waiting was hard.

The first of the five scouters from Central touched down against the outer door of Mercator's only fully equipped airlock. The second ship locked outboard of the first and the two were secured with a common passageway. The third, fourth, and fifth followed this procedure until all five formed a single unit stretching outward from Mercator. When all seals were tested and zeroed, the scouters' inner doors were cracked to equalize air pressure within the vessels.

The moment everything was reported ready, Captain Hartner opened a panel set into Mercator's outer door. The first code she entered on a number pad activated a small visual monitor screen. She verified that the airlock and the room beyond it were empty. The second code cycled the locking mechanisms inside. All good. The third armed a series of lethal gas jets in the rooms adjacent to the staging area her platoons would use to form up after entering. None of this would be necessary, she thought, if she'd been able to call ahead with the good news. No inmate would dare stand between Talon and freedom.

Captain Hartner rose and spoke to the man standing behind her. "Set, Lieutenant Ducaine?"

"Yes, Captain. All weapons locked and loaded. All masks tested and satisfactory. Radios checked and operable. Ready to crack the door."

"Very well. Crack the door." She stood aside as the lieutenant eased the outer airlock door open an inch. A few seconds passed as the air pressure equalized on both sides. "Ready to enter, Captain," he reported.

"Very well. Take your platoons inside, Lieutenant."

Hartner stood aside as men and women filed past her. There was a brief delay while Mercator's inner door was opened and the pressure to the staging area equalized. Then all five scouters were emptied of one hundred twenty armed platoon members, masks ready at their belts. Captain Hartner followed the last one through the hatch. When they were all in the staging area, she ordered Bravo Level to be aerated, and sent four of the platoons out. The pilots remained on station, with two crew members aboard each vessel standing by to secure all doors and to quick-release the scouters in case of trouble.

Sirens wailed and blared through all living spaces on Mercator. At the hatchway leading back to what had been Tench's territory, Talon and Joyner exchanged a look.

"Airlock," Joyner said.

Talon nodded. "Hartner."

"What will she do?" Corinne asked worriedly.

"That depends," Joyner answered. "If she sees my men out and armed, she'll open fire immediately. If they're still locked away, she may assume the fighting is over."

"No," Talon said. "All Hartner knows is that communications are out. I shut off both radios and all listening devices after launching the attack."

"Then she'll come in force," Simon concluded.

Joyner shook his head, visibly relieved. "This has happened before. The outside antenna needs repair every few years. If Hartner thinks it's merely a communications problem, she'll send only a repair crew and one platoon to check it." He turned to Talon. "How did you shut *all* the monitors off?"

She shrugged and smiled at him. "My agents began finding and rewiring the ones on your side quite a while ago. My controls were set to override yours, of course."

Simon watched as the general's face reddened slowly. "So I've seen," Joyner said. "I have work to do." He turned from her and spun the dog-wheel on the hatch, then opened it. It was pitch-black on the other side.

"Talon's coming. I told you she would." Gault pushed himself harder into a corner of the Duke's quarters.

"This is all so unfair," Clonus said in the darkness. "I . . . I know it's wrong to say it, but sometimes I wish Mr. Tench weren't here at all!"

"Are you crazy?" Gault hissed at him. "Tench is dead. So is Joyner, and that boy. They're either dead or they wish they were," he said grimly.

"Oh no! But they're good, Gault! Griffin and Simon. They're very good!"

"They're dead! And you're making me sick again," Gault shouted testily. "Keep your hackin' mouth—"

"Sssh! They'll hear!"

Gault felt a strong hand close over his mouth, and gave a muffled scream as he was lifted until his head banged against an overhead shelf. He went limp and silent.

"Oh . . . Oh!" Horrified, Clonus released him. "Oh, I'm sorry, Gault!" He placed an ear on his friend's chest and heard the heart beating, strong and regular. Then he checked his breathing and found it normal. He placed Gault gently down in the corner and moved a series of boxes around his friend to hide him. "They won't kill you too, Gault," he whispered. "I won't let them. I promise." To the others, he said, "Please, all of you be very quiet. I have to go and do something."

He left the room, and listened until the door was barricaded behind him again. In absolute darkness he walked without hesitation through the throne room, past the piles of bodies,

and down the corridor leading to his cell. Blackout drills had
been a regular part of life on New Sarajevo. Darkness frightened him, but he'd learned as a small child to memorize his
surroundings so that it didn't impede him in any way.

When he reached his cell he opened the hatch and dropped
down to the floor. After a few seconds of groping, his hands
located the holo-projector Simon had fixed. "Oh, Simon," he
whispered, as tears filled his eyes. "You were so smart, and
such a good friend to me. I told you I used to fix these sets.
Do you understand, Simon? I knew you weren't making it
work so I could watch the holo-tapes. I knew you were making a weapon. That was all right because it made you so
happy."

He felt for the battery slide-switch and pushed it on. The
projector hummed as power flooded its circuits. After a few
seconds the humming stopped. Clonus felt for the power button, careful not to press it. He took his hand away and tucked
the bulky but nearly weightless unit under an arm. Then he
jumped for the exit and pulled himself through.

"Captain, Leader Two. The lights are out."

Still in the staging room with Platoon One, Captain Hartner
keyed her radio. "Which lights, Barbara? Where are you?"

"Section Bravo Zero Six. Just above Tench's rooms. All
the lights are out."

"Can you hear anything?"

"No. Nothing."

"Send someone down to check the power boxes," she said.
Damn! The hatch leading down to Talon's area had been reported jammed shut. It was old, and probably nothing to
worry about. Except that now the only way to Talon was
through that madman's territory. All Hartner could think
about was Lindemeer's threats: The job. The pension. The accounts. Prison!

"Captain," the woman's voice came back. "I'd like to wait
for the other three platoons. Tench is doing something. I can
feel it."

"Just *feel* your hackin' portalights on and get your hackin'
butts to the power boxes and turn the hackin' lights on! Shoot
anyone in your way, unless it's Talon or her kid. Get down
there and do it!"

"Right."

Hartner keyed the radio to omnicast. "Leaders Three, Four, Five. Converge by numbers, Bravo Zero. Four, Seven, Eight. Expedite." She released the transmit button, wondering for the first time what it might feel like to be a hackin' inmate down there. It was a thought she quickly banished from her mind.

The platoon leaders reported in.

"Leader Three move to Bravo Zero Four, right."

"Leader Four move to Bravo Zero Seven, right."

"Leader Five move to Bravo Zero Eight, right."

Talon was fighting to control her temper. Her daughter had never spoken to her this way before. At least she'd had the intelligence to wait until they were alone. But the insolence!

"He is a child," Talon said as patiently as she could. "A child."

"And so am I, in your mind," Corinne snapped. "You're wrong about both of us, Mother. He is my choice." Her black eyes flickered, lighted with fierce determination.

"Corinne, we must have a good bloodline to continue the Hernandez clan."

"Simon is magnificent!" Corinne said angrily. "Didn't you see?"

"I saw a skillful boy fighting for his life," Talon answered calmly. "And that is all we know about him. He may be insane, as most men are. Or he may be a hollow shell as your father was." She said in a bitter tone, "Carter treated me as if I were a machine. I loved him, but his only concern was the value I added to his company. And Barrow has used you in the same way. Never forget that he was ready to sacrifice your life, merely to impress Tench. And he knows that he's alive now only because you care for him. Don't be fooled, Corinne. He would not hesitate to use you again."

"I barely remember Carter," Corinne said. "But you're wrong about Simon Barrow. I *know* him." She looked squarely into her mother's equally determined eyes.

"I'm sorry, Corinne. I can't allow it. There is someone much better for you."

"Here? Who?"

"General Griffin Joyner," Talon said. "We know his past.

We know his mind and his courage. We know—" Corinne burst out laughing. Talon flushed. "Child, how dare you—"

"Impossible," Corinne said.

"He is a fine man! Why do you think I sent you to observe Tench, and the others? It was to see for yourself, Corinne, that there is only one acceptable mate for you. And that is Griffin Joyner."

"Impossible."

Talon said angrily, "This is for the Family, Corinne. Everything is for the Family."

"You want him for yourself," Corinne said.

"Yes," she replied without hesitation. "But it's you who will bear our line into the future. Remember that I'm the prisoner, not you. General Lindemeer agreed to allow you here with me for a high price. You'll leave when you're twenty. But before I say goodbye to you, I want the future of our family to be in your womb. For that, Griffin Joyner is—"

"Mother," Corinne said. "I want Simon."

"You would marry this boy, and leave him here when you're free?"

"Never. Simon will leave with me."

"To use your own word, Corinne: Impossible. Don't you see? If you have no emotional attachment to Griffin, you will suffer less. This is best for you."

Corinne sighed. "I'm not the only one to be considered. General Joyner won't agree to this. And if he did, merely to please you, could you bear it? Knowing that he was with me, and not you? Even for only two years?"

"Yes," Talon said emphatically. "I chose him for you long ago. Recent events have altered the timing of my plans, but nothing else has changed."

"Of course it has. The way you behaved toward him—"

"I was unprepared for what happened," Talon admitted. "Griffin believed that he was about to die, and yet . . . Did you see him, Corinne? His strongest emotion was love. For me! I have never witnessed such a display of selfless courage." Clearing her throat, she focused again on the argument. "I was weak for a moment. It was a mistake I won't repeat. Yes, I can bear it."

Corinne, peering into the deep eyes of her mother, saw the invulnerable strength wavering. She said gently, "I know what you've had to do, who you've had to become, to protect me and the others. But beneath it all—" She took her mother's hand and held it tightly. "Beneath the witch-woman known as Talon, you're a human being. Just once, you can allow that to be so. Maria."

Through moist eyes, woman and daughter regarded one another.

She's not a child, Maria thought. *How long has that been so?*

Clonus sat in the middle of the huge chamber, in Tench's "throne". He was glad for the darkness. It was better not to see what he had to do when they came to kill Gault and the others. It was bad, he told himself over and over. What they were doing was wrong, and bad. For the first time in his life he felt no fear at all. There was only something very strange, and strong. He guessed it must be anger. With his finger near the power button of the silently vibrating holo-projector, he waited, listening for them.

"It's Joyner and Barrow." Griffin Joyner called out ahead of them as the two made their way slowly down the unlit corridor. After the first turn Simon had taken the lead, assuring Joyner that he remembered the rest of the way. The silence was eerie, now that the sirens had stopped again. Joyner had expected to encounter groups of his men before now. The power box that controlled this area was just around the next turn. His forces had apparently switched off the lights, as he'd trained them, expecting an attack—which would not come, now. But there should be advance parties in every tunnel. Where were they?

Joyner replayed in his mind that brief and incredible fight. Where had the boy learned skills like that? Joyner had trained half a lifetime in the martial arts, but he'd never seen a move like that against a sword, and he'd never seen anyone execute such a complex technique with anything approaching Barrow's speed and precision.

Griffin Joyner was a man who'd always kept emotion subordinate to intellect. But now he found himself nearly overwhelmed by the idea—no, feeling—that his future contained a great deal of happiness; on Mercator! He would learn everything Barrow had to teach him. And more than that: There was Talon.

He judged that they were approaching the power box. "It's here somewhere," he said, and began feeling along the wall.

Barrow bent over and scraped around the floor until he had a handful of loose stone chips. He stepped away from the wall and threw them all at once, in a spray-pattern that covered several square yards. A few metallic *chinks* located the panel. Stepping forward, he felt for the catch on the box. "Which ones, sir?" he asked.

"Left side," Joyner said. "Top, third, and fourth."

Barrow slid the top switch inward. Glowstones began to flicker at eighteen-foot intervals along the walls. After a few seconds the flickering stopped and the tunnel was filled with a dim cast of light. He looked up and down the corridor, and saw no one. As his eyes adapted to the light he hit the other two switches. After a short while the corridor was fully illuminated.

Joyner used the light to study the boy. Boy? No, he thought. He's quicker mentally and physically than anyone I've ever known. He behaves brilliantly, without hesitation. And under pressure he only gets better. Definitely not a boy. A very strange young man, and a very strange day.

"What are you laughing at, sir?"

"Nothing, Admiral Barrow. I was only thinking."

" 'Admiral'?" What had he done to earn sarcasm?

"Why not?" Joyner said. "I'm insane, not a criminal. For humanitarian reasons my rank was never officially taken away." He grinned. "So legally, I have the authority to appoint you a Peacekeeper. And promote you. Of course, the UN may not agree with your new title. So we'll expand it to the whole damn great domain of humankind."

Simon laughed. "Admiral Simon Barrow of the whole damn Great Domain. Thank you, sir. I believe I'll keep the title. And the hell with what the United Nations thinks."

"Allow me to be the first." Joyner snapped to attention and saluted. When Barrow returned the salute with exaggerated crispness, Joyner lost the serious expression he'd been trying to hold. He laughed longer and harder than he had in many years. Talon. Barrow. It had been the most eye-opening day he'd experienced since being sent to Mercator. And the most humbling day of his entire life.

The creaking of a distant hatchway could be heard in the pitch-darkness of the chamber. Clonus moved his fingers away from the power button, knowing he must not fire it too soon. He didn't know how powerful Simon had made it, or how many times it would work. The sound was coming from the ceiling, he was sure. How did Talon get her people up there? There was no air in Bravo Level, except when they were bringing in new inmates or work had to be done. There were a lot of rooms up there, he remembered. Maybe the rooms went all the way to Talon's side of Mercator. But how did she get the air? *Witches.* He was afraid again, but he wouldn't let the fear grow as big as the anger. He listened and heard the hatch clang open. They were coming in, dropping through the hatch. Then walking. Coming closer. A lot of them. Little lights formed and began moving along the wall of a tunnel that led into the Duke's chamber. His heart was beating very fast. They'll see me! What should I do? What would Simon do? He closed his eyes tight, and leaned back against Tench's chair. He stilled his breathing and pretended that he was dead, as he'd learned in the childhood games once played with such lighthearted joy on New Sarajevo.

"Captain, Leader Two. You need to see this."

Now what? "Report, Barbara."

"It's bad down here. The wiring to the lights has burned out, or been sabotaged. But whatever happened, it looks like it's over. They're all dead."

"What? Who? Who's dead?" Hartner decided instantly: If it was Talon and Corinne, she wasn't going anywhere but back to Central; take everything she could fit in a scouter, and get the hell away. Space was big; they'd never find her. She'd change her name, get new identity papers, and . . .

"Tench's men, Captain. We're finding piles of them everywhere."

"None alive?"

"No. And the ones we've checked have been mutilated. Left thumbs are gone. It looks like Tench and Talon were at war. And Talon won. All the dead we've found are men."

Yes. They're alive. "Have you found Tench's body?"

"Not yet."

"Has Platoon Four reached you?"

"Affirmative. Four is making a search of the other areas now. It may take a while, though. All we have is the portalights."

"Platoons Three and Five are on their way now, Barbara."

"Understood. As soon as this area's checked we'll work our way over to Talon."

"Very well, Two. I'm on my way."

At the sound of the first witch's voice Clonus pushed his fingers into his ears to protect himself from the spell she was casting. He made his mind think very loud thoughts so the voice couldn't get in. He heard the name, though. One witch said "Talon." And then he heard another one call back to her, "I'm on my way." The smart thing was to wait until they were all there. Then he could stop them from killing Gault and his other friends. But waiting was hard. He knew that if one of the little lights found him with his fingers in his ears, the witches would laugh at him. And then kill him.

Joyner and Barrow lit up the passageways as they walked toward what was once the Duke's throne room.

"Do you hear something?" Barrow asked.

They stopped and listened until the sound came again. "Overhead," Joyner said quietly. "It's coming from Bravo Level."

"Is that where the outside antenna is anchored?"

"The wires from the listening devices come together right about where the next tunnel joins the main area. From there it's a cable that runs through Bravo Level directly to the antenna box. But the box itself is over Talon's territory."

"So they started at the unit and are tracing the problem back to its source."

"That would be my assessment."

The sounds grew louder and nearer, then peaked and headed away toward the main room. "How many people would there be in a repair crew and one platoon?"

Joyner nodded. "You're right. I hear at least two platoons, maybe three. This could be bad. If the lights are out over there, and our people are anything but locked down and quiet, Hartner's going to start a massacre."

Not for the first time that day, General Griffin Joyner was wrong. The massacre began with the most gentle human being in the Gulag.

Clonus thought it might be smart to wait even longer—but he was sure that the witches' lights would find him soon. Or they would hear the thumping of his heart and the horrid noise that his thoughts were making. He eased his eyes open in the darkness, careful to keep his ears plugged, and saw the lights. Some were moving to one side and then another, going in little circles. They looked like supply ships waiting to land on New Sarajevo. Others were going straight and slow, like the constant tides of meteors in the sky he remembered. But it was wrong to think of home now, and it hurt. The real home was gone. All the people were moved away to where everything was different. Now Simon and Uncle Griffin were gone, too. There was no place anywhere that wanted him. Not a hybrid like him. But that didn't matter. He couldn't let Talon and her witches hurt his friends anymore. That would be honestly, truly and horribly, wrong. WRONG!

His fingers came down from his ears and closed over the projector's power button. His hands aimed the screen at a group of circling witch-lights thirty feet away. Taking a deep breath and holding it, Clonus pressed the button until it wouldn't move any further. The projector vibrated faster, as if it wanted to jump away from the evil thing he was doing. He could feel the humming through his legs and up into his arms, making his jaw tight and his ears buzz. Suddenly the casing CRACKed like splitting rock, then roared like a cave-in. The space ahead of him burst into white—quicker than sunrise at home, a thousand times brighter—and blinded him. A green afterimage burned in his eyes. He was nearly deaf. But he heard the screaming of the witches begin.

"What the *hack* was that?"

"A flash grenade! Get DOWN!"

"I can't see! I'm blind!"

"Over here! His head's gone!"

"Shoot! Shoot!"

"Where? Damn it, I can't see! WHERE?"

Clonus couldn't distinguish the words and was glad that
their spells would not reach him. But he was sure they'd
found him now. He squeezed the button again until the casing
split completely. The projector wasn't vibrating anymore. It
wouldn't fire. He threw the box at the voices and ran toward
them. It's all right to die this way! he thought as loud as he
could. His body felt like fire as fifty years of his own voice—
BE-QUIET-DON'T-EVER-HURT-ANYONE—blew out of
his pores. IT'S ALL RIGHT TO DO THIS AND DIE! He
charged at the voices with all the power in him, dimly hearing
sharp, cracking sounds and echoes that came from every direction. Blindly he slammed into a group of witches. They
fell away from him, cursing terribly, some sounding like men,
and he grabbed heads and cloth and arms and threw them as
hard and as far as he could.

"Platoon leaders, report! What was that explosion? What's
going on down there?"

"Flash grenade, Captain. They're shooting at us!"

"Who? Who's shooting?"

"Tench's men! They've got grenades and rifles!"

"That's impossible. They—"

"Hack you, Hartner! My leg's shot!"

"How did they get weapons?"

"They must have taken Platoon Four."

"Understood. Pull out. Assemble your troops and get back
up here. Do you copy?"

But the panic was complete. The shots were coming from
everywhere, ricocheting from stone walls and slamming into
troops and newly made corpses. Bodies flew in the air
through stabbing shafts of light as a bull of a voice roared,
"You're bad! You're all BAD! Go AWAY!"

In a corridor two hundred feet from the killing, Platoon
Four turned from its search and ran back toward the riot,
guiding itself with small cones of illumination. As the group
rounded the last corner, twenty inmates dropped onto them
from the overhead with knives, bludgeons, swords, and tools.
There was no time for the startled Peacekeepers to bring their
rifles to bear. The fighting was savage, and over quickly.
Eleven surviving inmates snatched up the weapons and lights,
and ran to hide again in the deep tunnels of Mercator.

Clonus strode unerringly through the cavernous black

room, flinging himself at group after group, pounding with his fists and throwing with his hands. He felt a witch's claw rake against his cheek, and then another one dig a hole deep into his shoulder. It didn't matter. He wasn't afraid of witches. Or anyone! He was going to make them go away and leave his friends alone. It was *all right* to die this way! He turned to run at more of them and felt three claws punched into his chest, one after the other.

The shooting and cursing and dying echoed around him as the green light behind his eyes went to the color of blood and he crumpled to the floor.

Aboard the scouters stretched out in a line from the surface of Mercator, the chief pilot was monitoring the radio. At the sound of a tremendous explosion he passed the word for all crew to stand by the quick-releases. As the unmistakable sounds of rioting came through the speakers, he directed the links between vessels to be sealed. After a minute, hearing nothing from Captain Hartner, he ordered the airlock secured. The five vessels broke away from the asteroid and took up a position parallel to the movement of Mercator. The chief pilot sent an emergency-status message to Central, and waited for further orders.

Joyner grunted and strained urgently at the hatch dogs. His neck and arm muscles stood out as thick cords while he pushed with one hand, pulled with the other, against the unyielding handles.

"We can switch places again, sir," Barrow said. Joyner was standing on his shoulders, with Barrow's hands locked around his ankles. The boom and ring of gunfire nearly drowned out his voice.

"Not yet," Joyner said through clenched teeth. They were confident that at least the section of Bravo Level above them was still sealed against space and aerated, because the platoons had passed overhead just minutes ago. Barrow had run back to alert Talon, then returned to help Joyner set up a flanking maneuver. But the hatch refused to give.

"Move aside," a female voice from behind them shouted over the noise. Barrow turned his head to see Ke Shan leading a strike-squad, nine of Talon's followers. The big woman said

impatiently, "Move aside, Joyner. Make room." She gestured
to one of her troops. The woman came forward and stood
while Ke Shan climbed to her shoulders. When she was in
position beside Joyner she gripped two of the hatch dogs.
"Together. One . . . two . . . THREE!" The metal shrieked and
moved marginally. "Again! One . . . two . . . THREE!" Now
the hatch wheel moved a quarter-turn. Twice more, and the
wheel could be spun until the hatch was opened a crack.
There was no rush of air from below. The openings to space
were still sealed—and would be, he knew, until Hartner finished her work and left. But this time, the leaving would not
be unopposed. The carnage he could hear going on was beyond the retribution Hartner always leveled for "trouble."
This was beyond reason or excuse. This was extermination.

Joyner pulled his head through the opening and looked. No
one in sight. He climbed the rest of the way into the upper
room. Within a minute the twelve of them were inside. The
hatch was secured behind them to guard against the massive
air leak that would occur if Bravo Level were vented to space.

Captain Hartner kept the radio switch set to monitor. The
gunfire had slowed, and finally ceased. There was no sound
now except for moaning and weak, anonymous voices calling
for help. She'd just dispatched Platoons One, Three, and Five
to the other entrance above Tench's area with orders to stand
by and enter at her command. She should have done this immediately, she knew, when Two had discovered that the lights
were out. But she'd been in a hurry, careless. There was no
more room for error. Too much had gone wrong.

The second-in-command of Platoon One stood silently beside her. Two platoon members came forward, each carrying
a sealed crate. They set the boxes down and stepped back.

"Captain," Lieutenant Ducaine said. "Again, I protest this
action. It is against procedure and unnecessary."

"And I protest your stupidity," Captain Hartner snapped.
"The inmates are armed. They've killed two full platoons. It
is my best judgment that if we don't stop them immediately
there will be a complete slaughter throughout Mercator."

"Captain, they were fighting us, not each other. The scouters will have separated from the asteroid by now. According
to regulations, we're to secure a retreat and report this to

Earth. Right now we should assemble the platoons and call back two of the ships, and return to Central. The inmates can't go anywhere."

But they can kill Talon and Corinne, you stupid hack! Hartner's mind screamed. *Tench is a madman, and armed! I'll lose everything!* Aloud she said, "Do your job, Ducaine. Or I'll courtmartial you for insubordination and cowardice."

The lieutenant stared at her, knowing that she had high-ranking friends who would stand by her no matter how flagrantly she violated procedure. He turned and nodded to the women with the crates. They unsealed the boxes and began taking out blue gas grenades. The five others in the room took two each.

"No," Captain Hartner said, deciding on a better course of action. "Use the red ones."

Lieutenant Ducaine flushed crimson. "Captain, those are lethal!"

"The gas is harmless after ten minutes," she said. "Platoons One, Three, and Five will have a safe area to stage for the next operation."

"But Captain Hartner, we—"

"This will kill only the rioters in China Zero and the ones in open adjacent tunnels," she said. "No one who wasn't involved will be harmed. That's why we have these, Lieutenant."

"But our people, Captain. Some of them may be alive."

"If so, they're hostages. There is only one response to hostage-taking. *No* exceptions." Her tone softened. "You're a good officer, Raynor. You know the regulation." She was calmer now. She knew that she'd handled the extraction badly and that an inquiry would follow. The idiot Ducaine's complicity would now force him to support her in any proceeding. But if she failed to extricate Talon and her daughter, nothing could protect her from ruin. "Sometimes we're forced to take action that we hate," she said gently. "But we have our duty. So. For the record: Do you still question my order?"

He looked down at his boots. "No, Captain. Your order is according to procedure."

"Then carry it out, Lieutenant."

Ten of the red grenades were distributed. At Ducaine's order the hatch leading down to China Zero, Tench's throne room, was opened. Ducaine peered down into a black pit. "Pull the pins on my mark," he said. "Counting down from five. Five ... four ...

Across from them a hatch eased open quietly. Barrow came through like a missile, pushing off from the hatchway with fists extended. Joyner and Ke Shan followed in the same manner.

"Captain!" a platoon member shouted, too late. Barrow's fists dug into Hartner's stomach. She lost the air in her lungs and flew pell-mell against the opposite wall. Joyner arrived a quarter-second later, opening his arms wide and hurling two of Hartner's people to unconsciousness against the same wall. Lieutenant Ducaine raised both hands in front of his face and bent double as Ke Shan swept into his midsection. The remaining five jumped for their rifles. Barrow and two more of Talon's troops dove and scattered them. Ke Shan caught two by the neck and butted their heads together. Joyner poleaxed one under the chin with a brutal uppercut that launched the man at the ceiling. He impacted with a dull crunch. The last two were taken down by Barrow, who ran with them trailing behind him, then slammed them into a wall. They crumpled and drifted slowly to the floor.

"Bring me the grenades," Joyner said. "Hurry!" He was holding three of them, the pins all in place. The other seven were found, two of them still in the air where they'd flown out of startled hands, and bouncing hard. All were safe. The radios were gathered up next.

Barrow walked to Captain Hartner. She was conscious, sitting against a wall and staring up at him. He bent down to her, and she flinched. "Number," he said quietly, an inch from her face.

She looked at him blankly. Barrow took her by the collar and raised her high off the floor. She froze, keeping her arms crossed and her legs tucked beneath her.

"Captain Captain," he said. "State your number."

It was a fast, nonlethal, and odorless gas, released from blue grenades quietly rolled into a direct ventilator line. Platoons One, Three, and Five were unconscious before anyone thought to put on a mask or could raise a radio alarm that would be heard by the scouters. Ducaine assured Joyner that four grenades would supply enough gas to remain potent in the room for twenty hours. The sixty-four men and women, on awakening, would wish for death after being gassed with a substance designed to control, and to punish, inmates. But they would be alive.

"He may live, Griffin," Maria said. "If infections don't set in. But I'm not a real surgeon. There's nothing I can do for his eyes."

Joyner stood as she crossed the room to him. As naturally as if they'd always loved one anther, he took her in his arms and kissed her forehead. "Talon," he said—and flushed. "Maria. Thank you."

"He'll be asleep for a few more hours. The anesthetic I gave him isn't as precise as I'd like, but . . ." She shook her head. "There were four bullets in him. It's incredible that none of them entered his heart or lungs."

" 'Incredible' is the right word," Joyner said in wonder. "Clonus stood alone against an entire rifle platoon, essentially unarmed. And won! He planned it and carried it out himself . . . Who would ever have thought . . . Clonus!"

Barrow listened, and was also surprised. But about Joyner, not Clonus. It had been apparent to him from the first that Clonus had no lack of courage or intelligence. Clonus lacked only confidence, and the ability to see himself apart from what others saw and judged in him. The big man loved people, and needed them. But within himself he'd always been an indomitable individualist—the "singular citizen" who formed the core of *War with the Mind*. Why hadn't Joyner made the same observation? Because, Barrow thought, putting a recent and vague uneasiness into direct terms, he is not the same Griffin Joyner who wrote the book. Brilliant and courageous, unquestionably. But not at the same levels. In all, not the same man. It was a heartbreaking thought, but a reasonable one. For as long as Barrow had been alive, Griffin Joyner had been locked away and slowly stagnating—isolated from the greatness he had lived and from the still greater challenges he needed. Who wouldn't deteriorate after sixteen years here?

It was a rhetorical question. Opportunity had presented itself, and could not be ignored. Details remained to be worked out—but to life or to death, Simon Barrow was leaving Mercator.

Maria said to Joyner, "Do you believe what Hartner told us?"

"I didn't at first," he answered. "But I had her radio Central and instruct her secretary to read back the order for your release and Corinne's." He remembered Hartner's stricken face when he'd given her that command. "As it happens, she hadn't yet received the formal written order. That's on the ship coming out from Phobos. All she had was an entry in a notebook she keeps locked away in her desk. But next to your names she'd marked 'Direct order, Secretary General UN.' "

Barrow had been thinking furiously, only half-listening to them. Now he gave his full attention to the conversation.

Joyner grinned. "The notebook also records the names of other inmates released, and the 'fees' she collected. Right now I don't know which she's more afraid of. Me, or having those records become public knowledge. It would destroy her."

That's not enough, Maria thought angrily. For years Hartner had kept the inmates on Mercator living like animals, forcing them to betray and to kill one another merely to remain alive. And she'd broken her promise to provide special protection for Corinne, who had never committed a criminal act. Like Tench, Hartner had much to pay for. And Maria had sworn that she would be the one to collect the debt; she would have her revenge.

"But," Joyner continued, "Hartner has no reason to worry about me. Not now. She seems to know about how . . . how much I love you." He finished the unfamiliar and uncomfortable statement, and found himself repeating it in wonder. "I love you." As Maria squeezed his hand he added quickly,

"She believes that I'll let her go, because she's taking you and Corinne to freedom. And she's right."

Maria stared at him for long moments. "I'm not leaving Mercator without you," she said. Her eyes were wide with surprise and disbelief. "How could you even think I would?"

He pulled her gently against him, and stroked her hair. "Thank you," he said. "Thank you. But my release isn't possible."

"Then neither is mine."

"But you—"

"Stop." She put a finger to his lips. Maria told him about her life: her childhood on Manhattan Island, her cousin Consuela and her marriage, her work at Fryeburgh Technologies, the reason she'd divorced Carter and left, and what she believed to be the reason for her release. "I'm not going back," she said finally. "Not without you, Griffin."

Barrow's heart jumped in his chest as he listened to Maria. And as she finished, everything fell together. He had the answers to his immediate future. "Excuse me," he said. They both looked at him as if shocked to discover that another human being shared their universe.

Barrow explained.

Twenty minutes later Captain Hartner shook her head forcefully from side to side. "No," she said. "Even if I agreed to try it, they'd know what was happening and blow us all to hell before we reached Central."

"I recommend that you change your mind," Joyner said. "This is the only way you're going to leave Mercator alive."

"Then kill me," she answered. "You lose, and I lose. But you can be rewarded for releasing me." She looked from face to face, searching for the fear and desperation she had been trained to use to her advantage. There was no hint of either. "Understand the situation," she said. "If I call down the scouters to transport me and my troops, and Corinne and Tal—ah, Maria—they'll come. But the moment I bring aboard three more inmates—"

"Thirty-one more," Barrow corrected her.

She turned to face him, then laughed. "This is all your idea, eh boy? I have a question. Why not the whole hackin' inmate population?"

"Thirty-one is the maximum number the scouters can carry," he answered. "There's nothing we can do about the rest." For now, he thought.

Hartner said to Joyner impatiently, "I don't believe you're willing to have Corinne and Maria killed by this boy's foolishness. Please listen to me. The United Nations Peacekeeper Correctional Statutes and Code has a principal tenet that has never been violated. Not once, in more than a century. We do *not* honor hostage-taking. No exceptions."

Maria spoke for the first time. "You're not a hostage," she said mildly. "Not at all, Captain. You are our personal guest." She smiled. "And we've been rude. Let me make you something to drink."

Hartner's face paled as her eyes widened.

Maria handed her the radio. "Call down the scouters, Wanda. And I insist that you have something to drink."

Corinne, Maria, and Captain Hartner were first to enter the inboard scouter secured at Mercator's airlock. After them came Lieutenant Ducaine and seven members of Platoon One. It took nearly an hour for the crew to carry out the sixty-four unconscious troops, and another half-hour to settle them safely in the cramped cargo holds for the ride back up to Central. Last to be brought aboard were thirty-one numbered food crates sealed with Captain Hartner's personal marker and labeled "Evidence." They filled every available space on the five scouters.

The chief pilot looked behind him to Captain Hartner and the two beautiful women seated next to her on the bench seat. "We're ready, Captain," he said. "We'll commence undocking procedures at your order."

She nodded weakly and spoke in a barely audible voice. "Go," she said, waving one hand while clutching her stomach with the other.

"Are you injured?" the pilot asked.

"Sick," she said. "Please, let's go."

"She'll be fine," Maria assured him. "I'm sure everything will be fine."

The pilot waited while the other scouters reported ready. The smiles on the faces of his two passengers were breathtaking. "This is a great day for you two," he said conversationally. "My name's Frank Giroux. How long has it been since you've seen the sky?"

He wasn't particularly surprised that neither answered. He'd made dozens of extractions before. Reactions were always strong, and filled the spectrum: elation, fear, shock, disbelief, anger. The most common seemed to be a combination of joy, worry, and shame. He understood it. These people never expected to leave here; Mercator was hell, but it was home. Now they were just beginning to think about a new life where most people had little regard for convicted criminals.

"Go!" Captain Hartner groaned.

Giroux turned his head and checked the status panel. The last of the lights went green. He shifted around in the seat and took the controls. "Separating, Captain. Central in twelve minutes. You'd better check into the dispensary, if you don't mind my saying so."

The pain that was spreading through her body was still minor. The sickness she felt was from the knowledge that it would grow steadily worse until she was given the antidote in a vial that Talon—she *is* a witch!—carried. It had been explained to her that within twenty hours she would be suffering indescribable agony. And it would be ten or more days later that she would finally, mercifully, die. Talon had promised to smash the vial if anything prevented Barrow and Joyner from completing their plan. There was not the slightest doubt in the mind of Wanda Hartner that the witch would do exactly that. It became less important by the minute to Hartner that she was facing the personal and financial ruin threatened by General Lindemeer. All that mattered was the antidote.

The station called Central looked like a small dim-white H from ninety miles out. As the scouters braked and closed the distance more slowly, tiny protuberances seemed to grow outward from the longer dimensions, and it could be seen that the longitudinal arm was dotted with lights. Corinne had last been there more than one-third of her life ago. On that trip Central would have been shrinking as fast as it now grew. But she had seen nothing from a dark cargo hold. She'd only heard the others crying and cursing as they all bounced against each other in free fall. Their arms and legs were bound with rope. She held onto her mother's rope with her teeth while Maria spoke her name like a soothing chant that could be heard even above the noise made by the others. Corinne remembered every moment and every thought of that day. She had been twelve, and afraid. But she knew that Maria would protect her, whatever they found in prison. That was the promise she'd made. And she'd promised to protect Consuela, who was nice to her but insane. Consuela had hurt some people who were against Carter's business. They had to hide her. But if Carter went to prison for those things, they would return and tell the Peacekeepers the truth. Then Consuela did more things. Maria tried to change everything so the Peacekeepers on Titan wouldn't take her away. But they found out about her. And a judge said that Maria was just as guilty as her cousin.

Corinne looked at the woman sitting beside her. She was so beautiful, and so strong. Maria had happily accepted the name "Talon," and built a reputation that protected all of the women who worked for her. This was the Family. There were rewards and punishments, even executions. But there was love. Not one of the huge family had ever been a traitor to another, or to their leader. Their loyalty was based on the knowledge that as Maria she loved them—and as Talon she protected them. They killed to create a mystique that kept them as safe as possible among predators who were stronger and more numerous than they were.

Maria taught her to understand this life, but never to accept it as normal; she would be free at twenty, and the world would be much different. And now what will happen? she wondered. She was away from Mercator two years earlier than planned. *But not free.* Was that important? She had never been free. Maybe someday. For now only two things were vital. Maria's happiness, and helping Admiral Simon Barrow of the whole damn Great Domain to realize how much he wanted to become the husband of Corinne Susanna Hernandez.

There were men and women standing by at Central to help with the unloading. Maria and Corinne were escorted to quarters prepared for them—offering food, a shower compartment, and clean clothing.

The unconscious troopers were carried to their quarters,

where they would begin reviving in ten to twelve hours under the care of the station doctor. All weapons were removed, as usual, and stored. Captain Hartner ordered the thirty-one crates taken to her office, where they were stacked side-by-side until they filled nearly all of the floor space. She refused to see the doctor and ordered everyone to leave. It would take all night, she told them, to organize and log the evidence against inmates whose executions she would demand.

After checking that the corridor leading to her office was empty, Hartner went back inside and locked the door. She found the crates marked '11' and '15' and knocked softly, twice on each. Barrow and Joyner released the inside locks they'd installed and pushed the lids open.

"Very good," Barrow said, looking over the office and stepping out. "Where's the schematic?"

Hartner opened a desk drawer and handed him a folded sheet. He pushed everything from her desk and spread it out.

Joyner knocked on three crates, then went to one more and opened it. Clonus was still under the anesthetic, breathing slowly but regularly.

Three former inmates emerged from their boxes, then set to work opening the rest. Those three, and eleven more being unpacked, were the best of what had been the guard force commanded by Joyner. All but one. Gault was the last to be released. He was warned again that he was there only out of respect for Clonus; and that if he did anything at all without a direct order, he would be killed instantly. He sat down in the crate and looked around silently, avoiding the sight of Hartner.

The other fourteen to emerge from the crates were Maria's followers. Ke Shan was the first of those out.

At the desk, Barrow and Joyner worked rapidly. They traced out the air and power lines, each memorizing one half of the schematic. Ke Shan came to peer over Barrow's shoulder. He pointed out to her the areas she was to secure with her thirteen women. The first were the two auxiliary power rooms, which were to be disabled before the main lines were shut down. Next were the three broadcast antenna complexes, each of which had its own power supply and backup. Joyner's men were to rush the arsenals and the four cannon emplacements located at the tips of the H.

"The fighting will be hand-to-hand, if we can hold the arsenals," Barrow said. "Our advantages will be surprise, speed, and knives. No station personnel carry weapons. Is that right, Hartner?"

"That's right. The maintenance people will have portable cutting tools in their belts, but this is third shift. Only four of them will be on duty. Firing weapons have never been carried inside except for repel-boarders drills. Even then, they're unloaded. One accident could do a lot of damage to the station."

"How many people are we dealing with?" Joyner asked.

"Two platoons were killed and three are unconscious," Hartner answered. "You're facing a total of fifty-one. All but nine are support personnel."

Barrow looked up from the desk. "You took *all* of your fighters to Mercator?"

"That's right. Our station complement is five rifle platoons of twenty-four each, including leaders. There are forty-two support people."

"That's insane," Joyner said.

"It's all according to a formula worked out years ago," Hartner said defensively. "Force has to be balanced against cost."

"She could be telling the truth," Ke Shan said. "Ten monkeys and a donkey are enough to operate this station, as long as we all stayed down on the asteroids."

Barrow was skeptical. "Hartner, I want you to think for a minute and answer again. How many of your people are here?"

"It's the truth. Damn it, *please* don't waste time. I need that antidote!"

Barrow and Joyner and Ke Shan looked at each other. Was it possible? Could anyone be that stupid?

Joyner turned back to Hartner. "Get me a uniform and have Maria and Corinne brought here. Then have everyone, and I mean everyone, report to this staging room." He pointed to a compartment on the schematic. "After that, I'm going to take a slow walk around Central, with the antidote. If I see anyone at all, Captain Hartner, I will break that bottle into a thousand pieces. Now tell me. Do you still feel safe with your answer?"

"Yes!" The pain was growing worse, as Talon had said it would. "But take a fast walk, please!"

"Good enough," Barrow said. "Hartner, can you disable all communication devices in that staging room?"

"Of course," she said. "I've commanded Central for ten years. I know every bolt and weld here."

"Can you get there without being seen?"

"There's nothing between here and there except work spaces. I told you, this is third shift. No one would be there now. Why? If someone sees me, what's the problem? This is *my* station."

"The problem is that you're stupid," Barrow said, "and so we have to send someone with you. You might overlook something. And if you did, you would die a very painful death."

She reddened, and then lowered her eyes. "Yes," she said.

"I was an electrician," Ke Shan volunteered. "I trained three years at Fujiwara."

"Give Ke Shan a uniform," Joyner said. He turned to the big woman. "Thank you. Follow several paces behind Hartner. If anyone comes toward you, turn and walk away. If your face is seen—"

"Break someone's neck," she finished. "But not Hartner's. She has something more interesting to look forward to."

"Exactly," Joyner said. "Check everything before you leave that staging area, then bring Hartner back here. Be careful and be thorough. You don't need to hurry."

"Yes we do," Hartner said miserably. "Let's go!"

Forty minutes later Ke Shan returned with Hartner, and nodded to Barrow.

"Get Maria and Corinne here," Joyner said.

Hartner made a call, cursed at the person on the other end of the line, and set the phone down. Within minutes, Maria and Corinne arrived with an escort. Hartner met them in the corridor and followed them into the office. Both were freshly bathed and in new clothes. Maria crossed to Joyner. They embraced, and then she turned to greet her followers. Corinne stood silently beside Barrow. The light pressure of her shoulder against his upper arm was distracting. And pleasant.

Simon nodded to Hartner. "Make the announcement," he said.

Hartner stepped to her desk and keyed the 1MC circuit. "All personnel," she began, her voice echoing back from outside the office. "All personnel. Report to Staging Area Niner immediately. All personnel . . ." She repeated the broadcast twice more and waited for three minutes. The procedure was followed again.

"Go there," Joyner told her. "When the head count is right—when you'll risk your life that it's right—order them to wait. Bring two airlock crew and the station doctor when you come back."

Behind him, Hartner saw three inmates holding blue grenades. At least, she thought, realizing that it would help her not at all, she wouldn't be tried as an accomplice to murder. A bolt of pain shot from her back to her chest. She left the office and half-ran to Staging Room Niner.

With the rerouted ship from Phobos still three hours away, Barrow and Joyner began one last inspection of Central. Along with the rest of their forces they were well fed, bathed and in uniform, with new haircuts. Simon was uncomfortable in the uniform he had come to associate with incompetence and cruelty. But it hadn't always been that way, he reflected; for most of its history the Peacekeeper Force had been a proud and necessary part of humanity. Perhaps, someday, it would again be what it was during the service of General Griffin Joyner.

Except for the lieutenant's insignia on his shoulders, Joyner looked as natural in the uniform as sand on a beach.

Everything was set. The engines to nine of the station's ten scouters were disabled. The tenth was ready for flight, in case they failed to take the FTL ship; it would be similarly sabotaged if they were successful. All but one of the communications rooms and antenna complexes were disabled. Every hand-held radio on Central was found and checked against an inventory printout until all of them were accounted for. Each of the former inmates received a radio, and the rest were packed away in crates they would take with them. Most of the weapons and ammunitions at Central were packed into airlocks, ready to be jettisoned into space. A small number of rifles were ready for transfer to the larger ship. Other crates were filled with food and medical supplies. When Barrow and Joyner were satisfied, they returned to the only still-functioning communications room.

"The ship made contact twenty minutes ago," Maria said. "ETA is forty minutes from now."

"Problems?" Joyner asked.

Ke Shan shook her head.

Maria smiled. "We'd have called you if there were," she said.

"I've done everything you wanted," Hartner pleaded from her seat at the console. "Can't I have the antidote? *Now?*"

"How many are aboard that ship?" Barrow asked her, ignoring the question.

"As you instructed, I offered to bring them a special meal aboard. They asked for fifteen. That's standard crew-size for these ships."

"And you told them about the injured man and the crates of evidence you need sent back to Earth?"

"Yes, Mr. Barrow! Their only objection was time. I said I'd have two squads ready to load them and bring out the meals as soon as they dock."

"Twenty people," Joyner said. "And with the escort they're expecting for Maria and Corinne, that's all of us. Good."

Barrow said to Maria, "The station doctor sends you her compliments. She expects Clonus to make a good recovery.

"What did she say about his seeing again?"

"She thinks it's possible, with an ophthalmic surgeon. For now he needs to remain under sedation to avoid moving and tearing open the wounds. We'll keep him asleep until we arrive at our destination."

"He'll do well, Simon. And I know you'll find a way to get him what he needs."

"Yes, I will. If it wasn't for Clonus most of us would still be on Mercator."

"All of us," Corinne said, turning to face him. Impulsively she took his arms and pulled them around her waist. She kissed him, and Simon felt as if he'd stepped barefoot onto a megawatt cable. He liked the feeling.

Blushing under Maria's arched-eyebrow glare, the two excused themselves and went for a walk.

The FTL ship arrived exactly on schedule and was directed in the docking routine by Captain Hartner. As the airlock opened, five uniformed Correctional Peacekeepers led by Ke

Shan entered from Central, with orders to inspect the ship for the safety of the two passengers. The vessel's captain accompanied them, assuring the stern-faced troopers that although his crew were mere civilians, he was a veteran who understood security very well. He voiced no objection to having his crew remain in their quarters while the personnel and cargo transfers were taking place.

When the walk-through was completed, Ke Shan returned and spoke with Barrow and Joyner for a few minutes. Maria and Corinne stepped aboard, flanked by eight escorts. Two more carried Clonus to the ship's dispensary, and remained with him there. Twenty of the forces came aboard carrying crates of 'evidence'—which they took to an empty cargo hold. Once inside, they sealed themselves in the hold and waited for the signal to come out again. Joyner and Barrow were the last to board, with fifteen boxed meals.

Captain Hartner directed the undocking from the communications room. Wishes for good futures and a pleasant trip were exchanged, and the vessel eased away from Central.

Seated behind the ship's pilot with Corinne at his side, Barrow pulled a small transmitter from his uniform blouse pocket. He keyed it three times. Small electrical explosions disabled the communications equipment still working on Central, along with the remaining scouter. At the same time two outer airlock doors opened and allowed crates of weapons to enter space.

Five more clicks on the transmitter activated a klaxon within a small locker that was identical to hundreds more like it, located in every compartment throughout the station.

Captain Hartner heard the klaxon and wiped a flood of sweat from her face. She released a breath she'd been holding and ran through the passageways of Central. She moved quickly despite overwhelming pain—pain that existed only in her imagination—until she located the shrieking locker, fumbled with a ring of master keys, finally threw them away and pounded and tore at the door with bloodied hands until the plate metal ripped open and she found a tiny, empty vial inside. Maria's revenge was complete.

⇒ 12 ⇐

The captain of the trade ship *Elsinore* opened a pouch of coffee and placed it at the mouth of the brewer. A hissing sound accompanied the quick intake of air that pulled the grounds inside. He shut the door and flipped a toggle to start the processing.

"This thing's older than I am," he said after a minute, turning to the man seated at the other side of a small wardroom table. "Works better, too." He took a seat and held up a hand. "No polite argument, please. Hell, General, I was the oldest major in the Peacekeepers. Knew a lot of people who worked for you. Never thought you'd turn thief." He turned again and filled two cups. "Be careful, this is hot."

"Thank you, Jacque." Joyner took the proffered cup and eased some of the scalding liquid to his lips. It burned with a burst of hard flavor that was at once new and familiar. He inhaled to cool his mouth and continued. "We won't harm your ship, or your crew. You have my word."

"I don't need your word, General. I need my ship."

"Then cooperate with us. Tell your people to do the same thing. Make the calls we talked about. They'll understand that all of this is against your will, and that none of it would have occurred—"

"If it weren't for that imbecile running Central," Jacque finished. "I know. But your plan won't work, sir. And they'll kill me and *Elsinore* and my family the same time they kill you. Damn it, even if they don't, they'll say I'm in this with you. Peacekeepers love scapegoats, General. You know that."

"Make them believe," Joyner said. "And hope that we're successful. It's the only chance you have."

There was silence until Jacque said, "More coffee?"

"Yes. Thank you."

After a while Joyner left the captain with a set of instructions
and one of the escapees to watch him. He found Barrow
where he expected to, in the ship's Control Center.

"How long will it take us to reach the transmission point?"
Joyner asked.

"Six hours nineteen minutes," Barrow said. "We have one
hyperdrive leg to run as soon as we're clear of the Belt. We'll
come out above the elliptic and take a position from which
the radio-delay will be only four seconds."

"You should sleep between now and then."

"Half of our people are already asleep. The other half are
watching the crew. Where is Maria?"

"She doesn't want to be disturbed until she's rechecked everything. Again."

"Then you'll want to rest. I'll stay on watch."

"I may doze in here for a while. When this is over, I'll
sleep for a year. Go ahead and find a cabin, Simon. I'll send
for you when we arrive on position."

They compromised. Each took a chair in the Control Center, and half-slept while *Elsinore* moved into position three-
quarters of a million miles from Earth.

"This is *who*?"

"Joyner, Mr. Secretary. General Griffin Joyner. My service
number is Bravo six five niner one eight seven two. We have
met, sir."

"I remember you, of course, Joyner. I was under the impression that you were in a sanitarium."

"I believe you know the details of my last assignment, sir.
It was your immediate predecessor who signed the order."

"Ah, yes. She may have mentioned it. I was not aware that
you were released, however."

"Mr. Secretary, there is no need for you to waste time. We
have your ships on screen. And I have provided General
Lindemeer with the circumstances of my leaving Mercator.
He agreed with me that you would wish to discuss this personally. May we do that?"

"Indeed we may, Joyner. First: As you say, we have ships
closing in on you. Second, they will arrive before you can
make a run into hyperdrive. Third, it is assumed that you have
stolen particle cannons from Central, despite your assurances

to General Lindemeer. At any sign of resistance from you, our ships *will* fire. Be forewarned. Fourth, you will present Maria Hernandez and her daughter unharmed when you are boarded. Fifth, you and your pirates will be taken into custody. Alive, if you do not resist. That is all we need to discuss."

Joyner exchanged a look with Maria and Barrow, then keyed the transmitter again. "Mr. Secretary, once more I ask. Are you prepared to begin our discussion?"

When the Secretary General's voice returned, the careful resonances of diplomacy had disappeared. "Joyner, there will be no concessions. Hostage-taking is not honored among a free people. Release that woman and her daughter. Then follow our instructions carefully, and you may survive this outrage."

"Very well, sir. I will begin." Joyner cleared his throat. When he spoke again he used the detached, rapid-fire cadences that penetrated minds like a rifle barrage. "You know that Maria is critical to your political survival. If that were not so, you would not personally have authorized her release. And you would not now be using a private and encrypted line to speak with me. You are fully aware that without her you will never deliver on the promises that you and UTIC have made to all of humankind. And that without her help, the next ship like *Shinar* you send out will be as useless as the first. Because without her, it will be another century, at least, before terraforming is possible."

Joyner paused, waited for a rebuttal which he knew would not come, and continued. "How long will it be, Mr. Secretary, before the public loses patience, and an eager politician launches an investigation of your administration, and UTIC, and you personally? Ten years? Five? One? And how many counts of bribery and corruption and secret arrangements will be uncovered and lodged against you? Fifty? A hundred? More? And how many witnesses will leap at the opportunity to testify against you in return for immunity? I won't even guess at that number, sir. You must achieve an immediate and successful mission into deep space, or you will not survive." He paused to let the barrage of words reach their target.

"Now. I will state the conclusion that you have already reached, Mr. Secretary. During the past nine years no one has been able to duplicate or add to the work Maria had done.

Therefore, without her willing compliance, you will never achieve the success you *must* have. For those reasons you will not take any hostile action against this vessel or its passengers." He changed his voice to a direct-command mode. "Stop wasting time. You have work to do." He released the transmit button and looked toward the man seated to his left.

"Perfect," Barrow said, smiling.

Joyner took a sip of the pungent coffee. "I'm a good pupil."

The radio was silent for nearly two minutes. When the Secretary General's voice returned, it had taken on a flat tone. "Is she willing to work for us, Joyner? And *can* she finish the work she started?"

A sigh of relief swept the table. Maria, Corinne, Ke Shan, Barrow, and Joyner grinned and kicked their legs like happy children.

Joyner took the radio again. "Mr. Secretary, we're going to transmit eleven pages of data to you. This is a continuation of the work Maria began before she left Earth. It isn't complete, but it will answer your questions. Have your best people run it up on a few of their computer models. If you like the results call us back on this frequency. If you don't, order your ships to blow us all to hell. Joyner out."

The call came back sixteen hours later. "General Joyner?"

"I'm here, Mr. Secretary."

"Please, call me Tomas. I believe we have work for all of you. Welcome home, Griffin."

2

HOME

➡ 13 ⬅

A.D. 2139

Lieutenant Commander Simon Barrow was uneasy as he read the console instruments in front of him. Something vital was missing from this part of the Universe. The meteor storm that had destroyed *Utic Shinar* was eleven years gone from this area; it seemed somehow wrong that there was nothing left to mark the area. The world was different now because *Shinar* had died, and he had not. Right here. There ought to be *something* left.

He'd had this feeling before.

Two years after Isaac and Neferti died, he'd made the journey from his combat school in Vladivostok back to Cairo. The house and shop from which he'd first seen the world was gone. But not completely. A new home was there, springing from the same ground. People were there. The sounds, the smell of the old neighborhood, were still there. He'd left with the comforting knowledge that there would always be something there that Isaac and Neferti had known—and therefore shared with him, even after their deaths.

But this was different. The screens showed nothing, and it wasn't right. More than eleven hundred human beings had found death here. Humankind was reaching out as never before; new worlds were being terraformed and settled because of events that had started here. But there *is* no *here*, his rational mind insisted. This wasn't a *place* at all. It was only a set of numbers that changed with fluid precision as he watched cold screens. It still wasn't right.

"Mr. Barrow."

He turned to see a blond, crew-cut young woman standing behind his chair. "Yes, Bridges. What is it?"

She took a step forward. "Sir, you asked me to remind you

117

about your class at 1540." Now she was standing, as she usually did, with her hands clasped behind her back—and closer to him than he found comfortable. A fellow officer, Francine Bellenauer, had advised him to ignore the sexual provocation: "She'll give up, Simon. And you'll be disappointed as hell when she does."

"Thank you, Bridges." As she smiled and took a step backward, he sighed, stood, and stretched. Another class. He hadn't slept in more than thirty hours and had taken four classes in that time. The instructors were good and the subject was fascinating. But it was also frustrating, in a way he'd never encountered; the learning came slow to him, and hard. He'd seen the terraforming process at work, most recently on New Hope. During ten days there he'd filled three dozen notebooks with formula after formula, details, exceptions, variables, constants, engineering considerations, methods, order-of-introduction for the chemicals and biomass; recording and adjusting, climatology, density, base-level gases, replenishment cycles ... it never stopped. How could even Maria keep all of it in her mind, when altering any one factor changed ten thousand others? But the problem isn't Maria, he thought angrily; it's Griffin. First General Joyner runs his officers the way Chief Woodley runs her engines. Fast, full-out, burn-and-replace, no rest and no ... He's changed in eleven years! And then Simon realized what Karen Bridges had been talking about. He smiled, relieved. "Tell them I'll be there in twenty minutes."

"Aye aye, sir." She snapped an unnecessary salute, executed a perfect rightabout-face, and walked away. He found his eyes following her; was it his imagination, or was Bridges wearing a uniform at least a full size too tight? He flushed at his thought—*You've been away from home too long*—and looked away, picking up three notebooks from the console. Clearing his mind, he turned and left the Control Center.

His quarters were in one of the "little wardrooms" outboard of the officers' galley. It was an eight-minute walk from Control, and he found himself wishing that they'd shut off the gravity for once. Again, First General Joyner's orders. In his heart he knew Griffin was right. Gravity maintained fitness. But his mind, nearing exhaustion, gave him an exhilarating picture of a young lieutenant commander boldly throwing his career away, standing straight and saying, "Ease off, Griffin, unwrap! Humankind is tired! Nine new worlds in six years is enough. Maria named that whole area of space the Pacifico Belt. *Pacifico*, Griffin! Understand? Peace! I need peace, and I need to sleep. And turn off the damned gravity!" The thought cheered him, as ridiculous as it was. No one would speak to First General Joyner in that way—with the probable exception of his wife, who had no title but at least as much authority. Certainly their son-in-law wouldn't.

The cabin he shared with two other officers was small. There was room for just the one bunk they shared in rotation, three small personal lockers, a desk with two chairs, and two computer terminals. He left the light out and bent his neck slightly to avoid the low overhead. This had been a storage area when *Celeste* was built three years before. Instead of its normal crew of twelve hundred the ship was carrying nearly twice that number. Most of the extra personnel were like himself, junior and mid-level officers sent out to experience, observe, and learn. The fourteen-month trip to four worlds-in-the-making was nearly over—Earthfall in twelve real-time days. But the pace had never slackened.

"Who is it? Simon, is that you?" The voice from the bunk was sleepy, and irritated.

"I'll only be a second, Francine. Change of uniform."

"Hurry up. And turn the light out when you leave."

"It *is* out." He flipped open the top of the locker and pulled out a jumper, sport shoes, and fresh socks.

"Well," she said groggily, "then . . . I forgot the formula! Quick, give me the ratios, chlorine to salt . . . what's in those bottles? . . . *Why are those trees in uniform?* . . . dirt . . . Who's there? Will you just *go*? I haven't slept in—"

She was asleep but still muttering when he pulled the door shut and headed for the shower compartment. Once inside, he set the dial to warm mist and pressed the button. He lathered quickly and increased the temperature until it was uncomfortably hot. With ten seconds left on the automatic shut-off he turned the dial fully to the left and set it for hard, vibrating spray. The water flew down in icy torrents that shocked him fully awake. For the final five seconds he positioned himself so that the water hammered directly against the back of his neck. He was invigorated, but knew it wouldn't last for long.

The energy wore away an hour into the class. He and a student were on hands and knees, head to head. Simon's face was directly over the student's right hand, which was open and palm-down on the deck.

"Sir?" the man asked again. "What do you want me to do?"

Simon shook his head and concentrated. "When you're ready, Litieri. Uppercut to my nose. Fast and hard. Surprise me."

There was a three-second wait. When he moved, Carlos Litieri was fast. His hand came up in a blur and began the turn to form a fist. Simon caught the wrist at half-rise with his left hand and straightened his arm. Litieri threw himself backward to avoid a dislocated shoulder.

"He wasted time," Barrow said to the onlookers as Litieri climbed to his feet, embarrassed but not injured. "These"— he held up his right fist and drew his left forefinger across the knuckles—"are minor parts of *a* weapon. This"—and now he touched his forehead—"is *the* weapon."

"I should have head-butted you, sir?" Carlos Litieri asked. His question drew mild laughter.

"Your head should have been involved before you acted," Simon answered seriously. "You took the weight off that arm early, and that's correct. But then you gave away your timing advantage. Try the same move again."

The two resumed their positions. Simon told him, "Don't waste the fraction of a second it takes to turn your hand over. Use the back of your wrist as the striking surface. When you're ready."

This time the wait was longer. Litieri tried a fake with his right shoulder, but Simon didn't move until the other man's hand left the deck. It came straight for his nose, wrist bent downward. Simon caught the blow three-quarters of the way to its target. *I'm tired!* he realized again.

"Much better," he said as Litieri again rolled away to avoid injury. Barrow stood and addressed the class. "Back of the wrist. Heel of the palm. In the time it takes to make a fist and begin a strike, you can deliver a blow with either one. Use the position your hands are in when the fight begins.

Changing slows you down, and telegraphs your intention. The principle holds true whether you're defending or attacking. Bridges, what's the difference between defense and attack?"

"No difference, sir," she recited brightly. "Unless you're programmed to lose."

"Exactly right. If you're not on the offensive before your body responds to the attack, your mind is not properly trained. If your mind is not trained, you're helpless."

"Sir," a student named Natalie Hassalem asked. "If the attack comes as a surprise—"

"No person within your sight can attack you without warning. Surprise comes only when you've missed the signs. Again, if your mind is not trained, you're helpless. We'll discuss this later in the class."

This was the third group he'd spent time with while aboard *Celeste*. "Training" was not a word that would apply. Each group received sixty hours of instruction, which was scarcely enough time to develop the concepts that would make real training possible. But General Joyner believed that even this limited exposure was beneficial for his Exploration Service personnel. Simon agreed. And the benefit was mutual: Some aboard *Celeste* would excel and ask for further work. From those, he was authorized to select a total of ten—ten to work with him intensively for three years, after which they could begin teaching still others, on a low level. From this would come more promising students.

But very few, he believed, would equal those who'd come to him after the waves of new trials for Gulag inmates. He'd trained ninety of them over a five-year period before joining the Exploration Service. Those were desperate, angry individuals whose level of motivation had been phenomenal. Even now the twenty best of them were operating ten small schools on Earth, Luna, Mars, and Titan, conducting classes in what he had taught them. And they were providing him with advanced students who themselves would one day be teachers. The specialized training and knowledge he'd received—and developed on his own—was now spreading geometrically among carefully selected students.

These people represented a gratifying challenge and necessary outlet for Barrow. For First General Joyner, they were a passion. It was his dream to build a generation of "singular citizens," using Barrow's skills to screen out the unfit, and to provide a shared standard of personal excellence for the fit. From this group, he believed, would emerge the best of the pioneers and world-builders humankind needed in unprecedented numbers and hardiness. Others would become leaders in industry, trade, science, the Exploration Service, and the United Nations itself. They would be the living embodiment of Joyner's first book—and of the one he was now writing, *Rebirth of the Individual.*

"Mr. Barrow, are you all right?"

"What? Ah, what was your question, Daniels?"

"I asked if you were awake. Sir, none of us would object if you took some time off. You could sleep right here for a few hours."

That would be a fine example to set, Simon chided himself, as his body urged him to make an exception. Just this once. "I didn't hear your suggestion, Daniels. Do you want to repeat it?"

"Ah, no, sir." Arthur Daniels was a thin young Engine-Tender with a promising career and a major flaw; he asked the indelicate questions others were thinking but wouldn't voice.

"Very well. Eight of you form a line." When they were formed up in front of him he said, "Come at me one at a time, and I don't want any attack repeated. Use your imaginations. The rest of you, be prepared to discuss the reasons that none of your classmates will succeed in striking me. Natalie, record this exercise on holo. We'll review it in slowed sequence for the discussion. Ready?"

Hassalem signaled when she had the recorder set.

Barrow turned his back on the line of students. "Begin."

After the end of the class he showered again, this time spending the entire thirty seconds under cold blasts of water. Four hours remained until the forty-hour work-cycle would be complete. He was looking forward to ten hours in his bunk, and then a virtual vacation. For the next seven "days" he would be back on Alpha Schedule: only twenty hours of duty, followed by ten long, luxurious hours of free time. Most of that would be spent asleep. The rest was his to do with as he pleased. There would be time—*Time!*—to write more letters to

Corinne and the children, and add them to the box that contained one hundred twelve others. There would be time to further develop three new combat techniques he had devised over the past months—assuming that his best student, Lieutenant Francine Bellenauer, was free to work with him. There would be time for anything—*everything*—he thought, nearly giddy with exhaustion. This last forty-hour cycle was the worst of the seven, as always. The first three cycles were relatively easy, now. It had taken a year to reach this point in endurance. His bodily cycles and rhythms had changed gradually, and were continuing to change. The number of times he ate and the amounts he consumed, even the foods he preferred—sometimes craved—were not what they had been at the beginning of the voyage. His heart and respiration rates were slower on average; but they responded more quickly than ever before, when the need arose. He thought, as the icy water shut off, It's almost as if my mind has been transferred to a body only now being made. As if . . . A light flashed on in his tired mind. Maria! This torture is *your* idea! You and your husband are *terraforming* us!

He laughed at the fine joke for the entire time he was toweling off. And he realized that, to a minor degree, he was doing the same thing with his advanced students. But it was their minds he targeted, by teaching them to perceive movement in new ways. Teaching them to hold the subconscious in the "ready" position at all times, to run a nonstop mental calculator that measured potential angles of incoming attack, force, effective ranges . . . that gave back available lines to an opponent, distance-to-target, environmental factors, avenues of escape. Teaching them that action and reaction are the same thing, separated only by the illusion of a moment's time. And that the mind is the key to dissolving—and creating—illusion.

After a quick meal in the junior officers' mess he reported to his last class of this cycle. It was a mercifully easy one, involving only astrogation and a written examination on particle-field mechanics.

Finally, alone in his cabin, he fell toward the bunk and was asleep before his body finished the trip.

• • •

"Mommy, why can't we see the ship? I want to see the ship! Why can't we?"

"I know why," Gordon Barrow said. "Can I tell her, Mommy?" Without waiting for an answer, he turned to his younger sister. "Jessica, you don't know about space and officers and ships because you're stupid."

"Gordon!"

At the look from his mother, the boy said hastily, "But that's all right, Jessica, because you're only four."

"Well you're only five!"

"But I know that Daddy's ship already landed on Luna, and you don't. And I know that he's coming down here in a shuttle, and you don't even know that. And I know that if he wants to drive the shuttle they'll let him because he's the best—"

"I know that! I do!"

"Do not."

"Do so! You *told* me. So I know! Ha! You're wrong!"

"That's not fair! Mommy—"

"Stop it, both of you," Corinne said quietly. "Randall is asleep. If you wake him up, you can both sit in the back."

"But then we won't see the shuttle!" Gordon whined.

"Then be quiet," Corinne said. She stroked his wiry red-brown hair. His dark eyes smiled up at her, and he whispered, "All right."

"I like the front seat," Jessica said, as solemnly as if she were giving away a special secret. "It feels good."

"This is Grandma's flyer," Gordon said. "It's a new one."

"I knew that!"

"Sshh," Corinne warned. She cradled eleven-month-old Randall against her. He made lip-smacking noises, then turned his head and went on sleeping. More than any of the three children, he resembled Maria. His hair was raven-black and he was smaller—and stronger—than the other two had been at his age. Simon had never seen his youngest son. What would he say? She smiled proudly at the thought of presenting the family to Lieutenant Commander and Admiral-of-the-whole-damned-Great-Domain Simon Barrow. First he would toss Jessica and Gordon into the air, and hug them tightly and answer a hundred questions all asked at once. Gordon would take his hat and wear it, and Jessica would scream at him. Then Simon would hold the new baby, and marvel at his clear eyes and powerful grip. Then he would embrace Corinne, and the two of them would become a little weak. And then self-conscious as the two older children laughed and tugged at their legs. On the way home he would ask, Why a new flyer? What went wrong with the old one? And then their joy would begin to end, because she would answer him truthfully. There would be more questions. And instead of going home to Quantico, Simon would pilot the flyer directly to the roof of the United Nations headquarters building—where First General Griffin Joyner was doubtless already waiting for him.

Corinne Susanna Hernandez Barrow knew her husband, down to the last detail. The reunion was as wonderful—and as short-lived—as she'd known it would be.

"Take the children home," he said as he stepped out of the flyer. "I'll catch a Service flight later."

"Simon, you weren't listening to me."

"What?"

"There *are* no Service flights. Go and talk to Dad. We'll wait here."

"They won't let a civilian vehicle stay longer than ten minutes."

"He's arranged clearance. Otherwise you'd have been warned off before you landed. Now go. The children will sleep."

General Joyner stepped out of the roof elevator, thirty yards from them. He met Simon halfway, then waved to Corinne. The two turned and walked side-by-side back to the elevator. No words were spoken until they reached the general's inner office.

Simon took several deep breaths before he spoke to the man seated across from him. In the fourteen months he'd been gone, Joyner seemed to have aged twenty years; his slate-gray hair was now totally white. He's seventy-three now, Simon thought. *But this isn't a matter of age. Something inside the man has broken.* The general's eyes were still direct and steady. But now there was a rheumy haze to them. Joyner sipped from a black porcelain mug that shook slightly as he raised it to his lips.

Simon swallowed some of the bitter brew and waited. "I'm sorry, General," he said at last. "What chances do the doctors give her?"

Joyner sipped more coffee. "None," he said quietly. "The poison was too strong. She's been in a coma since the day after giving birth. Eight months now. Her mind has deteriorated to ... She's breathing, but ..." His words trailed off to silence.

"Corinne told me it was Hartner."

Joyner's jaw tightened. "She'd just been released from prison," he said, looking down at the table. "They caught her. Wearing a nurse's uniform." He added, without explanation, "She's dead now."

"Good." Simon waited for him to look up again. "Your son is doing well?" He attempted a smile that wouldn't form. "Corinne showed me a holostat. He's a handsome boy, sir. And I like the name. Hector Horatio Joyner."

"No," General Joyner said. "It's Hernandez. Hector Horatio Hernandez. Maria wanted to continue the name. I'm glad now that I agreed. And I'm grateful that she had the opportunity to hold the boy. It was only for a few hours, Simon. So little time ... But I'd never seen her so deeply contented." He cleared his throat. "That's the way I'll remember Maria."

"I understand, sir."

"To answer your question, yes, our son is doing well. Did Corinne tell you that Clonus came in to help me take care of him?"

"No!" Simon brightened. Clonus hadn't left his home since the death of his mother, three years before. "How is he? Can he take the gravity?"

"It's difficult for him," Joyner said. He laughed weakly. "He said it's the first time he's ever understood what the word 'overweight' means. But he's still strong as an ox. And he loves Manhattan Island. A week ago he saw snow for the first time. He wouldn't come inside for six hours."

"I look forward to seeing him again."

"You and your family will come up next week, won't you? Clonus wants to prepare a special meal."

"Of course. Thank you." He sensed that Joyner would be more comfortable with another subject. And he was anxious to hear the details of other things Corinne had told him. There was so much, it was difficult to decide where to begin.

Joyner saved him the trouble. "You've been without news from home for more than a year," he began. "I'll start from the top down, so to speak. Secretary General Kali L'Awana lost the election eleven months ago. He was succeeded by Eleanor Douglas-Wycliffe."

"Yes, Corinne mentioned that." Douglas-Wycliffe was head of the Economic Party. She'd been blustering for years that the Exploration Service and everything it represented was a drain on world resources that could no longer be borne by humankind. "I never thought she had a chance of winning," he said.

"No one did. The voting was split almost evenly among all six major Parties. Douglas-Wycliffe managed to gain the backing of sixteen of the minor Parties and won the run-off. She won with seventeen percent of the total vote." He sipped at the coffee mug and straightened as the conversation moved to professional matters. His customary ramrod posture asserted itself as he spoke. "The Exploration Service budget has been reduced by ninety-one percent. Of our fourteen ships, we keep *Celeste* and *Majora*. In effect they'll be nothing but shuttles between Earth and the nine new worlds. The rest of the fleet has already been decommissioned."

Barrow was shocked. Corinne had not told him—perhaps did not know—that the damage was this extensive. He asked hopefully, "The ships will be sold for privatization, then? Commercial exploration and terraforming is an idea I've endorsed for years. As you know."

"I've half-agreed with you. But no, that's not what is happening. The twelve decommissioned ships have been broken up and the technology is being sold piecemeal to relatively small firms. They're forbidden by new laws to combine forces and send out the ships again."

"That's insane!"

"Of course it is. The rationale of the new administration is that this will broaden the base of research and allow us to consolidate the gains we've made in the past four and a half decades. And that eventually, when the problems of Earth and all of the settlements are solved, humankind will be fully ready to begin developing new worlds."

"Insane," Barrow repeated slowly. "It's insane."

"I agree. To destroy the momentum we've built since Dr. Lyndon's day is indefensible. But Douglas-Wycliffe has broadened her administrations's support during the past eight months. The public confidence suffered after ... The Economic Party has exploited Maria's condition. They've been very effective. A large part of the population has lost confidence in our ability to continue what we've started. They're afraid of a return to the era of UTIC. Massive waste and outright fraud. That's how the public is being led to think of us."

"But we've accomplished so much in six years. The evidence is so clear."

"This is politics, Simon," Joyner said. "There is no necessary correlation between political and literal truth." He finished his coffee and offered to refill Simon's cup.

"No, thank you, sir."

"Have you thought about what you'll do now?"

"I'll try to adjust," Barrow said. His smile was half-hearted. "Maybe there will be vacancies in the upper ranks of the Service. Who knows? In ten years I could be a *real* admiral."

Joyner's face paled. "Simon ... Corinne didn't tell you?"

It was instantly clear. "My commission."

Joyner nodded. "Five months ago. I'm sorry." He slumped in his chair. "I thought you knew. That's why Corinne has Maria's flyer. She sold yours because she doesn't want to touch the family savings. It's all she would accept from me."

"Corinne said it was a gift, and then she told me about Maria. And about some of the changes in the Service. But nothing about—" He sighed. "General, I don't understand this. My performance evaluations—"

"Have consistently placed you in the top one-quarter percent of the Exploration Service. I know. We're reducing our personnel drastically, but your commission should have been safe. I made that argument directly to Douglas-Wycliffe on two occasions. She never gave me a reason, but it's clear enough. The Steadhornes were strong backers in her election campaign. She owes them. Your dismissal is one favor she can grant easily."

Simon thought about that for a moment. "So this isn't a professional matter. It's personal."

"Nothing else makes sense. The Steadhornes expected Maria to work for them at UTIC, after her release. But because of the way she left Mercator, which they correctly attribute to you, she was able to refuse them. And then it was your public testimony that cost UTIC all of its government contracts. The Steadhornes lost their stake in space exploration, along with half their fortune."

"They should have lost much more." Barrow's face was deep red. "So. They struck back at me by jeopardizing the future of Corinne, Gordon, Jessica, and Randall. And Douglas-Wycliffe enabled them to do it. Just an easy favor." He said, looking away from Joyner, "Eleven years ago I learned how to respond to attacks on family."

Joyner sat up, alarmed. "Simon. This is not Mercator. That way of life is behind you. Behind all of us. Do you understand?"

"I'll agree," Simon answered angrily, "if you can explain Hartner's death."

"She collapsed and died in court, just after her sentencing. Massive heart attack."

Simon was taken aback. "I apologize for my remark, sir. I assumed—"

"I *wanted* to kill her, Simon. I wanted that so much, I stayed away from the courtroom. Corinne went, but I didn't trust myself." He said again, "Mercator is behind us. Do you understand?"

"Yes." That was foolish, he thought. I'm not a transparent child anymore. "I understand. Please excuse me, General."

"It's Griffin now," Joyner said. His smile was as weak as Barrow's had been. "That's worth losing a commission for, isn't it?"

"Yes, sir." He stood and shook hands. "Corinne and the kids are waiting, Griffin. We'll be stopping by the hospital before going home. When is Clonus making that special meal?"

"Wednesday of next week," Joyner said.

"That's Maria's birthday."

"Yes."

The Barrows made a pact that for seventy-two hours they would give the children their full attention, and say nothing of

the changing world around them—a world that seemed to be
shutting down, like a carnival closing its madly lit midway
and skulking off into darkness, leaving only darkness behind.

On the fourth day they pored over the messages Corinne
had received while Simon was away. Most were from friends
and students who communicated from every settlement in
what now was commonly referred to as the Great Domain—
and which Simon now thought to be grossly mislabeled. The
schools were doing well, he was delighted to learn. More than
two hundred students had now graduated past the first three-
year training level. The incomparable Ke Shan had personally
instructed fifty-one of them. They, Simon knew, would be the
best of the best.

His mood was so elevated by the news that Corrine was
reluctant to show him the final two messages. She set these
on the bed between them, and left the room. The dispatches
were identical, differing only in the date of transmission.
They were from the UN World Revenue Service demanding
payment of taxes based on a new assessment of the value of
their home and possessions—with penalties accruing from
the day of Simon's dismissal from the Exploration Service.
On impulse, he called nine of their neighbors; none had received such a bill. Corinne returned as he was making the
last call.

"I did the same thing," she said.

Simon listened without comment as she told him that she'd
found a buyer for their home. The negotiated price would allow them to pay all debts and retain a small amount for the
future, if he agreed to sign the document. Tight-lipped, he
agreed to consider it.

After a pleasant reunion with Clonus, followed by a som-
ber observance of Maria's birthday, the Barrows treated the
children to the finest vacation of their lives at Disney Universal and Star World.

Three days after they returned, Maria Regina Hernandez y
Estephan died without regaining consciousness.

First General Griffin Joyner took the call at work. Without
a word to anyone he packed his personal mementos into
boxes that the new administration had long ago ordered
placed outside the door to his office. He left a prepared letter
of resignation on the desk and carried the boxes down ninety-

one flights of stairs to a side exit of the United Nations head-quarters. Pulling into the mad traffic above Manhattan Island, he turned south and never looked back.

A month later, on January 1, 2140, the Barrows and family left Earth, having called it home for the last time.

3

THE DUELISTS

⇒14⇐

A.D. 2151

They came at Simon Barrow by threes, and they intended to kill him. Most of them at Site Alpha, half of those on duty and all of them in this makeshift arena, were drunk. The exhibition was not going at all as he'd planned. There was no opportunity this time to make a show of it, to finesse and bob-and-weave and banter, to create at least the illusion of a contest.

Without preamble, one of the miners swung a long metal bar at his head. Instead of bending his knees and simply letting the weapon pass over him, Simon was obliged to intercept it before the bar smashed into the face of the man approaching him from behind. He lowered his body and raised both hands over his head. The metal struck with tremendous power against his open palms as he pulled backward to diffuse the force of the blow. At the end of his arms' reach he pushed himself from the stone floor and rode with the bar as it completed its arc. His back slammed against the chest of the man approaching him. The man yelped like a startled dog and tumbled out of the white ring painted on the floor. Simon pulled the bar down to his chest as he found solid footing. Twisting his torso, he used the bar as a lever to throw his attacker from the ring. Now came the third man, charging at him with hands outstretched from a crouched position. Simon straightened to give the drunken miner the clearest possible target. He took the man's wrists as he moved into range, and stepped out of his path. The miner whirled, stumbled over his own feet, and was sent sprawling from the ring.

The next three, then the next, and then the last, were equally clumsy. There was no applause.

When it was over Clonus passed through the crowd collecting bets from those on his list. "Thank you. Thank you, ma'am, so very much. Thank *you*, sir."

The miners ranged in mood from sullen to semiconscious to bitterly angry. But no one argued with the large, polite old man who had opened the show by bending gear-wheels and twisting rocks in his hands until they snapped apart.

It was not so easy for Gault, who had spent a lifetime, without success, trying to inspire fear in someone—anyone. But he'd learned a technique that quieted most arguments quickly. When resistance was strong he turned and shouted to Simon, "We have another challenger, sir, at double the stakes."

After all bets were collected the three of them, along with fifteen of Barrow's students, left the work area. Simon was disappointed. In contrast to this dismal place called Site Alpha, most of these Beltway visits were great fun. Crowds became excited as the matches approached. There were shouts and catcalls and good-natured threats as opponents stepped into the ring, singly with his students, and in groups against him. It was usually possible to get the audience involved, shouting suggestions and encouragement and insults to the contestants. Often the wagers were paid with an amazed laugh, as the audience realized that they had not been betting, so much as paying for highly skilled entertainment. It wasn't unusual for a young man or woman to approach him afterward, with bright eyes and bursting curiosity. "How did you do that? Where did you learn it? Will you teach me?" And although it was rare—it had happened only four times over the years—he gained new students this way.

But even places like Site Alpha had their value. Students needed to see every aspect of the life they had chosen, and were training to enter. Although the name was often applied to them, they were not "prizefighters"; the term was too limited to describe what they did in their bouts with amateurs. They were combat artists, martial illusionists, whose challenge was to create the *impression* of a fight—where none, in fact, existed. The perfection of that art would require years of work. Most of these students would need to support themselves along the way, in just this manner. And while their enthusiasm and skill usually delighted rather than angered those who'd bet against them, there were exceptions. Site Alpha was one of them.

The mood was different when Simon entered the site boss's office with a double handful of pay-chits. With the fee for setting up the arena, the extra charge for full gravity, the administrative fee for coding the chits onto a money card, and the personal bets made that this quiet young man would win all bouts, Martha Havers was having a very profitable day.

"You can come back out here anytime," she said as she handed Simon's card back to him.

"Thank you!" Clonus said. "That would be wonderful. But we never—"

"Don't wait for us," Gault said, interrupting. "Even you people wouldn't bet against Simon Barrow again."

Havers ignored the insult. "You should have a name for your show, Mr. Barrow. You could call yourselves Barrow's Brawlers. Or The Fighting—something. You should listen to me, I can help you. For a small commission I'll contact the other sites and tell them about you." Her enthusiasm grew as she spoke. "I can get you onto all of the Dianymede sites. We've got forty-two that are still open. This is one of the smallest, you know. With my help you could do extremely well."

"No," Simon answered. "Thank you." The suggestions and offers were made nearly every time.

"But I . . . Oh, I see. If they know about what you people can do, you won't get any bets. I understand."

Simon shook her hand. "Goodbye, Martha. Thank you again." She had missed the obvious, as most did: Anyone looking to earn a great deal of money in the Asteroid Belt would concentrate on the few large sites still in operation, the major shipyards, or the established settlements. That was not his purpose. Barrow wanted as little attention paid to himself and his students as possible. More than anything else, this was for political reasons. Simon believed that at some future date his students would be welcome and appreciated everywhere in the Great Domain; his goal, his dream, was a formal Union that would establish codes of conduct, rules of engagement, and professional standards to be shared. The Union would also provide a secure future for Corinne and the children. But not now; at the present time, the formation of such a Union would never be allowed—because the UN government of Eleanor Douglas-Wycliffe bore a strong resemblance to the rule of Tarnon Tench on Mercator; suspicious and deadly toward anything it did not directly control. Any person or any group that stood out from the norm was considered a threat.

And so for the present, money was only a minor consideration. The small amount won on these trips served two purposes. It took care of expenses—and it gave his students a foretaste of the way most of them would earn a living, as individuals, after graduation.

After buying enough food and water to last for a nine-day trip, Barrow and his troupe loaded the old scouter and lifted off from Site Alpha. Years ago the journey home would have taken only five days. But the scouter's port engine was operating at less than forty-percent efficiency and the starboard could only be run to eighty. The needed repairs were easily within the capacity of Simon or any number of the former Service officers and enlisted personnel who shared his home. The problem was replacement parts; there were none available. Former mining sites operated by Dianymede and Basalt & Nickel and the smaller companies had been so thoroughly scavenged during the past six years of a universal depression that even junk was difficult to find. What could be found was remachined at one of the shops operated by Barrow's extended family. This scouter was one of only five remaining from a fleet of eleven. The others had been cannibalized to keep these running.

During the flight, Simon kept his students busy. He divided them into five groups of three and had them practice free-fall combat techniques in the scouter's cargo hold. They fought one against two, three on three, six on three, nine on six, with the groups changing fluidly at irregular intervals. He coached and worked them for twenty hours at a time, allowing six hours between sessions for rest and meals. He was proud of this group. It was a first trip for all but two of them, and each had done well. No student had lost a bout on any of the eight sites they'd visited.

The two senior students were Francine Bellenauer, once his cabin-mate aboard *Celeste*, and a twelve-year old phenomenon who invariably drew the longest odds and the most intense personal involvement of spectators and opponents. He was Corinne's brother, Hector Horatio Hernandez. The two were a strong contrast in performance styles. Francine was direct and humorless. She waited for an attack and responded accordingly. When her opponent showed skill and imagination, she would let the bout go on for a few minutes, probing and observing as if studying a specimen in a laboratory experiment. Those who tried to rely on brute power discovered that this rather small woman was eager to meet them on that basis, with astonishing strength. These bouts were typically of twenty seconds' duration or less.

Hector was special. He carried on conversations with his opponents before, during, and after the matches. His first bout always began slowly while the man or woman circled him, hesitant to attack a child with full force. Hector turned in place to face them as he asked about their homes, their ages, what they liked about mining, and eventually why they were so afraid of a twelve-year-old child. When they came at him he kept up the banter, making suggestions for the next attack as he threw them to the floor inside the ring. He laughed with them about things he'd seen, people he knew, places he hoped to visit one day. At some point those who spoke back, stopped talking. Their attacks grew more forceful, more desperate, sometimes armed and often with deadly intent. Hector continued joking with them as he evaded their blows, danced away from their thrust weapons, forced their hands to release knives and clubs, then politely offered them back as the opponent climbed up again from the floor. As the bout neared its six-minute limit he would say, "I've enjoyed talking with you." And that would be it. Within seconds the opponent would be out of the ring, very seldom standing. It was his habit then to escort them to their seats and congratulate their companions on the fine friend they had.

Hector's performances drew warmth, laughter, and rage, in about equal amounts. He was called a cynical little boy, and much worse. But those who accused him were wrong, he told them. He loved his sport, and appreciated the opportunity to practice on large people. If pressed he would explain that steadily unnerving an opponent was very much a part of his technique.

Home was just distinguishable as a separate asteroid when
Simon made the final radio contact before approach. He piloted to what was at present the sun-side and finessed the
balky scouter into the only operating airlock garage. After
the outer doors locked and sealed he waited while compressed air filled the fifty-by-forty-by-twenty compartment.
A green light above the inner door signaled when the pressure was equalized with the main dome. He opened a series
of hydraulic vents along the hull. Air rushed out until the
scouter's interior was equalized also. The troupe exited the
vessel and walked through the inner door, adjusting quickly
to the generated full gravity that permeated the dome and
living quarters of the original New Sarajevo—now called
Mari.

When Simon entered the family apartment Gordon and
Jessica Barrow were still in school. This was expected, but
the quiet was unsettling. He took a quick shower and shaved
off an eight-week growth of beard. After pacing the apartment
for several minutes he turned on some music and forced himself to relax while eating a meal the two oldest children had
left for him. It had been a good cycle for tomatoes and on-
ions, he was glad to see. The salad dressing was a specialty
of Gordon's. It was heavy to the taste and lumpy with a syn-
thetic cheese he'd invented. As he usually did, Simon put
aside the concoction, for later use with the asparagus mélange
that Jessica took so much acute pride in.

After the meal he picked up a stack of messages and took
them to his desk in the largest of the four bedrooms. There
was nothing about Randall's surgery, as he'd expected; the
administrative procedures for broadcasting a message from a
commercial liner were so extensive and time-consuming that
passengers were allowed only one. He and Corinne had
agreed that she would wait until after the last hyperspace
jump, when she'd know the exact time of her arrival. If all
had gone well, assuming that Griffin had succeeded in getting
the three of them passage on the liner, that information should
be coming within the next twenty hours.

The first message dealt with business, and the news was
good. The fusion chambers were in excellent condition. Har-
vests were up, as he'd guessed from the meal he'd eaten. All

five oxygen facilities were now on line. Within the year, the report continued, they would again be exporting the most lucrative of their cash crops.

He saved the school reports for last. Before reading them he opened a drawer and removed a ledger that was jacketed in black leather and titled with gold letters: GRADUATES. The well-worn book fell open to the last written page when he set the book on its spine and released it. Now he read the new reports, making notes as he went through them. When he was finished he stored the originals with others like them in the desk's bottom drawer. Then he began writing.

Onto the Three-Year list he entered five new names. He drew a thin line through nine others there, and flipped forward to the Six-Year section. He entered the nine names, grinning as he wrote them. Now he crossed off two names, and reentered them on the Instructor-Junior page. On this page he lightly circled two other names. These were ready to test with him for the position of Senior Instructor. He opened again to the Six-Year section and lingered over the names of his young brother-in-law, and two of his children.

Simon stretched out on the bed and closed his eyes, mentally reviewing his students. Here were faces and names and challenges and skills and breakthroughs, and numbers. Numbers. Seven hundred thirteen three-year graduates. Two hundred eighty-one six-year graduates. Fifty-one Instructors—thirty-seven Junior, fourteen Senior. Most of the six-year graduates were living independently now, traveling and fighting—"Anyone, Any Place, Any Way"—to support themselves. And sending new students to the ten schools, where the best of the best of them would someday be entered into the black leather book. He recalled the one thousand forty-five names in the ledger one by one until he drifted contentedly into sleep.

He slept soundly until he heard someone opening the apartment's outside door. An audible attempt to make no noise told him who the visitor was. Simon was up and dressed when a knock came at the bedroom door.

"Come in, Clonus," he said.

"Oh, you always know!" Clonus said as he entered the room. "Is there anything about Randall yet?"

"No. We should be hearing from Corinne soon. Have you eaten?"

"Of course! Traveling is such hard work, isn't it?" He eyed Barrow suspiciously. "Simon, did you remember what day this is?"

"Yes," Simon answered, hiding a smile.

"Well, I hope so! Are you ready?"

"Yes, Mr. Clonus."

"In the kitchen, Mr. Barrow."

Simon took his place, using his hands to hold himself up from the floor, legs forming a wide V, between two parallel chairs. Clonus went to a closet and brought back a yard-long alloy spring. He strapped an end to each of Simon's ankles. "Too tight?" he asked.

"Perfect," Simon answered.

"Then begin."

Simon lifted his legs slowly and began exerting inward pressure until the spring began to shorten. He pressed steadily, gradually increasing the force until it was half its original length.

"Good," Clonus said. He read from a small gauge at one end of the device. "That's one hundred fifty pounds exactly, Simon. Hold it there."

The first two minutes were easy. By the end of the third, his legs were beginning to tremble with the effort.

"One hundred forty-six," Clonus said disapprovingly.

Simon tightened the pressure as perspiration began to form on his forehead.

"One fifty-six! Simon, you're not concentrating!"

"Sorry," he said, straining. "How much longer?"

"Oh, I'll tell you when you're finished. Remember, Simon, when you get tired of pushing, pull! Make your *mind* do it! Push, then pull, then push—"

"I know! What's the pressure?"

"One fifty! Good, Simon! Hold it there like I taught you!"

Now his arms were shaking, and his abdomen felt like a steel ball collapsing in on itself. His legs were beyond feeling. *Dual* thinking, he reminded himself grimly. Dual! One set of muscles, one task, one result, two *different* commands, push-pull-push-pull, force the mind to believe the muscles were alternating, resting, pushing, pulling, a *dual* body, *one* purpose . . .

"Time!"

Simon released the pressure slowly. When the spring was fully extended again Clonus unstrapped the bindings. The familiar, odd feeling—his legs seemed to float upward and outward on their own—returned. He eased himself back to the floor and waited for a few seconds until he could walk without trembling.

Next were the arms, at an eighty-pound setting. These exercises were shorter, only three minutes each. First it was directly out in front of him, then over his head, and then behind his back. The final challenge was to sit on the floor with one end of the device held between his feet and the other beneath his chin. This was only fifty pounds, but the exercise lasted for seven minutes.

When it was over, Simon helped Clonus to go through his own program. The big man appreciated the company but didn't need the help. He'd been working with similar devices since early childhood. With the exception of his six years on Mercator he had used them, with other strengthening exercises, every day of his life. Clonus worked with settings that were exactly double those that Simon had attained during the past twenty-one years. Simon didn't undergo this torture as often as his teacher did; every fourth day was the frequency Clonus recommended for ". . . beginners and small people."

The two were sitting at the dinner table drinking iced tea when Gordon and Jessica opened the door and ran to hug their father. "Dad, Randall is all right!" Jessica shouted as he lifted her. "Did you hear?" She was light and compact, with thin arms that circled his neck powerfully. Her short hair was only now beginning to darken from childhood blond, and her freckles had nearly disappeared.

"He's all right?" The good news flowed through Simon like a warm tide. "Are you sure?"

Clonus clapped his hands. "Oh, good!"

"Here's the message," Gordon said as his feet left the floor. "It was under the door." At seventeen and already three inches taller than Simon, he found it embarrassing to be lifted at arm's length and then embraced like a child—as if he weighed nothing in the grip of his strong father.

Putting the young man down, Simon read the message at a glance. "Randall fine. Grandpa sleeping. Arrive Halcyon 0235 tomorrow. Love(s)."

"I'll pick them up, Dad," Gordon volunteered eagerly.

"That would take two days each way," Simon told him. "The shuttle will have them here late tomorrow. Besides, you and Jessica—"

"I know," he said, disappointed. "That's why Mr. Clonus is here."

Jessica turned to her big friend. "Can we start now, sir? I have a lot of study."

"Oh, certainly! I'll do mine, too!"

Simon left them and returned to his desk and began writing evaluation reports on the students who'd made this last trip with him. He needed the activity to silence a growing dread. There was nothing in Corinne's message to suggest it—but he knew that something was terribly wrong.

$$\Rightarrow 15 \Leftarrow$$

Carried from the shuttle to the scouter between Griffin and Corinne, Randall was sleeping face-down in a portable bed. Fine stubble nearly covered seven pin-sized incisions at the back of his head. After checking on his brother, Gordon returned to the small ships's controls and began the four-minute trip back down to Mari.

"They got them all? Everything?" Simon asked Corinne as they secured Randall's bed against the rear bulkhead of the pilot's compartment.

"Yes," Corinne said. She wore a half-smile that fought against the pain so apparent in her eyes.

The sense of dread returned, more powerfully than before.

He kissed her and held the embrace for long moments. "Were they able to give you a prognosis this time?"

Corinne didn't answer.

Griffin had been silently watching them. The old man shook his head. No.

Simon looked back to Corinne. This was his fault, he told himself. He'd passed on a genetic flaw to his beloved, innocent son. The doctors wouldn't say so, because the virus was officially dead—but this was the same disease that had killed Isaac and Neferti Barrow.

Randall had been strong, a healthy and exuberant boy with unbounded curiosity, until he was four. Shortly after his birthday he'd collapsed while playing with Jessica. They'd taken him to Mars while the final work was being completed on the original New Sarajevo, using Maria's techniques to restore the dead colony. The doctors found three tumors and removed them successfully. He was fine, for two years—until the disease struck again. On Earth, four growths were taken from his brain. Randall stopped growing at the age of ten.

This last trip had begun three months before.

"We'll go back," Simon whispered. "We'll stay on Earth."

"No," Corinne said, pulling away from her husband. "We've discussed this, Simon. We belong here. We're not giving up our home again."

"Corinne—"

Griffin coughed. "Excuse me, Simon, but she's right. There is no cure on Earth. You know they stopped looking for one, twenty-five years ago."

"The disease was reported to be dead," Simon answered tightly.

"I still have a few friends at the UN," Griffin told him. "They checked. There have been new cases every year. Not many, but a few have been reported."

"Not enough to look for a cure," Simon said bitterly.

"That's right. I'm sorry."

"Then," Simon replied, "we wait until this happens again. And again. Until our son—"

Corinne put her hand over his mouth. "Please," she said. "Don't say it. Don't *think* it. We can't go back again, Simon. Not to any hospital, anywhere. Not ever."

"What are you talking about?"

She hugged him again with all the strength she had left, while he held her and looked to Griffin.

"I signed away the last of my pension," Joyner began. "My annuities, savings, the property Maria and I owned on Long Island, all of it."

"Why, Griffin?"

"To pay for the surgery."

"But why? We bought lifetime insurance before we left Earth."

Corinne pulled back from him. "The policy is gone. *We're* gone. We're not in the system anymore, Simon. We don't exist. You, me . . . and the children!"

Simon's face reddened. "Thank you, Griffin, for what you did."

"There's no need to mention it, Simon. But I have no more resources, in case this becomes necessary again. All I own now is the principal share in this asteroid. But that's by Homestead contract. It can't be sold, except to the government. And they're not buying anymore, they're . . . We'll discuss that later."

"But how can they do this? It's . . . no, it's not impossible. But it's illegal!"

"It's done," Griffin told him. "And it's legal. All of the systems in the Great Domain are linked now. You have no identity. Therefore no action involving a person has been taken. Therefore no crime has been committed."

"The Steadhornes again."

"I don't think so," Griffin said. His breath was coming rapidly, in short angry gasps. "Those friends I mentioned, remember? They told me things. This has happened to thousands of people. Maybe tens of thousands. Potential political enemies, Simon. Erased. Powerless."

"I'm no one's enemy," Simon protested.

"You and your students have been noticed, apparently," Griffin said. "Judging from the mentality I found in the government, they probably decided you're building a private army." He added sadly, "No doubt I'm too old for them to bother with."

In the null-grav of the scouter, Simon felt heavy. He looked from the tearful face of his wife to the flushed and slumped

demeanor of Griffin Joyner. "There's more," he said in a subdued voice. "You have more to tell me."

"Yes," Corinne said.

None of them had noticed that the scouter was docking in
the airlock garage of home.

After dinner, when Griffin had had time enough to sleep,
Corinne and Simon walked to his apartment. The three sat
around his coffee table and continued the conversation as if
there had been no break.

"The Exploration Service is dead," Griffin said. "Assets
have been sold away. Some of the personnel were reassigned.
Most were fired."

"The ships?" Simon asked. "*Celeste* and *Majora*?"

"Stripped," Griffin told him. "In Lunar orbit. They'll be
structurally dismantled and sold within three months."

"But the settlements! There are nine new worlds out
there!"

"There won't be any more of them."

"I'm referring to the nine we have, Griffin. None of them
are ready yet to be isolated from Earth."

"I agree with you. But the UN says they *are* ready. The
argument is that this will force the worlds to develop their
resources more rapidly."

Simon shook his head. "That's garbage. With the reduc-
tions in personnel and supply that Douglas-Wycliffe started
twelve years ago, those worlds haven't had the chance to develop. They would have been self-sustaining by now, but they
were cheated."

"And now they're abandoned," Corinne said. "It will be
years before we receive any radio signals from that far away.
We may never know what happens to them."

"People won't allow it," Simon said firmly. "They'll force
her to rebuild the ships. Every person out on those worlds has
relatives back here somewhere."

"That makes no difference," Griffin said in disgust. "How
many people are directly affected? A hundred thousand? A
million? Add to that the populations of the Beltway and the
settlements, who are naturally sympathetic to the new worlds.
That still isn't many, counted against the nine billion people

on Earth. And even those nine billion can't do very much. Not now."

"Of course they can. Douglas-Wycliffe and her administration have poisoned everything they've touched. They've done it gradually, and that's the only reason people haven't reacted on a large scale. But abandoning those worlds is genocide, and citizens aren't going to accept it. Remember, the next general election is only a year away."

"No. The election has been canceled."

"WHAT?"

"That's right," Griffin said. "Douglas-Wycliffe has invoked emergency powers to deal with the economic crisis. And she's got the votes to support her. But even if elections were held, who are the citizens going to vote for?" He sighed and sat back, stretching his long legs beneath the table. "You already know how political enemies are neutralized. There was always a very thin line between world government and world dictatorship. Not anymore. The line has been erased. Earth belongs to the United Nations, and the United Nations belongs to Eleanor Douglas-Wycliffe. And the future has ended." He leaned forward and reached for the cup he'd emptied minutes ago. "The future has ended," he repeated quietly, looking at the floor. "That's an epigram, isn't it? Maybe I can make a wise and ironic book of it. Which would be as useless as everything else I've written." He sat staring at the backs of his hands, as if he'd read his destiny and now turned it away from himself. "Oh hell," he said.

Simon looked at his old friend in disbelief. Joyner had always been more than powerful, when strength was needed. Even after sixteen years of stagnation on Mercator he'd come back stronger than he'd ever been—due primarily to Maria, and the Exploration Service that was reborn around her. He'd commanded the Service with absolute self-confidence and unshakable vision. And then Maria went into a coma, and part of him ceased to exist. He'd kept his commission and power only to guarantee that Maria received the best care that Earth could provide. When Maria finally passed away, half of Griffin Joyner was buried with her.

But still he'd gone on, lecturing to Simon's students and writing his books for future generations. If Joyner's life were a fable, the moral would be that a person can be broken, can lose everything, time and again, and still keep coming back. But now it seemed that Griffin Joyner had done the one thing that no one would believe possible for him: He'd given up.

It was a thought Simon couldn't bear. And wouldn't accept. "You're wrong, Griffin," he said harshly. "There *is* a future, and it's ours. Earth has made a tragic mistake and will suffer for it. But Earth can deal with its own problems. We have our lives and our homes out here. We have what we need."

Joyner flushed and sat up straight. "Have you forgotten how to think, boy? Tell me what you're going to do if Randall gets sick again. No hospital anywhere will help him now. They're all under government control. And how long do you suppose it will be before Earth takes everything else? They need the ores from the mines, don't they? Did you know that the UN has already begun taking over Dianymede and Basalt? Who's going to stop them? And Earth needs null-grav research facilities, don't they? How long do you suppose Fujiwara and that new one, ProLab, will remain privately owned? And how long before the Homestead Acts are rescinded? How long before Earth confiscates this, and every home in the Beltway? Who's going to stop them? Earth needs something from every exporting settlement in the System. So why continue to pay for it? Why not take it all? And who's going to stop them if they want to let Randall die? You tell me, boy! *Who's going to stop them?*"

Simon stood up and paced the floor furiously. Everything Griffin had said was true. The process of Earth consuming itself was already underway—and accelerating, like the last stages of a star going supernova—with the same inevitable result. But accepting it like a half-dead dimwit was inexcusable. He faced the man whom he'd idolized nearly all of his life. "Look at yourself, Joyner! What the hell is wrong with you? 'The future has ended.' What kind of drivel is that? You're sitting on your hands and whining like—"

"Simon!"

"Let me finish, Corinne," he said, keeping his eyes on the placid face of Griffin Joyner. "Sir, when I lost my commission twelve years ago, I listened to you. And I did nothing. Not anymore, Griffin. I will *not* be still and allow what we've worked for, what every human being has worked for, to be taken away. I won't let *anyone* steal from my children, and condemn one of them to death! I will not allow it! They've attacked my family again, and I don't give a damn if it's only me and Corinne against everything Earth can throw at us!" Red-faced, he glared down at Joyner. "Ask yourself, Griffin: What would Talon do?"

Joyner stared back, saying nothing. This was the first time Barrow had ever shown disrespect. It was the first time in years Joyner had heard him raise his voice in anger. And it was about time. "I was worried about you," he said at last. "Sit down, Simon. I want your evaluation of the strategy I've mapped out."

⇒ 16 ⇐

The asteroid Mari had a revolving population of two hundred forty, of whom ninety percent at any given time were students and Instructors. Eight hundred twenty-nine similar men and women were scattered throughout the Great Domain. Three-year graduates, those now involved in the more intense second phase of training, lived and worked at or near the ten small schools Barrow had established. Six-year graduates were itinerants, traveling from city to city, settlement to settlement, earning their livings as entertainers and combat artists. In total, their number was one thousand forty-five. When Simon Barrow issued the first Domain-wide call, it was to the Senior Instructors and the itinerants. Corinne Barrow logged the call into the first of her journals under the date September 12, 2151.

On November 9 the last of the summoned combat artists, two hundred ninety-five in all, arrived on Mari. The three-

year graduates and their Instructors began leaving for their re-
spective schools, ready to be called if necessary.

The first day's business was scrapped when someone
pointed out that this was the first time all six-year graduates
and Senior Instructors had been together in one place at one
time. The spirit of reunion and comradery intensified as the
day progressed. Stories of combat tours grew from informa-
tional to anecdotal to competitive. Who'd won against the
highest number of amateurs? Who'd faced the most dangerous weapons? Who'd arranged and collected the most lucrative bets? What methods were best to keep the odds
favorable? The most lively subject of conversation dealt with
the ingenious off-world exits many of them had been com-
pelled to devise; on some of the outposts their farewells were
punctuated with rifle fire.

Simon Barrow had never known this degree of professional satisfaction. Although he was teacher to them all, he
found that in every conversation he held, or heard, he was
treated as "one of us." He was mercilessly chided about his
impending descent into senility and infirmity; his fortieth
birthday, they pointed out, was only months away. This was
a solemn event that must be met with dignity and despair,
and gifts. Suggestions varied from prosthetic aids to taxi-
dermy.

As the spirited day drew to a close, Ke Shan took Barrow
aside and whispered urgently to him. "Sir, I want your support. I've been with you since Mercator and I've given you
more and better graduates than any other Instructor. Will you
give me your vote?"

"Ke Shan, what are you talking about? Are you people
holding *elections* now?"

"You haven't heard?"

"No. But before you tell me about it, let me make two
points. First, this is not a democracy. It's a—a paramilitary
oligarchy, for want of a better term. Second, if we do make
any decisions by consensus, I won't have a vote. I'll have a
veto."

She huffed. "Well, that's fine. You listen to me, Simon Barrow. In a few days we'll all be out somewhere fighting something that's a million billion times bigger than we are and it'll

go on for years unless all of us get killed. But this is important!"

"All right. What is it?" He was tempted to laugh, but her expression told him that she was completely serious.

"Come with me, sir."

She led him to the main auditorium, where years ago Dr. Spinelli had stood to address the first permanent settlers on New Sarajevo. Most of the graduates and Instructors were already there, filling the front seats. Behind them were twenty of the support staff, along with Corinne and Griffin Joyner. Gordon and Jessica were seated in the second row, deeply engrossed in a conversation with the comrades around them.

Simon took a seat next to Corinne as the gathering was called to order. Senior Instructor Stewart Misiaszek was at the podium. He explained to those who were just arriving what the meeting was about. Now, Simon did laugh.

What they wanted first, what they demanded before this new adventure became too serious, was a name.

Suggestions were called out and recorded as Misiaszek recognized the nominators one by one. When Ke Shan stood, she looked directly at Simon. "This is the best one," she said. She turned to the podium and said, "Orphans of Earth." Then she sat and smiled proudly. The laughter began at the far side of the room—and stayed there, as Ke Shan jumped to her feet and glared around her.

As more suggestions were offered Simon vetoed most of them because they contained the word "Barrow." His intransigence nearly resulted in a good-natured mutiny.

Anton Kin'Te spoke from his seat. "Excuse me, but aren't we, ah, *against* dictatorship?" His lively eyes swept the room, as some laughed and others applauded. Kin'Te was a former Exploration Service officer, nicknamed The Great Kenyan because of his size, courage, and birthplace. The normally shy man stood and reveled in the applause.

"Don't be stupid, Anton," Ke Shan called back, still angry. "This is a *paramilitary oligarchy*. Right, Mr. Barrow?"

Simon stood and bowed to them as the ruckus picked up momentum. "Whatever you want," he said humbly while the noise diminished. "Whatever you want, graduates and Instructors, you have only to let us know. And please, be direct and forthright. General Joyner needs exercise for his own veto power."

Pounding on the podium, Instructor Misiaszek brought the laughter under control. "We have thirty-seven nominations so far," he said. "Who's next?"

"I am! It's my turn! Why won't you hacks give *me* a chance to talk?"

"Go ahead, Mr. Gault."

The rat-faced man stood. "It's my idea," he began, "that—"

"We can't hear you, sir."

"It's *my* idea," he said more loudly, "that, you know, that mind thing that I taught Clonus. Where you think twice at the same time and break rocks. That's what it should be. Right, Clonus?"

"Yes, Gault. I believe that will be the best name for them."

Gault cleared his throat. "This is what it is. The Dual People!"

"Oh, no!" Clonus whispered in a voice that carried through the auditorium. "That wasn't it at all!"

Gault bent down and faced the seated man. "Well," he whispered, "what the hack *was* it?" A second later he straightened again.

"I remember! It was Dualists! Dual people, you see? But just one word."

Clonus stood. "Isn't that good? It's a pun, and it's good! You fight a duel with a dual mind! If you write it down, you can see what I mean."

"What *I* mean!" Gault said.

Shaking his head and smiling, Simon turned in his seat to face the big man. "Clonus, that's very clever. But I don't think—"

"It's perfect!" Corinne said, pulling on his shoulder. "Simon, *that's* the name. It's the name I'm going to use for my journals," she added firmly. Uncharacteristically, she stood up and addressed the auditorium. "Duelists!" she said, and spelled out the word to them. "You people are Duelists!"

"It was my idea!" Gault shouted. His protest was drowned out by the applause, and then the chant that grew until everyone in the room was shouting it. "DUELISTS!"

• • •

"One more item," General Joyner said when relative silence finally returned. "One more item before we adjourn. There will be no vote and no argument. For this once, that includes Simon Barrow. Am I clear, Duelists?"

4

HITTING
BACK

➔ 17 ⟵

The next morning two hundred ninety-six Duelists, including the man who'd formed them and now bore a title—an official one—that embarrassed him, met again in the auditorium. The atmosphere this time was entirely different. Instead of the ebb and flow of conversation and boisterous laughter, the room was now filled with young men and women who waited with professional quiet. *Their backs are straighter*, Simon thought as he looked around from his seat beside the podium. It had never occurred to him to give them a name. They were all individuals who someday would go on with their separate lives—made better, he believed, by the training he'd given them. But now they were also a unit; bonded together by common experience and a name that represented years of arduous work and the unbreakable desire to transform their minds and bodies. Each one of them had now been told separately, without detail, of Joyner's plans. Every woman and man in the room chose without hesitation to become a part of the plans. So today they had a common purpose as well. Many of them, he knew—perhaps all of them—would sacrifice their lives to that purpose. *This must be done*, he told himself again. *This is right.* He looked out at the faces of Gordon and Jessica, who sat with the others and watched him expectantly.

Senior Instructor Stewart Misiaszek called the meeting to order. "Duelists," he said. "I present the first and foremost among us. Admiral Simon Barrow."

They didn't know whether or not to applaud. But when the applause started with one Duelist, they all joined in.

Simon cleared his throat. The "Admiral" bothered him. Before now it had been a private joke among himself, Corinne, Griffin, Maria, and a few others. Now the title was entered into Corinne's journal. And when the word was spoken, it was no longer with a smile.

"General Joyner will follow me," he began, "to discuss overall strategy and individual tactics. My purpose is to give you a picture of what it is we're going to do, and why. Some of you, like myself, have not been on Earth for many years. But you know what's happened there, and you know what the implications are. I'll mention just a few of them." He sipped from a glass of iced tea. "Humankind began this journey long ago. On Earth, someone discovered that fire can be harnessed and controlled. Someone else, perhaps thousands of years later and thousands of miles away, created the first wheel. Those two individuals were as united with one another as we in this room are today united. Perhaps they gave no thought to the future. Perhaps they never conceived of the notion that the future and the night sky were one and the same. I believe they did. But regardless, they began a march that has included every human being who has lived. We don't know where the march leads. But we know, deep within that part of us that has no name, that the march must never end. You and I were born at what may be the most critical time in humankind's history. Certainly, other generations have believed this to be true of themselves. And it is my fervent hope that future generations will also claim this distinction. But you and I will decide from *where* those future generations think of themselves. Will they be out among the stars, on hundreds, or thousands, of settled worlds! Will they be crossing galaxies, as readily as you and I travel among the asteroids? Will their numbers be billions of billions, not yet beginning to visit the infinite wonder and variety of the Universe?

"Or—" he said, pausing. "Or will the nine new worlds we've begun be the end of our march? Will they die of abandonment, with every person on them looking to the skies and asking, Why? Will what we call the Great Domain begin to shrink, to die also, as Earth reaches out—not as a nurturing parent, but as a twisted, mad and hungry, tyrant? And my first question, again. *Where* will the descendants of our children be? The answer is this. They will be out here with us, unimaginably beyond us. Or they will be choking to death. On a dreamless, bitter, and broken Earth.

"That is the reason we are here together." Simon drank

again from the tea, and then returned to the remarks he and Corinne had written. "I have told you why we are here. As to what we're going to do, I can tell you that in two sentences. We're going to break open the Great Domain. And we're going to kick the rubble from the path of humankind."

Of the two hundred ninety-six Duelists who'd met that November day on Mari, eighty-nine were veterans of the Exploration Service. The last of them had returned from their far-flung homes the previous week with whatever of their belongings they would need for the jobs assigned to them.

The final person to arrive before the first excursion could begin was Griffin Joyner. He was smiling, as Simon had not seen him smile in years, when he passed through the airlock between shuttle and scouter. In his hand was a valise, packed with documents he'd gathered from former friends and professional associates on Earth—who'd agreed to risk their careers and lives because *the* General gave them hope for a better future, and his solemn word that he would never reveal their names to anyone. To his dismay, Simon was informed that Joyner's promise extended even to him.

The veterans who hadn't discarded them brought back all of the Service memorabilia they owned. There were one hundred sixty uniforms in all. Eighty-one of them were given to Duelists—only a few of them Service veterans—after alterations were made and the distinctive emblems of the Exploration Service were removed. Three veterans found themselves promoted, and two former officers were now dressed as enlisted personnel. None of the Duelists were pleased to be looking like Peacekeepers, knowing what that formerly great organization had now become.

Admiral Simon Barrow—in seven weeks he'd become accustomed to the title—went through two scouters as the Duelists settled in for the flight to Dianymede's Bravo Three site.

"Good," he said as he finished with each of the two groups. "Stow the uniforms and let's go."

The site boss at Bravo Three had been with Dianymede Mining Company since its establishment in 2102 by Grace, Alicia, Dominia, and Matilda Hoffman: The Four Sisters, whose portrait hung from at least one wall on every facility they owned. There were only forty-two sites now, down from a high of over two hundred.

Most of his career had been spent as an executive and corporate negotiator on Earth. Now Mylo Edelman worked for a third of his accustomed salary, and saw his children and grandchildren only once a year. At work, he made the expected comments to his crews about injustice and the lack of appreciation they all felt. But in truth he considered himself fortunate to have a job at all. A year from now, if government interference and trade restrictions continued, Dianymede would be out of business.

And so when a radio call from two distant scouters announced that they were Peacekeepers, his heart began pounding harder than it had in the seventy years of his life. It became worse when they warned him that no other sites were to be notified of their arrival on Bravo Three.

As the scouters taxied to the airlocks he noted with grim satisfaction that they were old and worn-looking. Good, he thought. Times are rough for them, too. He met the Peacekeepers in the arrival area after ordering gravity to be set at half, the standard procedure for greeting important visitors. The Peacekeepers began filing into the room and Edelman's heart began its heavy pounding again.

"My God," he whispered to the crew chief beside him. "They're Commandos!"

This was the fittest group of human beings he'd ever seen. Every one of them was razor-straight, and walked with a confident, catlike gait. He'd never seen Peacekeepers like this; not a jowl, not a protruding belly, not a slouch among them.

"Mr. Edelman," Francine Bellenauer said, advancing on the two.

"That's me, Major," Edelman said. Without a conscious decision to do so, he took a step backward.

She reached for his hand and shook it—which was clearly a surprise to the man. "I'm instructed, sir, to ask you if you have contacted anyone regarding our arrival."

"Absolutely not," Edelman said. He wished now that he had; but of course they'd have monitored the call and arrested him immediately. Then, why the question?

"I see," Bellenauer said. "Please come with me, sir."

She turned and walked back toward the airlock door. Three

paces away she stopped and turned again. "Now, Mr. Edelman. If you please."

Simon was waiting for them in the inboard scouter's pilot compartment. Francine stopped at the door and motioned for Edelman to enter. When he was inside she shut the door, leaving the two of them alone.

"This is a serious offense," Barrow said without preamble.

"What is, Colonel? I don't know what's going on here." This colonel confirmed Edelman's suspicion that he was dealing with Commandos; the man's eyes were steady and clear, and absolutely confident. He was not large or overtly muscled, but there was about him an unnerving combination of casual ease and ready, explosive power.

Barrow snapped a switch at the radio monitor panel. "Listen to this recording." A husky, whispering voice came out of the speaker: *Clayton, listen and don't respond. The Peacekeepers just arrived. Edelman says—*He cut the switch. "Mr. Edelman, why did you disregard my order?"

"I didn't!" Edelman said. "Colonel, I swear to you I did not!"

Barrow's eyes narrowed. "You're under arrest, Mr. Edelman. The property and assets of Dianymede Mining Company are seized, by authority of the United Nations and the Peacekeeping Force. In addition ... Oh, this is becoming a bore. Do you insist that I quote the statutes and regulations, as all the others have?"

Edelman flushed and shook his head.

"Good. I'm beginning to make that speech in my sleep. Here, read it for yourself." He passed the site boss a document from Joyner's valise. "Pay particular attention to Item B, paragraphs 3 and 5."

"Colonel, what are you *doing* to us? Why?"

"Read it!" Barrow snapped. He watched Edelman's eyes as the man read the document, which was genuine. He sympathized; his family's home on Earth and citizenship had been lost this unfairly and abruptly. But he kept his feelings away from his eyes and voice.

When Edelman looked up again his face was tight with barely contained anger. "I believe I have the right to authenticate this, Colonel."

"That is your right," Simon agreed. "Is anyone on duty in your radio room?"

"Yes."

Simon handed him a handset. "Have them patch you through. You know the department you need to contact."

Edelman nodded. "It's becoming routine now. Every message-group we receive has new laws and regulations and 'clarifications' from you people. If there weren't that station on Mars, all my time would be spent waiting for radio confirmations."

"Do it."

When the connection was made, Edelman gave the call sign for Bravo Three and then read out the authentication code at the bottom of the document. "Wait one, Mylo," the voice answered. Forty more minutes passed, during which time Barrow ignored his visitor and pretended to be reading a novel that Francine had brought along. He didn't let it show, but he was beginning to worry. This was much longer than should be required for radio-time. Mars and Bravo Three were nearly at closest-point. What was causing the delay? Joyner's associate had assured him that she could insert the new document's code into the system by this date—even though it was not yet in effect, and highly classified.

Finally, the voice came back. "Sorry to keep you, Mylo. That number's in the batch we're inputting now. Yes, verified. Repeat, Document code verified. Out."

Simon released a breath. This plan was the easiest, and the safest for the miners. But there were others ready, just in case. "That's your copy," he said. "Read it to your crews and post one in every office and barracks here."

"What do I do now?" Edelman asked. He was speaking to himself. The anger in his face was gone. Now it was despair and resignation that dominated his features.

Barrow spoke sharply. "First, you will increase your output by a minimum of twenty percent. Beginning now. Second, you will receive supplies and crew rotations from Dianymede as always. But you will *not* on-load ore to those ships. Store it here. A government freighter will pick it up when we're ready. Questions?"

"You—you're taking everything . . . the government has freighters?"

"We will. Soon." He said, "You will not communicate with anyone about this. Be warned, Edelman. You and your crews are criminals. A second violation will not be tolerated."

The site boss was silent. His future—more importantly, the future of those who depended on his income—rested with this man now. There was no escape, and no one to whom he could appeal this treatment. "Your Commandos are staying here to enforce this?" he asked, alarmed at the sudden thought. "You're turning my workplace into a prison?"

"Why would I do that?" Barrow asked. "You won't break the law again." He smiled. "Would you like me to convince you?"

"No!" Edelman said. "There's no need to hurt anyone, Colonel." He swallowed hard. "Please."

"I agree, that isn't necessary," Barrow said, relieved that this was so. "You'll be watched, Edelman. We have our agents in place." He hit the monitor switch again. A husky, whispering voice said, *Clayton, listen and don't respond. The Peacekeepers just*—He closed the switch.

"That was *your* man!" Edelman shouted, red-faced.

Barrow laughed. "And there are others, among your crews. Your government is very thorough, sir. I trust that you are re-assured. And warned." The smile left his face. "Do your jobs, Edelman. And don't communicate this to anyone except on-site personnel. I would prefer a peaceful arrival at our next site. But if there *is* resistance . . . you've seen my troops."

"Yes," Edelman said bitterly. "I'm not going to give you an excuse to kill innocent people."

"Good. Now get out."

When he'd left, Francine Bellenauer entered the pilot compartment.

"Did you hear everything?" Barrow asked.

"All of it. You were right, it was simple."

"It won't be that easy every time. And remember, it's crucial that you convince the site bosses that they're among the last to be taken over. That will make them less likely to notify anyone off-site. And they'll be angry that no one told *them*. Also, be sure that they see our people. The visual impact is important."

"That's clear, sir."

"Are you ready to take command?"

She flushed. "Of course I am, Simon. My rank was nearly the same as yours in the Service. And even if it weren't, I'm a Duelist. Anyone, any place, any way. Any*thing*."

He smiled at her, thinking that this shared name had become more valuable than he'd thought at first. "As soon as you're satisfied that Instructor Misiaszek is ready, give him half of your people. Forty should be enough, on these small mines."

"It's going to take a lot of time."

"This has to be done personally, at every site. But we can speed the process. As soon as we've, ah, borrowed a few faster vehicles, I'll have two of them delivered to you."

"I recommend Peacekeeper cutters. They're hyperspace-equipped, and they create a stronger impression than these piles of scrap."

Simon grinned at her. "You've read my mind." He said seriously, "All of the mines have to be reached. I'm estimating that once you have the faster ships, you'll finish in two months."

"We should be leaving now. Your pickup will be on station by this time tomorrow."

"Right." It wouldn't be long, he knew, before this action would begin to have real effect. Griffin Joyner had forecast the stages that events would take: The miners would work diligently at first, under an apparent threat, to meet the new quotas. Ships arriving to deliver supplies would be sent away empty after the site bosses displayed the document and repeated Simon's orders. The mining companies were sure to protest—but very weakly, after authenticating the UN order; and they would be ignored. If anything, they'd be given a standard and official denial that any of this was taking place. The companies, without recourse, would be silenced. Eventually the stockpiles of ores and the anger of the mining crews would lead to on-site slowdowns. By the time the site bosses were desperate enough to communicate openly with one another again, the momentum would be unstoppable. A first-ever Belt-wide strike of the mines would already be underway.

⇛18⇚

Prometheus Shipbuilding and Drydock Company was a relatively new facility. The huge manufacturing station orbited Mars, where it could take advantage of the metal mills on the planet, which were gradually replacing the ones on Earth because of the shorter average distances between Mars and the various Beltway mines. And because not all of Earth's bureaucratic restrictions were in effect on Mars. Yet.

Thirty Duelists arrived at PSDC as an entertainment troupe. They wore new and colorful tunics that caught the attention of everyone who saw them. That was especially true of the two boys who marched ahead of the waving and smiling performers, calling out to all passers-by and pressing into their hands flyers that promised amazing feats of acrobatic and combat skill. One of the boys was very young. "Join us!" called Hector Horatio Hernandez. "The Duelists have arrived! Join us!" He was so enthusiastic and engaging that dozens of the onlookers left their off-shift routines to follow along behind this new attraction. As they went, the Duelists performed hand-walking routines and formed human pyramids that collapsed, rolled, and then formed again, with uncanny precision. The parade continued through all levels of the family and recreation areas throughout the mammoth space station. Before the day was over every man, woman, and child at PSDC knew that something fresh and exciting had come to their small world. After that, the entertainers broke up into small groups and began paying courtesy calls to the executives and senior Peacekeepers who operated PSDC.

The next evening an unusual, profitable arrangement with the station's Director emptied the four-tiered concourse that served as shopping mall and main area for bars, holo-houses, and restaurants. Only a squad of twenty Peacekeepers remained inside, to watch the newcomers as they set about erecting a stage. The platform was located at the center of the main concourse, where it could be seen by looking over the guardrails from the upper three levels.

At every entrance to the area Duelists sold advance tickets for the upcoming performance, only two hours away now. They bantered with the swelling crowds and challenged them to come and be a part of the "Best Show in the Great Domain! Guaranteed!" And they said hundreds of times, in answer to a repeated question, "Yes! That boy will be here! Are you coming to the show?"

Each carrying a flight bag and dressed in similar working clothes, Simon Barrow and fifty Service veterans—with the exception of Ke Shan—arrived at the station by way of a shuttle that came up from the planet below on a six-hour schedule. The Duelists went immediately to one of the mall entrances and raised angry protests by stepping to the head of the line. "They're roustabouts!" the Duelist selling tickets explained as she let them enter, then locked the door behind them. "They're setting up your show!"

Once inside, the new arrivals quickly overpowered the Peacekeepers. These were stripped of their radios and left tied and gagged in the back of one of the restaurants. Ten minutes later fifty-one Duelists put on altered Service uniforms, filed out through one exit, and began the long walk to the main shipyard. The corridors were nearly deserted, as they'd hoped.

Barrow stopped the group just before they entered the last passageway. He reviewed with them information provided by the blueprint and timetable that Griffin Joyner had brought from Earth. "The cutters should be power-up now," he said in summation. "The real transporting crews are due on the next shuttle. If any of the ships aren't ready, don't waste time. Go to the next one and—"

"Sir, we've been through this," Karen Bridges said. "We're ready." A murmur of agreement passed through the rest.

"Good enough. I'm going in now. The rest of you come in by tens. Ke Shan, you know which power lines have to be rigged. And—"

"Admiral Barrow, we *know*!" Ke Shan said.

He looked from face to face, and nodded. Turning for the

door he murmured loud enough to be heard, "How quickly they grow up."

Simon passed through the doorway and walked to the far end of the corridor, to the Peacekeeper sitting at a desk. "You're missing the show, Corporal," he said pleasantly.

"Yes, sir. I'm junior in my squad. You're here to inspect the ships?"

"That's right."

"I'll need to see your identification."

"Certainly." Simon reached inside his uniform blouse. "I hear those Duelists are—" His free hand back-fisted the corporal below the left temple before the man could react. He crumpled without a sound. Simon propped the unconscious man forward in his chair, putting his head down on the desk with his arms tucked as pillows beneath him. A few seconds later Simon had disconnected the alarm switch beneath the desk and disabled the portable radio. The next group of Duelists to pass this way would cut the communications lines that ran through the corridor. One of them would put on the corporal's uniform and take his place at the desk, until everything was prepared.

Stepping through the doorway, he entered a small room that contained nothing but three elevator doors. One was open. He selected the fifth level and turned around in the cab to face the transparent rear wall. As the elevator began ascending, the gravity eased until it was gone. After a few seconds the shipyard came into view. His destination was visible now, two hundred yards away and sixty feet above him.

The supervisor's cubicle was paneled with glassite on all sides, affording a panoramic view of the mammoth work area that was open to space. From this distance he could see a small figure, alone, seated at a desk.

Enclosed flexible tunnels ran like strands of silk along the dozens of catwalks leading to and between the five new cutters. Simon marked all positions mentally, and stepped out of the elevator at the fifth level. He entered the last of the open entrances to his right. Within the six-foot-wide tunnels were guy-lines that ran along each side. Simon pulled himself along the right-side wire as the passageway gradually inclined. This was a quick way to travel, but it was uncomfortable. It gave him the eerie feeling of being on Mercator again, passing through long tunnels with little or no gravity. Guided by the memorized schematic, he took the first intersection and then changed direction to straight "up." Only two people passed by during the six-minute trip, neither paying any attention to him.

He pressed a buzzer beneath the floor to the supervisor's cubicle and waited until the hatchway was opened.

"You're early, Major," the shift supervisor said as he climbed through. She was a young woman with short black hair and dark complexion. "We weren't expecting you on this shift."

"Is there a problem with the units?" he asked. The eerie feeling returned as Simon looked at her. If her name sounded anything like 'Corinne,' he'd be sure that he was dreaming.

"Oh, no! Not at all."

"Then we can proceed." He kept his voice low-pitched and spoke in clipped, half-barked sentences. Too many questions at this stage could be dangerous for everyone. "My crews are coming in now."

"But the schedule—"

"I'm ordered to begin now," he said impatiently. "What is your name?"

"Caravelli, sir. Linda Caravelli."

"Supervisor Caravelli, I am prepared to accept delivery. Verify these release codes, and stop wasting my time." From his uniform blouse he removed a sealed envelope bearing the logo of the UN Peacekeeper Force. "You will attest that the seal is unbroken," he said, passing it to her.

"Yes, I can see that the—"

"Open it, Caravelli. There are five sheets inside, one for each vessel." Despite a lifetime of combat training and discipline, he felt absolutely vulnerable at this moment. If Joyner's 'friend' on Earth had been wrong, or if the intrusion into the computer system had been detected—or if they'd changed any of the seventeen-digit strings that filled each page, a supervisor's check would alert the station's Peacekeepers immediately. The Duelists had prepared several avenues of escape. But there would be casualties—and no ships. Simon took a deep breath and released it slowly as Caravelli fed each of the five sheets into an input tractor. They both watched the computer screen while the data was matched against the encrypted information inside. Code strings flashed across the surface, too fast to read. After five seconds the screen went blank, then turned a solid red and began flashing. There was no sound. Were alarms sounding elsewhere? Simon tensed, ready to begin the escape procedure.

Caravelli turned to him, the fear plain in her eyes. "I can't release the ships to you, sir," she said quietly.

"That's unfortunate," he said sincerely.

Abruptly, she turned and crossed to a filing cabinet.

"What are you doing?" He had no desire to hurt this woman. But if she was reaching for a weapon . . .

As he stood beside her, ready to move, she began taking out stacks of documents. She handed them to Simon. "I don't have the authority to sign these," she said. "The Director is Mr. William Burnside. He has to—"

Instantly he understood, and was back in character. "Call him," he said harshly, conscious of a dry rasp in his throat. "Get him here. But first order your crews out of those ships. And release all mooring lines except the fore and aft hawsers. Do you have the authority to do *that*, at least?"

She glared at him as she crossed to the intercom banks. Simon ignored her and began signing the papers. With his back to her, he smiled as she began issuing the instructions. When she'd finished, she went to her desk. "That's odd," she said.

Simon turned to face her.

"The phone is out." She clicked the button several times.

"That gives me great confidence in these cutters," he said sarcastically. "By chance, do you know how to use a radio?"

She made the call. "Mr. Burnside is at the show, Major. Everybody's at the show. I sent a messenger down to get him."

"I heard the conversation," Simon told her. "Thank you, Linda." She had done everything he needed her to do. There was no longer any reason to put on the act that he genuinely hated. And she *did* look like Corinne. He regretted what he had to do next. He finished signing the papers and turned to the windows. Already the shipyard crews were out in force, taking down the moorings. Simon looked at his chronometer and saw that Ke Shan's group, the last of them, would be boarding now. That meant that the power to Caravelli's radio was disabled, along with all main communication lines. "I'll

take these with me," he said, stacking the papers neatly.
"When Burnside arrives, tell him I'll be aboard number five."

"Goodbye, Major," she said stiffly.

"Goodbye, Supervisor." He knocked her out as painlessly
as possible and set her gently on the floor. Next to her he
placed the sheaf of papers. He hoped she'd understand that
for her sake, it had to appear that she'd acted under threat to
her life—and that her signature appeared nowhere on the
forms releasing the ships.

In the mall area, the show was just getting underway. The
tiers were fully packed with off-duty workers and their families. Jessica Barrow and Hector Horatio Hernandez were
standing at the center of the stage, surrounded by larger Duelists. The audience was shouting out suggestions for the im-
provisational scenes taking place.

One woman shouted above the others. "Two, with saps!"

Two of the circling Duelists snatched up short bludgeons
from a pile of weapons and ran at the two. Jessica and Hector
turned back-to-back and waited. The first Duelist to attack
them was Anton Kin'Te. As he reached them, each of the
children bent sharply to the right, creating an open area above
them. Kin'Te rushed into the opening and was lifted as
Jessica and Hector each grabbed an ankle and pulled upward.
They spun in tandem and threw the Duelist from the stage
and into the audience.

The next one circled more warily. At a quick wink from
Jessica, Delores Nancarrow charged. Jessica put her hands behind her, on Hector's shoulders. She jumped, lifting her legs
and pushing against Hector as the Duelist approached. Her
body shot forward like a spear and her heels dug into the
charging woman's stomach. When Jessica hit the floor she
rolled over and pushed up with her hands, again straightening
her body. This time her heels caught the larger Duelist in the
chest and knocked her backward to the stage. Instantly Jessica
was on her. She grasped Nancarrow's uniform at shoulder and
crotch, and lifted her high over her head. The audience applauded the little girl's unexpected strength as she walked to
the edge of the stage and threw her opponent twelve feet
through the air.

"More! More!" William Burnside, PSDC's Director,

stamped his feet and clapped in amazement. These two had introduced themselves to him before the show began. They'd seemed so small, and harmless!

Another thirty minutes passed while the performers switched roles, then went to a set of acrobatic maneuvers involving all of them at once.

Rolling away from the peak of a collapsing forty-foot human pyramid, Hector looked questioningly at Gordon and raised his eyebrows. Gordon checked his chronometer and nodded twice. Hector returned to center stage and raised his hands until the applause stopped.

"And now," he said, filling the mall with his strong voice, "do you want to see something *really* good?" He waited while the renewed shouts and applause quieted. "I talked with Mr. Burnside, and he said you deserve something special!" The audience turned toward the station's Director, who waved cheerfully back at them from his prominent seat in the first tier. A woman beside him whispered in his ear. He shouted something at her that was drowned out by the crowd, and she turned away.

Hector continued. "And so we ask for your patience, friends, while we prepare. We're going to turn out all the lights for five minutes. And you people behave yourselves in the dark!"

Again, when the audience was quiet, he laughed and held up his hands. He said in a voice quivering with excitement, "When the lights go on, you won't *believe* what you see! Are you ready?"

"Ready!" "Show us, kid!" "Nobody touch my husband!"

The lights snapped out.

Three seconds later, on the far side of PSDC, the lights went out also.

"Now, just wait, all right?" Hector's voice called out.

The crowd laughed and joked, waiting expectantly for the next round of fun. And they waited, and waited, while thirty Duelists quietly slipped out an exit and began running. The few people they encountered were rendered unconscious with a minimum of force as they hurried through corridors toward the service vehicle hangar.

•　　•　　•

Simon strode through a transparent tunnel to the cutter's main entrance area, noting that the pier-panel was nearly all green: The engines were active, environmental systems operational, and the ship was functioning entirely on the power of autogenerated hydrogen fusion. Only two lights remained red: Some of the moorings were still in place—the fore and aft hawsers—and departure clearance had not been received.

"This happens occasionally," one of the station crew told him. The man shrugged and looked to his four companions for agreement. "You know how management is. Shouldn't be much of a delay, Major."

From where he stood, Simon could see only one side of one cutter. As he watched, the forward hawser separated from the vessel and began floating free in the null gravity.

"What happened to the main lights?" Simon asked. "Everything's dark over there." He pointed back toward the banks of elevators, which he knew were also without power.

"Oh, that's the electrical gang," the man said, grinning. "They're mostly idiots here." He turned and made a sweeping gesture toward a secondary station two miles away across a gulf of open space. "I used to work there at Smallcraft, and I tell you we never—"

He was the first to go. The other four were taken out just as swiftly, only one of them raising his voice in shock at the blur of hands.

Karen Bridges stepped from behind the airlock door at the cutter's entranceway. "Everything's set, Admiral. We're casting off the lines now."

"Secure the airlock behind me and take your station," Simon told her.

"Yes, sir."

As the cutters began lifting away from the piers Simon keyed the intraship speaker system. "A reminder, Duelists," he said. "These cutters are yard-ready, but they haven't been through space-trials yet. Check everything twice. Units One through Four, you're clear to enter hyperspace as soon as you can safely do so. You all have your charts marked. I'll be joining you soon. Good luck."

"Yes, Admiral."

"Thanks, Mom."

"Good luck, sir."

"You're a saint, Simon. Nothing else explains your luck."

Simon turned to the man seated in the co-pilot's chair. "Litieri, I'll give you the controls as soon as we've made the pickup. When the radio challenges begin, ignore them."

"Yes, sir. Ah, gravity, sir?"

"Yes." As internal gravity built he piloted the cutter out from the shipyard, watching as the other four reached open space and increased speed. Within a few seconds they'd passed below the station's horizon and were out of sight. As the ship began its swing around PSDC Simon keyed the 7MC circuit. "Bridges, ready at number three airlock?"

"On station, Admiral. Ready."

"Very well."

Seven minutes later a small utility ship came into sight, blinking its emergency lights as the cutter approached. Simon flashed a return signal and began the docking maneuver.

"This is Prometheus Peacekeeper Station," the radio blared. "Vessel X-Ray November China, you are ordered to stop and shut down engines immediately. Do you copy?"

Simon concentrated on the small vessel just now moving out of his view along the starboard side. He held course and reversed maneuvering jets, feeling himself pulled forward by the abrupt change in inertia.

"Vessel X-Ray November China, we read that you have complied with our order to stop. Be advised that a boarding party is on the way. ETA your position, six minutes. Please shut down your engines. Out."

There was no physical sensation as the utility ship's airlock door mated with its counterpart on the cutter. Only a soft buzzer and blinking blue light indicated that the cutter's airtight integrity was unstable in number three airlock. Now that the vessels were joined, Simon gradually brought up speed and began easing away from the mammoth space station to starboard.

"X-Ray November China, cease your motion immediately!"

"Admiral, we have thirty passengers aboard," Bridges reported. "We've released the smallcraft. Airlock secured."

"Understood." Simon heeled the cutter around and broke for open space, adding speed as rapidly as possible. The ship responded beautifully. G-forces pushed him back into the padded seat, deeper and deeper, until his vision blurred.

"X-Ray November China! We have four cutters closing in on you. Stop!"

"Admiral, this is Radar. Negative on the four pursuit cutters, sir."

"Negative, aye." Simon laughed. He said to Carlos Litieri, "Prometheus only *has* four cutters. They're chasing our friends, not us." The vessel stabilized near maximum normal-space speed. Simon checked the instrument panels as the pressure eased away; all good.

"Ah, sir," Litieri said. "May I take the controls now?"

Simon hesitated. "Are you sure you can set up for hyperdrive? If you'd like, I'll walk you through it again."

"Sir—"

"Yes, yes. I'm transferring control to your station." He was reluctant to leave the helm. It had been years since he'd been an integral part of such smooth, incredible power. No, he reflected, that's wrong. Now I'm a part of something stronger than any machine ever built—dedicated human beings, with a purpose. The Duelists.

He walked back to the Maneuvering Room and checked with the two Service veterans on duty. All gear was running at specs, they assured him; the ship would be in hyperdrive in forty-one minutes.

Simon had already decided on a name for his cutter. It was a natural choice, considering the fight they were beginning—to protect the future of a great family, against immeasurably superior forces.

The ship would now be called *Talon*.

⇉19⇇

The five cutters remained outside the elliptical plane for six weeks, far enough out that the chance of a Peacekeeper unit finding them was infinitesimal. During this time the fifty-one Service veterans drilled and trained, until any Duelist could perform at any shipboard station. While not training or sleeping the Duelists went through every part of the ships, locating and removing the secret ID-beacons which would respond with a coded signal to an encrypted inquiry from another Peacekeeper ship. Food was a concern. Only minimal supplies had been onboard for the transport crews. Rationing was the order of the day, and was the only aspect of their experience which the Duelists did not find exhilarating. Each crew, after much deliberation, named its ship. Along with *Talon* they were now *Lion, Fury, Breaker,* and *Defiant.*

When he judged that they were ready, Simon dispatched *Lion* and *Fury* to find Francine Bellenauer and Stewart Misiaszek among the Beltway mines, and to give them a time schedule and a rendezvous point. With the rest of the ships he set a course for Mari—knowing that it would be deserted.

Talon verified the presence of the Peacekeeper ships around Mari shortly after coming out of hyperdrive, while still thirty-five million miles out. Radar screens were empty.

Simon went directly to the radio room.

"I'm picking up ID-request codes," the operator said as he stood behind her.

"Good. It's a general broadcast. No doubt been going on for weeks. Are we responding?"

"Negative, Admiral Barrow. It looks like we disabled all of the automatic beacons."

"Very well, Simmons. Send the message."

"Aye aye, sir." She played the recorded message twice, en-

175

crypted and matched to a pre-set scrambler at home: *Griffin, please respond.*

Six minutes later a reply came back. It was a male voice, husky and doing a good job of imitating the well-known First General. "This is Griffin. Welcome home. When will you arrive?"

Simon picked up a handset. "It's good to hear your voice, sir. We'll be there in forty-one hours. Is everyone well?"

After another pause. "Yes. Were you successful? Are the cutters all with you?"

"Affirmative, sir. All five. I'll give you a tour as soon as we're home. Out." He replaced the handset in its bracket. "They'll wonder for a few minutes why they can't get an ID return," he said. "It's likely that they'll call you back. Record whatever they send, and don't respond."

"That was clear, sir," Simmons replied. "They'll assume we're making one last jump."

"Right."

"And they'll call in reinforcements from Mars and other parts of the Beltway."

He looked at the young Duelist, pleasantly surprised. "I never said that."

"It's reasonable, sir. You wouldn't have made the call without a good reason."

Simon clapped her on the shoulder and left the radio room. Long ago he'd followed Griffin Joyner to Talon's side of Mercator, thinking the same thing: There must be a good reason for this. He hoped his plan was better thought-out than Griffin's had been. Luck wouldn't be enough, this time.

The Duelist forces were scattered in five groups now: Two crews of forty each were paying calls on the Beltway mines, twenty were aboard *Fury* and *Lion* as they went to link with Misiaszek and Bellenauer and thirty-one were aboard *Talon*, *Breaker*, and *Defiant*, heading out to unite with the last group: one hundred forty-six Duelists and twenty-four others who had left Mari.

Fifty hours later the ships arrived at an isolated section of the Beltway. There were no habitats in this area; normal-space traffic would be virtually nil, occurring only during planetary alignments that put the sector between major ports. For now, there were only great rolling behemoths and smaller travelers that formed a river of broken rock, all flowing together in an endless journey around the distant sun.

In the radio room, Simon stood behind Simmons as she placed a tape in the broadcast slot. "Lowest power," he reminded her.

"Yes, sir."

The radio sounded, an unintelligible squawk that was repeated twice. After five minutes it was broadcast again, as *Talon* moved at slow speed in the direction opposite the asteroid flow. Radio interference would be high in this area due to the thousands of metal barriers racing past them. Contact would require a nearly direct line between transmitter and receiver. "I'll be in the Control Center," he said as he turned to go.

After twenty minutes the call was answered.

"Same sequence played four times, sir," Simmons reported over the intercom. "It's them."

"Thank you. Contact *Breaker* and *Defiant*, tell them to break off their search and proceed to the rendezvous point."

"Aye aye, sir."

Standing behind the radar operator, Simon released the handset switch and watched intently as five of the dots filling the screen began moving together in a new direction. There was silence in the Control Center as those present watched five scouters negotiate the dangerous passage up through the flow. When the ships were clear of the most concentrated streams, everyone breathed a collective sigh of relief.

"Bridges, return to the helm," Simon ordered.

"They'll have food, sir?" she asked.

"Yes. They harvested everything. The scouters will be packed. Now, expedite! Expedite!" Over the ship-wide 1MC circuit he passed the word, "Litieri, Hassalem, stand by your airlocks. Prepare to receive passengers."

Randall was the first of them to enter *Talon*'s Control Center. He hugged his father tightly, and then Jessica. "Oh, I feel so heavy!" he said. "It's wonderful! Where's Gordon?"

"He's aboard *Breaker*," Jessica told her brother. "He was hoping he'd be the one to pick you up."

"Ah, I knew it would be Dad. He was right! The Peacekeepers were looking for us! It was exciting, Jessica! We heard them for weeks on radio, and they even hit us with radar, twice! But we just stayed right against the rock. Dad knew when they'd stop looking, you know," he said proudly.

Corinne was next to come in, carrying a small suitcase. She and Simon embraced reservedly, each conscious of the eyes watching them: Randall, and four snickering Duelists. "Griffin's scouter is the last in line," Corinne said. "He wants to see you as soon as he's aboard."

"Griffin Joyner can wait another hour, Mrs. Barrow. I want to give you a tour of our new home." He whispered in her ear, "We start with the captain's stateroom."

"But Simon—"

"Private shower," he said quietly, pulling her close and grinning.

Corinne repeated the words reverently. "Private . . . shower." Picking up the suitcase again, she turned to her daughter. "Jessica, watch your brother."

Simon turned at the hatchway. "Bridges, take us, ah, well, somewhere!"

"I know, sir," she called back, grateful that he couldn't see her face as she readied the helm. "Rendezvous point."

"Right! Excellent idea!"

Simon had forgotten to tear out the shower's fifty-second shut-off; it could be restarted, but not overridden. Eventually it ceased to matter as they bathed one another, each overwhelmed by the nearness and the need of the other.

After dozing deeply and contentedly for a while, Simon was listening to the sounds of his wife sleeping beside him. He was at ease beneath the comfort of her arm draped across his chest. She murmured something from deep in a dream, and pulled herself closer to him. Her arm and hip were warm against his skin. What was she dreaming about? he wondered. He recalled her silence while he'd told her his plan for taking the five Peacekeeper cutters. Nothing like this had ever been attempted, he'd said, and then explained that this was an advantage: both sides were starting even, with no precedent for the Peacekeepers to follow in developing their security plans, and no expectation on their part that such a thing would be attempted. Corinne didn't respond to his enthusiasm. She asked if he planned to take Gordon and Jessica and Hector along, and didn't wait for an answer. Then she said, "After you leave Prometheus, they'll have your pictures on surveillance cameras. They'll identify most of you. We'll have to leave Mari."

"Yes," he said.

Now, watching her sleep and dream beside him, he reflected that he'd cost her two homes since their marriage. The first, on Earth, he'd lost because he didn't fight back. The second he'd lost because he *was* fighting back. It wasn't necessary to ask himself which course was right to follow. And he knew that Corinne understood. But after a childhood spent in prison, and losing two homes that she'd loved, and Maria's slow death, and Randall's illness, how much more could she bear? Corinne was a quiet and strong person. But the fight was only seven months old now, from the day the Domain-wide call to Six-Year students had been issued. Now they were known, and hunted. And they were just beginning. A buzzer sounded across the cabin. From habit, Simon leaped for it.

Corinne woke up at the sudden movement and pulled the sheet tightly against her. She smiled when she saw her naked husband reaching over his desk, and remembered where they were: Safe for now, and together.

"Barrow," he said as he opened the intercom switch.

"Admiral, this is Control Center. We've reached the rendezvous point, sir. We're back in normal-space."

"What? How long have I—?" He looked at the chronometer set into a cabin bulkhead. He stared in disbelief. Nineteen hours had passed since he'd followed Corinne here. "Thank you, Control," he said. "The other ships?"

"Both on station, sir."

"Understood."

"Also, General Joyner asked me to mention that he's still waiting to see you."

A sleepy voice from behind him said, "He can wait another hour."

Simon turned as the sheet flew across the compartment and landed at his feet. Corinne was standing, stretching and yawning, wearing a pair of slippers. "Our anniversary is only eight months away," she said. Smiling and holding her arms out to him, she asked, "Does our new home have any waltz music?"

Catching his breath, he keyed the intercom. "I'll be there in two hours."

Three hours later, with the new Duelist ships formed up and linked together, Simon gave a grinning Griffin Joyner a point-by-point report on the mission to Prometheus.

⇥20⇤

Talon, Breaker, and *Defiant* spent five weeks waiting on station for *Fury* and *Lion,* using the time to drill and to make plans for the next phase of their quest to break open the Great Domain. One of the first things they needed to do was to arm themselves. Although the ships were equipped with particle cannon, they would remain unpowered until Joyner and Barrow devised a way to have them activated at a Weapons Depot. Food was a more immediate problem. Supplies dwindled to the point that, except for the children, only one small meal per day was available. Clonus was weakening dramatically. But of two hundred and one persons aboard the three ships, only Gault mentioned the hunger. His tirades amused, and only sometimes disturbed, the others.

The day of their scheduled departure arrived, with no signal from *Fury* or *Lion.* Griffin Joyner and Simon Barrow called for a vote, and promised that this time, no veto power would be exercised. The vote was unanimous; they would wait.

Ten days later, hungry but concerned much more about the Duelists aboard *Fury* and *Lion,* the three ships made ready to get underway again. The signal came in one hour before the first hyperspace jump was scheduled.

A relieved Corinne Barrow recorded the reunion of the five ships under the date July 7, 2152.

Francine Bellenauer and Stewart Misiaszek made no formal report until hundreds of crates of food were distributed to the other ships. And then they stood at the end of *Talon*'s wardroom table and watched as other Duelists finished the first full meal they'd had in weeks.

If those two would stop grinning, Simon thought as he cut into a third slice of something that was uncannily like beef, *I'd ask them.* Later—over ice cream and coffee—he did.

"We warned each of the mines," Misiaszek began, "that they'd be tested by other Peacekeepers in the area, to see if they were breaking the law again. They all thanked us for the tip-off, and swore they wouldn't complain about or even mention their new status as government-owned."

"Also," Joyner said, sipping coffee and nodding his gray head in satisfaction, "they wouldn't believe that five cutters had been stolen, no matter what the 'other' Peacekeepers told them. After what they've all been through during the past years, the government has no credibility. The mines will assume that such an unlikely story was a trick of some kind, another excuse to tighten security." His crinkled smile said, *Just as I'd planned.*

"We finished a few days early," Bellenauer said, as the grin returned. "We decided to make one more visit."

Simon's eyes widened.

"Oh, did we mention?" Misiaszek said, raising his eyebrows innocently. "We have guests aboard *Lion*."

Simon sat back and looked at them closely. "Tell us about it," he said.

The trial of Mr. William Burnside, Director of Prometheus Shipbuilding and Drydock Company, was over before the first gavel fell in the General Assembly Court of the United Nations. A portly man, Burnside nearly filled the same glassite defendant's booth that had held a young and angry Simon Barrow, almost a quarter-century before. There were a number of similarities. In each case, the verdict was decided upon and written before the proceedings began. In each case, the defendant shouted into a switched-off microphone while detailed accounts of wrongdoing and evil intent and stealing from the world's people were read aloud and discussed. In each case, the defendant at first wondered why the UN was directly involved. But there were differences as well. Barrow's trial had lasted for three days, and attracted thousands of spectators. Burnside's ordeal went on for only forty minutes, and was played out to an empty auditorium. Barrow had been innocent of all charges. Burnside was guilty on every count, with the single exception of evil intent: He loved his company, his job, his employees, and even his government. He bore them no ill will at all; not for one moment of the nine years he'd been stealing from them.

The investigation had opened with the charge of criminal negligence. But as one falling domino leads to the collapse of all the others in line, so it was with Mr. William Burnside. Investigators wondered about Linda Caravelli's suitability to supervise a full shift, and looked into her background and the circumstances of her assignment. They learned that she was grossly unqualified—and Burnside's niece. And that while the payroll department allocated the salary that her position required, her filed income statements reflected substantially less. The difference, she confessed, went to Uncle William. And on, and on, from supply to cost overruns to accounting procedures that truly impressed jaded investigators who'd believed that they'd seen it all. The final surprise uncovered was that despite his being a consummate thief, Burnside built ships of exceptionally high quality.

When the trial was over, Mr. William Burnside was given a number which entitled him to spend the remainder of his life in the Gulag.

And then adding to a day of perfect disaster, he was taken upstairs thirty floors to meet Eleanor Douglas-Wycliffe.

The Secretary General was a small woman. This fact surprised everyone who met her personally for the first time. Whenever she gave a public address she stood on a platform hidden from her audience. When her image was broadcast, or captured for a portrait, she was alone and presented alongside the visual imagery of authority. In person, she was not physically impressive. But as Burnside stood alone with her, before her desk—The Desk—he was more frightened than he'd been at hearing his verdict and sentence read to the court.

She ignored him for several minutes while she filled a sheet of paper with quick, decisive strokes of a silver pen. From the corner of his eye—he did not dare look away from her—he saw red and black and gold elegance: paneled walls, a tapestry, deep carpeting, rounded furniture of wood and leather.

"3123-5566-344QJCL," Douglas-Wycliffe said at last, still writing. "That's your name, we believe." Her voice was low and brittle.

"Yes, Madam Secretary."

"What is a Duelist?"

"Ah, Madam Secretary, they are entertainers. I believe they were involved with the theft of those ships."

"From whom were the ships stolen?"

"Ah, from me?" When she didn't answer, and still didn't look up, he tried again. "From Prometheus Shipbuilding and Drydock Company." No response. "From the government?" She went on writing. "Ah, Madam Secretary, from the people of the Great Domain?"

Now she looked at him. Her gray face was impassive. "You attended the Duelist's show."

"Yes, Madam Secretary. I believed that the station was secure at that time, although I should point out that technically, the responsibility—" She hadn't moved or changed expression at all, that he could see. But she'd interrupted him as surely as if she'd thrown a rabid dog into his face.

She lifted an envelope from beside her and emptied it onto the desk. Two holostats tumbled out, face-up. "Tell us about these children," she said.

"Jessica and Hector," Burnside replied at once.

"This one is Hector Horatio Hernandez," Douglas-Wycliffe confirmed, pointing to the boy's image. "He is the son of General Griffin Joyner. The other one we have not identified. What can you tell us of them?"

"I spoke to them before the show. They were very engaging. I would even say charming. But deceitful," he added bitterly.

"We have heard you described in similar terms."

"Ah, yes, Madam Secretary."

"Go on, 3123-5566-344QJCL," she said. Her rapid-fire delivery of his new name sounded like a muted plate-hammer.

"I can add only that each of them is stronger than any adult I've known." He wished she would come to the point of this interrogation. Certainly, she had seen many of the holos of the performance that had been taken by the spectators. All of them, he knew, had been confiscated as evidence in the most expensive theft in history. Every employee of PSDC had been interviewed time and again, even the children. Miraculously, he had been the only civilian arrested. The Peacekeepers did not fare as well; all of them had been courtmartialed and reduced in rank and reassigned, except for the senior personnel—who were already on Ellis Island, locked inside a military prison.

In an abrupt transition, Eleanor Douglas-Wycliffe said, "A number of the Beltway mines are in rebellion against their government. They have refused our legal orders to recommence shipping. We see that you were once employed by one of the major mining companies. We fail to comprehend your appeal, but your records indicate that you were held in high esteem by your colleagues. Perhaps you can be of service to us."

A faint, distant hint of light hovered somewhere in the darkness that his future had become. Sweat beaded on his forehead and began to run freely. "Yes, Madam Secretary," he said, shaking with hope and gratitude. "I was the Executive Vice President at—" He stopped, in panic. She would know his record. "I, ah, was one of the Associate Vice Presidents at Basalt & Nickel. My career with them spanned thirty-one years."

"And they never uncovered your thefts."

Burnside hesitated. Surely, he was not here to add to his punishment. Perhaps she knew the truth, perhaps she did not; the risk was too great to take. "No," he said. "They never knew." He held his breath and waited.

"Go back to them," she said after a pause. "You are our liaison. Within two weeks' time the companies must order the mines to obey the law. Tell them that we will no longer accept the lies and assurances they have offered us. You may not negotiate in our name. But you will inform them that mass arrests will take place at all company offices on Earth and elsewhere, and that armed action will be taken against the mines themselves. You know these people, Burnside, and they trust you. Convince them."

He nearly fainted at the sound of his true name. "Ah, Madam Secretary, my prison sentence? When I'm successful, will I be—" Again, she hadn't moved. He said quickly, red-faced, "I'm sorry! Thank you, Madam Secretary!" When he could control his voice he said, "Ah, may I ask—"

"The children."

"Yes."

"A challenge, Burnside. We would classify you as an ingenious thief. Our investigators were highly complimentary. But you were surpassed by these Duelists. Therefore, emulate them. In your own words, you are to be engaging, charming, let us say 'resourceful' in place of 'deceitful,' and stronger than any adult you know. As you have seen, even a child can do it."

When Burnside was gone, Douglas-Wycliffe turned the two holostats around to face her. Although she'd not yet clarified the thought, she was convinced that this band of thieves was somehow connected to the trouble at the mines. It might be productive, she decided, to arrest a few dozen of the recalcitrant miners and see if they could identify any of these Duelists. She studied the two young faces looking up at her from the desk. "Children," she muttered angrily, and swept the two holostats to the floor.

An hour later Peacekeeper Commanding General Anna Chakheya stood at rigid attention before The Desk, at which her appointment had been confirmed six years before. This was the first time since that day she'd personally seen her boss.

"We have read your reports," Douglas-Wycliffe said dryly, writing with her silver pen. She looked up. "Please explain to us, General, the military definition and consequences of insubordination, desertion, and mutiny."

"Madam Secretary, those words appear nowhere in my reports to you. I have attempted to convey a condition of low morale, and mistrust, and confusion. Many units have not been relieved for months, as detailed in the reports. Also, I believe that imprisoning those officers who served at Prometheus was only a recent example—" She stopped and flinched.

Douglas-Wycliffe repeated, enunciating every word carefully, "Please explain to us, General, the military definition and consequences of insubordination, desertion, and mutiny."

It was to be a long day. The Secretary General's next appointment was interrupted by the intercom. "Yes," she said testily. She listened for a moment. "Tell the Steadhornes that they may go to hell," she said. "You may quote us." Releasing the intercom key, she looked back to the Peacekeeper Colonel she'd been listening to. "Incompetence, kidnapping, theft, and a criminal insurrection on ProLab," she repeated. "Tell us about it."

⇒21⇐

"This is all new to me," Griffin Joyner said dubiously. "None of my friends on Earth has ever mentioned anything like this."

"It's new to everyone, General Joyner." The young man across from Joyner and Barrow was bald and thin, with a blunt nose and wide mouth. His eyes were sharp behind thick glasses, blue and moving quickly from person to person as he spoke, then back down to the schematic spread out across the wardroom table of *Lion*. "The research for this was personally ordered by the owners of ProLab."

Simon sat up straight. This was an interesting bit of news. More and more with each passing year, Fujiwara and ProLab had been losing the independent and competitive character which had created them and made them indispensable to human progress. Had there been a recent change in UN policy? He asked, "Does that mean there is no government involvement, Dr. Harding?"

"It means exactly that, Admiral Barrow. This project is in-house, from start to finish."

The dark woman seated beside him nodded. "I cannot imagine in modern times an official sanction for anything of this, er, rather undramatic nature. Can you, gentlemen?"

Simon looked up at her. He'd never seen a woman so tall.

But her features gave no hint of gigantism; photographed alone, she would appear to be an average-sized, attractive woman who somehow conveyed the impression of royalty.

"I agree, Dr. Bey. My question is really, does the government know about this?"

"Ah," she said. "That is more precisely worded, sir. The answer is no, with the customary caveat regarding the use of paid informants. I am aware that such individuals are retained extensively by the Peacekeeper security personnel."

"What do we need to install this and test it?" Joyner asked.

"Merely common tools, and your patience," Dr. Bey answered. "This is a matter of conversion, you see. Full charging is not necessary. A minimum of power will enable you to achieve the intended effect."

"You two can do this?" Simon asked.

"Of course. Dr. Harding and I are not technicians per se, although I believe we are adequate to the task."

"We're grateful," Simon told her. "May I ask why you're willing to give us this technology, at high personal risk?"

Dr. Bey smiled at him. "This is rather a grand adventure, is it not? But of course, personal stimulation is not a noble pursuit."

"We talked with some of your, ah, Duelists," Dr. Harding said. "We were prisoners at the time, but the conversation became more distracting than our captivity. We both agree that you and your people are doing work that's beneficial, and necessary. I believe a lot of others will support you also, if you make your position widely known. There's a lot of desperation out there, Admiral."

Barrow nodded at him without speaking. What Dr. Harding had just suggested was very much a part of the Duelist strategy. Soon, they would be announcing themselves—and their purpose—to a number of the Beltway site bosses.

"Your Francine Bellenauer delivered a most impressive account of your ambitions," Dr. Bey said. "And she was demonstrably concerned with the well-being of those of us who at that time were in some measure of danger. I found the combination to be quite compelling."

"How long did she hold you hostage, Dr. Bey?" Simon asked. Direct endangerment of civilians was to be avoided, if humanly possible.

"Oh, excuse me, Admiral Barrow. I have not spoken clearly. Francine Bellenauer was a prisoner as well."

"Peacekeepers," Dr. Harding explained. "A number of us were in Labspace Fourteen when they followed Francine and five others there. The doors were locked, and the air supply was shut off. I have no doubt they were planning to use gas," he said angrily. "Some of us would have died, sir. I have severe allergies. And there were old people in there, too." He cleared his throat and took a sip of cold tea. "We're scientists and technicians and administrators, and families. And yet we've been subject to martial law for more than three years. Recently we saw how little our lives are valued. I don't believe anyone on ProLab trusts the Peacekeepers now."

"Others of your group rescued us," Dr. Bey said. "To return to your question, Admiral Barrow. Dr. Harding and I believe that this technology will enable you to widen your struggle."

"Yes," Simon answered gratefully, reaching out to shake hands with each of them. "Yes, it certainly will."

"This is too much," Joyner said, shaking his head and grinning again. "Too much for simple coincidence. They're right about you, Simon. 'Luck of the Saints.' Get used to it, Saint Barrow."

Simon stood behind Carlos Litieri at the radio console. "Send out the ID request," he ordered. "Only once."

"I understand, sir."

This was the fifth time in three weeks they'd maneuvered *Talon* and *Defiant* to match the orbits of behemoth asteroids in an area of the Beltway that was relatively free of small debris. So far, they had received no answer to the bait they were offering. At the beginning of this watch Litieri volunteered for radio duty; he was certain that his own luck, added to that of his commander, would make the difference.

He was right. One hundred nineteen seconds later *Talon* received an answer. "Got one sir!" A few seconds later, he said, "We've got his ID code. I don't know what it means, but we've got it. Now he's asking for ours."

"Good. Send him gibberish. Make it close to the code he sent us."

"Aye aye, sir." After a second, "Done."

"You have a good bearing on his transmission?"

"Yes, sir. Solid bearing. He's well above the elliptic."

Two minutes later another signal was received. Litieri clapped his hands and whooped. "He's ours! He verified our ID as authentic and wished us a pleasant trip. The lying bastard! I'd bet my mother's house he's on his way."

"Very well."

In the Control Center, Simon approached the old man sitting behind Hassalem at the radar station. Joyner was holding a closed notebook loosely in his hands, looking over the shoulder of the young woman seated at the console. He turned to face Simon, showing sleep-weary eyes. "You found one? How far?"

"The transmit-receive time was just under two minutes, sir. That places his range at about eleven million miles."

"Are you sure he'll find us? Will he suspect a trap?"

"As we discussed, sir. With mutually good bearings and transmit-receive times, he'll know where we are. And he'll believe that we're testing our ability to penetrate the Peacekeeper identification system."

"Out of the elliptic?" Joyner asked.

"Yes. He wasn't transiting, he was looking for us. If he runs up to hyperspace right away, he could enter in less than an hour. He'll allow plenty of normal-space room when he comes out again. He could be here within two hours. My guess would be slightly longer than that."

"If he responds directly," Joyner said, absently shifting the notebook from hand to hand. "He may wait for help."

Simon was surprised at the comments and questions. They had discussed all of this at length, again, only a week ago. "No sir, they want us badly. No Peacekeeper ship will take the chance of letting us go. And he won't call for help, because we'd hear him before he gets to us."

"You're confident that he's alone?"

"The ID responses are not controlled by the ships' captains," he said patiently. "They're intended to control the captains. If there were more of them in range, we'd have received other responses as well. And we may, in time. But this ship will reach us first."

"Well, yes," Joyner said after a moment's thought. "Of

course that's true. I told you about the ID system myself, didn't I?"

"Yes, sir. It's a new development. If you hadn't obtained that information, we'd never have known. Nothing we've accomplished would be possible if it weren't for you."

Griffin flushed. "Don't patronize me, Barrow. I've lived for eighty-six years, and I have endured much. But I won't endure that." He stood and walked stiffly from the Control Center.

Simon watched him go, and was ashamed of himself. It was inexcusable to condescend to a person like Griffin Joyner, no matter what the intent. But up to now, he thought, it had been inconceivable that anyone could. He pushed the problem away for the time being, and began rehearsing the crew of *Talon* for what lay ahead.

Two hours and seventeen minutes later the radar screen recorded a new blip.

"I see it, Hassalem," Barrow said quietly. "We'll assume he's picking us up also." He spoke into a handset. "Radio, stand by to respond with our ID code the moment he requests it. Inform me immediately.

"Aye aye, sir—there it is, Admiral. Sent and acknowledged."

"Very well." He switched to another handset and keyed the 7MC circuit. "Maneuvering, stand by to give me maximum speed. Weapons Rooms, activate all units. I'm planning a starboard-side-to approach. I say again, Starboard Weapons Room will shoot first." The instructions were repeated back to him.

Turning to Karen Bridges, he said, "Helm, move us to put the asteroid between us and that ship. Give it one minute, then launch the target-can as if we were coming out from behind the far side. Slowly, same speed we rehearsed."

"Aye aye, sir."

"Radar, as soon as he goes off our screens, cease broadcasting. Switch to listen-only mode."

"Aye aye, sir," Hassalem said.

Minutes later *Talon* was concealed from the Peacekeeper's radar, and replaced with the target-can which would transmit the same radar signature and return that the Peacekeeper ship had been receiving from them. Simon turned at a sound be-

hind him. Clonus was standing at the entrance to the Control
Center. He held a half-eaten apple in each hand, and there
was a worried expression on his face. When he saw Simon
watching him, he smiled. "Good luck to everyone," he said
quietly, and left. He's growing old too, Simon thought. Clonus
was nearing his seventy-fifth birthday. He had gained back
some of the strength he'd lost when food had been severely
rationed. But he was smaller now, as if his body were collapsing in on itself; gravity was a continual strain that he refused
to leave, even for brief periods of time in the null-grav training room. "Oh, I'll adjust," he would say. "It takes time, you
know. And persistence." The gentle man's habitual smile and
good cheer were still there, but now seemed weak and forced
at times. My dearest friends, Simon thought. They're here,
and I can't be with them.

After a ten-minute wait *Talon*'s instruments again picked
up a signal from the Peacekeeper's radar transmission.

"He's coming around," Simon intoned quietly. "Still following the target-can."

"He won't pick us up, sir?"

"No, Hassalem. We're just a part of this asteroid, until we
move or broadcast." Into the 7MC handset he said, "Maneuvering, on my mark. Full speed."

"Ready, sir."

"Bridges?"

"Helm ready, sir."

He held the key down on the handset, watching the movement of the Peacekeeper on the passive-radar screen. "Steady
. . . steady . . . steady . . . GO!"

Talon seemed to draw traction from the fabric of space,
tearing itself from behind the asteroid and leaping like a beast
of prey at the Peacekeeper. Watching the visual screen above
the helm, Simon felt a momentary shock. This was a cruiser!
Seven hundred twenty-one feet long, he recalled instantly, and
one hundred five at the beam. Full personnel complement,
four hundred sixty. Two hundred lifelaunches and four
armored scouters aboard. Slower to maneuver than a cutter.
The thought took less than a second. Within that time the
quarry had spotted the hunter, but it was already too late.
Talon swept by close aboard to the vessel, still accelerating.

"Starboard Weapons, shoot!" Simon called into the handset.

The Control Center lights dimmed as the altered weapons drew power from the reactors and sent volley after volley into the Peacekeeper ship. "Three hits, sir!" a voice announced. "Good hits!"

"Helm, come around, portside-to pass. Stay close. Now! Maneuvering, reduce speed to one half. Now!"

Talon swung around in a tight arc as the acceleration eased. Simon held his breath, waiting for the shock that would announce the Peacekeeper cruiser's return fire. "Port Weapons, stand by! On my mark." He watched the screens. "Steady . . . steady . . . shoot!"

Again the lights dimmed. "Maneuvering, full speed!"

"Full speed aye, sir."

"Four hits, sir! Good hits!"

"Helm, break away. Steady as you go, take us out of range."

"Aye aye, sir."

After two minutes of steady acceleration, Simon ordered the engines slowed to dead crawl. An intercom check revealed that *Talon* had received no damage.

"He fired twice, Admiral," Weapons reported. "No hits."

"Very well." Simon took in a deep breath and let it out slowly. "Good work, Duelists!" he said, and shook hands with each of them in the Control Center. "Helm, resume local control of speed. Radar, range to cruiser?"

"Seventy-one thousand, sir. He's not moving."

"Understood. Bridges, let's go back. Half-speed, then slow to one-eighth when we're within twenty thousand."

"Helm aye, sir."

Litieri's voice sounded from a speaker. "Sir, he's broadcasting a distress signal."

"What status is he reporting, Radio?"

"He's operating on auxiliary power only. I guess it's 'she,' though. The captain's name is Von Velt. She's calling to another captain, by name. Martinson."

"Put me on a standard frequency, Litieri."

"Yes, sir." After a second's pause he said, "Go ahead, sir."

Simon keyed the transmitter. "Captain Von Velt, this is Simon Barrow, aboard *Talon*. Do you copy?"

An infuriated voice answered. "Yes, I copy, Captain Barrow."

"Ah, actually," he said, smiling, "it's 'Admiral.' "

"Well, *Admiral*, what in the hell did you shoot at me?"

"Minimum power, Captain," Simon replied. "According to our instruments"—he grinned around him, and shrugged, *why not*?—"you have sustained no structural damage. Your Chatterly-Wang engines are disabled, and your reactors are out."

"Your instruments? What in the name of ... what kind of instruments do you have?"

"The kind that tell me that aside from a few minor scrapes," he said, improvising, "your crew has suffered no casualties. Are you prepared to surrender, Captain?"

"Absolutely not, Admiral. I've radioed for help. If you come within range of me, I'll kill you. I have enough stored power to fire the weapons."

"Dying with your ship is your prerogative," he said coldly, while watching the smiling faces around him. "Captain Martinson will never reach you in time."

"We can wait, Barrow. Come closer, if you dare."

"Captain, I advise you to check your engines and reactors. The field you'll see developing will detonate them within the hour."

"That's ridiculous."

"Check them!"

"I ... Wait one."

She was gone for ten minutes. "I can't confirm your last statement, Barrow," the radio speaker said.

"Which is another way of saying that your people have never seen a field like that," Simon replied. "Fifty minutes maximum, Captain Von Velt. The process cannot be reversed. We're prepared to take you and your crew aboard. Let me have your answer before it's too late for us to complete the transfer safely. Don't wait more than three minutes."

"I ... Wait."

From behind and over him, Simon heard a new voice in the Control Center. "Our contribution has operated satisfactorily, Admiral?"

"Perfectly, Dr. Bey," he said, turning and looking up at her. "The engines and the reactors are seized shut."

"Not precisely," she said. "Our 'weapon,' if you wish, merely induces a field which affects elements that are common to both, and produces magnetic flux and temperatures beyond operating tolerances. I hasten to remind you that the effect is transitory, with the duration depending upon the strength of application." She smiled at him. "The discovery involved is a rather modest one. But your imagination has added to it, quite nicely. My, that is a large ship!"

"Thank you for your help, Doctor," Simon replied. "Again."

"You are welcome. The intent of our assistance to you is to save, rather than to cost, human lives."

"Of course. May I ask you a personal question?"

"I am seven feet tall, and five inches," she said pleasantly.

"No, that wasn't it. I'm curious about your accent, Dr. Bey. My parents had trading partners in most of the nations on Earth. My guess is that you're from Swaziland."

"You are quite correct, Admiral. You are a linguist?"

"I don't speak any of the Bantu languages," he said. "You're of the Zulu, aren't you?"

"Yes. The Bey family has produced physicians for five generations. I am the first to enter another field, or to leave our homeland. My father humorously refers to me—"

The radio speaker sounded.

"Barrow, my crew is boarding lifelaunches. This is not to be interpreted as an act of surrender. We will wait until Martinson arrives. I don't believe you'll fire at us."

"I won't. And that's irrelevant, Captain. Those lifelaunches can't take your crew a safe distance before your ship explodes. But I'll respect your decision. Good luck. Barrow out."

A second later she replied. "Admiral Barrow, I need the assurance that my crew will be humanely treated."

Simon smiled at the radio, and then at his companion. "Excuse me, Dr. Bey. Business. Perhaps we can talk again later?"

"That would be most agreeable to me, Admiral Barrow." She turned to leave.

Simon picked up the handset again. "Captain," he said with mock impatience, "if my intentions were otherwise, we would leave you to die. Disarm your people and have them standing by in the portside airlocks. Understand that I'll know immediately if you charge any of your cannon to fire. And you will transmit no messages. Expedite, Von Velt. There isn't much time."

"Yes, sir. And I've *got* to see those instruments!"

The transfer of personnel was completed thirty minutes after *Talon* pulled alongside the Peacekeeper cruiser. There were five hundred ten aboard, Simon noted with satisfaction; more than the normal complement of combat troops. They were strengthening the hunt for him and the other cutters, obviously hoping to disable and board them—and knowing they'd need a lot of people to deal with Duelist crews.

The cruiser personnel were searched and locked into five compartments that held nothing critical to the ship's operation. When all was secure, *Talon* began the enabling run up to hyperdrive. A short radio message was sent on low power to Captain Anton Kin'Te aboard *Defiant*. The second cutter detached itself from the sheltering body of an asteroid and prepared to transfer half of its crew to the ship they were already calling *Serendipity*, the newest member of Saint Barrow's Fleet.

From the cruiser's inventory Kin'Te left behind three radiation bombs, which would drift together in space and then detonate an hour later, at one-second intervals.

Talon winked out of hyperdrive three hours out from the System's most distant outpost. It was called Triton, although it was not Neptune's moon of the same name; that moon rotated at speeds that excluded colonization, and was unsuitable in other ways. The settlement called Triton was an artificial station, much smaller but similar in construction to its owner, ProLab. Scientific research and observation were its reason for being, but years of neglect from Earth had reduced it to a core population of employees waiting for better times while minimum activities were carried out.

Captain Von Velt was surprised that she was not questioned at any great length by her captors. Nor did she know how many of them there were. She and her officers were kept in one large compartment of the cutter and provided adequate food and water. She spoke with the unusual man Barrow only once—unusual, because while he obviously came from a military background, his demeanor was nothing like the

Peacekeeper officers she'd served with during her thirty-three years of service. She guessed that he had been trained in one of the elite services, perhaps the Commandos or the Exploration Service. But he answered no questions about himself, his weaponry, the unheard-of instrumentation on his ship, his crew, or his intentions. He asked only one thing of her—and that, primarily for the safety of her own crew. After considering his request she had agreed. She provided him with an authentic ID code, one still in her memory from a recent encounter with a cutter now operating in the Beltway. She knew he was intelligent enough to realize that he could use it only on this one excursion; that as soon as she could, she would let the Peacekeeper Force know that the code had been compromised. She would also recommend that the system be scrapped entirely, assuming she could remain out of prison long enough to make a full report.

During their short conversation she realized that she and Barrow shared a mutual respect, and that—grudgingly—she liked him. He was a strangely distant and intriguing man. Under other circumstances, she told herself, she would pursue him as a lover; but as it was, she hoped that one day she would have the opportunity to kill him.

There were no challenges as *Talon* approached the station called Triton. To be safe, Simon broadcast an ID request. It was acknowledged. Short pleasantries were exchanged with a vessel they determined to be a minimum of ninety minutes away. As they neared the docking station Simon handed Von Velt a radio handset.

Before keying the transmitter she said, "I can't offer you thanks for endangering my career, Admiral. But on a personal level, I appreciate the treatment of my crew." She managed a smile. "I would also have appreciated a tour of your Weapons Rooms and Control Center." The smile disappeared. "I want another shot at you, Barrow. You won't surprise me again."

"I understand, Captain," Simon answered. "Go ahead and make the arrangements. We don't want to be here for long."

Von Velt keyed the handset. "Triton Base, this is Senior Captain Ingrit Von Velt, Peacekeeper Force. I have five hundred ten personnel to transfer—"

The Duelists slipped back into hyperspace two hours later. In *Talon's* wardroom Griffin Joyner and four ex-Service officers sat talking and sipping coffee, telling stories of childhood and friends and plans they'd once made for a future that had seemed without limit.

When Simon entered the room the conversation stopped, but he sensed immediately the easy and relaxed mood of his friends. It was understandable. They'd scored a major and unexpected coup in their struggle. It felt damned good. The cruiser they'd added to their arsenal was one of only five left operational by Douglas-Wycliffe. This, and other things, they learned from listening to the recorded conversations of the Peacekeepers they'd taken aboard *Talon*.

"Here's one you haven't heard yet, sir," a Duelist named Bob Judd said as Simon drew a cup of coffee and sat down with the four. Judd touched a button on the cassette. There was a mass babbling of noise as the tape began to play. A few seconds into it, two people had apparently wandered closer to a recessed microphone.

A man's voice could be distinguished. ". . . told me these people are murderers. I don't believe that now. They took us off our ship, and they didn't have to. That's what I mean."

A second voice, also male but deeper than the first said, "My cousin Walter was on Prometheus, Hoggins. They tied him up with the rest and locked him in a restaurant. Could've killed him. Easy, he said. Didn't."

"Sure, sure. That's what I mean, that's it."

"So what are they doing? They can't sell the damn wagons they stole!"

"I got a theory, Terry. I think they're trying to hack up the government. And I think there's thousands of them."

"Why?"

"Well, it's my theory. You know the trouble at the Beltway, and ProLab, all of that?"

"You think it's the same people?"

"Sure, sure it is."

"Hmm. I don't know, Hoggins. If the idea came from anybody but you—"

"Hack you, Terry! I'm saying they got an army. Thousands. Maybe ten times that many, you think? And who knows how many hips they have now? A hundred? You think the Brass is gonna tell us about an army that big out there? Don't grow old waitin', that's what I mean. And you *know* the weapons they got! And also instruments that can read right through the hulls."

"I heard that. Don't believe it."

"Kersky heard Von Velt herself say it. Straight stuff, Terry."

"They beat us, that's sure."

"And we're alive, you see my point?"

There was a laugh. "They're not much of an enemy."

"What I think is maybe they don't want to be."

A third voice, a woman's, was heard. "Hey, Hoggins, did you see my gloves? I left the hackin' things—" Judd switched the tape off.

Simon nodded and finished his coffee. "I've heard a few like that. Some of them hate us, and others don't know what to think."

"But," Joyner said, "they all believe we're tens of times bigger than we are." He grinned and rapped on the table with his fingers. "And in war, Saint Barrow, that means we *are* tens of times bigger."

Simon flushed slightly at the name, used for the first time as a form of address. He saw Judd, Delores Nancarrow, Gary Henault, and John Marconette watching him for a reaction. The question was plain in their eyes. Would he accept it silently, or admonish Joyner, and publicly humiliate the great man? *And why are you behaving like a stone-for-a-heart prig? Who the hell are you to admonish Griffin Joyner?* Self-consciously, he began to smile. And then it was easy. And then it was unstoppable. The six of them stared at each other. It was impossible to know who started it—but in seconds they were all giggling like giddy children.

Dr. Augustus Arroyo bit back the words that formed in his throat. As a research physicist for fifty-one years and Chief Administrator at ProLab since its beginning in 2122, Dr. Arroyo considered himself separate from, and above, the violent nature of humankind. During the past thirty years he had shared quarters and workspace with the finest and most brilliant minds the species had yet produced. Theirs was a world complete unto itself. Dr. Arroyo's realm was the sublime dream of the god of architects, cast in *faux* marble columns and glistening sweeps of steel and grand acres of flatness, with domes that swelled and families that lived in paradise. His home lay in the orbit of Saturn, where the gas giant hung like a winged sun across twenty degrees of brilliant sky. The fourteen major and minor moons were silent friends to Augustus, friends who combined to tell him the date and the time, and who reassured him that nothing stands still in the Universe: Everything he hated about what his life had become over the past years would pass. The suffocating bonds that choked him, and choked all of the scientific community, would open again. Peaceably. With no need, no excuse, for violence.

And yet he knew, with a measure of self-loathing he could not endure, that if he had the opportunity he would murder the person standing two feet away from him. End life. Kill. Cause to exist no more. All without a moment's reflection or hesitation. It's the drug, he told himself again. But he knew it wasn't; his hatred was real. The drug only kept him awake, and made him tell the truth. Why didn't this fool see that he *was* telling the truth?

The hand slammed against his face again. It was only a dull pressure now, not the sharp pain it had been at first.

"*Tell* me!" Colonel Galard shouted at him. "*Tell* me!" Her face was an inch from his nose.

A detached part of his mind told Dr. Arroyo that she was nearing apoplexy. Good. "There is nothing more to tell you," he said weakly.

"Liar! We have eyewitness accounts, Arroyo! Hundreds of them! Your *weapon* caused a cruiser's reactors and engines to seize, and then detonate!"

"Not possible. Not—"

"When Captain Martinson arrived, *Doctor* Arroyo, there wasn't a piece of *Kali L'Awana* left big enough to register on radar! There was nothing there but radiation. Explain that!"

"I can't."

"And your instruments were able to monitor the conditions aboard, including the personnel! You have withheld this technology, Arroyo, and that is treason!"

"I . . . I don't work for you. I—"

"Then you admit it!"

"Nothing of what you are describing exists, Colonel," he said tightly.

"Not anymore!" she snapped. "The research has been erased. When did you do that?"

"I did not. I told you—"

"Where are Dr. Bey and Dr. Harding?"

"Gone. They left with—"

"Your fellow conspirators?"

"No. I've *told* you, Colonel. What is missing are the designs for a shut-down device. It is *not* a weapon. It merely induces a field—"

She slapped him again. "You spent years of work," she sneered, "so that Peacekeepers can halt fleeing criminals without killing them."

"That is one application, of many," he said. "From a safe distance, one can now stop a fully automated test vehicle directly at the power source, without depending on radio to operate interior controls. This could alleviate many deaths that occur—"

"STOP!" This time the blow was to his temple, and too hard. He stared at her, uncomprehending, until his eyes rolled upward and his head sagged to his chest.

"Oh, shit," she said quietly, feeling for a pulse. "Don't be dead. The witch will kill me."

⇥22⇤

"I strongly disagree with you," Joyner said. "We've established a momentum. To abandon it now would be as inexcusable as Douglas-Wycliffe ending humankind's expansion into new worlds. Or interrupting it, if we prove to be successful. And we may not, Simon, if you go ahead with this."

Simon flushed. "Sir," he said slowly, "we have an opportunity we could not have foreseen. And you're entirely out of line to make that comparison."

Both men sat in tight-lipped silence. Finally, Joyner spoke.

"We have one cruiser, Simon. One! There are nine worlds out there. You visited four of them, on a fourteen-month trip. This cruiser could visit *one*, in the same amount of time. It would take years to travel to all of them and back."

"Sir, those people could be dying. It will be decades before any radio signals reach us from out there. But you're right, we can only go to one of them. New Hope is the nearest to us. We'll take a minimum crew, and maximum provisions. If it's necessary, we can bring back a thousand settlers."

"That isn't much, compared to the level of help they may need."

"It's a thousand more than we're helping right now," Simon answered firmly.

Joyner sighed. "If only they hadn't butchered *Celeste* and *Majora*." He grunted. "With your luck, you could probably get them by asking with a nice smile."

Corinne spoke for the first time. "Dad," she began, "you know Simon is right. Those nine worlds out there are a large part of the reason you two sat down together that day and spent ten hours discussing strategy." She tapped a finger on the topmost of a pile of journals on the wardroom table between them. "Should I read back some of the comments you *both* made about their importance?"

Joyner shook his head. "I'm not senile, Corinne," he said in a soft voice. "I remember what was said, and why all of this was started. My reluctance is a matter of timing. In one year we've accomplished more than we'd planned for the first five. We have six hyperspace-capable ships, one of them a full-dressed cruiser. We need that cruiser here, and now. The pressure against the government of Douglas-Wycliffe is building exponentially. Already we've got ninety percent of the mines on strike. They'll know soon that we tricked them, but they'll also see that if they stand together they can outwait Douglas-Wycliffe. ProLab and Fujiwara are at a virtual standstill. The Peacekeepers know we're not murderers and they believe we have impossible weapons and numbers. It won't be long before they refuse to come after us at all. Add to that the plans we have for Mars and Titan and the other settlements, and it all comes to this: We're winning. *Winning*, Corinne! We can't slow down. Not now. Not for a year."

"Not for the thousand lives we may save?" she asked.

"They may be dead already."

"They may not, Dad."

Joyner looked away, not answering.

Simon was thinking about a conversation he'd had with an old woman just before he'd arrived at Mercator, so many years ago. What was her name? He'd promised her that he'd remember. DurNow. Alicia DurNow. She'd told him things then, words he'd listened to because she'd been kind to him, and because listening helped to keep his mind off the fear that threatened to unmask the terrified child he was. "Everything serves a purpose," she'd said. "Everything." And it seemed that she was right. Because Joyner and Maria and Corinne had been there on Mercator, and because Maria had been strong and ruthless enough to survive, and because she'd been brilliant and needed by the outside world, and because Captain Hartner had been a coward and stupid, and because Clonus had been brave and loved them all . . . the chain of circumstances and people and events went on and on, culminating in the creation of the Duelists and the work they'd begun that could be only years away from collapsing a System-wide dictatorship, and suddenly they had a full-dressed cruiser that would allow him once again to pass by the "place" where *Utic Shinar* had died—and to rescue people who were on New Hope, *only* because Joyner and Maria and Corinne had been there on Mercator, and because Maria . . .

"Simon, did you hear me?"

"No sir, I'm sorry. What did you say?"

"I asked where and how you intend to acquire the store of provisions we'd need."

"Peacekeeper Supply Depot Six, of course," he answered. "We'll go in with *Talon, Breaker, Lion,* and *Fury* to disable the station and any defenders, as we did against Captain Von Velt. We evacuate the depot and the ships we've disabled. Easy, because the personnel will have heard about our special weapons, and will be anxious to leave. *Defiant* comes in later to destroy the ships we evacuated. We can clear the area in under two hours. The Peacekeepers we release will spread the same rumors that began with Von Velt's crew. It couldn't be simpler. Why do you ask? Have you changed your mind?"

"Yes. For three reasons. First, we *can* spare the cruiser for a while. The cutters can continue harassment and disruption. Your Duelists are good, Simon. Bellenauer and Misiaszek especially, as they proved at ProLab. They can work without us for a short time, as much as it disturbs me to say so. Next, we need visible symbols that will *infuriate* the people living on Earth against Douglas-Wycliffe. If we can return with a thousand of their friends and relatives from New Hope, they'll have a deeper understanding of how insane, and wrong, it was to abandon those worlds." He paused and scratched at his forehead. "Analytically speaking, the effect will be the same, whether the people on New Hope are alive or, ah, not. All that really matters is that you bring some of them back."

"I hadn't thought of it in those terms. I'm assuming that at least some of the colonists are still living. But I see your point, sir."

"Historic precedence," Joyner answered. "In every mass disturbance or war, all factions respond best to a cause outside themselves. People will fight and die for their own property, food, or even money. But they combine and become unstoppable when the motivation is both practical *and* abstract; personal *and* universal. They see pain inflicted on themselves, and *wrong* inflicted on those they care about. Do you understand?"

"Yes, sir." Simon remembered that Joyner had phrased the concept better in his book *War with the Mind*, but the principle was correct. And again, Simon remembered Alicia DurNow. Against all probability the Duelists were in possession of a cruiser—and their purpose made necessary a mission that required a cruiser. *Everything serves a purpose*, he thought again. "What was the third reason for changing your mind?"

Joyner looked at him blankly. "Ah, I don't recall now. But two is enough, I think." In truth he remembered exactly what he'd realized a few moments before, but was now ashamed to mention it: That he'd been unwilling to "waste" a year; he wanted to win quickly, and to see Barrow and the Duelists in full triumph before his life was over.

The raid on Peacekeeper Supply Depot Six took place four days later, and was more successful than the taking of the cruiser; surrender was virtually immediate. And this time, scores of the six hundred and two Peacekeepers they evacuated asked for private conversations with the Duelists. One hundred nineteen volunteered to join their army—which they all believed numbered between five and ten thousand at present. Joyner spoke with these men and women individually. When the interviews were concluded he met with Barrow in the spacious wardroom of *Serendipity*.

"I want to stay behind," he announced abruptly as the two sat down.

"I see." Simon wasn't particularly surprised, although he was disappointed for personal reasons; it had always been good to know that the old man was nearby. But now he saw a light in Joyner's eyes that he hadn't seen for a long time. He suspected the reason for it, and he was right.

"Spies," Joyner said excitedly. "Officially I've turned all of the volunteers down. But there are thirty-nine I can use. These, I'll go back and speak with again. I'm going to organize them into a fifth column. Also, there are another forty-one you should take on your trip to New Hope. They're good people, Simon. They've been waiting years for a chance to prove that." He paused and searched Barrow's face for a reaction. "And," he added, "there are another two. Physicians. I'll keep one of them here."

Simon watched him, enjoying the moment. This was vintage Griffin Joyner: Fully engaged in challenging work, already conceiving and choosing and polishing plans for contingencies. Like a chess grandmaster, he was looking far ahead to move, countermove, end game. Checkmate.

Finally Simon broke the silence. "Thank you, General. I recall your admiration for the ancient Chinese general Sun Tzu."

"I was having the same thought. Sun Tzu wrote his masterworks on espionage more than twenty-six hundred years ago. No one has yet improved on them."

" 'The three secrets are simplicity, simplicity, and simplicity.' "

Joyner nodded. "That's my phrase, but I believe it captures the spirit of his work in that area."

Uncomfortably, Simon changed the subject. "Sir, I have a favor to ask."

"Certainly."

"Gordon wants to stay and serve aboard *Fury* with Francine Bellenauer."

Joyner laughed. "Personal, or professional?"

"Both, I think," Simon answered, returning the smile. "Corinne asked him the same question. It's the first time I've seen my oldest son blush."

"He's of the age," Joyner observed. "He's three years older than you were on Mercator."

Simon sat back. "Good Lord, that's true!" It was a heart-stopping thought. Ah, he reflected. But it was a different time then. I was forced into maturity, to deal with adults and . . . *so was Gordon Barrow.* And he's nineteen. Face it. They're right when they call you "Mom."

"What favor can I offer?" Joyner asked.

"Transfer your operations to . . ." He stopped. *Am I insane?* Griffin Joyner would never serve aboard another cutter while *Talon* was available. It was only a name, but the attachment was real. "Actually," he continued, "I withdraw the request. Gordon is a man now."

"I agree. Francine Bellenauer will help to develop his every potential."

Simon smiled wryly at the double entendre. He reached across the table and shook hands warmly with his old friend. "We'll miss you, Griffin."

"Come back in a year, Simon. We'll mind the store while you're gone."

"You'll what?"

"Read more history, youngster. It helps you to grow old gracefully."

Six weeks were spent organizing the five cutters into a disruption, harassment, and "store-minding" unit. Bob Judd assumed command of *Fury*, The Great Kenyan Anton Kin'Te skippered *Defiant* as before, and Delores Nancarrow remained in charge of *Breaker*. Francine Bellenauer took command of *Talon*, along with overall operational responsibility. Gordon Barrow remained aboard the ship, starry-eyed and self-consciously carrying himself like a much older man. A precocious Hector Horatio Hernandez joined the crew of *Lion*; he was to learn command tactics from Stewart Misiaszek, and electrical engineering from Ke Shan. Joyner—complete with veto power—would act as strategic and tactical advisor, while concentrating on his fifth column of spies and *agents provocateur*.

As *Serendipity* completed the enabling run for the first hyperspace jump, Corinne Barrow began the fifth of her journals. The opening entry was headed December 14, 2152.

⇉23⇇

Many of the thirty-nine Peacekeepers now working for General Griffin Joyner found their assignments to be simpler than they'd anticipated, despite the old man's lectures. As expected, all of them were reduced in rank and sent to diverse commands. Former watch commanders found themselves tending engines for the first time in years. It was no great effort to rewire a heat monitor so that it gave a false reading, or to add metal grindings to precision gear boxes. Others became personnel clerks. They'd all been victims in the past of misplaced transfer orders, or incorrect pay amounts, or illegible re-enlistment contracts. In a system as complex as the one they now dealt with, it was virtually impossible to trace the reason for seven hundred Peacekeepers from all over the Great Domain being suddenly assigned to one small cutter—or hundreds more receiving quadruple their normal pay—or still others learning that they had signed documents pledging themselves to fifty more years of service with no opportunity for promotion. These were small things, easily corrected when discovered. But they added to a growing cacophony of clatter and discontent within the ranks. And they happened over and over again.

The simplest of all assignments was the one they all shared: Speak with a combination of fear and admiration, of the ten thousand or more astounding warriors who followed Admiral Simon Barrow. Yes, they assured their co-workers privately: They'd never mention it to the Brass—of course they know, but do you think they want *us* to know?—but they personally had seen some of the weaponry that was standard aboard all of the ships in Saint Barrow's Fleet. It was like nothing they'd seen before. How many ships were there? No one knew. But fifty or more, that was certain. At least fifty. And did you hear about it? They just killed two of our ships, crews and all, for attacking a mine. God help us, friend.

But as General Joyner had carefully explained to them, the concept of "simplicity" was not to be confused with "safety." Many were caught, and became the first Peacekeepers executed in more than a century.

It had required months of work for hundreds of specially assigned agents traveling to every part of Earth and the settlements to reconstruct the identity and life of a man photographed by cameras on Prometheus Shipbuilding and Drydock Company, and identified by Captain Ingrit Von Velt and numerous witnesses as one Admiral Simon Barrow. No computer in the System contained information on anyone who matched the name, rank, and photographed likeness.

Others of the criminal band were readily identified after Prometheus, and traced to the now-deserted original New Sarajevo, held through Homestead rights by Griffin Joyner and others. But this "Admiral Simon Barrow" could not be found in any part of the System-wide tracking system. He was clearly the leader of these thieves, and Douglas-Wycliffe wanted him. She was familiar with the name, of course, and the link with Griffin Joyner was conclusive. But she remembered Simon Barrow as a lieutenant commander in the Exploration Service. As a small favor to the Steadhornes she had fired him '39. In '51, for the same reasons, she'd designated him as a political enemy and ordered his family's citizenship revoked. It was a simple, minor act that had required less than a minute of her time. How could it have caused such difficulty? She'd been furious to discover that her orders had been carried out so thoroughly; even the World Population data banks no longer contained any mention of him.

In February of 2153, while struggling with levels of economic challenge and rebellion she was sure no predecessor at the UN had endured, she received a final written report detail-

ing the life of this Simon Barrow. It was hand-delivered and
read aloud to her by Undersecretary for Security Damis
LaMothe.

"Barrow was born April 4, 2112 in Cairo, Madam Secretary. His parents expired thirteen years later of natural causes.
The family business was liquidated by the World Health Organization to offset research expenses involved in their disease. Barrow supported himself for three years by teaching a
form of martial discipline in Tel Aviv and Vladivostok. At the
age of sixteen he was involved in the destruction of *Utic
Shinar*. You recall the details, of course." When she didn't answer, he continued. "It appears that after his marriage and
commissioning in the Exploration Service, Barrow established
a few small martial schools at which—"

"When do you plan to capture him?"

LaMothe released a breath, calling upon his decades of diplomatic experience to provide outward calm. More than his
career was at risk. His citizenship, the official right of him
and his family to exist, depended on the whim of this woman.
Douglas-Wycliffe had always been a difficult administrator to
serve. At first her energy and vision had been exhilarating,
and seductive—if not draining. She intended to consolidate all
of the System's resources and produce an era of prosperity
and social justice never experienced by humankind. But as
time progressed, her energy transformed itself into a zeal that
recognized no bounds. As her policies began to have broader
and wider reach it became apparent to almost everyone that
adjustments and compromises were needed. Her reaction had
been to purge the UN of hundreds of public servants and to
redouble her efforts in every direction. She personally managed details of administration that traditionally were left to
mid-level bureaucracy. And never did she recognize that her
point of exhaustion had long been passed.

The situation had grown critical since the theft of the five
cutters from Prometheus nearly a year ago. Since that time,
Douglas-Wycliffe had become obsessed with personally directing the efforts to capture these anarchists. She was convinced that they were behind every problem her administration faced. The Beltway mines had been striking since June of
'52. Even armed attacks and mass arrests had provided only
partial relief for an Earth whose own mining facilities had be-

come unproductive decades ago. Earthside manufacturers were closing. Those surviving were desperate for new materials, and prices had risen as never before. Fortunately, she had delegated some of the responsibility for seeking a solution; William Burnside was a crafty wizard, and LaMothe believed he would eventually succeed. He hoped fervently that this was so; as they never had during his forty-three years as a public servant, whole segments of people Earthwide were turning to civil disobedience—as jobs, manufactured goods, clothing, and in some areas even food, became little more than memories. There simply weren't enough Peacekeepers to handle them all.

And what about the Peacekeepers themselves? Enlistment levels had never been so low. Career personnel were clamoring for early retirement. Desertion and sabotage were rampant. Many units had refused outright to attack the masses of criminals on Earth or on the rebellious mines, or even to provide more direct enforcement of martial law on ProLab and Fujiwara. Hundreds of Peacekeepers were arrested, some executed—hanged!—as agents of this Duelist horde that now apparently numbered in the thousands.

A decades-long steady flow of new technologies and materials had come to a virtual halt. Earth was starving, and angry.

"We have asked you a question," Douglas-Wycliffe said irritably. "When do you plan to capture him?"

LaMothe chose his words carefully. "Madam Secretary, as you know, our enforcement units are spread rather thinly in the Beltway and elsewhere. Also, we have had no direct evidence of Barrow's presence anywhere since he destroyed Depot Six, four months ago."

She interrupted him. "Evidence need not be direct to be convincing. Barrow's presence is certainly verifiable. We have signed confessions indicating that Barrow's people helped to plan the first insurrections at the mines, one year ago. We have others from individuals who saw him and General Joyner personally, and agreed to work for them. There can be no doubt that Barrow and his conspirators are at present fomenting much of the unlawful activity which you, Mr. Undersecretary, are incapable of ending. Now, we ask you for the final time. When do you plan to capture him?"

Perspiration beaded his forehead as he thought frantically. "There are plans now underway, Madam Secretary—"

"Students," she said abruptly.

"I beg your pardon?"

"We quote what you have told us. 'It appears that after his marriage and commissioning in the Exploration Service, Barrow established a few small schools.' We assume you are referring to this martial discipline that he taught in Tel Aviv and Vladivostok."

"Yes. There were ten schools, three of them here on Earth. None of them is presently in operation."

For the first time in his life, LaMothe saw Eleanor Douglas-Wycliffe smile. He stepped back, shaken.

"Find the students, Damis. Some of them will not be of a criminal mind, and will therefore not be with him now. Wherever they are, track them down. Arrest them all."

He saw her plan immediately. "Yes, Madam Secretary! They will provide us with the linkage we need—"

"Of course." She picked up the silver pen and opened the detailed report on Simon Barrow, underlining parts as she flipped rapidly through the pages. LaMothe turned gratefully and left the office.

Simon stepped back from the pilot's auxiliary control station aboard *Serendipity* and motioned for Jessica Barrow to stand beside him. "All controls are set to neutral," he said. "Ready?"

"Yes, sir."

"Simulate full speed, make all preparations for entering hyperspace." He stepped back. "Begin."

While he timed her, the eighteen-year-old Duelist began resetting the dozens of switches, knobs, and levers on the four consoles that formed an open box above, on both sides, and in front of her. She moved quickly and methodically, going from console to console as she adjusted one system at a time. When her hands stopped moving she stepped back and let her eyes sweep the boards. "Done," she announced.

"Two minutes twelve seconds," Simon told her. "Very good, best time this watch. Now let's check your accuracy."

"You don't need to bother," she said confidently. "It's all correct."

"Are you certain of that?"

"Yes. You trained me, didn't you?"

"I trained you always to *check*, Jessica."

"I did, sir. That's why it took so long."

There was quiet laughter from five Duelists and seven former Peacekeepers standing behind them. Even Dr. Janet Reilly, at most times painfully shy except with Randall, joined in. Simon took a minute to verify what he already knew; the settings were perfect. From behind the others, Clonus said, "Ha, Simon! I think she's even as smart as you!"

"But is she as lucky?" Dr. Reilly wondered aloud.

Simon turned around, and the snickering stopped. He stepped away while Jessica set all the controls to neutral again.

"Next," he said.

A new crew member, a stocky young man named Shaeffer, briskly stepped forward. Simon looked at him for a long moment and handed Jessica the stopwatch. Without a word he turned to leave the huge Control Center. He wondered, again, if he were overtraining them. Each of the fifty Duelists aboard, taken in equal numbers from the five cutters, was already qualified in every aspect of cutter operation. *Serendipity* was larger and more complex, with vastly superior capabilities. But the principles were all the same, with most of the gear different only in details. And the forty-one Peacekeepers whom Joyner had recommended were exactly as he'd observed: good people, waiting for a chance to prove it. They'd been poorly trained in limited areas. But they were all intelligent and eager to learn.

The problem, he thought, was alleviating boredom. The Duelists among them went through strength and combat technique drills daily. The former Peacekeepers ate, slept, stood watches, and practiced in areas they'd never learned. They were fascinated by the astounding physical prowess of their new shipmates. And they provided the Duelists with a reminder of what they had attained over the years. It was a good, symbiotic relationship. All of the crew were adapting well to life aboard a cruiser. But except for himself, no one aboard had ever made a trip this long; *Serendipity* had been in transit for nearly four months, and boredom was a constant threat to preparedness. It was necessary to keep the crew busy—partly to diffuse the worry they all felt about events and conditions that were now light-years behind, but never out of mind.

Most of them enjoyed the holo theater on *Serendipity*. That was especially true of the scientists Doctors Bey and Harding, and Clonus and Gault. These four operated the projector, argued over the features to be shown, and had even installed a cooker and beverage dispenser. At first Simon had been opposed to the theater's use; fiction and spectacle had never interested him. But at Corinne's good-natured use of the words "stodgy" and "antiquated," he'd relented. Now the theater was used as a performance-incentive for the former Peacekeepers. To the Duelists, the concept of exterior incentive was alien; the holos were thought of as a distraction, and used sparingly by them.

The world called New Hope was only five real-time weeks away.

As he entered the stateroom they shared, Corinne looked up from her small writing desk. Seeing the expression on his face, she closed the journal. "Jessica?" she asked.

"No," he said, surprised at her question. Then, thinking about it, he said, "How did you know?"

Corinne shrugged, smiling at him. "You're a father."

"And she's a child," he said. He sat on the large bunk and removed his boots. He'd seen the way that new crewman, Shaeffer, stood and straightened his posture whenever Jessica entered a compartment. And smiled, and deepened his voice when he spoke. And watched her like an idiot, listening to every word she spoke to anyone. What bothered Simon more than anything was the coy way that Jessica pretended not to notice the young man. Most of the male crew members, Duelist or not, paid special attention to Jessica. But she ignored *this* one in a different way. Simon didn't trust him. But he knew better than to mention this to Jessica.

"She's—" Corinne began.

"Please don't tell me that she's only a year younger than you were when we were married," he said quickly. "Griffin said something similar about Gordon, before we left." He stretched out on the bunk and propped a pillow beneath his head. "But I was *older*, Corinne. So were you."

"Why, thank you, Simon!"

"What?" He sat up and looked at her.

"If I was older *then*, how ancient am I now?"

"No, no," he said quickly. "I meant—"

She jumped from the chair and threw herself at him, laughing as he allowed himself to be pinned at the shoulders. "You insulted me," she said, grinning down at him. "I demand satisfaction." She lowered herself against him and whispered in his ear. "Pay, villain."

He reached for the light switch and then decided to leave it on. He was grateful, for once, that Corinne enjoyed watching the holos.

⇒24⇐

The star Zed Centauri seemed to erupt from nothingness into blazing glory as *Serendipity* winked out of hyperdrive. The planet called New Hope became visible as a faintly red egg-shape suspended in the night against a background of glistening, distant jewelry. Simon had visited the world-in-the-making over fourteen years ago. Then, it was an enthusiastic and hopeful experiment, one of nine designed to test new theories of terraformation devised by the brilliant Maria. This was the same planet he'd hoped to see even earlier, aboard *Utic Shinar*. And like that doomed ship, it seemed that New Hope was an unlucky world—with its first human visitors killed before arriving, and the second group abandoned.

"Anything?"

"No, Dad. Only background noise." Jessica listened through another sweep of the spectrum. "They're not communicating with each other by radio. No transmission at all."

"Very well. Commence broadcasting. Let me know immediately if you receive a reply."

"Aye aye, sir."

Serendipity's Radio Room was three times the size and

twice the complexity of its counterparts on the cutters. During the five-month trip from Earth's Beltway, Jessica had emerged as the most skilled technician and operator of the equipment. As a result, and much to her dismay, she'd been assigned overall responsibility for the area and for training crew members in the intricacies and codes she'd mastered. As time passed she'd confided in her mother that she came to find the position rewarding; not only did she enjoy the work, but it provided her with a new opportunity to impress an already awe-struck Kellan Shaeffer. Corinne assured her it was merely coincidence that her father found important work to do there whenever the young man was on watch with her.

All of the ship's off-duty personnel were in the Control Center when Simon entered. Doctors Harding and Bey were speaking in low, excited tones at the prospect of seeing the work of Maria Hernandez. They held hands as they spoke— and then self-consciously broke the contact as they looked up to see a number of people watching them. Why, Simon wondered, were they so publicly shy about this mutual affection? It was known throughout the ship that the two had discussed marriage.

Randall sat next to Corinne, watching as she wrote in her journal. Dr. Reilly had examined him in the ship's dispensary and found no evidence of new tumors, although his body was neither maturing nor growing. At nearly fifteen the boy looked as he had at the age of eleven. He still bore a striking resemblance to Maria, with the same complexion and eyes, and the same softness of skin and muscle tone. But his personality had developed in a way that made no concessions to the disease that slowed his body's development.

Randall had always been a natural mimic and storyteller, within the confines of his immediate family. But the shyness that had been so much a part of his childhood was passing. During the last month of transit Simon had seated himself many times in the back row of the holo theater and watched as Randall performed from an elevated platform and interpreted historical events: an hilarious depiction of Madam Curie discovering an unfamiliar isotope of radium on her husband's shirt collar; a frustrated Harry Lyndon kicking the Locket Rocket to get it started; Douglas-Wycliffe rehearsing a political address on her gradually sickening dog. Some of his stories were more serious, and gripping in their intensity: Moses crossing the Red Sea; the final words of John Brown before he was hanged; General Griffin Joyner's trial at the United Nations.

The Duelists accepted him as one of their number. Unable to perform as they did, he understood the principles and techniques behind their combat training, to the extent that he was valued as a coach and advisor. Among the former Peacekeepers, he was a bridge into the new society they'd joined. He mentioned his disease rarely; once to Simon, in a tear-filled attempt to understand why the ". . . five women I love *desperately*," behaved toward him as if he were only a warm and funny child. An hour afterward, he was lampooning his father's command mannerisms in front of a shrieking audience as the crew of *Serendipity* celebrated Simon's forty-first birthday.

Everyone in the Control Center watched expectantly as Simon walked to stand behind the pilot's station. "We've received nothing from New Hope," he announced. "Jessica is broadcasting now."

Natalie Hassalem turned back to the consoles she was preparing for the approach. "Full speed, sir?" she asked.

"Yes," Simon replied. "You'll be on watch when we reach the atmosphere. You've studied the charts I drew?"

"I have, sir. Latitude and longitude of the colony are preset." She dialed in the course and speed changes and enabled the controls.

"Those figures won't reflect precisely in *Serendipity*'s navigation system," he reminded her.

" 'Approximately twenty degrees south of the equator, smallest continent, northeast corner, forty-mile peninsula shaped like a horse's head,' " she recited.

"There may be no lights to help you find the settlement."

"I can do it by sight, sir, if it's on the day-side when we get there." Hassalem cleared her throat, turned quickly, and winked at Simon's youngest son.

On cue, Randall said, "That won't matter, Natalie. Infrared. Ground-search radar. Use *all* your tools."

"Excellent suggestion, Randall," she said.

Now he's in love with six of them, Simon thought. And, he added to himself, I'm becoming entirely too predictable.

He looked around him at those in the Control Center, and felt a deep pride in each of them. Despite their outward ease, everyone aboard was apprehensive about what they'd find on New Hope—and what that could imply about the other eight new worlds in what was called the Pacifico Belt.

Anxiety levels were high as they prepared themselves to face a world on which every human being might have suffered a slow and painful death; the absence of any normal radio communication was a strong indication that their worst fears were about to be justified. But that dread was held firmly in check as *Serendipity* made its full-speed approach to New Hope. As it had been for millenia, the discipline of those facing the unknown voiced itself in quiet, casual tones. His crew joked among themselves, enjoyed the company of one another, and did all of the small things that were normal in a close family.

As New Hope grew larger on the visual screens, members of the crew left for duty stations or sleep, and were replaced by others. Simon dozed sporadically in the command chair. At the end of her duty cycle, Jessica came to stand next to her sleeping father and watch the screens. She didn't wake him up; there was nothing to report.

Natalie Hassalem returned to the Control Center and took control of the pilot's station again. With steady, expert hands she reduced speed at the proper time and brought *Serendipity* into an equatorial orbit at the edge of the thin atmosphere of New Hope. Locating the smallest continent and then the peninsula required less than thirty minutes. It was just past noon, local time.

The cruiser returned to a high position while Simon and twenty-one other Duelists put on full suits and climbed aboard two of the ship's armored scouters. Leaving *Serendipity* behind, the craft streaked downward toward the surface.

The settlement, itself called New Hope, was a sprawl of interconnected below-ground tunnels that reached between residential areas, warehouses, schools, a hospital, and myriad work stations and laboratory spaces. Above-ground, New Hope showed itself as a twenty-acre glassite dome. Simon recalled small patches of soil where ongoing tests were conducted that would eventually lead to dome-wide stable crops of oxygen-and-food-producing vegetation. Animals and insects waited below for the day they could be released to become a natural part of their new world. Because glassite and metal framing were easily manufactured from minerals found in abundance on New Hope, the pioneers themselves would construct the next, larger dome. And then the next and the next. Eventually—Maria had estimated eleven decades—the domes would no longer be necessary.

New Hope represented a luxury not known on Earth or anywhere in its System: unlimited expansion potential, for centuries to come. There was a reason the settlement and the planet shared the same name; they were intended to become the same entity.

As the two scouters sped closer to the ground, Simon hoped to see evidence that a second dome was under construction. With a deepening sense of dread he saw that this was not the case. The scouters flew around and above the dome in a slowly descending spiral as a sudden gusting wind rose from the south. Within seconds, sweeps of sand were skirting the surface and washing in waves over the dome. Nothing inside could be seen in any detail. The scouters switched on piloting radar as the swelling sandstorm came up to meet them.

"Stay two hundred yards behind me, Marconette," Simon radioed as visibility closed around the vessels. The sand-laden gale was strong, but now steady; easy to adjust for in controlling the scouters. "We'll touch down near the northside airlock. There should be some relief from this wind there."

"Understood, Admiral."

Another radio frequency was activated from *Serendipity*, miles above them. "Dad, that storm is small. Unless it intensifies, you should be clear in fifteen minutes or so."

"Thanks, Jessica," Simon answered. "We're coming around the lee side of the dome now. I can see well enough to proceed."

"Yes, sir. Be careful."

Simon keyed the radio twice in acknowledgment. He eased the scouter down gently, edging close to the airlock. "Marconette, the wind is shifting. I'm losing visibility again. Land a hundred feet behind me. I'll radio when we're all inside."

"Aye aye, sir."

The Duelists checked their suits for good seals, then paired off for rechecks. When all of them were ready, Simon led the first two through the scouter's small airlock and waited in blowing sand until they were all outside. The dog-wheels on New Hope's airlock offered no resistance. This meant little, Simon thought as he spun the wheel open; even if this entryway had not been used or maintained recently, corrosion would be minimal in air that was so deficient in oxygen. The inner door was the same. Simon stepped through and looked around in semidarkness while the others followed him in. As he'd feared, the vast, open area was unlit and empty. Beneath his feet were crumbled brown remains of what once had been vegetation. He keyed the mouth-mike in his suit's helmet. "Come on in, Marconette. We're going to need help."

The twenty-two Duelists separated into small groups and stayed in radio contact as they fanned out in different directions, using their suit lights to guide them after they descended from the dome. An hour later they found the first of the settlers, a group of thirty, in one of the family apartments. There was no way to know how long they'd been clustered together here. Like the metal on the airlock doors, the corpses were perfectly preserved in lifeless air. The expressions on the gaunt faces drove Simon from the apartment at the first sight of them.

The images would remain with him forever: Mothers and fathers with empty, hope-dead eyes. Children in their arms, clinging to their parents with the final human strength of rigor mortis.

All of the colonists were found in one residential complex.

The crew of *Serendipity* worked for thirty hours, operating the four scouters in shifts. There were a total of 4,193 bodies to bring aboard the cruiser as it hovered above the empty dome. More than a third of the new passengers had been born here, light-years from the planet they'd have been taught to revere. The settlers of New Hope were photographed individually and then stacked en masse in the ship's berthing compartments. The compartments were then sealed and emptied of the Earth-brought air that would only corrupt humankind's first world-builders.

Corinne returned to her journals and began entering the names beneath the heading of April 29, 2153.

In the Control Center, Simon watched grimly as New Hope seemed to withdraw from sight on the visual screen. *Serendipity* continued the enabling run to hyperspace while an egg-shaped, blood-colored image became indistinguishable from the dark Universe beyond.

For the first time since she'd begun training in the special arts taught to her by a man who'd studied for years under Simon Barrow, Shelly Bascombe was unable to stop a fight before serious injury occurred. There were four of them. They burst in through both doors, front and back, at the same time. Shelly leaped out of bed and listened in total darkness. Within five seconds she heard weapons fire, and knew that they'd killed her husband as he sat downstairs at the kitchen table, working on his accounts as he always did in the pre-dawn hours.

The killers called her name as they searched the small house. They were Peacekeepers, they shouted. With a warrant.

Two of them could be heard coming up the stairs. She entered a hallway closet and left the door cracked open. Breathing slowly and evenly, focusing her mind on the strategy that seemed to come without conscious thought, she climbed to the top of the closet. Then, bracing her arms and legs against opposite walls, she inched upward until her back was touching the ceiling. One of them was coming closer now, while the other walked toward the far bedroom. A stream of brightness entered the closet as the hallway lights were turned on. They were still calling her, kicking in doors and overturning furniture. She watched as a hand came into view on the doorknob below her. It was a tall, broad man who eased the door open and peered inside. He bent to look beneath the line of hanging clothes, reaching with his free hand to probe between the garments. She touched him first with her hands as she dropped to his back. One hand covered his mouth and choked off a startled cry. The other found the wrist of his weapon-hand. She jammed a knee against the back of his elbow and pulled until tendons ripped and the joint shattered. The man struggled to pull away, biting at her smothering palm, pushing backward and pinning her against a wall. With her legs squeezing his chest until she felt his ribs begin to crush, she put the wrist of her free hand against the back of his neck and pushed. With her other hand she took the bottom of his chin and jerked her arm backward. His neck snapped like a pistol-shot.

A female voice came from inside a room at the far side of the hallway. "Gus, what was that? You got her?"

Looking quickly into the empty hallway, Shelly left the closet and ran silently toward the woman's voice. She caught the second one as the bedroom door opened. Shelly charged through, knocking the Peacekeeper back into the room. As the woman stumbled backward Shelly spear-handed her face, crushing the bridge of the woman's nose, driving the cartilage upward into her brain. She was dead before she slammed against the wall behind her and fell to the floor.

Leaving the bedroom, Shelly ran to the top of the stairway and stopped, listening. There was only the muffled sound of her name being shouted as before; the other two were in the basement, she decided. She climbed out a window onto the roof and verified that there were no more of them waiting outside. She entered again through the same window.

There was no hurry now.

Taking her time, she moved silently to the basement entrance in the kitchen. Neil Bascombe lay with a small paring knife in one hand, an orange in the other. Half of his face was gone. She turned from him and walked into the pantry, where she opened the main power panel and switched off all power to the house. The shouts stopped.

Shelly waited until they were both in the kitchen, searching ahead of them with portalights. One of the lights lingered for a moment on the body of her husband. She waited until he was left in dark peace again, and then she moved. This time she was not as gentle as she'd been with the first two.

Weeks passed as Shelly Bascombe tried covertly and unsuccessfully to contact friends with whom she'd trained. They'd decided over a year ago to close the schools and wait to be called into action alongside their Senior members. Since that time, they'd been in communication with each other only briefly, and never in a group. Shelly located some of their relatives, but no students. All of them were gone; a few dead, most arrested, some hiding. She knew where to go.

Arriving in Australia and making her way westward to the city of Freemantle occupied a full month of careful travel. She found sixty students already there, from five other continents. No two stories of lethal encounters with Peacekeepers were exactly alike, but they all had two things in common: The fights were over and the students were miles from their former homes or workplaces before they felt anything at all. And each of them had realized in that same moment that there was no longer any reason to wait for a call from Simon Barrow. The group formally took on the name used by the world's media to condemn their Senior comrades as thieves and murderers. They were all Duelists, now.

Anton Kin'Te stood rigidly straight at the helm of *Defiant* as his life poured out onto the deck in washes of redness that already filled his boots. Standing out from his back like a third shoulder was a nine-inch wedge of shrapnel. *Please, Lord God*, he thought, shaking as an unbearable weight pulled him down. *Please, don't let me die . . . yet. My friends have called me The Great Kenyan. Let it be so, this one last time.*

The image on the visual screen dimmed and paled, growing larger but lighter while all color drained from his vision. He willed his legs to hold him for a moment longer, and his arms to stop their shameful trembling. *So easy*, he told himself. *To stand and to reach, for a moment more, just a few seconds, please God keep me alive so they don't have to die with me . . . Push legs, pull arms, push arms, pull legs, one mind, one job to do, two commands, Dual mind!* Oh, *Blessed Saint Barrow I'm not going to last . . . yes I will! I will!*

Because his eyes were nearly lifeless, he could not see that the Peacekeeper ship chasing *Defiant* had firmed up on a course directly behind him, as he'd prayed that it would. But he felt it happening. And so he fell forward, pushing with the last of his strength so that his body would strike the helm yoke *just so*.

Defiant's maneuvering jets swung violently to one side, spinning the ship around on its axis and pointing its prow at the killer that was now too close to escape. As he fell to the deck, Anton Kin'Te felt an explosion of joy and peace purer than anything he had known. *Thank you, God, for their lives.*

Lion careened into a tight half-speed turn that threw the two of them in the Control Center against the braces they gripped. The face-plate of Hector Horatio Hernandez smacked hard against a metal stanchion, but held. Air in the compartment hissed as it escaped through tiny cracks in the portside bulkhead. At least, he thought, the fire will go out.

He turned the helm again, now slowing to one-eighth speed and aiming the ship directly at the last attacking Peacekeeper cutter. He'd just seen the other one erupt into thousands of pieces as Anton Kin'Te turned his vessel and rammed head-on into the Peacekeeper.

"Wait," Hector whispered to the image on the screen in front of him. "Hold course, damn you. There is no reason to be afraid of a fifteen-year-old child." He was certain that the last volley from *Lion* had temporarily disabled the enemy's reactors, and one of its Chatterly-Wang engines. The Peacekeeper was slower now, and had used the last of its stored main-weapons power. They were shooting at him with only small cannon. Still, the armor-piercing projectiles were enough to tear his ship apart. He could outrun the Peacekeeper, but true escape was impossible. *Lion* was too severely damaged to enter hyperspace, and all of the crew would be dead before *Talon* or the others members could respond to a distress call.

"You turn aside first," Hector intoned. "Now, please, or we all die, as my friends on *Defiant*. Yes, turn ... turn ... you should do it ... NOW!" The Peacekeeper began a quick veer to port. Hector keyed the mouth-mike. "Starboard Weapons, shoot!" Lights dimmed as the Peacekeeper flashed by close aboard on *Lion*'s starboard side. The outer hull rang from the hammer-blows of shells that ripped through the ship's outer skin and exploded against the thicker bulkheads inside. The last of the air screamed out of the compartment, clearing the smoke away.

"We scored one hit, sir!" the radio speaker in his ear reported. "Good hit!"

"Very well," Hector said. He kept *Lion* on a straight course and increased speed to Full. Turning to watch the radar screen behind him, he saw that the Peacekeeper was slowing. Slowing, but not turning. From the corner of his eye he saw the suited form of Stewart Misiaszek slump to the deck. He cut speed to slow and began a sweeping turn, programming in the course he wanted to follow.

"I think we are safe now," Hector said as he stepped past his commanding officer and into the Radio Room. He keyed the monitors and heard the distress call immediately.

". . . been hit by that damned weapon of theirs. My crew is boarding lifelaunches. *Volga* will detonate in forty minutes but it'll be clear of us by then. Tell Douglas-Wycliffe that we lost *Pampas*, but I got the sons of a bitches. We killed one and crippled another. Do you understand? He can't escape! Come get us, and we'll go after him." The call gave *Volga*'s position, and then began to repeat itself as the automatic re-broadcast took over. Hector recognized the voice from taped conversations he'd heard. It was Captain Ingrit Von Velt.

Back at the helm he came to full speed to go after the Peacekeeper cutter. Still accelerating as he passed the lifelaunches, Hector ignored them. He was strongly tempted to radio Von Velt and explain to her that any explosion they might detect would be the final *adios* of the Duelist ship *Lion*.

It was an hour later, as the last of the dead was loaded aboard *Volga* and they were starting the run to hyperspace, that Hector Horatio Hernandez began to feel anger. Stewart Misiaszek had suffered a concussion. His eyes were unfocused and dilated, but he'd regained consciousness. Ke Shan's legs were broken and she appeared to be bleeding internally. Arthur Daniels had been blinded. Four others were injured less severely. Hector thanked the luck of Saint Barrow that any of their suits had held. Most had not, as exploding projectiles created storms of shrapnel in the compartments of *Lion*. There were a total of twelve survivors from a crew of forty Duelists. No one who'd served aboard *Defiant* was alive.

With his last breath The Great Kenyan Anton Kin'Te had delivered a message to the Peacekeeper cutters that unquestionably had saved Hector and the others: Duelists do not back away.

"I have always dealt kindly with my opponents," Hector explained to the twenty-eight torn bodies laid together in a berthing compartment. "No more, my friends. No more." He touched each face gently, saying their names along with the forty-two who'd perished aboard *Defiant*. When he'd spoken the final name he whispered a prayer for the dead that Corinne had learned from their mother.

Of the twelve survivors, four besides Hector were capable of standing watches. He conferred with them along with the seven injured.

"*Talon* and the others won't be at the new rendezvous point for another two days," Misiaszek began. His level of alertness was not constant, but the pain was. His head was bandaged according to illustrations in a medical manual they'd found in *Volga*'s dispensary. Ke Shan's legs were set with the help of the same manual. She was extremely weak, and pale. Arthur Daniels wore a dressing over his eyes and moved his head as if watching Misiaszek speak. "There is something we can do while waiting to see the doctor," he continued. "But Hector, you're going to do it. I'm declaring myself unfit for command. Temporarily."

"Then I will choose our targets and method of attack."

Misiaszek hesitated only for a second. "Yes, sir."

"First," Hector said, "we have to compensate for the Peacekeepers' new tactics. Apparently they aren't using the ID system any longer, and they're hunting for us in pairs. We have to take back the advantage of surprise. So now when we leave hyperdrive we will try to come out right *on* them."

"I hope you're joking," Ke Shan said.

"No, I'm not. The system isn't accurate enough for us to hit them, do you understand? But we may be close enough to gain a few seconds before they can react."

"Or," Daniels said, "we'll reenter normal-space in the path of a thousand meteors. Wouldn't it be easier just to shoot ourselves? The Peacekeepers will die of worry because they can't find us."

"We could come out of hyperspace on a collision course with one of their ships," Ke Shan pointed out.

"If our enemies are bearing down on us, we'll be ready, but they won't," Hector explained. "We'll catch them when they make short hops in normal-space, above the elliptic. They'll be away from the main meteor flows. I'll monitor for them in passive mode, out of their detection radius. Assuming a standard transit speed, we can use a line-plot and get a good course and range, then project their position for any time we choose. If we determine that we can get into hyperspace and intercept them before they approach the Belt again, we aim at them and go."

"Maybe we can get close," Misiaszek said, after considering the plan. "And maybe we won't kill ourselves in the process. But if we're not in weapons range, surprise will do us no good."

"Then we run at full speed back to hyperspace. We try again, when we locate more of them. We have two days to test this out, and then we'll link up with *Talon*."

"Speaking of that," Misiaszek said. "This ship can't disable, it can only kill. Admiral Barrow isn't due back for another two months. And neither Griffin Joyner nor Francine Bellenauer has authorized lethal attacks."

"What does that matter?" Ke Shan snapped. "Your head is foggy, Stewart. Seventy of us are dead. For the first time the Peacekeepers have evidence that we can be beaten. We've got to kick up the charge. Apply all the force we have. I know this is a 'paramilitary oligarchy,' but I vote with the plan. Let's do it."

Misiaszek looked at her, offended. "I lost the same number of friends everyone else did. But we're crossing a major line here."

"You were appointed by Simon Barrow," Hector said. "The Orders of Engagement he gave to all the ships' captains were clear. You and I have discussed them for hours. So I understand, you have no choice but to say these things. Very well. You've done your duty, and advised the new captain. Now let's go hunting."

"Good," Misiaszek said, wincing as he tried to nod his head. "Everything's done and legal." He stood slowly, waiting for the dizziness to pass. "I'll be in the Forward Weapons Room. Call me when you've got something for me to kill."

Hector's tactic was half-successful. The Duelists found two different pairs of Peacekeeper cutters in transit, and were able to come out of hyperspace much closer to them than had ever been attempted. But the range each time was still too great for the element of surprise to be a factor. After two days of hunting, *Volga* abandoned the search for targets and went to meet

the other Duelist ships. There was a lot to discuss with Griffin
Joyner and Francine Bellenauer.

Talon, *Breaker*, and *Fury* were waiting as scheduled when
Volga came out of hyperdrive, broadcasting a low-power recognition signal. They kept their Weapons Rooms poised to
fire until Hector's voice reached them.

The three ships had been engaged in blockade-running,
carrying supplies taken from Depot Six to the mines along the
Beltway. Mylo Edelman on Bravo Three, now fully aware
of—and in agreement with—the Duelists, had given Joyner
news that was encouraging: Even though the mine crews were
forced at times to on-load ores to Earth-bound ships, there
weren't enough Peacekeepers to intimidate them all while simultaneously hunting for the Duelists. The miners resisted
when they could—and on-loaded low-grade ore and useless
rocks when forced into compliance.

The deaths aboard *Lion* and the total loss of *Defiant*'s crew
were a shock to all of them. At a brief memorial service Hector again recited the names and repeated publicly the prayer
he'd offered on the day of the loss. For the first time in his
life, Griffin Joyner listened to a prayer, and thought, Maybe.

Joyner and Bellenauer made crew reassignments to alleviate the shortage on their newest ship. A reluctant Gordon Barrow transferred to *Fury*; Bellenauer insisted that she'd taught
him enough to command a ship—and that Bob Judd would
provide him with the practical experience he still required. On
the recommendation of Steward Misiaszek, pronounced too
severely injured for immediate return to his former position,
Hector Horatio Hernandez was given command of *Volga*—
now called *Avenge*.

The four ships remained light-months away from Earth's
System and rehearsed new tactics, moving frequently and
waiting for the return of Admiral Simon Barrow.

September 2153

There were seventy-two of them now, new Duelists, as they
split into squads of eight and left the port city of Freemantle.
Standing with the group she now led, Shelly Bascombe felt a

lightness and ease she hadn't known since before the Peacekeepers had murdered Neil.

All of them shared a deep commitment to strike back at those who'd murdered family members and friends. And all felt the familiar anticipation of entering a combat situation. Their minds were clear, eager, and ready.

Ahead of the Duelists, a line of young people waited with cheerful impatience to board a glistening white passenger liner standing four hundred feet away. From their conversations Shelly learned that most of the young men and women were students from Manhattan University. The ship looked as if it were already airborne, riding on waves of heat that floated up from the tarmac. A slight breeze stirred. The moving air felt odd, brushing directly against the back of her neck. Unconsciously she raised a hand and felt for the long hair she'd worn for years; it was gone, as she constantly had to remind herself. Neil wouldn't recognize me now, she thought. This was one of the few times she allowed him to enter her thoughts. But she knew he'd approve of her decisions, and have a good long laugh at her new appearance. Besides replacing her shoulder-length brown hair with short blondness that scarcely covered her ears, she'd changed eye color. The deep smoky blue he'd loved was now hidden by colored contact lenses that flashed a bright green each time she passed a mirror. And he'd be hysterical at the new name: Melodina Sommersby; it sounded like a puffed-up European opera star. She and the real Melodina, a tourist, were very close in size and age. Unfortunate for Melodina. But the woman would get new travel and identity and money cards eventually.

"They're opening the gate," a shabbily dressed young man in front of her announced. He turned and spoke to Shelly. "I'm glad to be leaving. It's been a terrible vacation."

"Worst I can remember," she agreed.

"Hotels out of food, lines everywhere, people striking, local police and Peacekeepers watching everyone. It'll be good to be home again."

"It's no better there," she said.

"True," he said, nodding thoughtfully. "Not better for most. But my family's in government. We're rich." He smiled broadly and offered a handshake. "I'm Burton Frank. You're not from the University, are you?"

It was clear that the young man was lying to impress her. They'd been better at this, she thought, in her own University days. She shook his hand and spoke in a low, confidential tone. "No. I'm a spy from another galaxy. I plan to disrupt the government you serve."

He looked at her for a moment, then down at his clothing. "All right," he said, grinning. "I'm not rich. My parents are janitors at the UN. So am I, when I'm not studying. But why not pretend for awhile? Life is too grim, don't you agree? I have an idea. We'll sit together on the trip. I'll be the Secretary of something, and you'll be an alien anarchist. When we get to Manhattan Island we'll introduce ourselves and start again. Yes?"

"Yes," she answered, warming to him and recognizing the opportunity. "First, I will beguile you into telling me about every square foot of the UN building. You'll never suspect a thing."

⇒25⇐

During the trip back to Earth's System, Corinne spent hours of each day in transit with the personnel records from New Hope. When at last she was finished, each of the four thousand one hundred and ninety-three pages she'd compiled contained two photographs—one a child or adult pioneer, the other an emaciated corpse—of the same person. Corinne placed the last of them into an emptied food crate and noted the event in her journal: October 7, 2153.

Other sources detailed the slow death of New Hope. The last supply ship from Earth had arrived in 2139; the next was expected two years later, but never came. And yet the settlement had done well for nearly a decade. Personal diaries and official records revealed years of gradually lessening anxiety as the work they were performing began to take effect. The colonists' writings reflected a sense of optimism; Maria's theories were translating steadily into observable success. They all knew that two more shipments of essential minerals were needed to bring the developing ecosystem to the point of perpetual regeneration. But it was also known that because of their early success they could afford to wait for years, until the next ships arrived. There was wide-spread speculation about the ship's delay. But nowhere did Corinne read of a single person who doubted that Earth would send the needed supplies. That changed in 2148.

Severe food rationing kept them all alive. But over a seven-month period a critical mass of colonists became too weak to carry out the hard work required to supply enough power, water—and at last, on the final day of life—air. Every human being on New Hope had suffocated, clustered together in one sealed residential complex.

Simon spent a lot of time reading and thinking about the fate of the colonists. He recognized parallels between what had happened on New Hope and what was now taking place at home. All of humankind was vulnerable to what had killed those four thousand pioneers. Without the chance to grow, to open up new territories and to soar beyond old horizons, the human species would one day find itself in the same place as the people of New Hope: clustered together, weak, dispirited—and suffocating.

The journey back to the Earth System had occupied one hundred fifty-five days, with only ten to go. The crew was afflicted with a condition traditionally referred to as "channel fever"; eager anticipation of home, and a youth-in-the-springtime buoyancy of spirit and excitement.

As a way to direct and contain the heightened levels of energy, Randall devised a ranking system that added to the already strong sense of competition among the Duelists aboard. He proposed a tournament, with himself and Simon as judges: a two-day event, giving all Duelists a chance to compete, and everyone else the opportunity to be a spectator at some of the matches. Enthusiasm was immediate throughout the crew.

The rules of mutual engagement were identical to those of

training: For blows delivered, the rule was "Speed Maximum, Power Minimum." For holds and throws, it was "Remember, This is Your Friend." The tournaments produced pain for the participants and work for Dr. Reilly, but no permanent injuries.

The Duelist who emerged with the most points, Carlos Litieri, was designated by Randall as Grade 1 Expert. The next four were Grade 2, and the progression continued down to the last group of four: Grade 12. The five lowest-ranking Duelists bore the title of Grade 13, Novice. Simon watched their faces closely as the results were read. Next time, he knew, the fighting would be more intense. He lightened the mood by announcing that these ranks were temporary; a formal tournament would be held later, when the other ships' crews—and their teacher—would compete also.

Jessica left the compartment while the others were already making plans and predictions for the next competition. She had emerged as a Grade 3, and she was furious. The judging had been fair, she knew; both Litieri and Bridges had landed blows that should never have slipped past her guard. With the others, she had lacked the aggression that normally characterized her combat style. Her anger was directed at herself. Yes, she'd looked forward to seeing *his* eyes as she won the final bout and was declared the winner. But Kellan Shaeffer hadn't been there at all. She was angry that his absence had disturbed her as much as it had—and still did, she admitted. Why hadn't he come to watch? He wasn't on duty; she was as familiar with his schedule as she was with her own. Perhaps, she thought, she'd offended him somehow. Again. Kellan was too reserved to say so directly; a flaw in him that she tolerated, despite the time wasted on trying to guess what he was thinking. But time was precious now, with only a week to go before the trip was over. She decided to find him.

Time, she thought angrily, an hour later. It takes too much time to look through a 720-foot cruiser. No one had seen Kellan, or his friend Roger Minton; the two were studying somewhere, most of them guessed. Jessica was beginning to develop a dark suspicion about all of this that had no relation to "studying." In her search through *Serendipity*, there were a few others she hadn't seen. The only woman among them was Lauren McKay. Lauren was twenty, Kellan's age, and attractive, Jessica admitted. But she wasn't even a Duelist! The thought struck her seriously for the first time: Maybe Mom was right! Maybe Kellan *needs* to be stronger, more capable than the woman in his arms. What a sick mind! Thinking about it as she walked throughout the ship, Jessica realized that her jealousy was ridiculous—even if her reasoning was accurate. She decided to continue the search, however. And if she found Kellan and Lauren together, she'd accept it rationally. She'd turn without a word. And walk away quietly, calmly. And then go to see Grade 1 Expert Duelist Carlos Litieri. And beat the hell out of him.

She found Kellan Shaeffer, after another thirty minutes, in Auxiliary Machine Space 3. Or rather, above AMS 3. The compartment was empty as she passed through it. But just as she reached the hatchway leading to the tunnel through Reactor Compartment 4, she heard movement coming from above the overhead. Thinking that a watchstander was up there, she climbed the ladder and opened the hatch. This typical overhead space was only a yard high, twenty feet by twenty, and was crisscrossed throughout with ventilation ducts, piping, and wiring conduits. Now it contained lashed-down food crates as well, from the oversupply they'd on-loaded for the trip to New Hope. Jessica stood on the ladder with her head above the hatchway.

"Have you seen—" she called out. And then she saw him from the chest down, on hands and knees, partially hidden by a thick vertical support stanchion ten feet away next to the outboard bulkhead. "Kellan, what are you doing here? And who's with you?"

He crawled backward until he came fully into view. As he smiled at her, his face reddened. "Ah, hello, Jessica."

It dawned on her that he was wearing a full tool belt. And now she saw that his hands were dirty. Well, she thought, relieved. No need to worry *too* much.

"There's no one with me," he said. "Why?"

She was embarrassed. "Oh," she said, thinking quickly. "It's because . . . you know the rules. No crew goes into the overheads alone. You could get hurt. No one would know." He wasn't hurt, she saw happily. "What are you doing?"

"Do I have to tell you? Isn't it obvious?"

"Yes, you do," she said. "And no, it isn't."

"All right." He reached behind the stanchion and pulled back a folded sheet of paper. Jessica recognized it as a schematic drawing of the communications systems. "I'm tracing out lines, finding components," he said, now sitting with his back against the stanchion. "In each of the last five off-periods I've spent at least three hours at it, while you were on watch."

"But why?"

Now he flushed again. "Jessica, who knows more about these systems"—he pointed to the schematic—"than anyone aboard?"

"I do," she said.

He grinned at her. "Not for long."

She thought for a moment, and laughed. "You're doing all of this, using your off-time . . . to *compete* with me?" *What a wonderful mind!* she thought proudly.

"That's right," he confirmed. "This is the only way I *can* compete. You've been through all these spaces, haven't you?"

"Of course. Dad and I traced them all out, on the trip to New Hope."

"I knew you'd been here," Kellan said. "I could feel it."

Now it was Jessica who flushed. "Kellan. Kellan, I have to be on watch in twelve minutes. Otherwise . . ." Her eyes finished the statement.

"You'd better go," Kellan said huskily, going back on his hands and knees and moving toward her. "As you said. 'Otherwise . . .'"

She blew him a kiss and pulled the hatch closed.

Kellan Shaeffer waited and listened for five minutes before moving again. He crawled back behind the stanchion and opened the schematic drawing again. "She's gone," he said quietly.

Roger Minton answered from just below him, outboard toward the hull. "Good. Give me the snips again and another five connectors. This one's about finished."

October 2153

"3123-5566-344QJCL," William Burnside answered again, this time raising his voice. The rod against the back of his neck was activated.

"Louder!"

"3123-5566-344QJCL!" He screamed, as amperage shot down his spine and outward. Perspiration ran freely from every part of his body. The chair he was strapped into overturned as his legs spasmed and pushed him backward. The hard jolt of hitting the floor caused him to bite through his tongue. One of two blue-uniformed men kicked him onto his side as he began drowning in blood. Stepping away from a spreading red stain, the other man reached down to drag the chair upright again.

"Enough. Leave him there this time." Douglas-Wycliffe looked up from the notes she was reviewing and set her silver pen down unsteadily at the side of the notebook. Both of her hands were shaking in quick, short tremors. An eye tic made her normally immobile face even more difficult to watch than it had been before.

General Anna Chakheya and Undersecretary Damis LaMothe stood quietly, neither one daring to move or to speak. Burnside wept, eyes shut tightly, as he moved weakly in spastic attempts to free his arms and legs from the thin bands of metal digging into his flesh.

"We acknowledge small accomplishments," Douglas-Wycliffe said to Chakheya and LaMothe. "But your government cannot survive on meager and intermittent effort. Do you understand us?"

"Yes, Madam Secretary," they answered together.

"That is doubtful," she said. "General, let us review. You have succeeded against how many of these Duelist ships?"

"We've eliminated one that we can verify, and we know that another sustained crippling damage."

"You were unable to find the second vessel."

"Yes, Madam Secretary. Two of our cutters searched for seven days. My judgment is that our ships are better deployed in searching for other targets."

"How *many* other targets, General?"

"Four, we believe, from the five cutters stolen at Prometheus. There is no direct evidence that these people are using civilian ships."

Uncharacteristically, Douglas-Wycliffe flushed. Her voice sharpened as she spoke in clipped tones. "As we have observed before, evidence need not be direct to be convincing. We have provided *evidence*," she said, pointing a shaking finger at Burnside, "that the mines have a strong network of support. Do you doubt that these Duelists are providing that support, General?"

"No, Madam Secre—"

"In nineteen months you have have attained one, and only one, measure of success." She glared at Chakheya. "Our patience with you was based on the fact that you once served with Griffin Joyner. It seemed reasonable to assume that you had learned enough about him to be in some way effective against him. And against his protégé, Simon Barrow. Our patience has not been rewarded, and has therefore expired. You are relieved of command. We will decide your next assignment, when it is convenient to do so. In the interim you will wait with others of your staff at Ellis Island. We believe you have a military stockade there?"

"Yes, Madam Secretary." Chakheya executed a sharp about-face and left the office without a look back.

Douglas-Wycliffe turned next to LaMothe. "How many of Barrow's students have you incarcerated?"

LaMothe steeled himself, recognizing his fate in the treatment of Anna Chakheya—whom he considered to be the finest of the commanding generals he'd personally known. He resolved to go, as she had, with dignity. "As you know, Madam Secretary, one hundred nineteen."

"And how many have provided you with information we can act on?"

"None of them has a criminal background. There are no legal charges—"

"That was not our question."

"Yes, Madam Secretary. My point is that we have held some of them for months. It has become clear that they know nothing of Barrow's activities, other than what has been presented in the media. I believed that this was an avenue worth pursuing, but in fact they're of no use to us. We should release them."

"We agree with you, partially," Douglas-Wycliffe said. "There is no further reason to keep them. But they can serve us, nonetheless. Beginning tomorrow they will be declared guilty of criminal conspiracy and murder."

LaMothe paled. "Of the many who escaped arrest, some committed murder, yes. And all are guilty of resisting lawful restraint. But surely the ones we have in custody, who surrendered without incident—"

"They will be publicly executed," she said, ignoring him. "Hanged. At the rate of two per day. We have arranged for universal media coverage." She lifted her pen in a trembling hand. "Damis," she said evenly, "the citizens demand answers and solutions from their government. You must learn to respond to them. And when necessary, to warn them." She lowered her voice. As before, her smile was unnerving. "We, also, require much of you. You must learn to satisfy us."

Before LaMothe could answer, Douglas-Wycliffe continued. "This man," she said angrily, again stabbing a shaking finger toward the quietly sobbing Burnside, "has informed us that the mining companies and rising percentages of common people are resolutely supportive of Barrow. He claimed that he has been unable to sway them, and has pleaded for another opportunity. We have decided to grant his request. He will deliver one more statement from us."

She nodded toward her uniformed bodyguards and pressed a button on the arm of her chair.

Damis LaMothe turned his head away when he realized what was happening. As a large office window slid silently open, the bodyguards lifted Burnside and hurled the bound and screaming man through forty-two stories of cool autumn air, down to the angry streets of Manhattan Island.

Stunned, LaMothe was silent until the window slid shut again. "Madam Secretary," he said slowly to her expectant, grotesque smile. "I—"

"We will send for you this evening," Douglas-Wycliffe said. "For now you will prepare the necessary documents to begin the executions. Go." Instead of looking away as was her custom, she watched him. She was still smiling.

LaMothe lowered his eyes and turned for the door. He would prepare a document, he told himself. In addition to the one she expected. As the decision firmed itself in his mind he was surprised by a sudden and overwhelming emotion—not fear, but relief.

"Damis." He was stopped at the door by her voice. "Be a dear, would you? Select a pleasant fragrance to wear for this evening."

Without looking back at the chuckling bodyguards, he nodded his head and walked briskly through the door.

⇒26⇐

Serendipity arrived at the prearranged position two weeks ahead of the schedule that Joyner and Barrow had agreed upon; transit time was immutable, but Simon had expected to remain on New Hope for longer than two days. There was no surprise, then, to find no one waiting as the cruiser completed the run in normal-space to the established coordinates.

Emotions were running high among the crew. For the Duelists it was the anticipation of seeing friends again, after nearly a year—and informing them that until formal tournaments could be arranged, they were all ranked below Grade 13 Novices. For the "civilians," once Peacekeepers, it was the hard realization that they could not return to their homes; they would be listed either as missing, or—more probably—as traitors. For all of them, there was one overriding question: What had happened during their absence?

On watch in the Radio Room, Jessica went through the routine of verifying that all power to transmitters was off, and that all monitors were working properly. Kendall Shaeffer assisted her. When the checks were complete the two sat talking, discussing a future that was uncertain for both of them.

"We'll win," Jessica assured him, holding his hand. "It won't be long before you're home again." She cleared her throat. "Do you think your parents will like me?"

"I think everyone in Ireland will like you. But I won't be with you when you go."

"Don't say that!"

"Sorry." He was quiet, while she stroked his hand. "Do you still have those holostats of home I gave you?"

"Of course I do. They're beautiful."

He smiled at her. "Did I ever point out the oak stand where the leprechauns have their kingdom?"

"No!"

"I'd better show you, then. Stepping on leprechauns is a sin past forgiving. Duelist or not, you don't want to face the Little People when they're angry. Why don't you get the pictures and bring them here?"

"We'll look at them later," she promised, hoping his brightened mood would last. "I'm on watch now."

"Jessica," he said, "your father spent more than two hours with me in here, trying to find a reason to turn me down for watch qualification."

"He was very impressed," she said truthfully.

"So I think I can be trusted not to break anything while you get the pictures."

"But Kellan, I'm on duty."

"Then I relieve you," he said.

She thought about it; nothing improper, just unusual. "Sometimes," she said, standing and kissing him again. "Sometimes you do." She raced from the room as he grabbed at her.

When she'd gone, Shaeffer worked quickly. He shut down all radio monitors ship-wide and altered the automatic maintenance recorder to ignore that, along with the events of the next two minutes. Next he wired and activated a console switch that had been disconnected since *Kali L'awana* became *Serendipity*. He waited with the switch "on" for twenty seconds, holding his breath and sweating, then threw the toggle back to "off." Thirty seconds later three short lengths of wire he'd brought with him were in his pocket, hidden again.

On the fourth day of waiting for contact from the other ships, Simon and Corinne were called by Dr. Janet Reilly to the cruiser's dispensary. They entered the compartment with growing dread, each knowing what they were about to hear.

This was the first time the physician had asked to see them in her office; and she'd examined Randall only an hour before.

As the door from the processing lab opened, Simon and Corinne reached across the foot of space between their chairs to grasp each other's hand. Dr. Reilly entered the room and sat on the edge of her desk directly in front of them. She said nothing. There was no need to; her expression was eloquent.

"How many?" Simon asked. "And how far have they progressed?"

"Six," Dr. Reilly answered. "They're small, barely readable on the scan. But the facilities we have aboard—" She shrugged. "Better equipment would have alerted us before they formed. But even then, I don't have the tools, or the knowledge . . . They're all inside his brain stem. I'm sorry."

Corinne felt the blood drain from her face as she slumped forward. Simon caught her, and pulled the two chairs together until she was leaning against him with his arm around her. "There's nothing?" he asked, clearing his throat. "There's nothing we can do?"

"Only monitor," Dr. Reilly said. She leaned forward and took Corinne's trembling hand. "I love him too," she said. "Please, listen to me. From what you've told me of his past episodes, there may be weeks before symptoms begin manifesting themselves. Or if we're lucky the disease could go into remission again. The polyps may not advance into tumors this time. It's reasonable to guess that this has happened many times, with no further developments. All we can do is wait."

"No," Simon told her firmly. "We'll take him to a hospital. We'll find a way to—"

The ship-wide 1MC circuit blared: ADMIRAL BARROW TO THE CONTROL CENTER. HOSTILE CONTACT. ADMIRAL—

He was out the door—BARROW TO THE CONTROL CENTER. HOSTILE CONTACT—and running through the passageway—ALL HANDS TO BATTLE STATIONS. ALL HANDS TO BATTLE STATIONS—already envisioning the action ahead. *How did they find us? How many?*

Making his way forward, he passed crew members running in both directions as *Serendipity* made itself ready to fight.

"Situation?" he called out as he arrived at Control.

"One Peacekeeper, sir," Hassalem reported from the radar station. "His reading doesn't match any of our ships. This is one of the older and larger cutters, according to what I'm getting." One of the advantages to having a ship that had been in commission, as opposed to the cutters that were fresh from the shipyards, was the specialized technology already installed and usable. *Kali L'Awana* had come to them with the capacity to distinguish among target-types—as could all of the Duelist vessels, now.

Simon noted the range on the radar console. "Why did you wait this long to call me?"

"Sir, he was well within detection range before he showed on the screen."

"Malfunction?"

"That's my guess. He's still well out of weapons range, though."

"Yes, I see that."

"Control, this is Radio," Jessica's voice came from a speaker. "The contact is broadcasting a recognition signal, sir. It's *Lion*'s signal."

"Confirmed?" Simon asked into a handset.

"Yes, sir. Verified twice."

"Give him our acknowledgment," Simon responded. "I say again, you are authorized to make a single transmission."

"Message sent and receipted for," Jessica announced five seconds later.

"Sir," Hassalem said. "He's slowing and turning away."

"Interesting," Simon whispered. "Helm," he called out. "Come about. Minimum speed. Stand by to go Full and run at him, on my order."

"Aye aye, sir," Bridges acknowledged.

Simon keyed the 7MC circuit. "Weapons, ready on all particle cannon?"

They all reported ready.

Jessica's voice came back. She was laughing. "Dad, it's Hector."

"Say again?"

"It's Hector, sir. He says a big ship like us shouldn't be afraid of a fifteen-year-old child."

• • •

The wounded were brought aboard *Serendipity*, along with the dead—who were placed in a small compartment near the ones already filled, from New Hope.

The utter coldness of these bodies was a shock that Simon wasn't prepared for. He'd seen death before; swift and brutal on Mercator, slow and cruel with his parents. The tragedy at New Hope was beyond comprehension. But these had been personal friends—his children, in a way. He'd watched them, tested them, chosen them, trained them; seen their reluctance to try the impossible, and then their astonishment at seeing the impossible happen within themselves. Every Duelist had known that some of them—perhaps all of them—would lose their lives. But that had been abstract knowledge. This was real. He could not reconcile himself to the knowledge that these friends would never be seen, heard, touched, again. The sorrow and anger strengthened his resolve to complete the work they had begun.

After a memorial service Simon Barrow followed Hector Horatio Hernandez aboard his new command.

Avenge was a decade older than the Duelist cutters, but fairly well maintained. It was apparent immediately that this had been a squadron commander's ship. The wardrooms were luxurious by comparison even to the newer cutters. And the yeoman's offices were crammed with piles of printed orders and regulations—obviously for distribution to the settlements and mining sites—and stacked with crates of blank sheets, for creating even more bureaucratic noise. It would be interesting, later, to penetrate the squadron commander's personal records code and read in detail the plans and procedures of Ingrit Von Velt. But Simon was most interested in the functioning particle cannon, which—along with the weaponry aboard *Serendipity*—added a new and deadlier dimension to their potential. He would wait for Joyner and Bellenauer, he decided, before agreeing to, or rejecting, the new Orders of Engagement they'd developed and rehearsed while he was in transit. He was pleased with Hector's ingenuity and satisfied that he'd done everything humanly possible to prevent the deaths aboard *Lion* and *Defiant*. But it disturbed him that the young captain had deliberately come out of hyperspace so close to *Serendipity*. He admonished Hector for the unnecessary demonstration of his proposed tactics—all the while recalling a young Simon Barrow, whose "quest for adventure," in Griffin Joyner's words, had led him to "stunts" that were far less reasonable—the unauthorized passage aboard *Utic Shinar*, chief among them.

Hector, chastened and unusually quiet, turned to leave his new wardroom.

A thought occurred to Simon. "Wait," he said. There was an opportunity here to give the eager young man something interesting and challenging to do while they waited for the other Duelist ships to join them, and to finish the work Corinne had begun as they'd left New Hope.

As Simon explained his idea, Hector's grin spread until his small face seemed in danger of cracking. He shifted from foot to foot impatiently as the plan grew in detail. Finally he could contain himself no longer. "Sir, I understand! I volunteer! May I go? *Now?*"

"Yes," Simon told him, fighting back the temptation to begin the explanation again. He was still upset with Hector's stunt, but simultaneously grateful; it seemed that the young man's innovation was exactly what was needed at this moment. All were agreed that the personal biographies and photographs of New Hope's settlers would be a powerful psychological tool. The question had been how to deliver them for the broadest possible distribution.

Now there was a way.

The settlers' biography sheets were transferred to *Avenge* and duplicated to make one hundred sets. These were loaded aboard an equal number of lifelaunches taken from the ample spares aboard *Serendipity*. When all was complete, Hector and his crew departed—to flash into normal-space close to the Earth, release the lifelaunches, and run again into hyperspace.

Some of the launches would be intercepted by Peacekeeper vessels, it was assumed. But there would be too many to stop without using lethal firepower. And by the time those intercepted were opened, the rest of the tiny craft would be scattered and gone. These would follow their individual programming to the oceans and remote areas of Earth, where their distress beacons would summon fishing ships and local rescue authorities.

Within days, the New Hope settlers—as vibrant pioneers,

and then as grotesque images of betrayal—would be seen again and remembered by every part of the Earth.

When *Avenge* returned five days later, the ship first contacted *Serendipity* from what Hector had pledged would be a "respectful distance." But there were three other Duelist cutters on the way, whose captains had not made the same promise.

Fury was next to arrive, twenty hours after the return of *Avenge*. Captained by Bob Judd, the ship came out of hyperdrive even closer that Hector had, the first time—nearly within weapons range. Battle Stations was canceled after the ship was positively identified. Half an hour later an exasperated Simon Barrow called both ships' captains to the wardroom of *Serendipity*. While Judd stood quietly at attention and Hector nodded with the solemnity of the recently converted, he explained to the new arrival that such tactics were to be used only against an enemy—on his orders.

"Understood, Admiral," they said together.

"Good. Stand at ease." Simon asked Judd about the performance of his oldest son, Gordon.

"Ah, may I speak freely, sir?"

Simon peered at him, saying nothing.

"Sorry," Judd said. He cleared his throat. "Gordon knows every square inch of that ship, sir. He's an excellent navigator and engineer, and without question the best pilot aboard. That includes me. He has a talent for precision flying that exceeds anything I've ever seen, or heard of."

"But?"

"And the crew respects him. Again, that includes me. I have no doubt that in time he'll be a superior commander."

"But?"

"He's impetuous. At times he's a little too quick to act. Sir, it's as if . . ." Judd took a deep breath and spoke quickly. "It's as if he needs to prove that he's your son."

Simon replied after a moment's thought. "I see. Thank you." It took him several seconds to recover from Judd's remark. "Go back to your ships, gentlemen. And I remind you of our discussion. The hyperspace tactic is to be used only on my orders."

"Yes, sir." They turned and left the wardroom. Simon knew

that they would follow his order—and that within ten minutes they'd be discussing new techniques to bring their ships even closer to an unsuspecting target. Judd's reference to Gordon was disturbing; was it possible? His oldest son was a man now—certainly with no need to "prove" anything. The best thing, Simon decided, would be to have him come aboard *Serendipity* for the evening meal; and see how the conversation progressed. For now, his wife and his *other* son needed him.

He'd just begun walking aft to check on Corinne and Randall when the 1MC circuit blared again: ADMIRAL BARROW TO THE CONTROL CENTER. WE HAVE THE LAST TWO ARRIVALS, SIR. Ke Shan's voice continued with obvious amusement. ALL HANDS TO BATTLE STATIONS. AH-GAIN, PEOPLE. Furious, Simon turned and ran past crew members who flattened themselves against bulkheads to avoid his full-ahead run. He was there in less than ten seconds.

"How close this time, Hassalem?" he asked angrily as he came to a stop behind the radar station. He'd been sure that Francine Bellenauer, at least, would know better.

"Best yet, sir," Carlos Litieri called out from the helm. "I've got them on visual already. They're within—" As Simon turned to watch the screen, Litieri called out: "Sir, there's a flash . . . they're firing!"

At that moment *Serendipity*'s lights dimmed, then flickered. A low-level jolt could be felt through the ship's decking.

"Helm, ahead full!" Simon ordered. "Come about, take us out of range."

"Aye aye, sir. Helm is ahead full. Turning now." The flickering stopped, and the lights held steady.

"Very well. Ke Shan, pass the word over the 1MC. All hands into full suits. Hassalem, designate these hostile contacts Targets One and Two."

"Aye aye, sir."

Simon grabbed for the 7MC handset. "Port and Forward Weapons Rooms—"

"Ready, sir," each of them responded immediately.

"Shoot at will, both targets. Full spread, full power."

Another jolt, this one stronger.

"Firing, sir." A second later, "Sir, Port Weapons Room. We

have a portside reactor failure. I'm working on stored cannon charge."

"Understood."

"Sir," Hassalem said, "both targets are turning. They're going after *Avenge* and *Fury*."

"No!"

Simon turned to see Bob Judd standing behind him, next to Hector. The eyes of both men were focused on the visual screen above the helm. *Avenge* was firing back and taking evasive maneuvers. *Fury* wasn't visible yet. It dawned on him, then, what an incredibly stupid thing he'd done: Keeping Judd aboard *Serendipity*, he'd forced Gordon to command a ship under attack—a ship with no means of returning lethal fire.

"Helm," Simon ordered. "Come around. Take us between Targets One and Two." Into the 7MC he said, "Starboard Weapons Room, we'll pass Target One on your side. Shoot as soon as he's in your sights." Everyone in the Control Center braced as *Serendipity* swung around, still accelerating. Simon watched the screen as the cruiser swept toward the two Peacekeeper cutters. Bolts of intense light streaked from the screen's sides and bottom as lethal energy reached toward the enemy. Return fire from both vessels appeared as steady streams of brightness that flashed out toward the cruiser.

"Control Center, this is Port Weapons Room. I'm out of stored power, sir. Shooting projectile cannon only."

"Hold until we're closer, Port," Simon answered. He was jarred roughly on the shoulder. As he turned, Gault shoved a full suit into his hands and bent to pull another from the box at his feet. Clonus was across the compartment, already suited, passing out more of them.

Both Peacekeeper cutters veered outward as *Serendipity* closed the range. Deciding instantly, Simon ordered, "Helm, come right, bring us around Target One for a starboard-side-to approach." If the Peacekeepers formed up again, he'd have them both to starboard. Simon climbed into his suit and took the helm while Litieri quickly stepped into his own.

Serendipity fought to overcome its ponderous inertia as the ship heeled around in an accelerating turn. In a close-in fight like this the smaller vessels held a powerful maneuvering advantage. A cruiser would normally use its superior speed and firepower to retreat and fight from a distance. But Simon couldn't allow the two Duelist cutters to fight the battle alone, even for the time he'd need to move away; *Avenge* was older and slower than the others, while *Fury* had only disabling weapons. And neither ship had its commanding officer aboard.

"Control Center, this is Forward Weapons Room. We took a direct hit. All of my guns are out, sir." The voice sounded distant and tinny through the suit speakers.

"Very well, Marconette. Evacuate and seal the compartment." He steadied on course, quickly closing the distance to the Peacekeeper cutter ahead. Target One was slowing; there was a good chance that it had been hit, but they were too distant to view any damage.

"Negative on the evacuation, sir. Compartment's already sealed. All the air is gone. We'll just relax and enjoy ourselves in here until this is over."

"Understood."

Litieri was now at the radar station while Natalie Hassalem put her suit on and adjusted the helmet. "Sir," he reported, "*Fury* has completed a sweep-around and is coming in on our port quarter. I think he's using us as a screen."

"Good," Simon answered. *That's the way, Gordon!* He wondered why the ship hadn't advised him of its intent; this was a tactic they'd rehearsed before. He keyed a helmet transmitter. "Radio, transmit to *Fury*. Message is 'Count twenty, starboard tack.'" In twenty seconds *Serendipity* would veer to the right, allowing *Fury* to sweep around the Peacekeeper as the two Duelist ships moved to outflank the vessel on both sides. After a moment Simon repeated the order. Still no reply. "Jessica, do you copy?"

From across the Control Center, Clonus answered. "I'll go see if anything's wrong, Simon."

"Thank you."

The big man made his way, breathing heavily in the uncomfortable suit, down the fifteen-foot corridor leading from Control to Radio. He pulled off his helmet and saw her as he opened the door. Jessica was sitting at the main console, slumped forward and face-down on the keyboard. The back of her head was matted with seeping blood.

"Oh, my!" Clonus stepped into the room and reached for her. Something heavy and hard came down twice against his skull before he could turn or react. As he fell, the wrench struck again, this time glancing off his right shoulder. Kellan Shaeffer dropped the wrench and turned from the crumpling old man. He reached for the switches and levers that would open up all of *Serendipity*'s frequencies, effectively jamming the transmitters. The first of the toggles was opened when he felt a movement against his right foot. He screamed into his helmet as vise-like hands closed around each of his ankles and squeezed until his bones were crushed to splinters. Shaeffer went into instant shock and fell backward. He was caught at the belt as Clonus struggled to remain conscious.

"Clonus, what the hack are you . . . CLONUS! JESSICA!" Gault stepped the rest of the way into the compartment and was shoved violently ahead as Roger Minton charged in behind him, slamming the door. The rat-faced man stumbled across the room, tripping over the dropped wrench and kicking it ahead of him as he fell. He landed hard on his right shoulder and turned to see his best friend crawling toward Minton, who had opened a panel and was beating against the controls inside with a rubberized machinist's mallet. As Gault struggled to his feet, Clonus reached Minton and groped for his legs. The young man kicked at the strong hands reaching for him and raised the mallet. Screaming, Gault lifted the wrench and charged at him. He threw the wrench and missed, but caught Minton squarely in the chest with his left shoulder. They fell to the deck, with Minton clawing at the furious old man above him.

Gault hissed through clenched teeth as his hand again found the wrench. "You think these hackin' Duelists are tough, boy?"

Minton, by far the stronger of the two, was terrified by the spitting, twitching, demonic face above him. He'd just managed to bring his hands up when the wrench came down again, and then again, pulverizing his hands against his face. He was jerked from beneath Gault then, as Clonus took hold of his belt and yanked him away.

Painfully lifting his torso from the floor, Clonus swung Minton outward until the young man's head impacted against the base of a metal console. After a second Clonus released the unmoving form.

W. C. Gault rolled over onto his back and clutched at his

chest, gasping for breath. A sharp and crushing weight squeezed his heart as sweat poured out of him and his vision dimmed. The pain was excruciating. But it wasn't important. "Did you see, Clonus?" he managed to whisper, overwhelmed by what he'd done. Not dreamt about—*done*!

"Yes," Clonus said. "You got one of the ah, hacks. Truly, my friend. You saved my life."

"Damn right I did," Gault said. He was falling backward, sinking into blackness. "He was afraid of me, Clonus. You saw it. You can tell them that." With his last breath he added, grinning broadly and no longer in pain, "You tell all those hacks."

"I will, Mr. Gault." Clonus wept as he reached his friend, knowing that it was over. He turned away. "Oh, Jessica, please, *you* be all right, truly," he whispered, and began to crawl up onto his hands and knees while streams of blood ran down the back of his neck and into his suit. Jessica's chair overturned and dumped her on top of him as *Serendipity* lurched suddenly to one side. They were both thrown powerfully against the opposite bulkhead, and lay still.

In the Control Center, Simon watched the screen in frustration. Target Two had just completed a tight looping maneuver that placed *Avenge* between itself and *Serendipity*.

"Turn and shoot," Hector said quietly, watching his ship on the screen. He was careful not to key a helmet transmitter. "Please, slow and turn quickly, my friends, and shoot."

Beside him on crutches, Ke Shan cursed softly to herself as *Avenge* increased speed and began a gradual turn, obviously trying to lead the Peacekeeper into turning away hard, giving *Serendipity* a broadside shot.

"No," Hector said. "No." As he knew it would, the Peacekeeper came to full speed in an equally narrow turn and closed in on the slower cutter. Hector watched as intense tracer-lights flickered from the Peacekeeper to his ship.

"Helm," Simon ordered, "put us on an intercept course with—"

All ship's main power went out at once as Target One braked, turned, and fired from ahead of them. It took a moment for eyes to adjust to the auxiliary lighting.

"—intercept course with Target Two," Simon continued.

Litieri acknowledged the order. "Sir, I recommend cutting speed for the turn. Otherwise—"

"Slow to one-eighth," Simon agreed immediately. "Go back to Full when we've come around."

"Aye aye, sir."

Clonus had been gone for two minutes. There was still nothing from the Radio Room.

"Aah, NO! *Merde!*" It was Hector's voice, loud enough to be heard through the helmets. Simon snapped his head up from the radar screen. *Avenge* was tumbling now as plumes of fire from escaping oxygen appeared and died instantly in the vacuum of space. The ship erupted in a final, silent burst of light, and was gone.

"Hector!" When the shaken young man turned, Simon ordered, "Go to the Radio Room. I've got to coordinate with *Fury*. Give me a direct channel."

"Yes, sir."

Natalie Hassalem's voice sounded in Barrow's helmet speakers. "Admiral, we've got two new contacts."

"Identification?"

"Same type as ours, sir. But so were the first two."

"Understood. We'll designate them Targets Three and Four until we know for sure." He keyed a second transmitter. "Hector, are you on station?"

"Yes, sir. I'm switching everything manually to auxiliary power. The automatic override didn't operate."

"Expedite, Hector."

"Yes, sir. Admiral, I'm calling in the doctor."

"Judd, Ke Shan," Simon ordered, avoiding the thought that was suddenly uppermost in his mind, "go and give him whatever help he needs."

On the 1MC circuit Hector called: "Dr. Reilly to the Radio Room."

"Sir," Litieri reported. "Targets Three and Four are hostile. They're shooting at *Fury*."

At the same moment Hassalem's voice sounded. "Two more, sir! These are cruisers! Headed straight at us! I say again, *two cruisers coming into weapons range!*"

"Helm, take us to Targets Three and Four," Simon answered quietly. "Full speed." He braced himself as *Serendipity* heeled around again in an accelerating turn. It wouldn't be long, he knew, before the stored charges for the two remaining particle cannon were gone. For all of his life Simon Barrow had been trained, and then trained himself, to feel no emotion during combat. But now there was amazement, and a sense of wonder—at how quickly, and how well, the Peacekeepers had adapted the hyperspace tactic to their own use. And there was something he'd never encountered before, during a fight: Fear. Gordon was aboard *Fury*—and Simon was not confident that he could protect his son.

She called for him at midnight, as she had every night for the past seven. Damis LaMothe carefully set down his pen. He was mindful not to touch its fine tip against the metal holder. The pen was part of a calligraphy kit his wife had given him two decades ago, a year before she sued for divorce and left him. He sat for a moment, looking over the document on his desk. A fine job, he thought again. The penmanship was crisp and clear, giving no hint of the anger and frustration—curiously combined with relief—that had guided his hand. He lifted the pen once more and added the new date, the seventh he had entered. Every evening for a week he'd returned to his desk and carefully erased the numbers he'd inscribed the night before. This time, he thought firmly, this time I will certainly resign. To strengthen his resolve he took up another pen and hastily scratched out one more document. He signed and dated it for the day before, wondering if this one, too, would need to be changed on a daily basis.

The Undersecretary for Security stood and walked to a silver-framed mirror that rested on its own pedestal against a wall. This had also been a gift, from the Mayor of St. Tropez, given on the day she'd replaced him in office and wished him *bon chance* as he left for a minor, but new and thrilling post at the United Nations. Forty-three years, he thought. I have done well. He smiled ruefully at the old man looking back at him from the mirror—and recalled a younger self, hopelessly in love with humankind, vowing to serve with diligence and honor. And believing, in his heart of hearts, that he would someday be a revered servant to them all, a Secretary General they would cherish throughout history.

But the vagaries of fortune, he thought sadly. If any future citizen recalled his name at all, it would be with loathing:

LaMothe, the dog who served Douglas-Wycliffe; who shares
the blame for those poor wretches from New Hope. LaMothe,
who signed the orders to hang two innocent young people every day for a week now. LaMothe, who did nothing as a glorious and heroic future collapsed between the crushing pillars
of stupidity and malice. They would despise him, as billions
did now.

They didn't understand, he thought bitterly. They never
would. He was an *Under*secretary. His job had always been to
serve, and to obey. What could *he* have done about New
Hope, and the other abandoned worlds? Ah, but how much he
could have done for them all, if they'd recognized his desire,
his abilities! His love! Perhaps when they read his resignation
they would . . . No, he thought, they'll never understand me.
I alone will know that I served loyally, for every moment of
my tenure.

Using his moist palms, he smoothed back the hair at the
sides of his head. He took a deep breath and turned for the
door. As he was about to leave the office he remembered, and
returned to his desk. He lifted an atomizer from its mahogany
case and sprayed himself with yet another pleasant fragrance
she'd sent him.

In the elevator he nodded absently at two janitors sharing
the cab with him, and watched as the display lights climbed
upward to forty-two. When the door opened the janitors excused themselves and passed around him.

Rude, he thought, as he followed them down the plush
hallway. They stopped at the door that was his own destination, and spoke to a uniformed security guard.

"You two," he called after them. "Where are you going?"

"The Secretary General asked me to call them here, sir,"
the security guard answered. He was a young man, who
brushed loose strands of fine blond hair from his forehead as
he spoke. "This is Burton Frank. He heads the floor maintenance on this shift." He added, raising an eyebrow at Burton,
"They're two hours late."

"We're here to clean a carpet," Burton said laconically.

His partner was a woman who nodded her head vigorously.
"That's right!" she said. "For her! Isn't it exciting?"

"I have business in there," LaMothe said brusquely. He remembered the blood stains left by Burnside. They would

never come out, he thought, disgusted. Why hadn't she just
replaced the carpet, as he'd suggested? "Go," he said. "Come
back tomorrow."

The man shrugged. The woman said, "But, sir!"

"Go, go," LaMothe said, motioning with his hands.

The guard said, "You heard the Undersecretary. He has
pressing business." He snickered at his own wit.

LaMothe glared at the man and stepped past him to open
the door.

When he'd passed inside and shut the door, the security
guard turned to the maintenance people and grinned. "I'm
sorry I can't let you two listen with me. Now go away."

"Yes, sir," the woman said, disappointed.

They'd walked halfway down the empty corridor when
they turned around and approached the guard again.

"What is it?"

"We were thinking," the woman said, smiling at him.
"What if we *pay* you? Could we listen then?"

The guard took a long moment to let his eyes travel the
woman's body. He decided not to tell them that he'd been
joking; the door was as soundproof as the walls. "You,
maybe," he said, leering openly. "But him—" Burton's fist
caught the guard in the stomach as the woman quickly put
one hand over his mouth and the other behind his neck. Pulling him toward her, she drove a knee into his midsection and
then released his neck, using the hand to back-fist his temple.
The man went limp, and she lowered him silently to the
floor.

"Burton," she whispered angrily, "I told you to let me do
this! You nearly let him call out!"

"I'm sorry, Shelly," he said. "But you saw how he was
looking—"

"Sshh!"

They listened at the door, and opened it an eighth of an
inch. A man's hoarse shout could be heard, followed by
grunting. Burton Frank grinned. "Energetic old bastard," he
whispered.

Shelly eased the door open slowly, ready to charge ahead
if the bodyguards were still present. A woman's voice cried
out, tapered to silence, and was followed by heavy breathing.
How does a Duelist handle *this* situation? Shelly wondered, as

the man beside her laughed quietly. *Quickly*, she answered herself.

She nodded to Burton. He bent and took the unconscious security guard by the arms, pulling him toward a closet.

Shelly pushed the door open forcefully and rolled to the center of the room, seeing it all as she moved. There were no bodyguards. The gray-haired man was alone. He was standing at an opened window, looking down. After a moment he winced and pulled his head back. As Shelly stood up he turned to face her and smiled, bowed with an exaggerated flourish, and fell backward into death.

Francine Bellenauer stood behind Griffin Joyner as the old man made the final preparations for coming out of hyperdrive. His hands moved confidently over the pilot consoles, and she watched with approval as he took the time to refer to the manual on his lap. During weeks of study and endless rehearsals on the auxiliary station, he'd been nervous about a complex task he hadn't performed in decades. But as ever, when practice became reality, it felt right. *Right.*

"Ready, Captain," he said at last.

"Very well, sir. Engage."

There was no physical sensation as the shift took place. But the difference showed itself immediately on the visual screens. Where there had been nothing, suddenly blackness appeared, lit by thousands of silver points.

"Commence radar search," Bellenauer ordered, turning to watch as the navigation computers went to work and gave her *Talon*'s new position.

"Excellent work, sir," she said as the numbers settled. "We're right at the point."

"Captain!"

Francine moved quickly across the Control Center to the radar operator. "Four ships, ma'am," the young Duelist reported. "At the edge of our . . . There's a fifth one. Two more . . . They're—"

"Call Battle Stations, everyone in suits," Francine ordered. As the word was passed on the 1MC she watched the screen. Three of the ships she recognized as cruisers, from the characteristic returns. One was alone, apparently being chased by the other two. The other four ships were cutters; impossible to know whose, yet. But it was clear that a dogfight was taking place.

"Helm," she called over her shoulder, "full speed toward that single cruiser."

"Aye aye, ma'am."

She ordered Radio to broadcast *Talon*'s recognition signal.

Aboard the Duelist cutter *Breaker*, Captain Delores Nancarrow finalized the procedure for reentering normal-space and ordered the system engaged. She watched, fascinated as always, as nothing became blackness, and then stars. Two of them were impossibly close.

"Sir," Hector reported over the intercom, "we're in contact with *Talon*. I've identified us and given a situation report. *Fury* has done the same."

"Coming on screen now," Hassalem confirmed from the radar console. "Ah! Yes! Admiral! We—"

"Got him, got him, we *got* him!" Litieri called out. "Target One is dead, sir!"

"Very well," Simon responded. "Radio, advise *Fury* to head for *Talon* at full speed. We'll do the same." The order was acknowledged.

"Coming about," Litieri said.

"New contact, sir!" Hassalem's voice nearly deafened him. "Close aboard Targets Three and Four . . . Collision, sir! They've collided!"

"Sir," Litieri reported. "The cruisers are shoot—"

Serendipity rocked with the impact of two focused beams slamming the vessel from astern. Simon felt his fingers tearing as he fought to hold himself against the bracing stanchion while the Control Center shuddered violently. The compartment filled with smoke as Simon's head smashed against the stanchion. With his ears ringing, he blinked several times to clear his vision. We've still got air, he thought, as circulation fans switched on and began swirling the smoke into columns that poured into the compartment's emergency ducts. He turned toward the helm to see how far they'd been thrown off course. Litieri was down, one arm reaching up toward the ship's controls, faltering, then collapsing.

Simon rushed to take his place and careened *Serendipity*

around again to charge at the oncoming cruisers—giving them
the smallest possible target, and attempting to pass between
them. "Port Weapons, Starboard Weapons," he ordered,
watching the visual screen. "You'll have targets in eighteen
seconds."

"Port aye."

"Starboard aye."

"Sir," Hector reported from Radio. "I have a broadcast
from *Fury*. He's coming up on our port quarter again."

The young Duelist's voice carried an uncharacteristic note
of alarm. Simon felt his legs weaken beneath him. "What is
it, Hector?"

"Gordon said, *Dozo*, Admiral. 'If you please.' "

"No, Hector! Tell him NO!"

"I did, sir. Immediately. Gordon reports that most of his
crew is dead. The survivors are unanimous in their decision.
He said goodbye, Admiral. For all of them. And . . . and he
said, 'Thank you, Saint Barrow. I love you.' That was all,
sir."

"Call him back!"

"There's no response, sir. I'll continue trying."

"Understood, Hector."

Fury came on visual screen at full speed, flashing from behind *Serendipity* like a bright arrow loosed from an invisible,
celestial archer. As the Duelist cutter rushed ahead of *Serendipity*, it was seen by the two enemy cruisers at the same moment. Bolts of illuminated, charged particle fire lashed out at
the small intruder who dared to step between the great beasts
of this fight. *Fury* bored straight ahead as Simon watched,
horror-struck and helpless.

The brief life of Gordon Barrow ended in a head-on mael-
strom of torn metal and bursting, brilliant sheets of fire. Both
ships flew apart. *No sound*, Simon thought, unable to turn
away from the screen. *My son died and there was no sound!*

"Sir!" Hassalem's voice broke into the silence. "Admiral!"

"Yes," Simon answered. "Yes, Natalie."

"We're on a collision course with that remaining cruiser,
sir."

"Good." Simon stared at the screen. "Come at me," he
whispered calmly, watching the cruiser. "Steady . . . Come
ahead . . . WHAT IN THE HELL IS THAT THING?"

Hassalem's voice, "Say again, Admiral?"

"Port weapons shooting, sir!"

Simon made no response. *Serendipity* continued its straight course, flashing past the Peacekeeper cruiser as it veered to starboard.

"Admiral?" Hassalem shouted. "Sir!" After another second with no response she keyed a different helmet speaker. "Radio, this is Radar. Hector, Admiral Barrow's hurt. He needs relief at the helm." Her ear-speaker squelched twice in acknowledgment.

Hector was there ten seconds later, pulling a frozen Simon Barrow away from the helm station. He glanced at the radar and visual screens and understood the situation immediately. Ahead of *Serendipity* was empty space. Behind was the cruiser, rapidly leaving the center of the radar screen. Further out, but not in the path of the cruiser, Target Two was making a run toward the distant *Talon*. He slowed to one-eighth speed and began turning to pursue the Peacekeeper cruiser.

"Hector . . . what was . . ." Looking up from the course indicator, Hector saw Barrow take a hesitant step toward him.

"Please sit down, sir," Hector said.

"I . . . yes, I'll sit down." He lowered himself toward the deck, then stood straight again. "I'm all right, Hector. I was stunned for a moment. Keep the helm." He stepped away briskly to the radar station, still seeing flashing, colored lights in his eyes.

"The cruiser's maintaining course and still accelerating, sir," Hassalem reported. "I don't understand."

"We hurt him," Simon answered, hoping he was right. "Port Weapons, report," he ordered.

"Port, sir. We scored multiple hits, projectiles only."

"Very well." The chances of severely damaging the cruiser on one pass were miniscule, he thought, especially with only projectile fire. But . . . *Lucky again, Saint Barrow!* he thought bitterly.

To the helm he ordered, "Hector, ignore the cruiser for now. Reverse course and take us to *Talon*. Full speed." Target Two was charging directly at Bellenauer's oncoming ship.

"Aye aye, sir."

Simon stared at the radar screen. The cruiser was maintaining a straight course, away from them. But if it came around at them again . . . he would leap from the shell of *Serendipity* and crush the bastards with his own hands. No more of us will die today, he thought. No More!

"Radio Room, this is Control," Simon called. "Judd, is Dr. Reilly still there?"

"Yes, sir."

"Litieri is down. Can you take him to her?"

"On my way, sir."

The new situation on all radar and visual screens changed the equation, and was immediately recognized by both sides of the battle. Alone now as the surviving Peacekeeper cruiser continued accelerating away, Target Two abandoned its charge toward *Talon* and broke for open space. *Serendipity* changed course again and raced at full speed toward the fleeing cutter. Simon's head throbbed from the mild concussion he'd suffered. Tired and grief-stricken as he was, he knew it had been an illusion—that incredible, beautiful *thing* hovering behind the Peacekeeper cruiser. He'd seen—or imagined—it, just a moment after his son and the remaining crew of *Fury* sacrificed their lives to save *Serendipity*. Of course it was illusion; but why that particular one? He thought of the old woman Alicia DurNow, and knew that only she would listen to him describe it and not pronounce him insane.

The memory disappeared as he watched the inevitable result of the chase unfolding on the screens. With the loss of main power, *Serendipity*'s speed advantage was gone. *Talon* was still too distant from the others to have an effect on the outcome. As the seconds passed it became clear that there was no choice. Simon keyed the ship-wide 1MC circuit and ordered the crew to begin damage assessments. They were to remain at Battle Stations. But for now, he advised them, the fight was over.

And it could be over permanently, his rational mind told him as the rest of him shouted for attention. He refused to listen to any voice that named his son. *Never mind . . . that . . . for now. Think! Other lives depend on you.* At last, years of training prevailed, and discipline returned.

Coldly, the assessment came: It was over. The Duelists would lose. There was no possibility of replacing the ships that were lost. The pseudo-weapon provided by Doctors Bey and Harding was no longer intimidating to the Peacekeepers. Worse, Hector's tactic was unstoppable; superior numbers and competent ship commanders would be enough for the other side to prevail. The mystique and the momentum achieved by the Duelists was broken. The Peacekeepers could beat them now.

Ingrit Von Velt expressed none of the anger she felt. *That was my ship! Kali L'Awana!* She'd had nearly a day to think about it and to confer with the Peacekeepers at ProLab, after the old ID-code had been received. Still, she'd refused to believe it. Another trick, she'd decided. But . . . Sons of bitches! And Simon Barrow had been commanding it. She was certain of that; no one else could have survived the coordinated attack she'd planned. But he was lucky, she thought. What idiot came out of hyperdrive right on *top* of her ships? And who had ordered those cruisers in? Imbeciles! If the survivor repaired its damage, fine. If not, they could die. And good riddance. She'd *told* her superiors not to interfere!

Her own squadron had rehearsed the hyperspace tactic intensively since the Duelists had tried it twice, three months before. It was breathtakingly dangerous; and even better—oh, how it worked!

Von Velt calmed herself. Despite the incompetence of her superior officers, she had a major victory, and crucial information, to take home. Could there be any doubt now that Douglas-Wycliffe would appoint her to replace Anna Chakheya? No! She smiled in satisfaction, picturing the terror on the face of that smug bastard Simon Barrow when they met again.

With none of her thoughts reflected in her practiced command voice, she said, "Engage."

The Peacekeeper cutter winked into hyperdrive, turning a starlit Universe into nothing.

Serendipity's crew loaded food crates and their personal belongings as quickly as possible aboard the one remaining Duelist cutter.

Clonus, Schaeffer, and Minton were carried to *Talon*'s dispensary. Jessica followed, bandaged and walking with difficulty. A weak and shaking Randall was borne on a stretcher between Corinne and Dr. Reilly. The physician had said that she believed his present condition was brought on by the trauma of battle and the shock of Gordon's death; but she could make no guarantees.

Simon was the last to leave. He paced through the engine compartments, unnecessarily verifying what he already knew: Hyperdrive capability was lost. Both Chatterly-Wangs had sustained irreparable damage. It bordered on miraculous that *Serendipity* had kept any speed at all for as long as it had. Lucky, he thought sullenly. But whatever had kept the engines going—luck, or a fiercely competent crew—he was grateful. Corinne, and Jessica, and Randall and Clonus were alive. But so many others were not. Gordon was gone. The young man with the "talent for precision flying" had saved their lives, all of them. But Gordon was gone!

Still refusing to allow his mind to tell him the extent of this damage, he walked quickly, heading forward past the berthing compartments. Sealed inside were most of the more than four thousand colonists from New Hope. The others were floating in space, torn from their resting place by a blast from Peacekeeper weapons. Even in death, they couldn't escape what Earth had become. In another compartment, with the comrades who'd gone before them, were the thirty-nine newly dead—eleven Duelists and twenty-eight civilians—lost in the battle. Among the civilians lost was Gault, a man who in death had finally accomplished his life's goal: To be feared. Lost also were the two scientists who'd risked everything to help them, when they needed it most: Dr. Bey and Dr. Harding. Only the day before they had finally summoned the boldness to announce publicly their love for one another—and were stunned to learn that everyone already knew.

In the Control Center, Simon programmed and locked the helm according to analyses provided by the navigation computer. Then checking everything and looking back one last time, he left for the airlock connecting the cruiser to *Talon*. If nothing interrupted its slow course, *Serendipity* would reach the Earth System and deliver the dead, and their final personal message, in slightly more than three thousand twenty years. But if he could, Simon would return for them; they deserved better than this.

Talon disengaged from *Serendipity* and began its enabling run to hyperspace. Behind them, impossible to see, were the speeding, broken remains of *Avenge* and *Breaker* and *Fury*, and the friends who'd died aboard them.

Two hundred ninety-six men and women had answered Simon Barrow's call and proudly named themselves Duelists. More than half of them were now dead.

Corinne was stiff and quiet as she entered the new names in her journal under the date November 22, 2153. Simon watched over her shoulder, remembering a face, a voice, and something unique and good about each one of them. And as he feared that he would, he saw the face of a smiling boy with red-brown hair—who thought he needed to prove that he was Simon Barrow's son. Who proved instead, at his moment of death, that his need to love was far greater than his need to live.

Corinne's hand refused to write the name of her son alongside the others. Standing, and leaving the pen on an empty page, she said, "You do it." Without a glance at her husband she walked from the stateroom.

Simon lifted the pen—and then fell to the floor, weak and helpless as an infant. He clutched his knees to his chest and held the anguish inside of him for as long as he could.

⇒27⇐

"The tool belt," Jessica said bitterly. "Kellan wasn't tracing out lines to impress me. I should have known he was lying, when I saw the tool belt."

"Yes," Corinne said gently.

Simon cleared his throat. "Jessica, I can't fault you for not understanding at once. I remember my parents, and how, ah, irrational, they were at times. And your mother and I, as well. But you did believe that Shaeffer was alone in the over-

head. And you knew that to be a violation of clearly understood rules. Those procedures were established for a number
of reasons, including the fact that we had forty-one new people aboard. You should have reported the incident to me."

"Yes, sir. I trusted him. I—" She lowered her head, grimac-
ing at the pain of her wounds, the deepest ones being Kellan's
betrayal and the loss of Gordon and so many other people
she'd loved. She looked at her father. "There are no excuses
for my actions, sir, and I offer none. Please tell Mr. Clonus
again that I'm glad he's all right. And I'm sorry."

"He's not angry at you, Jessica," Corinne said. "He's told
you that many times."

"May I go now?"

"Yes," Griffin Joyner said.

Fighting back the tears, Jessica turned and walked unsteadily from the wardroom of *Talon*. Behind her, both Simon and
Corinne rose.

"No," Joyner said. "Let her go. She needs to think." He
sighed. "Her heart will mend. But the damage to her spinal
column . . . it may be years before she gains back the full use
of her legs."

"The one depends on the other," Corinne said. "If she'd
only work with Dr. Reilly . . . But she won't, until she can
stop blaming herself."

"Corinne," Joyner said. "She'll understand, eventually. It
was me. I recommended those Peacekeepers to Simon."

"It was my decision to accept them," Simon told him.
"You're not responsible for what happened. And neither is
Jessica."

"That's not good enough," Joyner said. "As a younger man
I would not have made that mistake. Shaeffer and Minton
would never have got past me. Somehow, I'd have known
what they were."

"They were murderers," Corinne said bitterly. "But I'm
sure that in their own minds . . . You spoke to them before
they died. Did they try to excuse what they did?"

"Yes. They were proud of themselves. They called us 'ter-
rorists.' The type of people who tore Ireland apart for centuries. According to them we were doing the same thing to
Earth."

"Bastards," Corinne said harshly. "Well, the others of their group apparently don't have the same opinion. And," she added, "neither do the miners or most of the people anywhere, from what you've told us."

"That's true. But we can't support and defend them now as strongly as before. Their opinions of us will change when the Peacekeepers are no longer afraid to attack them. They'll see us as weak, and then as criminals again." He asked Simon, "I'm curious. What would you have done with Shaeffer and Minton if they'd lived?"

"Kept them locked away in the dispensary, for their own safety. Whatever we are, we're not executioners."

Corinne flushed, thinking of a wise and strong woman who'd known how to deal with those who attacked her Family. But Corinne said nothing to Simon or Griffin. Her mother had never revealed more than necessary to those weaker than herself. And neither would the daughter of Talon—nothing about Wanda Hartner fourteen years ago, and nothing about Shaeffer and Minton, three days ago.

Joyner nodded at Simon and finished his coffee. "Yes. 'Whatever we are.' Suddenly that's become a good question."

This time, Corinne lost the self-control she'd fought so hard to maintain. She slammed both palms down on the table. "You two . . . you sound as if it's over. As if you're *planning* to lose!" She turned to Simon. "Maria was right about you," she said coldly. "You used me to stay alive, and then to escape from Mercator. I gave you everything I could, Simon. *Everything*, including a beautiful son who died so that you could keep going. And win! Now you're ready to give up, to make his sacrifice mean *nothing*." She stood. "You disgust me. Both of you." Glaring at the two, she strode from the wardroom, pulling the door forcibly shut behind her.

Neither man spoke, or moved. Long minutes went by while each weighed Corinne's hot anger against cold reality. And each decided, privately, that Corinne was right; impossible odds were no excuse for surrender. Not when so much was at stake.

Above them, the intercom sounded. "Admiral Barrow, we've arrived in normal-space. I'm picking up a broadcast. It's in General Joyner's code."

Simon exchanged a questioning look with Joyner, then

stood and reached for the panel. "Thank you, Francine. We're on our way."

An hour later *Talon* was in hyperspace again, for the long journey back to the Beltway.

"That's him," Griffin Joyner said positively. He referred again to a slip of paper in his hand, and reread the confirming code just reported by Jessica to the Control Center. "Definitely."

Up to now indistinguishable from the metal-laden meteors whose path it paralleled, a scouter separated itself from the flow and moved toward *Talon*. It grew quickly on the visual screen as the Duelist cutter closed the distance.

The man who stepped through the airlock door a few minutes later was greeted warmly by Joyner. As the two shook hands Joyner said, "Mylo, I believe you remember Admiral Barrow."

"It was 'Colonel' then," he said, reaching to accept the proffered handshake. "But yes, I certainly do remember the man who scared the hell out of me on Bravo Three."

"Hello, Mr. Edelman. I've been told about your support during the past year. I'm grateful."

"Please, don't thank me. Without the supplies and protection that Griffin and your Duelists gave the mines, we could never have kept going."

"And we'll continue to do what we can," Griffin said firmly. "But ... we have only one ship now, Mylo. Twelve days ago—"

"Yes, I know about your losses. I'm very sorry."

Simon looked at him, surprised. "You know?"

Edelman nodded his head. "A lot has happened in those twelve days. That's why I've been broadcasting and requesting this meeting. Ah, Griffin, do you have any coffee aboard? Real coffee?"

"Yes, in the wardroom."

"I'll follow you two." As they walked, he said, "I once served aboard a ship about this size. Of course, when I was in the military ..." He laughed. "I've told you all those lies by now, haven't I, Griffin?"

"Simon hasn't heard them," Joyner answered as they entered the wardroom.

"Ah. Well. Time for lies later." He sat down and waited while Simon filled three cups with coffee. "Thanks." He tasted the brew and grimaced. "Awful. Unfit for human consumption." He breathed an appreciative sigh. "Shipboard coffee. Just like I remember."

"Mylo—"

"I'm getting to it, Griffin. Let me savor the moment, will you?" He sipped again and smiled. "Now. It all starts with the fact that Douglas-Wycliffe is dead. You didn't know that, did you?"

"No!" Joyner said, nearly choking. "We only came back to the System a few hours . . . What happened?"

"Wait." Simon crossed the wardroom to an intercom panel. "Jessica, are you copying the media broadcasts?"

"No, sir. Why bother? All they do is—"

"Begin now, and record."

"Yes, sir."

He sat down again. "Go ahead, Mr. Edelman. What happened to Douglas-Wycliffe?"

"One of your Duelists got to her, Mr. Barrow. Killed her, along with Damis LaMothe."

"WHAT?"

"Twelve days ago, the same time you were in that battle." Edelman grinned. "Griffin, I wish you'd told me long ago that you had Duelists operating on Earth. And all the way out to New Hope! Knowing there are so many of you would've made it easier for me to hold the mines in check. Some of them were ready to resume normal shipments. Of course, that was before New Hope, and before we heard about Douglas-Wycliffe hanging Duelists. Both of those factors convinced everyone that you people were stronger and working in more places than we'd even hoped. And of course the hangings told us what Earth would do to us, if we didn't win. Thank God, we held on."

"But Mylo—"

Simon interrupted. "Excuse me, sir." There was nothing apparent to be gained by destroying the myth that somehow the miners had come to believe. What had happened was clear—a foolish move that had backfired. Douglas-Wycliffe had been desperate for a victory—or at least the appearance of a victory—over the Duelists. Desperate enough to claim that she'd captured and executed some of them—despite the fact that no Duelist had been to Earth since the group was formed over two years ago. And now, whoever had assassinated her and LaMothe had found a ready-made scapegoat. The apparent result was that the mines, and perhaps even Fujiwara and ProLab and the other settlements, were more united against her administration than ever before. A faint hope arose in him; it was more than he'd felt in many days.

He asked Edelman, "What else has happened?"

"Only everything, Mr. Barrow. To begin with, Anna Chakheya was released the day after Douglas-Wycliffe died. You once served with her, didn't you, Griffin?"

Griffin Joyner sat up bolt-straight. His heart was suddenly pounding in his chest. Then it *was* true. She *had* been arrested. The news had come like a fatal blow. But now . . . He said to Simon, as casually as he could manage, "She was a friend of mine at the UN."

"A *friend*?" Simon asked, stressing the word. Joyner had never identified the 'friends' who'd provided him with documents and information on his last trip to Earth.

"That's right."

"Well, that's interesting, isn't it?" Edelman grinned at Joyner again, misunderstanding the exchange. "I hope you left her with warm memories, Griffin. She's Secretary General now." He waited, watching their stunned expressions. "LaMothe had written her release orders and his own resignation before he was killed. That made her eighth in line for the position. The other seven apparently decided that they'd be wise to resign, given the assassinations and the mood on Earth. Those pictures from New Hope are everywhere now, and they've stirred up more anger than I've ever seen. Although if you were to ask me, I'd guess that Chakheya had something to do with those seven resignations, as well. But to return to my main point, the new Secretary General took the oath of office eight days ago. She's fired nearly everyone who worked for Douglas-Wycliffe. And there have been mass resignations among the General Assembly delegates who supported her. A new election is scheduled for six months from the day she took office."

Joyner and Barrow stared at their guest.

It was Joyner who broke the silence. The surge of hope nearly overwhelmed him. He spoke tentatively, fearful of giving too much information to Edelman. "Anna was a strong supporter of the Exploration Service. I wonder if she'll—"

"Already did," Edelman said, nodding. "She's written orders for two of the old shipyards to be activated again. With more to follow. To begin with, they're planning to rebuild *Celeste* and *Majora*." He sipped his coffee and smiled. "There's already talk among the shipyard unions of putting up statues of her. And I," he said, inclining his head in a bow, "in a more modest role, have agreed to instruct the mine bosses to begin shipping down ores again. Real ores."

Simon refilled Edelman's cup. He could barely contain the flood of emotion that caused his hands to tremble. Gordon, the others . . . their deaths *did* mean something.

Joyner spoke again, exploring every syllable as if he were blind and reaching for something totally beyond comprehension. "Then we, then, we have . . . won."

"No," Edelman said quietly. "I was hoping you'd understand without my telling you directly. I'm truly sorry, my friend. But *you* haven't won."

Simon Barrow looked from Edelman to Joyner, and understood. Why hadn't he realized it immediately? *Simpleton!* "The killing of Douglas-Wycliffe and LaMothe," he said finally, as much to himself as the other two. "Chakheya can pardon us for everything else. But not that. If she did, she'd never escape the suspicion that she herself was involved in the assassinations. It would cripple her government."

"That's part of it, but not all," Edelman said. "Please understand why I insisted on this meeting with you two, Griffin. You've been a good friend. God knows what you people have accomplished . . . There'd be nothing to *fight* for, if your wife hadn't given . . . and then you, and Barrow . . ." He swallowed more coffee as his voice began to rasp. "It was only right that I bring this to you personally."

"Thank you, Mylo," Joyner said. "But we didn't assassinate anyone. Anna Chakheya will provide an honest court. We can prove our case." He understood Simon's concern, but in the same moment he realized that a false accusation meant nothing. Not anymore.

Edelman shook his head. "I'll believe you didn't order it,

Griffin, if you tell me that's true. But they have the testimony of a security guard, and DNA analyses. As you said, Anna Chakheya is an honest person. None of this has been fabricated. Everyone believes that. Including me."

"The assassins were not Duelists," Joyner said resolutely.

Simon began to wonder. And as he did, his pulse raced. "Were any names reported?"

"Yes," Edelman said. "A janitor named Burton Frank. And a woman identified from fugitive files. Shelly Bascombe. She's the Duelist who murdered Douglas-Wycliffe and LaMothe. And she killed seven more security guards before she and her accomplice died in the fight. You trained her well, Mr. Barrow."

"Shelly . . . Oh, no. No." Simon lowered his face into his hands. He'd miscalculated, terribly. From the beginning he'd left his junior students out of the fight—"for their own safety," he'd thought. They were innocent of any crimes. But Douglas-Wycliffe had been hanging them. And one of them had retaliated. He felt as though his heart were tearing from his body. *We came so close to winning!*

He raised his head again. "Everything you said about Chakheya's plans. You phrased it all as if it were conditional."

"Yes. As I said, there's more than the assassinations." Edelman cleared his throat and spoke with a slower, more formal tone. "Mr. Barrow. While she was Commanding General of the Peacekeepers, Anna Chakheya made every effort to defeat you. You were able to choose your targets and strike at will. And you eluded or beat everything she sent against you, for two years. Until recently you'd lost only one ship. No one knows what type of weaponry you have, but it's clearly superior to anything the Peacekeepers can deal with. I always thanked God for that. But . . ." He paused and scratched at his forehead, concentrating on his next words.

"You sent one of your ships directly to Earth, where it released those lifelaunches. They could have carried bombs instead of paper. Your ship escaped, untouched. Security procedures were immediately changed, of course. But the point is that time and again, you have come up with innovations that were not anticipated. And then that battle. Anna

Chakheya read Captain Von Velt's action report on the day she took office. You lost three ships. But in the process you destroyed a fully armed cruiser and three top-of-the-line cutters. Another cruiser is still missing, and presumed lost. That encounter has convinced her, gentlemen. She can't beat you. Not with force."

"How did you know all of this?" Simon asked. But as he spoke, the answer revealed itself.

"Mylo—" Joyner began.

Edelman held up a hand. "No one knows how many ships, how many Duelists, you have left. You say only one ship. I believe you have at least two. This one, and *Kali L'Awana*. But that's irrelevant. What matters is that most people think you have dozens more. Do you see? Because of your successes, you're unknown—I should say, 'unknowable'—and you're powerful. That makes you an unacceptable threat."

"Mylo, we . . ."

"Please, Griffin. Let me continue." He faced Simon. "And to the point you mentioned earlier, Mr. Barrow. Yes, everything is conditional. As I've said, Chakheya wants to open up the Great Domain again. But she can't possibly win the coming election, without first bringing you to justice for assassinating a Secretary General. At the same time, she won't risk another war with you." Edelman sat back, raising his hands palm-upward. "I'm sure you can appreciate her position."

Simon was certain now that he'd guessed correctly. Edelman had spoken directly with Anna Chakheya. And of course, she'd given him only limited information. But she'd told him part of the truth; she honestly did not know the strength of the Duelists—how could she?—and she was afraid of them.

Feeling betrayed by Chakheya, Joyner said through clenched teeth, "If what you're suggesting . . . No! And it wouldn't help if every Duelist *did* surrender, Mylo. You said it yourself. No one will believe that that's all of us."

"That's right," Mylo said. "The Secretary General has made the same assessment. As you surely understand by now, I am acting as her personal emissary. My instructions in part were to inform you that she has taken steps to accomplish what you've told me all along were your own goals. That is evidence of her good faith. She wants an equal gesture from you."

"But all we have left—" Joyner began.

With a quick look, Simon cautioned him to say no more.

Edelman stood and reached into a breast pocket. From it he retrieved a sealed envelope.

He said, "Anna Chakheya is an intelligent woman. She knows that if you decide to continue the fight, in effect becoming pirates with no purpose but your own selfish interests, she would be forced to devote an unacceptable level of resources in the effort to stop you. I've spoken with her, and I am convinced. She wants to end this war, and to release the Great Domain from policies that were choking all of us. And to begin again the outward expansion of the human race. Do I need to repeat myself, gentlemen? These have been *your* goals, as well."

Edelman looked from one face to the other. *They're tired*, he thought. *My God, how tired they are.* He said, hating the words as he spoke them, "Griffin. And Simon, if I may. You are honorable men. And for that reason, you have no choice."

He handed the envelope to Joyner. "When hostilities have ended, the Secretary General will make this document public. She will formally pardon all of the Duelists and the others who followed you. In return she requires only two surrenders. That would be you, Griffin. And Admiral Simon Barrow."

⇌28⇋

The six of them stood facing one another in two lines of three. No eyes met. They were all strong individuals, but there were moments when eyes could not be trusted. A droning buzzer sounded, and a green light flashed above the hatchway. They turned their heads as the dog-wheel began to spin.

From *Talon*'s 1MC circuit came a series of tones that was centuries old. The bosun's pipe finished its call as the hatch opened.

Joyner stiffened his posture and held a salute. "Welcome aboard, Madam Secretary."

Anna Chakheya stepped through the hatchway. Like Joyner and Barrow, she was in formal military attire, white trimmed with gold. The uniform seemed to be a natural part of her, Simon thought, as he had whenever he'd seen holostats of her over the years. She was taller than he'd realized, and wore across her chest dozens of ribbons awarded during her forty-five year military career.

Behind her followed an elderly man with short-cropped gray hair and wide, inquisitive eyes.

Chakheya swept her gaze to include the six who formed her honor guard. She stood in front of Joyner and returned his salute. "Thank you, Griffin," she said, and extended her hand to him. "It's good to see you again. But please, we've known one another too long to stand on ceremony. Call me Anna."

Joyner stepped from the line. He said proudly, "May I present my son, Hector Horatio Hernandez. And Admiral Simon Barrow, and his family."

As he spoke their names they greeted her in turn when she stood before them and offered her hand. Only Randall broke the discipline. "My dad didn't do anything wrong," he said, as his eyes met firmly with hers. "Do you hear me?"

She put a gentle hand on the boy's shoulder and motioned for her companion to step forward. "Randall, this is Dr. Lindseth. He is one of the best physicians on Earth. When I heard about you, I asked him to come with me."

"I don't need him," Randall said. "I need my dad!"

"Mrs. Barrow," Dr. Lindseth said to Corinne, "may I speak with you, and your children? I believe I can help. And I would like very much to do that."

Looking from Joyner to Simon, Corinne nodded. "Yes. Hector, would you come with us?" The four of them left, each turning to face Simon and Griffin as they stepped through the doorway and out of view.

"Now," Anna Chakheya said, turning to Simon. "Admiral Barrow, please notify your Control Center that my ship is leaving."

"I will, Madam Secretary. But why?"

"My name is Anna," she said. "And to answer your question, Simon, my purpose is twofold. I want to avoid any chance of misunderstanding between the ships' captains. My crew does not trust yours, and I'm sure that their caution is reciprocated."

"Another demonstration of good faith," Joyner said.

"It may be premature," Simon replied carefully. "Griffin and I have discussed this at length."

"And you've discovered the major flaw in my proposal."

"Yes."

"Of course. That, gentlemen, is the more compelling reason for my gesture. None of us will be successful without mutual trust. I'll return to Earth aboard *Talon*, or not at all."

"And Dr. Lindseth?"

"I'm confident that you can spare a scouter, even if you refuse my offer and keep me as a guest. But no matter what you two decide, I've arranged for your son to accompany Dr. Lindseth to Manhattan Island Institute. With your family, and with full pardons for them already published. That includes Hector, of course. I want your surrender. But it will be based on reasons other than fear for your wife, Simon. And I do not accept children as my enemies."

"Thank you. Anna."

"May we go to your wardroom? Mylo Edelman has promised me that your coffee is authentically awful."

"I won't ask," Simon began as they sat down, "what level of help you gave us. And of course it will never be mentioned again, regardless of the outcome. But I do know that you saved lives. Ours, and your own forces. I'm grateful."

"Griffin Joyner was always a persuasive man," Anna said. "I hoped, without believing, that he'd win. But please don't attribute your successes to me. I provided you with documents and information at the beginning. After that ... My personal belief has always been that a commander who *can* be beaten, should be beaten." She shrugged, and stirred the steaming coffee. "But life isn't so simple for a politician, as I now find myself. In truth, you beat me. But history will record that it was you who surrendered."

"That hasn't been finalized," Joyner reminded her.

"Yes, I know."

Simon voiced the objection. "Griffin has known you for years, Anna, and he trusts you. That's all the assurance I need on a personal level. But with respect, you're only one person. If we surrender and the Duelists disband, all of the plans you've announced could unravel in a day. Nothing you've done so far is irreversible. And whatever our decision, there's no guarantee that you'll be in office six months from now."

Chakheya nodded her head and smiled at him. "Yes, that had to be it." She cleared her throat. "Simon, none of this depends on me, personally. Let me explain. In the shipyards I've called forty thousand people back to work. So far. During the ten days since you spoke to Mylo Edelman, the keels have been laid for the new *Celeste* and *Majora*. It won't surprise you to hear that we've already received ten times more applications to crew those vessels than we can use. And the moment I have your formal surrender, I'm dispatching two fully supplied cruisers to those worlds that were abandoned. It may be too late, but we can try. Next. The mines are shipping more high-grade ore than we can process with existing facilities. And so I've ordered the creation of more, on both Earth and Mars. Manufacturers will need all they can produce, and more. ProLab and Fujiwara have said goodbye to their Peacekeepers and have instituted private security forces. There will be no further government interference. They will enter contracts when, and with whom, they please. The result will be that they accomplish more than ever before." She held up a hand as Joyner began to interrupt.

"But," she continued, "relatively speaking, these are very small steps. And so you're right, Simon. Nothing I've done is irreversible. But think, both of you. What you people have accomplished *cannot* be reversed. Griffin, your Maria made true terraforming possible. This was at a time when most of humankind believed that it would be interesting and exciting to see how far we could reach into the Universe. But you and your Duelists, and I hope to receive partial credit after I'm dead, have demonstrated conclusively that we *must* find out. Do you understand? Recall the argument made by Douglas-Wycliffe when she first dismantled the Exploration Service. She claimed that the nine new worlds should be self-sustaining. Well, isn't it ironic? It's *Earth* that can't sustain itself! Not without the mines, and new technologies. Not without the support of people who believe, and continue to believe, that they're on the best possible path. Most of all, not without the freedom 'to *go*, to *reach* for what's out there, and to *do* whatever is necessary to go even further.' You recognize your own quote, don't you, Griffin?"

"Yes."

"Go. Reach. Do. That is exactly what you people have done, as individuals. Twenty years ago, Maria's work proved that the same thing is possible for the entire human race, on a scale as big as the Universe itself. And now Barrow's Duelists have proved that it's essential!

"The point is, Griffin, that I can't undo what I've started. Nor can my replacement, if I lose the election. You and Barrow have made that impossible. And for the best of all reasons. The people won't let me. They have another chance to do what must be done, and can be done. And they won't let anyone stand in the way. Except—"

Simon looked across the table at her. "Except for us. The Duelists are the one remaining threat." He laughed at the irony. "We're the 'rubble in the path of humankind.' "

"We're not a danger to the very things we've been fighting for," Joyner said. "How could we be? Anna, we've served together. You know me. And you know what our intentions have been from the beginning."

"Griffin, if you're seen as unbeatable, you're a threat. That's very basic, isn't it? You've pointed out on many occasions that an uncontrolled force must be judged by ability—not by intent, which can change at any moment. I agree. You and Simon and your Duelists have proved yourselves to be beyond my reach. With all due modesty, it can be said that this places you beyond the reach of anyone. And since I can neither control nor monitor your intent, I must deal with your ability. That is to say, I must end it. There are no alternatives. For these plans I've outlined to go forward, the Duelists must disband. And the two of you must surrender yourselves to authority." Anna Chakheya was quiet then, having presented her case just as she'd rehearsed innumerable times in the past ten days. Now it was up to them. It remained a shock that she'd been beaten militarily; and that after two years, she knew nothing of her enemy. She only knew that if these Duelists could be broken now, she would have to *keep* them broken. And that would be impossible, she knew, if she failed to keep her promises to them. When she judged the time to be right, she asked, "Griffin, Simon, do you still see a flaw in my argument?"

Joyner answered. "Only that it's leveled against Simon and me, and is therefore not necessary." He sighed, tapping the table with his right hand. Overwhelming emotion—relief and elation—was growing in him, and it was difficult to conceal. For the first time in his life he felt no shame at the tears building in his eyes. "But from a military and political standpoint, of course you're right."

Anna Chakheya said to both of them, "The citizens love you. They're grateful for what you've done. But they're afraid of you. On a personal level I feel the same way. That changes nothing, of course."

Simon Barrow stood and hesitated for a moment, watching the face of his old friend. He'd known this great man for a quarter of a century. And he was sure that they were thinking the same thing: Anna Chakheya could easily take them by force now; it was the mystique they'd created around the Duelists that prevented her from knowing that—and which also condemned Barrow and Joyner. But what mattered most—the only thing that had mattered since that incredible conversation with Edelman—was her offer. Simon was convinced now that she was sincere. And that what she would do, for the Duelists and for humankind as a whole, was worth infinitely more than the price she demanded.

Joyner looked up at his friend, pupil, and teacher. He nodded. And although his impulse was to leap onto the table in all the virile power of his youth, and to cry out in triumph over all that the gods had sent against him—he remained calm. He said hoarsely, with a straight, sad face, "It has to end, Simon. It's time."

With the same measure of self-control, Barrow reached out and keyed the intercom. "Francine, tell the crew they're going home. Take us to Earth."

Griffin Joyner was in uniform for the third time in fifteen years. He stood straight, jaw set firmly and shoulders back at rigid attention. Steady were the old eyes that had watched his world build, then shatter around him, then miraculously grow again with love and hope—and then break yet again, to rise once more through the power of Simon Barrow and the Duelists. And now the larger world—the Great Domain—was moving, rising again, to catch the strong wind of destiny. It mattered very little to him that Griffin Joyner would have no further part to play. He had lived, had given himself without reservation to those ideas which he knew to be noble, and best. He was content. He grieved for the recently dead; but he envied them, also. Because if the Universe were truly great— more than infinite and eternal; truly *great*—they would be together in some radiant and peaceful place, with his beloved Maria. Oh, how he envied them!

But for Hector, whose wise, dark eyes had spoken so eloquently of love and pride ... and for Corinne, and Jessica, and Randall ... his heart was breaking.

The man standing next to him was as rigid and unmoving as he. What is he thinking? Joyner wondered—and realized that he'd never known the answer to that question. Perhaps that had been the luckiest thing about him; until now. Ironic, that the same quality which allowed him to win everything, was now to cost him everything. But for a newly reborn Great Domain it was the height of all good fortune that no human being had ever been able to know, or to anticipate, the mind of Simon Barrow.

From forty feet above them in the cavernous court of the General Assembly a voice came from an overhead speaker. As Joyner had expected, it came in a quiet, almost apologetic monotone.

"Guilty as charged," it said. "The prisoners will be taken into custody."

Twelve thousand spectators, who'd spoken not a word during the one-hour trial, stood. Their silence held as the two men were led to family and friends. It held while hands were grasped, long embraces given, and unheard whispers exchanged. And then it shattered as two fifteen-year-old boys began to cry.

EPILOGUE

A.D. 2166

The small stars above Mari flowed across the heavens in the tight, disciplined ranks they'd agreed upon for millions of years. Beyond them, smaller by sight but infinitely greater, the suns of the Universe glistened through a night that was deep enough to hold them all, and an eternity more. *He's out there*, she thought, willing her eyes to see the impossible. *And he knows I'm here.*

"Mother, are you asleep?"

Corinne Barrow lowered her eyes from the dome reluctantly. "No, Randall. I'm glad you're home. Please come and join me."

The tall, muscular man walked between dense rows of flowers that filled the air with perfume. They seemed to glow with an inner fire beneath the strong starlight. He stood next to her, waiting for her to see him. "Are you all right?" he asked. "Jessica said you haven't spoken to anyone since the funerals. I'm sorry I left so quickly, but—"

"Don't apologize," Corinne said. She lifted the two journals from her lap and set them on the ground beside her. Sitting quietly for a minute, she was looking at the spot in her garden that was bare; the flowers were now covering three new graves in one of the smaller domes. "I sent a message to Chakheya, thanking her for ... for having Griffin's body shipped here. And Maria's. How strange, that they arrived an hour before Clonus died. It was as if he were hanging on, to say goodbye to them one last time." She lifted a fallen petal from beneath her chair and held it in her open palm.

"Grampa died peacefully, Mother. He accepted what had to be."

"Yes, I know. I read his diaries. At the end, all he wanted

was to come home again. To be remembered by his son, and buried beside Maria. He's content now. And so is she." Corinne closed her hand around the petal, then let it drift back to the ground. "That's what I want, Randall. When it's time. I want the same contentment for your father and me."

"Mother, please don't think about that. You and Dad—"

"I want your promise, Randall."

"And you have it," he said quietly. "Of course you have it. But please, don't—"

"How is your wife?"

"Navina's doing very well," he said, responding immediately to the change of subject. It was a relief. "She'll finish her internship at Manhattan Institute in three months."

"We're all proud of her, Randall." Corinne laughed, as she did each time she thought of the delightful young girl. "But since she doesn't approve of either fighting or gambling ... well, it's not really gambling, is it? Still, I wonder how long she'll allow you to practice your own profession."

"I'm working on that," Randall said, bending down to kiss the top of her head. It was good to see her smile again, to hear her laugh. "I think this will help." He cleared his throat loudly.

She looked up at him then, and gasped. "Randall! That's ... why, it's beautiful!"

"I brought them back with me," he said, grinning self-consciously. "But please don't use that word when you see Hector." Randall was wearing a short tunic that was royal blue—the signatory color of a Grade 1 Expert—and trimmed at the edges with white. Below gray trousers, leggings of fine leather were tucked into wide black boots. Around each of his thick wrists was a small iron buckler engraved with a crossed pike-and-sword; designed by Jessica, it was now the family crest of the Barrow clan and the insignia of all the loosely associated—by force of law—individuals who'd earned the title of Duelist.

"Everyone has the uniforms?" she asked.

"All but Ke Shan," Randall said. "She swears the tailor made hers three sizes smaller than she'd ordered. Her husband is leaving for Earth tonight to have them done again."

"Poor Stewart."

"Actually, he has another reason for going. Francine

Bellenauer has been promoted to flag rank in the Exploration Service. Karen Bridges and Natalie Hassalem will be joining her staff at the end of the ceremony."

"Yes," Corinne said. "I'd heard something about that."

Randall hesitated to say the most important thing he'd come to tell her. He'd considered waiting until everyone on Mari could be present, but he knew that Corinne could easily lapse again into the silence that gripped her so often, and held her for so long. And, he thought, it was fitting that she hear the news first.

"Mom," he said. "There's one more thing." He waited until she looked up at him again, and was sure that he had her full attention. "The Secretary General sends you her best wishes."

"I still don't know whether to hate that woman, or . . . You spoke with her?" Corinne's expression was frozen between surprise and dread. "Is . . . did. . .?"

"No," he said hastily. "No." When she was calm again, he continued. "I've been asked to present the news to you, Mother." Taking a deep breath, he said, "Griffin's letters and yours have finally persuaded Chakheya that they may need us again some day." As her eyes widened, he smiled at her. "That's right. We can open Dad's schools again. The General Assembly of the United Nations has accepted our charter application. The Duelist Union will be formally recognized. In one year."

Corinne stared at him, unbelieving. It was what they'd all waited to hear, for so many, many years. She reached for his hand, trembling. "Then they admit that he was right."

"That won't be in the language of the UN proclamation, but yes. That's what it means."

"Public vindication," she said, drawing out the words. "For everything he did. Everything he believed." She spoke next in a whisper, looking up again through the starlit dome, "He's won." *And it will be known that Gordon died in an honorable cause*, she added to herself gratefully. *They will mourn him, too.* Tears flowed over her cheeks as she wished with all her heart that Simon Barrow could share this with her. There was so much that she needed to say at this moment—but she could not tell him. He would never know. *Damn you, Anna Chakheya!*

Corinne looked away from the dome and into the eyes of

her son, the eyes that were so much like Maria's. "One year ... that's not so long to wait, is it?"

"No, Mother. That's a very short time. It's barely enough to get ready."

"Oh, yes! There's so much to do! But first Carlos and Jessica are expecting another set of twins, and ... Why couldn't they wait! And the media will attend, of course. We'll have a reception here, in the garden! And ..." She refused to look away from his handsome, smiling face, for fear that this would be only another dream. "Randall," she said breathlessly. "Your father has won."

"Yes," he said, pulling his mother gently to her feet. He held her while she clung to him, shaking, and allowing the years of lonely anguish to come out of her. At last. His own tears mingled with hers and he said again, "Yes."

Maria Hernandez and Griffin Joyner had provided humankind with tools, and inspiration. In return they had what they'd wanted most; they were at peace, and together.

But in the end, Randall knew, it was Simon Barrow who'd been the indispensable catalyst; the "singular citizen" around whom the players and circumstances of his time had gathered. He had given the Great Domain its future; so that it too had what it most wanted: freedom, and infinite space to grow. And in return—because it feared him—it had taken from this man the one thing he'd valued above all else.

But now, Randall thought, now there would be something good and lasting for the woman who had waited for so long, and had lost so much. Now she would fulfill the last promise she'd made to her mother, in a way that Maria could never have imagined: The clan would go on. Already, the Family of Corinne and Simon Barrow numbered in the hundreds.

"Yes," he said. "Dad has won."

It was called the Pacifico Belt: Four strong stars, light-years apart, each sending into the Universe furies of radiation and power that for billions of years had meant nothing to a distant, tiny phenomenon that became human life.

Nine planets around these stars became worlds and were given names, and children to nurture. And despite a regional name that meant "peace," a world once known as New Hope had renamed itself Belli—"from battle"—because its new residents wanted always to remember how their world had come to be reborn. These people of Belli were proud and aggressive, scientists and builders; and they were fiercely combative, but only against the slow pace of planetary evolution. Every day they worked to exhaustion, knowing that in that one day they accomplished more than a procrastinating Nature would do for them in a thousand years. And at night, before falling into sleep, many of them would come up to the dome and stand together, staring at a distant star that seemed to grow dim, to become less important, with every sighting. *We love you and we're grateful*, they would think. *But we're afraid of you. And we don't need you anymore.*

There was one exception. One man came to the dome on every night that offered a clear view into the heavens. He stood alone and found the same star the others did. But his thoughts were very different from theirs. For thirteen years he'd counted nights such as this, on one new world of exile after another. The citizens of these worlds revered him, and they called him Saint Barrow. He returned their affection. But always, his thoughts were on that one star: the one that for now gave light and warmth to all that was truly important in the Universe.

Remember me, he was thinking on this night. *Remember me, my loves. I'm coming home.*